AVENGING DEVIL

PART 1

Satan's Devils MC - San Diego Chapter #3

COPYRIGHT

Disclaimer

This is a work of fiction. Names, characters, businesses, places, events and incidents are either the products of the author's imagination or used in a fictitious manner. Any resemblance to actual persons, living or dead, or actual events is purely coincidental.

Warning

This book is dark in places and contains content of a sexual, abusive and violent nature. It may not be suitable for persons under the age of 18.

PRODUCTION ACKNOWLEDGMENTS

Cover Design by Wicked Smart Designs

Edited and formatted by Maggie Kern @ Ms.K Edits

Proof reading by Darlene Tallman

Photographer: Golden Czermak of Furious Fotog

Model: Curtis Presley

CAST OF CHARACTERS

Officers

Lost – President

Dart – Vice President

Grumbler – Sergeant at Arms

Salem – Enforcer

Scribe – Secretary

Bones – Treasurer

Blaze – Road Captain

Hard Token – Computer Expert

Patched Members

Brakes

Deuce

Dusty

Keeper

Kink

Niran

Pennywise

Reboot

Snips

Prospects
Connor
Curtis
Kid
Wrangler

Old Lady's and Children
Alex (Dart's): Tyler, Isla
Patty (Lost's): Beth, Connor
Mary (Grumbler's): Alicia

Club Girls
Cindy
Eva
Pearl
Tits

Members Out Bad
Bastard
Crow
DJ
Rattler
Tinder

Deceased Members
Bird (ex-Prez)
Gator
Poke (ex-SAA) Dispatched to Satan
Shark
Smoker
Snake (ex-Prez) Dispatched to Satan

SATAN'S DEVILS MC

CHAPTER ONE

Saffie

How did it, or rather I, come to this?

My hands twist in my lap as I sit on a filthy couch in the clubroom of the Crazy Wolves MC in Nevada, scared and nervous, with every fibre of my being on alert. Flinching when I hear his voice, I try to keep my eyes lowered, but they rise automatically as I hear his tone. I look down again fast.

He's angry. No good ever comes of that. My quick stolen glance at least shows, for once, his ire isn't directed at me. Instead, his focus is on a poor prospect standing, shaking in front of him.

"There's a scratch on my bike," Duke sneers. "What the fuck did you do to it?"

Around him stands Knife, the prez, Slit the sergeant-at-arms and other members of the MC looking on. Their arms are folded, and all have the same expression of anger on their faces. I know immediately, the prospect won't get any sympathy or support from them. No one goes against Duke.

Jude, a pleasant young man who's only been trying to earn his patch for a couple of months, holds out his hands in supplication. "I cleaned it, VP, that's all." When his voice croaks, he clears his throat, but he's not successful in hiding the tremor. "Th-th-there was already a scratch on it. I didn't do it. Honest to fuckin' God, I didn't." He glances around as though looking for help, but no one steps forward.

Duke moves fast, his large hand circling Jude's throat. The prospect stands stoic and valiantly pretends he's not choking. "You're a fuckin' liar." Holding Jude in place, Duke's eyes encompass the men standing impassively around. "Anyone here want a man who can't tell the truth as a fuckin' member?"

"Or who takes the Lord's name in vain."

"You fuckin' what?" Slinger throws at Stoat, who shrugs and goes red, while a few others snort.

Yeah, God and the Wolves don't have much of an understanding. I reckon He abandoned the club when it was founded and there's no chance of Him listening in, let alone being offended. I know, none of my prayers have been answered, and I've sent up too many to count.

Slit spits on the ground. "A man who can't admit the truth has no fuckin' business in an MC, VP."

Since when? I ask myself cynically.

But I'm the only doubter as, "Too fuckin' right," is echoed around him.

As though coming to realise he's in danger of losing the chance at his patch, and maybe more than that, Jude tries to defend himself, stressing again, "It was already there. I left the bike how I found it."

I could have told him it's not worth the breath he's wasted. Once Duke's mind is made up, nothing will change it.

As for the scratch, Jude was right, I could confirm it. I'd noticed it yesterday and had almost asked Duke how he'd gotten it last night. Almost. Luckily, I know better and had kept my mouth closed, as I do now. I'm probably the undeserving woman God thinks I am, as heaven help me, but I stay dumb, even though I suspect I know what's coming.

This isn't about a scratch, real or imagined. This is something worse. The signs are all there. The muscle in Duke's jaw ticks, a sure sign he's itching for violence. Prewarned by my prior experiences, it's certain if I declared the prospect was right, it would be me feeling Duke's fists raised in anger. Call me a coward, but those I've felt too many times before to speak up and face them again.

I'm Duke's old lady. I wear his patch. My more correct title would be his punching bag.

How did I get here?

Inwardly, I shake my head as I ask myself the question again, zoning out of the here and now, which is something I wish I could escape from.

Five years back, I had met a different man, one who in no way resembled the man in front of me now. One who was kind, charming and loving, and who'd appeared in my life at the exact right time. I suppose, having already been let down by my cheating ex-husband, I was ripe pickings for anyone who'd appreciate me. All it had taken were a few kind words, special smiles seemingly only for me, and all given by a handsome man who behaved like a gentleman and was generous with compliments as well as his money. That was the man I'd met, not the monster in front of me now.

I had known that Duke was a member of a motorcycle club from the start, and it hadn't bothered me. My ex had been a banker and his respectable profession hadn't stopped him from taking off with his PA ten years his junior.

When I'd told him my sorry story, Duke had declared he'd never trade me in for a younger model, assuring me I was the only wife he'd ever need. Over the past five years, he's proved himself right. Duke didn't need to cut me loose or try to deceive me. No, he was completely up front, having both his cake and eating it. He kept me, and if he wanted to plant his dick elsewhere, he never bothered to make a secret of his infidelities, often using the club whores in front of me. More than once he'd suggested I could learn a lot from them.

Why did he want an old lady? I've never really figured that out. The one benefit I could see was my use as a shield to stop any other girl from getting ideas above their station. I was some kind of trophy, someone good brought into his evil world. Someone he could corrupt and treat however he wanted. Or at least that's what I supposed. He's never enlightened me as to the truth of the matter. I know part of it was to punish my dad, something I wasn't responsible or asked for.

While my mind's been wandering, Duke has been letting the prospect's torture play out. It's not the first time I've seen him use this ploy as he stands silent, his eyes focused on Jude, giving him time to wonder if he's going to be offered some way to make recompense for his imagined crime.

Knowing Duke too well, I hold no optimism on that count. If anyone heard my story, they'd ask why I stay, why I put up with the moods, the anger, the striking. Why I allow my body to be a mass of bruises and healed broken bones from the too-many-to-count beatings. Do you think it's by choice?

If I had a way out, I'd take it. Truth is, I'm trapped. I'm Duke's property, not my own person anymore. I've no other identity except that of his old lady and wife. None of the Crazy Wolves MC would so much as lift a finger to help me get away.

Believe me, I've tried to escape, more times than I can count. Always I'm caught and dragged back, screaming and kicking. I always get punished. Still, I try. Freedom is worth the risks that I take, though the penalty worsens each time. A few weeks back, I'd tried again. When I'd gotten no further than just beyond the fence of the compound, Duke had dragged me back. Being a master of torture, he'd left me to languish for a couple of days alone in a room at the back of the clubhouse. When he'd next appeared, he'd taken me violently, then while I was still catching my breath, he'd taken a baseball bat to both of my legs, then had laughed when he left me incapable of moving. *That will stop you escaping again,* he'd callously told me.

At least he'd lost interest in using me while my legs were in casts. Apparently annoying to have around, I'd been left in that room, isolated with only the prospects to care for me, with them being issued with strict instructions not to engage in conversation, and only to provide the minimum of care.

Painful though it had been, those weeks had been like a vacation. For Duke, I'd ceased to exist. I was more often cold and hungry, but it had been a break I cherished, a distance from the man I hate with everything that I am. He never visited me, and I never asked to see him.

I dreamed he was dead. But when I was healed, it was only to find I was still living my nightmare.

The prospects had obeyed him blindly, seemingly immune to the helpless state I was in, doing the bare minimum to keep me alive.

All except for Jude.

Jude, the newest prospect who retained an element of humanity about him, and who was even then becoming uncertain about his place in the MC. Jude and I had become friends. No funny business, I'm almost old enough to be his mother, but when he was sure he wouldn't be missed, he'd stay with me longer than he was strictly allowed.

We'd talked, at first my voice, unused, was rusty. During our brief conversations, I'd found he was trapped as much as myself. Despite the promise that prospecting goes both ways, a chance to get to know the club, and for the club to vet their prospective new member, Jude had discovered no one gets away from the Crazy Wolves. Not once they've got you in their clutches. The only ways out are to become a member or die.

Jude could do nothing other than do as instructed, and work to gain his patch. At least he had that way to improve his lot, unlike me. As no woman becomes a member, and Duke's made it clear he'll never let me go, only death will end the torture of being Duke's old lady. I half dread, half long for it every day.

Jude fucked up though. Duke has eyes and ears everywhere, and somehow he learned that Jude gave solace to me. My gut churns as I'm forced to watch the scene play out. Unless hell has iced over and I'm mistaken, Jude's going to end his career with the Crazy Wolves tonight. Whatever sympathies I have for the prospect-come-friend, there's nothing I can do to prevent it. Any interference would make it worse not just on him, but also on me. *If it has to happen, make it quick,* I plead in my head, while knowing here any prayers go unanswered.

As so often is the case, silence stretching out needs to be broken.

"I'll fix the scratch." Jude breaks first, his eyes urgently searching the men surrounding him for any sign of compassion or an indication they'll spring to his defence. They won't. They'll likely all know how Duke's bike got scratched and that it wasn't his fault, but none of them will say a word to help the unlucky prospect. As bad as their VP, they'll more likely be chomping for blood. Their nostrils are already flaring as though they can already smell it.

Duke growls, a tone I know to interpret as a warning. "You? You're gonna fix nothing. You'll never again touch my fuckin' bike. Or any of my *property*." He stresses the last word with a quick glance toward me. Then to Slit, he instructs, "Hold him."

It happens so fast. It's not in the slightest bit fair. Given no chance with his hands pulled tightly behind him, Jude doesn't get an option to fight back. Duke, a big muscular man, lets his fists fly. As blow after blow rains down on the prospect, Duke barely pauses to draw breath. When Jude slumps, Slit drops him, and

Duke uses his feet. The sounds of flesh being pulped merge with the cracking of bones.

What had been a man a few minutes ago, quickly becomes an unrecognisable corpse on the floor. Duke continues long after he must have killed him, only stopping at the point when he gets bored.

He's breathing heavily when he issues his next instruction. "Prospects! Take the fuckin' trash out!"

Jude. Knowing I must, I'd sat stoically, trying to divorce my senses from reality as though what I was watching was a film. But hardened as I am to Duke's excesses, Jude's painful and so unnecessary demise is too much, and a sob escapes me. Part of me wishes I'd spoken up, though nothing I could have done would have prevented the senseless killing that had just taken place. If I had tried to defend him, there'd probably now be two dead bodies on the floor.

If I were braver, maybe I would have said something and allowed death to be my escape. Maybe it would be easier than existing like this, day after day, week after week, year after year until I can't remember who I was before I met Duke. That Sapphire wouldn't have watched on as a man had his life beaten out of him. That woman would have spoken up.

That woman has since learned.

CHAPTER TWO
Saffie

With my head in my hands, my view of them dealing with what remains of the prospect I'd taken a liking to is hidden. Covering my ears also blocks some of the sounds of his body being dragged across the floor. Shrunken into myself, I miss the approach of my man.

The first sign that he's in front of me is when he wrenches my hands away from my face and cruelly grabs my jaw.

"Enjoy the fuckin' show?" he snarls, his tone showing me his rage hasn't abated. "What's this I see? A tear for that fuckin' sorry excuse of a man?" Wrenching my head up, he turns it this way and that, as if checking on me.

My hands grow sweaty and my heart thumps hard, but I try to keep my voice steady. "Just let me go, please, Duke." My eyes plead with him. "I feel sick."

"You feel sick, huh?" Suddenly he lurches forward. "Sick with fuckin' fear, I hope. Jude's been eye fuckin' you for weeks, ever since you were laid up. Makes me wonder what you did to encourage him."

He might be just guessing; he wouldn't care if the facts matched the truth or not. I'm damned whatever I do. If I defend myself, protest any conversation between us was innocent, which it most definitely was, he'll still believe whatever he wants. If I stay quiet, my silence might damn me. *Jude's gone,* I reason. *He can't get hurt anymore.* No words of mine would make his life easier. As for my life, I'm not sure I still want it.

"Your little boy toy's gone now," he sneers. "Along with any plans the two of you were hatching." My horror-filled eyes watch his hands go to his belt which he starts to unbuckle, taking his time about it. "And you, *baby,* have some fuckin' amends to make. Starting with sucking my cock."

He's going to treat me like a whore.

In the scheme of things, it could be worse, and it's not like it hasn't happened before. Hell, he's even fucked me over the pool table in view of everybody to make a point. For a serious infraction, he's even let the other members fuck me.

I hate this. It isn't who I am, or rather, who I was. While knowing it's fruitless, I try to appeal to a better nature he doesn't possess. "Duke," I begin, anxiously looking around. Keeping my voice low, I stress, "I'm your *wife.*"

In the brief space that follows, I pray I've gotten through to him, but no. His face darkens. "You really want to play that card? When you've been fuckin' around behind my back?"

"I didn't!" As soon as my involuntary rebuttal escapes my mouth, I know it's a mistake. I could plead that with two broken legs there was nothing I could do, but Duke will believe whatever he wants to rationalise the violence he's about to dole out. His appetite for causing pain hasn't been satisfied by Jude's death. He wants more, and I'm the only one here who can assuage his dark hunger.

I brace but can't do anything more. Recently, his attacks have become more violent and more regular. While I may wish for death, I don't relish the pain that will accompany it. This time I fear that tonight I'll be following Jude into his grave. All the signs are there that he won't stop. I want to wail at the unfairness of it. Neither of us did anything wrong or even thought about it. Not Jude, twelve years my junior who just had his life so cruelly curtailed, and certainly not me. After Duke's less than tender administrations, I never wanted sex with a man ever again.

But hurting me isn't his immediate priority. I'm part relieved, part disgusted when he states, "Spilling blood gets me hard. Now suck me like the fuckin' pro you are." His dick now out, he steps closer, grabbing hold of my hair and wrenching my head back. "Open your fuckin' mouth."

I'm worth more, my internal voice screams. *I'm no whore.*

A violent jerk on my hair which will leave me missing a few strands has my mouth opening automatically. His cock enters, not gently, not slowly. He rams it into my mouth and down my throat. I retch, he laughs, holding himself there until I start to choke, then he draws back, letting me grab a breath then starts fucking my mouth in earnest.

He's wound up tight, heated by the death of the man he murdered in cold blood. On edge already, it's not long before he's swelling and flooding my mouth. When he pulls out, he slams his palm over my mouth, forcing me to swallow. I gag and almost choke on my own vomit in an attempt to keep it down. Tears stream from my eyes, my nose is blocked, and I gasp, desperate for air when he at last removes his hand.

Is my penance done?

It seems not. Now with the hand still twisted in my hair, he pulls my face up and lets his other fist fly, hitting my nose, the crunch and blinding pain telling me he's broken it. He throws me on the floor and kicks me in the ribs, in the stomach, my legs, and my head.

I curl up, trying to protect myself, even now conscious that out of all the men standing around, not one of them makes a move to stop him or to save me. Punch after punch, kick after kick, the pain assures me this time he'll go too far, and I'll be buried alongside the prospect.

Pain, agonising in its intensity is my whole universe. Blows follow one after the other until they seem to merge. My hope for a quick death is denied to me, and my punishment seems to go on for hours, until a welcome darkness descends.

I'M ALIVE.

When I come to, I'm uncertain whether that is good news or bad. My body is a ball of pain. It's hard to breathe, and there's no part of me not screaming in agony. I'm vaguely conscious that the bed, more like a cot, feels familiar. The blankets I'm lying on are scratchy and smell unwashed. My senses tell me I'm in the clubhouse, in the room they put me in when my legs were broken.

But where I am is of no matter now. I might have survived the beating, but my instincts tell me Duke's gone too far. It's not just painful to take air into my lungs, it's fast becoming impossible.

I'm dying.

Self-preservation makes me gasp, trying to suck in air and failing. Panicking, my lungs burn as if I'm drowning. There are people around me, and I try to cry out for help, but my voice doesn't work.

Familiar voices reach my ears. "Nah, can't do that. Prez would fuckin' kill me. That's if Duke doesn't get to me first."

"Croak, she's got a fuckin' collapsed lung."

"Treat her, doc. You fixed her last time."

"Last time he didn't do as much damage as this. Does Duke want her to die? 'Cause that's where she's heading."

"You fixed her lung, what more do you want?"

"She's got half my fuckin' pen in her chest. It's a temporary solution. I can't leave her like that, Croak."

Oh God, I'm dying. Won't anyone help? In my dreams, my

death was always peaceful, perhaps a blow or a bullet to the head, not lying helpless and conscious, feeling my life leeching out of me, slowly dying a painful death inch by inch. I try to open my eyes, but they feel glued shut. My ears are in full working order as I hear a thumping when heavy boots approach.

"Prez." Croak sounds relieved. "Duke want her finished? If not, Doc says she needs to go to the hospital."

Knife sighs heavily and there's a pause before he responds. "Fuck. No, she can't die. You know how Duke gets. She's his fuckin' property. He patched her for life."

Yeah. So why the fuck did he just half kill me?

"Never saw her fuckin' around with the prospect," Croak speaks again. He sounds confused.

Now a laugh comes from the prez. "Of course she fuckin' didn't, but that's the VP for you. When he has a hankering for bloodlust, he'll use any excuse. Easier to just let him get it out of his system. Doc, you sure she needs to go in?"

"Can't treat her here, Knife. Just look at this fuckin' place. My fix won't work for long. She'll drown in her own blood if she doesn't get professional help. Then there's a risk of sepsis."

Take me to the hospital. Please, let me go.

Even if it's just for a day or so. To get off the compound would be enough medication in itself. To be with normal people, people who wouldn't hurt, degrade or humiliate me. That's all the medicine that I want.

Do I pass out, or does Knife just take a long time deciding?

Whatever, it seems forever before I hear those glorious words. "Oh, for fuck's sake, get her out of here. Tell the hospital it was a mugging, or someone out to get the club. I'll clear it with Duke. One fuckin' body already today was enough."

Decision made, they don't waste time springing into action. It's Croak who says, "I'll get her. You bring your car around, Doc."

"Be care—"

Though I doubted I could do it, a piercing scream leaves my mouth when Croak picks me up. Once again, mercifully, I pass out.

The next couple of days I don't care where the hell I am, as time passes in a blur of machines beeping and pain, then wooziness as the pain meds kick in. Unaware of the passage of the hours, I only find out how long I've been here when I finally struggle up to full consciousness, seeing the relieved looking nurse, and, for the first time, am able to understand what she's saying.

While she catalogues my injuries, I tune out, not relishing hearing the damage he's inflicted on me. From what I do let sink in, it sounds bad. I don't even feel lucky he hadn't caused mortal injury. If he'd finished the job this time, it would have prevented me going through this again. There can be no doubt, once I'm healed, it will only be to go through more abuse.

I lie still, lost in my abject misery, wishing I were dead. Or I do until some more words spoken by the nurse register.

I try to speak, but my throat is dry. After sipping at some ice she holds to my lips, I manage to get some words out. "You're kidding me." She has to be.

Trying to focus on her face, through eyes I can only just open, I see her smiling. "No, I'm not. Though how the baby survived is a miracle. It's early days, you're about six weeks."

A miracle. Mine. Only mine. She starts to busy herself as if to leave me.

"My h-h-husband," I stammer out. "Does he know?"

Her eyes sharpen. "I don't think so. Honey, you were so badly hurt, I'll be honest, it's been touch and go. We've given him reports on how you're doing. We honestly thought even if you'd make it, you'd lose the baby."

"Is… is there still a chance I could miscarry?"

Compassion floods her features. "I can't lie to you, but the baby's made it so far. He must be one determined little soul to keep hanging on in there."

How, I don't know, but I'll do everything to keep it that way. "Please." Injecting as much pleading as I can into my voice, I beg her, "Don't tell my husband."

Duke's been ambivalent about wanting a child, sometimes ruminating about an heir, a son he could mould to be a reflection of himself. But when that became a reality a year after our marriage, after his first moment of elation, he'd kicked the baby out of me. Then, of course, he blamed me for infuriating him so. It was my fault I lost his baby, not his violent and uncontrollable urges.

After the loss of that baby, it seemed all Duke had wanted was me pregnant again. He couldn't fuck me enough and kept me full of his semen. I couldn't risk it, unable to bear the thought of losing another to this irrational man, already knowing carrying his child was no protection.

So, I'd taken precautions. Duke would kill me if he knew, but on the pretext of needing women's necessities that members didn't want to purchase for me and women's problems about which they didn't want to know, I'd managed to secretly go on the pill. The pill I'd not had access to during the weeks of captivity while my legs had healed.

The nurse looks at me, her brow furrowed. "I won't tell him if you don't want me to. He's here, though. It's up to you if you want to share the news yourself."

He's here. Of course he is, playing the concerned husband role. He can do that very convincingly. Using his charm was what had originally allowed him to reel me in and foolishly accept his proposal. At that time, I'd felt the luckiest and most treasured woman in the world.

My face must betray how I feel about my husband being close by and probably a whole lot more as her face fills with commiseration. She tilts her head to one side, considers me for a moment, then asks, "Do you want me to tell him you're not up to seeing him?"

I'd love that, but no. He'd only break down the door if he thought he was being kept away from his property. Analysing it fast, I realise I'm safe right now, hooked up to monitors that will alert someone if he so much as raises my blood pressure. "I'll see him."

She gives me another assessing gaze, then nods, albeit with a trace of reluctance. "I'll send him in."

When she goes out, I gather what strength I have, and focus my mind on how to get out of here. I'm determined not to lose this baby. It might be Duke's seed, but it's my womb it's growing in. This baby belongs to me, and it's up to me to protect it. Which means, whatever the odds against me, this time I have to escape.

With the Crazy Wolves controlling most of the surrounding area, how can I get away? I run through my problems in my head. I've no money. He controls all my documents. The only clothes I have here are the ones I was brought in wearing, and they'll be bloodied and soiled and that's if they hadn't been cut off and destroyed.

But whether I have to run in a hospital gown and beg strangers to help me, I have to not only try but succeed. It's not just me. It's my baby. *A new life inside me.* As the realisation sinks in, so does my determination to get out of his clutches.

When the door opens again, the air grows heavy around me, and I don't need to open my eyes to see who's there.

"Fuckin' cunt," he hisses. "Have you any fuckin' idea how much trouble you caused me? Jeez, why you insisted on coming here, I don't know." As he kicks a chair, I don't explain I had no choice in the matter. He'll blame me in any event. "Cops want to talk to you. I told them you were attacked by a person unknown. That's all you fuckin' tell them, you got me?"

"I got you, Duke." I know how this goes.

"Hmm. Well, once you've seen them, I'll break you out of here and take you home."

"I might need to stay in. I'm… I'm hurt pretty badly."

"I don't fuckin' care how bad you're hurt. Your place is with me." He moves forward and leans over the bed, letting me feel his warm whisky-tinged breath on my cheeks. "You do whatever you have to do, Sapphire. Tell them you want to discharge yourself. Hell, refuse treatment. I don't care how you do it, but you're coming home. I want you back tomorrow, you feel me? You can lie around in this bed feeling sorry for yourself for twenty-four hours. Then I'm bringing you home."

CHAPTER THREE

Niran

PRESENT DAY

Arriving back at the clubhouse just in time to catch the end of Grumbler's band's set, I stand a few steps inside the doorway and grin. As they finish on a crescendo that has hands clapping and boots stomping, I shake my head. *Who would have known the old man would have it in him?* But hell, his vocals are good, and as for the way he plays that guitar? He's as good as any rock star I've seen. The whole band is excellent. If they went professional, they could probably make a killing.

But they won't. Content to say their time has passed, they're happy just playing a couple of times a month at the clubhouse, belting out favourites we all enjoy.

As usual, Grumbler jumps off the makeshift stage and stops first to kiss the fuck out of his old lady, Mary, who grins and returns his affection wholeheartedly. When he finishes, the PDA that has had Alicia, his adopted daughter pretending to wretch, he pauses only to run his hand over Mary's extended belly, the one carrying their surprise child, before heading my way. I grin at him, musing, *Grumbler's the epitome of the old saying, there's life in the old dog yet.*

Stepping forward with a hand extended, I meet him halfway. "Sounded good tonight, Brother."

His thumb locks with mine. Pulling me in, he slaps my back, and a little hoarsely, turns to the bar and demands a beer from Connor. Then glancing at me again, he asks, "Were you in time to catch much?"

Grimacing in regret, again I shake my head. "Just the end. That job was a fuckin' bitch." I'd stayed late at the auto-shop to ensure a rush job was completed for the customer to pick up in the morning.

He grins. "Guess you didn't notice our fuckup, then."

I suppress the desire to roll my eyes. I doubt any fuckup was worthy of note, and probably only noticeable to the musicians themselves.

A movement to the side catches my eye. "Fagan, my man." Stretching my hand out to the drummer, he takes it in his. "On form as always."

At Grumbler's beckoning, the other two members of the band wander up, as anxious as he to wet their throats. It's no hardship for me to greet Jon Boy and Kurt as well. The three are only too welcome at the club, where no one actually cares if they fuck up anything. Their music enlivens the clubhouse, and the only payment they'll take is beer and snacks.

I wait on the sidelines while Grumbler dissects the set with his bandmates, tuning out completely when they start to discuss C minor sevenths and shit like that. I might appreciate music but haven't the first clue how to play it. As for singing? Let's just say, people would pay not to hear my voice.

Instead of listening to the conversation that's going way over my head, I examine the changes in Grumbler. Less than a year back, he was staring sixty in the face, his only companion and interest his motorcycle. Now, while he's added a year to his age, you'd easily take him for someone years younger. He's been given a whole a new lease on life and looks the better for it. It seems like in a flash, he'd resurrected his music hobby he thought abandoned, gained a wife, a stepdaughter, and currently has a kid on the way. Shows even old farts like him shouldn't give up on life.

I've got him beat in years, of course. I'm thirty-seven to his fifty-eight, but otherwise there are many similarities between us. A few years back, I thought I was made for life, a solid Marine rising through the ranks until a stateside accident took my leg. Lost, feeling washed up and abandoned, with no future to look forward to, I was adrift until I'd stumbled on the club's beach ride out. Finding the Satan's Devils had saved my life. Where would I be without them? I can't even imagine. I wasn't cut out for civilian life.

Not that joining the Devils was easy. Prospecting was hard, but my background as a Marine meant I could take all of their shit. It hadn't been the first time I'd gone through hazing. It had been worth every moment and I'd never looked back. Now I've been a patched member for getting on two years, and I fucking love it. Society might have turned its back on a vet having no further use for him, but the Devils made up for all that.

"See you in the week, bros." Grumbler's finishing up with the band. "Practice on Wednesday? Yeah, hell. I'm up for that."

"See you, Niran." Fagan mock-salutes as he walks past.

"Bye, man." I exchange a chin lift with Jon Boy, a man totally misnamed as he's in the same age bracket as Grumbler.

"Keep it shiny side up." Kurt gives a sharp nod as he follows the others.

Outside, their van will be waiting, already packed with all their shit. Well, what are prospects for if not to do the grunt work? I think having resident roadies is one of the reasons they enjoy playing here.

"So, Grumbler," I begin once I have his undivided attention. "How's it all hanging? How's Mary doing?"

Before he answers, Grumbler casts a look over his shoulder as though to check for himself. "She's in good shape. But," he taps his forehead, "I'm scared she worries too much. She says she's being realistic, while I'd prefer her to just relax."

Mary recently turned forty-eight and is six months pregnant. If the medics are to be believed, that's pushing it to deliver a healthy baby. It hadn't been planned, of course, and had been a surprise to them both. It still amuses me how folks their age can be caught out by, of all things, an out-of-date condom.

I think Grumbler had been in a state of shock when he originally found out, but he and Mary had been pragmatic, continuing with full knowledge of all the risks that came with a late pregnancy. Now he's fully onboard with the idea, there's nothing more he wants than his kid to be alright, and his wife to come through safely. Unfortunately, there are risks that can't be ignored or discounted.

"What's the doctor say? She happy with how it's going?" All of us are following the situation carefully, prepared to give the couple all the support they need.

"Doc's keeping a close eye on her. Mary's got another checkup on Monday. As you know, she goes regularly. But so far, so good, Brother. So far, so fuckin' good." Another quick glance behind at his wife as if to make sure he's still telling the truth, then there's an abrupt change of subject. "You get that beast tamed then?"

We shoot the shit for a few moments about the bike I've spent the evening fixing up, then, one of Grumbler's frequent checks over his shoulder has him narrowing his eyes.

"Mary's tired. I don't want her to overdo it. I'm going to get her home."

"You do that." I grin. "Take care of them both, Brother."

With a hefty back slap, he's gone.

Grumbler, Mary, and Alicia aren't the only ones leaving. As though a signal has been given that it's the end of the evening—for anyone other than members, that is—Dart, the VP, and Lost, the prez, along with their women, Alex and Patsy have followed fast on the tails of Grumbler and Mary. Now that the clubhouse is empty of old ladies and civilians, the club girls and some of the hangarounds who'd stayed in the background while the band had been playing, take their place in the limelight.

Deuce, patched in a year before me, sidles up to Cindy, clearly ready to commandeer her for an hour or so. Tits and Pearl make their way toward Salem and Pennywise, who each pull a half-naked girl onto their laps. My lips curve at the way they manage to carry on their conversation without seemingly pausing for breath.

Eva, the oldest, makes her way across the room. She's heading my way.

When I first came to the clubhouse, I admit it was with a sense of outrage that I found club girls in residence. Women, whose only purpose in life is to make themselves available for any man to use them. In the beginning, I wondered whether I should report the club for keeping sex slaves, but it soon became clear that they were here by choice. While I still can't fathom why any woman would choose this life, I've spoken enough to them to know they rate it better than working on a checkout or being a street walker.

During my time, I've watched them. Far from believing they're not worth much else than earning their keep on their backs, the girls here take pride in the services they provide, going so far as to chase hopeful hangarounds off. It makes me chuckle at times when I think how possessive they are about their bikers.

Then there are others—hangarounds, we call them—girls from town coming to club parties looking for a good time. Several of them are here at the moment, often coming when the band is playing, a free chance to hear live music. I watch as a gaggle of giggling girls gather around Dusty. Yeah, the good-looking fucker's going to get lucky tonight. Idly, I wonder which one he'll choose. Bones, sniffing and wiping his nose, approaches optimistically.

Uh oh. One is pulling free of the throng and coming straight for me. Narrowing my eyes, I brace.

"Get lost, Susie," Eva snaps, her arrival coinciding with the hangaround's. She backs up her words by placing her hand on my arm in a gesture of ownership.

Susie bites her lip and looks up at me pleadingly, but I give a violent shake of my head. I've been there, done that, and had immediately regretted it. Hell, I didn't even remember it, just woke up with a sore and obviously well-used cock and her lying next to me looking like the cat that had gotten the cream.

If it had been that good, wouldn't I have remembered?

While I didn't want an encore, she had, and for some reason believed she deserved it. But anything she thought I owed after that night was all in her head. In fact, I think it was me who had been wronged and taken advantage of, though I have nothing and no way to prove it.

Yet I was the man, the one assumed to be the aggressor. Despite not believing it was my fault, I'd let her down gently. Did that put her off wanting a repeat performance? Like fuck.

"Susie," Eva growls. She literally snarls at her. I choke back my laugh, and turn my head to the bar, vaguely conscious that Susie's heeded the warning as the scent of her overpowering perfume recedes. While remorseful for my part, I have no qualms sending her off. She'll soon be warming the bed of someone else with an eye to wearing their patch.

Before I became a Devil, I was a Marine, and sure, I got more than my share of casual fucks. I'm no prude, but there's something distasteful in going with a girl who's just been with one of my brothers, and after me, will probably move on to someone else immediately without waiting another sunrise and sunset to pass.

That night with Susie? I'd been in one of my despondent moods—thankfully now occurring less frequently—and she'd caught me when I was down low, and simultaneously high on a bottle of Jack. I suppose I must have grabbed at the fuck to bring me out of my funk. I hadn't a clue what I'd been doing or thinking until I woke up with her in my bed. A bed I soon kicked her out of.

As a prospect, I was forbidden to touch the whores, then as a member, I could take my fill. But I didn't—with the one notable exception. That's a mistake for which I'm still paying. For some reason, Susie keeps trying to get her hooks into me. My drunk self must have been quite impressive.

I'm no saint, I've hooked up occasionally in town, but casual isn't what I'm looking for. Sometimes, though, nature drives a man to take what's on offer, but I'm not tempted by the club whores. Eva and the club girls know the score.

At the end of the day though, they see me as one of theirs, and don't want anyone poaching. That's why Eva had rescued me. The thought makes me smile. I could have spoken for myself and told her to get lost, but why should I when I had Eva to do it for me?

"How are you doing, Niran?" The lightening of her tone confirms Susie's disappeared.

"Good. You?" I respond, as Eva pulls up a stool and sits down.

"I'm okay." The wipe of her hand down her face belies her certainty. I raise an eyebrow to encourage her. Seeing I've seen through her act, she drops the fake lightheartedness and grimaces. "Lost a kid today. Cancer." She grimaces. "We knew it was coming, but it's still hard, you know?"

Eva's the exception within the ranks of the club girls. While one of their number, she's also a mom who amicably shares parenting with her ex, as well as being a nurse, and a fucking good one at that. But when her ex has her son and she's not at the hospital, she's at the club, working on her back. She's a conundrum I can't quite work out. Why does she do it? Fuck knows.

Ignoring the services she performs for the club, I concentrate on her professional occupation instead. "That sounds a hard call, expected or not."

Her mouth twists. "He wasn't the first, and sadly won't be the last. But hell, seeing that waste of life, Niran, he was only thirteen."

Placing my hand over hers, I give it a squeeze. I know she won't misinterpret my touch. She knows the score. I'm never going to involve myself with the club girls, but hell, I don't mind playing the role of friend when they need it.

"Grumbler give a good account of himself tonight?"

I allow her the change of subject, knowing I'd probably want to do so myself. "By all accounts, yeah."

"I'm sorry I missed it." She sounds genuine, but then I expect she would, considering what she had been doing. Watching a kid taking his last breath must be soul destroying, whether you get paid for it or not.

She takes an opened bottle of beer from Connor and brings it to her mouth. Feeling sorry for her, I wonder whether I could make an exception and take her back to my room to help her forget her troubles for a while. I'm almost tempted, Eva's a beautiful woman, but then I remember that after leaving my bed, she'd go with the next brother who asks.

If I'm going to have a woman, I want her to be mine, and mine only. Not that I'm looking for permanent, but for however long the relationship lasts, I'd be faithful, and would expect her to be likewise. If I suggested that, Eva would laugh in my face, and remind me she'd once tried that and didn't care for it.

"Hey, Niran!" As I turn to greet the newcomer, Eva slides off the stool and taking her drink, makes herself scarce.

"Kink, my man." We exchange back slaps, then I look around and finally down at his feet. "No pets tonight?" The brother often has at least one naked woman in tow.

"Even a Dominant sex god needs a break sometimes." He winks. "Need to recharge the batteries."

"Or no one wanted to play," I tease him.

Placing his hand over his heart, he shakes his head. "You wound me, Brother. Fuckin' wound me."

Signalling to Connor I'd like another drink, I crease my brow. "I've been meaning to ask, what do the girls get out of what you do, Kink?" For the life of me, I don't understand how they allow Kink to humiliate them. What's more, he seems to have no shortage of volunteers.

As the prospect passes two beers across, Kink takes the stool Eva had just vacated. Casting a look at me, I presume whether to check I'm serious and not yanking his chain, he takes a breath and starts to explain. "I'm Dominant as fuck, Brother, which means I give the bitches what they need."

Scoffing, I respond, "And they have a need to go crawling around after you?"

He shrugs. "Know anything about BDSM, Niran?" When I shake my head no, he continues, "Everything in our world is based on communication which means being honest with yourself, being able to understand what you need rather than what you want and being able to ask for it. That goes whether you're submissive or Dominant."

I shake my head in confusion. "But you're the Dom, isn't what you dole out up to you?"

"Nah, Brother. I'm Dominant, yes, but that doesn't mean I'm an asshole." He gives another wink. "Well, not all the time. I get off on pleasing the submissive who's servicing me. By giving her what she needs, I can take her out of her head for a while, and by doing that, I get out of mine. Subspace and headspace aren't just terms, the states exist."

I don't think he's answered my question, or not in a way I can understand. "You humiliate those girls when you bring them here."

"Ever considered humiliation is just what they need?" His eyebrow rises quizzically. "Subs find a Dom who suits them." When I clearly am not on the same page, he continues to enlighten me. "Remember the girl last week?"

"The one with the big boobs, short bob, and curvy ass?"

He snorts. "You noticed, huh? Yeah, her. Well, by day, she's a fuckin' bank manager." My eyebrows rise. And there I'd been thinking she was a nympho just one step away from a street corner. Kink gives a sharp nod as if he can see into my mind. "Makes all these decisions that affect people's lives. A loan approved here, one denied there. Has to listen to sob stories or grand ideas all the time and deals with the fallout when the customers don't think she's got it right. She finds it hard to turn off from her day job. Takes her work home with her every night, if not physically, then mentally. Her work plays on her mind. Man needs money to pay off his debts? She might judge it would just land him in more. He rants and raves as he sees no other way out of it—brings up his starving kids, his dying wife, the whole damn lot. Her first duty is protecting the bank's money, but in doing so, she makes judgement calls which affect someone's life. Sometimes it's hard to live with such thoughts going around your mind."

He's caught my interest. I wiggle my hand to show him I want to hear more.

"In real life, she's so far from submissive it's a fuckin' joke, but after work, she can only relax by giving up control, entering a space where for a time she makes no decisions, but more than that, is taken to a place where she can totally clear her head. Might be temporary, but when she comes down, she's better able to compartmentalise than she was before." He checks to make sure I'm following him. "Some subs find their release with

Shibari—that's being tied up in ropes, unable to move and forced to submit to their Dominant."

"Sounds like abuse," I mumble, taking another sip of my beer.

"Abuse? You're so fuckin' wrong." He pauses and brushes back his long hair with his hand. "But also, right. Done by the wrong Dom, it can be. That's why clubs exist. It's a safe place, and everything's consensual. Good clubs that is. Some attract assholes. But in mine, everything's negotiated and agreed up front. The girl, or man—gender doesn't come into it—agrees with the Dom before anything takes place exactly what will happen and give their consent. The Dom will know the sub's hard limits, what to avoid, soft limits where he might push her, and of course, what she really enjoys."

"Sounds like a lot of work just to get your rocks off." Of course, when I get down and dirty, I check the woman is into it, but prefer to work on the fly. If something feels good, and it gets the response I want, I'll run with that.

Kink chuckles. "Work? Nah. While everything's negotiated up front, there still remains leeway. Think about it as acting out fantasies, but knowing you'll only go so far as both partners want."

I grimace. "Still don't understand how some women like humiliation."

"Not just women, it works for some men." He stares at his beer bottle. "Some people need the adrenaline rush from extreme sports, others wouldn't sky dive if you paid them too. Kinks vary, Niran. Think for a moment about what I do. Can you imagine how much trust a sub must put in their Dom to crawl naked in a room of bikers looking on? Knowing their Dom will protect them? Knowing men can look, but not touch?"

"But what does she get out of it?"

"The idea she's desirable, that I want to show her off. That she doesn't have to think about anything, and I'll take care of her."

I snort. "Then you take her back to your room and fuck? Seems like you do a lot to get a twisted kink satisfied, Brother. Me? I'd go straight to the good stuff."

"And again, you're wrong. Sometimes sex isn't involved. My kink, as you term it, is the heady feeling I get from knowing how much trust is placed in me. I would never hurt a sub, nor push her further than her set boundaries."

"And here I was, thinking you were just showing off." I chuckle.

"The club's a great place to bring my subs," he says, seriously. "None of you fuckers would touch my property, but there's an edge, as the sub doesn't one hundred percent know that. She has to trust me that I won't allow anyone close. The exhilaration she feels is equal to that adrenaline rush I was just talking about. That glassy expression in my subs' eyes you must have seen? That's when they've let all their doubts and everyday worries go, and have placed their trust in me, their Dom, completely."

To be honest, I'd often thought they were stoned.

I still can't comprehend fully, but he's opened my eyes. "So, it's a kind of therapy?"

"Kind of. Back to the case of the bank manager. She goes home, is able to switch off and get a good night's sleep. The next day, she's back at work making decisions logically, instead of her emotions having kept her awake."

"So, your expertise is humiliation?"

He snorts. "Some Doms prefer one kind of shit over another. Some aren't programmed to do what I do, but I won't say that's my only forte." He turns and stares at me. "Being a Dom is a heavy responsibility. It's not just sex. If I wanted that, I'd go with a club girl and get my balls emptied in record time. Negotiating, learning what a girl really needs, then carrying it out, all takes time. It's not a quick release, Brother, and that's if I even get there." After a moment, he nods, seeing I'm taking it in. "You've got a Dominant streak in you, Niran. If you're interested, we can speak more."

Having just taken a large swig of my beer, I choke. When I've recovered with the aid of a hefty back slap, I look him in the face. "Seems like too much darn trouble to me."

He laughs. Sliding off the stool, he rests a hand briefly on my shoulder. "Offer's open anytime, Brother."

CHAPTER FOUR

Saffie

When Duke left my hospital room, I was terrified. How the hell can I escape when he's given me just one day? In his mind, the time limit was probably generous, and if I refuse to leave, I've no doubt he'll carry out his threat to abduct me. Hell, I wouldn't put it past him to hire a private ambulance and forge papers to say I was being transferred. Nothing ever gets in Duke's way.

Twenty-four hours. That's all he's given me.

What the hell can I do? I'm hooked up to machines, a catheter in place. Even if I wanted to move, it's too painful to do much more than breathe.

I'm trapped. Just as I've been for the last five years and will continue to be until Duke has enough of me.

The same nurse who was in earlier comes in again and checks the monitors and the fluids dripping into me. Letting her get on with her job, I focus on worrying about myself.

Could I call my parents? Would they help?

I only wish I could, but according to Duke, they've washed

their hands of me. While I wouldn't give much credence to anything uttered by him, I know it's probably the truth. I may not know the details, but Duke used me to get revenge on my father. It's all my fault I enabled whatever had happened by being taken in by his lies. As for my mother, she swears that a marriage vow once uttered can never be rescinded. I disobeyed once, when I divorced my cheating ex, and last time I saw her, she still hadn't forgiven me. She definitely wouldn't approve of me leaving another man, and if she knows I'm with child, whether or not she likes Duke, she'd insist that he be involved with his child.

No, it's too dangerous. I can't take the risk they've disowned me as their daughter and can't rely on them to protect me from him.

"Sapphire, may I speak plainly?"

Lost in my thoughts, it takes a moment for me to realise I'm being addressed. Awkwardly turning my head, I focus on the nurse.

"Your husband did this, didn't he?" Her lips are pressed tightly together.

"It was a mugging." I parrot what I've been told to say.

She grimaces and ignores me. "If it was your husband, I can get you help."

I'm already expecting a visit from the cops and I know better than to tell them something other than what Duke had suggested. He's got some of their rank in his pocket. He boasts often enough about that, and how he could literally get away with murder.

"No one can help me." I turn my head back the other way, not wanting her to see the tears of defeat in my eyes. Anyone offering assistance is likely to go the same way as Jude. Even if I could make an official complaint about him, he'd have to be convicted and put away if I were going to be safe. They might arrest Duke, but they wouldn't arrest his brothers, and they, protecting their VP, would do whatever it took to stop me from testifying against him.

The nurse, though, isn't put off by my dismissal. "There's a group I've heard of that helps women like you get away. Women who can't involve the authorities."

"It was a mugging," I stubbornly repeat.

"Sapphire. Your man was wearing his cut. He's one of the Crazy Wolves. I've heard the rumours, hell everyone around here has. I can well understand why you don't want to go to the police, but please, trust me, there is a way out."

With embryonic hope, I turn back to her. "You're taking a risk if you help me."

She shrugs. "I won't be doing anything but putting you in touch with the Freedom Trail. I'm sure, if they can, they'll get you out of here."

The Freedom Trail? I've never heard of them. But what could they do? "I've no time for anything to be arranged. And if they helped me escape, what then?" I'd still need to be in a hospital, and being moved to a different one wouldn't help. Duke would still find me. Crazy they might be, but one asset to the club is a disgraced ex-fed, whose computer skills can find anybody.

"Just leave that to them." The nurse is not at all put off. "If they help you, you'd be given a new identity. You'd be moved far away, and Sapphire Marshall wouldn't exist anymore. You'd have a fresh start. Both you and your baby."

I don't allow myself to get excited, but I'd be lying if her words don't give me hope and something to think about other than the desolation of my situation. *There could be a way out?* My eyes widen as the idea settles in my head. "Are you sure they'd help me?"

"Honey, you're one of the worst cases I've ever seen. You don't have to tell me this isn't the first time he's beaten you.

You're covered with scars and healed broken bones. They'll help you, I'm certain."

"He's going to come for me tomorrow," I warn her.

The short timescale doesn't seem to put her off. "Then we'll need to be quick. Please say yes, honey."

Just one nod, one little rise and dip of my head, and that's all it takes for her to beam at me.

As she disappears without delay, presumably to kick-start arrangements, I start to daydream about having help to get away. I don't give a damn about changing my name or my whole identity. As long as Duke's nowhere close, I'll be free.

How could this work? I'm in no state to be moved. Not even by Duke. Under normal circumstances, a patient would expect the medical staff to explain my condition to concerned relatives, and said relatives would agree, the hospital was the best place for me. But Duke's never been described as normal. Come morning, I know he'll arrive and take me away. My future will comprise of little more than a cell and whatever medical care he deems necessary, and that only being provided by prospects again. Prospects who'll have witnessed Jude's demise and know better than to become friendly.

Don't get your hopes up, I tell myself. I'm out of my mind if I think I can escape.

But I've got to try.

And do it despite the pain I'm in. What's far worse is the worry about the new life I still can't believe is growing inside me, and what would happen if Duke ever found out about his impending fatherhood. Either of his possible reactions would have horrific consequences. Like before, he might kick the baby out of me, or he'll decide it's time to be a dad, and look forward to having an heir. A child I wouldn't put past him to take away from me.

What's certain is I'll be little more than an incubator, having no influence on how my child grows. A son would be groomed to follow in his footsteps, a daughter, well, her future would depend on how best she could be used. My baby, like me, would be nothing but his property.

If this Freedom Trail offers a way out, I have to take it. Alone, I've no chance, even if I wait until I've healed. I've been trying to escape Duke for five years, but he's never given me sufficient freedom to make a successful attempt. When I'm allowed off compound, I'm always escorted.

If he takes me back, it will only be a matter of time until he puts his fists on me again. Now I definitely can't risk it, not least because I know I'm only alive as they decided to help me. Only a few more minutes without the correct treatment, and I might have died. But most of all, I now have a baby to think of. A child who could be killed along with me.

The cops come to see me, but like Duke had instructed, I lie. *It was a mugger. They took my bag. No, I didn't know who, they came up behind me.* Something inside was crying out for the cops to see through my lies, but if they did, if that was a glimmer of doubt I saw in their eyes, they dismissed it as a domestic dispute between husband and wife.

After them, a stranger comes to visit me, a middle-aged woman, whose eyes are sharp. In soft tones she explains what using the Freedom Trail will mean. I'll be unable to have contact with friends or family or anyone from my current life. No problem, I reassure her easily. Duke's kept me isolated. I've had no contact with friends for five years, and any which I thought would show pity for me, I wouldn't risk putting up against the man I so foolishly married.

I've been lonely throughout my ill-fated marriage. I can cope with more now. To only worry about myself, to be able to concentrate on growing my baby, seems a luxury to me.

When she leaves, satisfied with my response, I wonder how my disappearance will be accomplished. Whether I'll be caught.

Whether Duke will get wind of my plans. Whether he'll turn up and kill those trying to help me.

In the end, my worries were in vain. It goes smoothly, showing I'm certainly far from the first person they've helped. I'm moved in the dead of night. On a gurney, I am wheeled out of the hospital and into an ambulance. It's not the normal type, but one painted black.

Doped up on painkillers, I'm only vaguely aware of the apology that I'm being transported in the same way as they would a corpse.

I pass out for most of the journey, and when I come too, see sunlight streaming through windows of yet another hospital. It's light and airy, and I take it as a premonition, a sign my future is looking bright.

I'm reassured by yet another woman from the Freedom Trail that things had gone to plan, and I have gotten away cleanly. I don't ask for details of the mess I left behind.

Duke must be out of his mind with rage, but I don't want it confirmed. I know he'll desperately be trying to find me. A man like him won't let his property go lightly. But the image of him, tearing the hospital apart in an effort to find me, I try to wipe from my mind. *He'll be beyond furious.*

My fear he'll succeed taints my sense of victory, and the stress can't be good for the baby. I try hard to chase all thoughts of my possible failure and his likely success out of my mind, putting my faith in the group of people who assure me, they've successfully liberated people like myself before.

Determined I'll do nothing to rock the boat, I do everything they ask, follow every instruction to the letter just to make sure that I and my baby are safe.

Do I feel remorse it will never know its father? Hell no. I'll make up some excuse, some fiction, whatever light it paints me in, having already decided *father unknown* will be written on the birth certificate. I'd rather be thought a whore than leave a trail for anyone to follow.

I'm Sapphire Marshall no longer.

Saffie was the name I used to go by until I became a precocious teen and insisted on everyone using my full name. Even my parents never refer to me by my childhood nickname, and Duke's never heard it. I suppose there's some comfort when I hear it used after so many years, some sense of returning to a time when things were easy, and I'd felt safe. When my only worry was would I be forced to eat peas yet again, where I'd misplaced my favourite toy, or whether the teacher would yell at me for forgetting my homework. Everything was so much simpler before I became an adult.

Jones is my new surname, something so common it's hard to be traced.

It takes two weeks for me to become fit enough to cope with what lies ahead. When I'm asked where I'd like to be located, I don't much care, but if the choice was mine, I'd prefer California. Safe, warm and vibrant, or so my tortured mind paints it to be.

The Freedom Trail is a well-oiled machine and take pains with preparing me for my new life ahead. I've become well versed in the use and exchange of passwords to make sure anyone helping me on my way are who they say they are. I listen carefully, ultra-cautious—it isn't just me in this now.

Finally, armed with only a small suitcase of donated clothes, I travel across country partly chauffeured by strangers in cars, and then left to my own devices to complete my journey by Greyhound, mysteriously finding tickets ready at every stage, and arrive at my final destination with my new ID and details in hand.

Somehow, miraculously, it had all gone to plan, and I successfully found my way to San Diego where I got into a cab and headed for my new address.

My apartment is small, clean and nice—a perfect place to stay and bring up my child. I've also been set up with a job, one suitable for skills I don't possess. I'd gone from my parents to a marriage where I was a trophy wife, and from there, lived off my settlement until I'd met Duke. I'd never worked in my life. Although I think I must be capable of something better, stocking supermarket shelves is about all I'm qualified for.

It's when I compare the amount on my paycheck to the rent that I need to pay, I realise I should have insisted on going to a cheaper state. How could I prepare for the birth of my baby while putting food on the table and a roof over my head? Skimping on food isn't an option. I have to think of the new life inside me.

It isn't long before I realise that if I'm to buy the vitamins and healthy food that's recommended to nurture my child, I have to move to save money. In the back of my mind, I think having an address not even the Freedom Trail know of might add an extra layer of protection. I'm constantly terrified that Duke will find me, unable to shake the impending sense of doom.

Of course, cheap is never perfect and I know the place where I end up isn't the ideal situation. It's cheap, and that's all that matters. Inside my apartment, I have all that I need. Outside? Well, I'd worried about that as soon as I moved in. But so far no one's bothered me, seemingly uninterested in a pregnant woman, who drives the cheapest car she can afford. On my part, I ignore the drug deals which go on day and night, and the fights I have to evade when I pass.

It's not much, but it's mine, and allows me to put part of my salary aside to cope with what lies ahead.

Days pass, weeks go by, and I can't hide my pregnancy now. Despite its simplicity and monotony, I enjoy my job. I like the boss I work for. Shelly is understanding and spotted my condition early on, and now she's set me to work on the tills which isn't such physically demanding work.

Life without Duke is perfect, and not a day passes when I don't thank the Freedom Trail and the anonymous people who helped me. At the back of my mind though, I can't shake the worry, that somehow, some day, Duke will find me. I take every precaution, keeping to myself, using cash to pay for everything, friendly enough when coworkers chat to pass the time, but wary of getting close to anyone. When leaving the apartment, I disguise my appearance as much as I can.

Do I grow more confident as time goes on? Not really, though I try to put my fears aside. That's not easy, when a loud male voice speaking too loudly can make me startle and kick off a panic attack.

Introspection does me no good, neither does revisiting the past and bemoaning how I got here. Instead of thinking of myself, I force every thought to be for the precious cargo I carry. Instead of looking back with regret, I look forward to when I will hold my child in my arms.

I sing to my baby at night, stroke my stomach as I go about my life, living only for him or her.

The thing I'm not is lonely. My years of being locked up and ignored serve me well, as I'm fully capable of amusing myself and not getting bored. How could I? I've access to a television and more books than I can ever hope to read downloaded on my Kindle. Reading becomes my escape. Where else can you find hours of pleasure for the price of a coffee?

Home from work, I cook and eat a healthy dinner, then settle down with a book. Finishing it, I purchase another by the same author.

Big mistake. To my horror, I've accidentally stumbled into a new-to-me genre, MC Romance. I read as much as I can before throwing the book down in horror. *She'd gotten so much wrong.* How can she write of respect for women when in a real MC there is none? And that clubhouse she was describing was nothing like my experience. I want to contact her and tell her how much she got wrong.

I don't of course, I just put down the book and stop reading. I can't afford to come out of hiding, even anonymously to someone on the internet.

But I read blurbs carefully from now on, watching out so I'm not lured in by such books again. MC Romance doesn't exist, or not like the authors portray it.

But then, I rationalise, if fiction reflected real life, who'd want to buy it? Who'd fall for a cruel murderer, or want to redeem a man who makes his living abusing, buying and selling women?

Instead, I read books about mothers and babies, and lose myself in the fantasy of having a man in my life who'd accept me as a single mom. Then I realise I'm being stupid and would never be able to trust myself with a man again, and definitely not with my baby. I've made mistakes twice. How could I ever trust my judgement? As for sex, the thought makes me shudder. Duke had turned that act of pleasure into a nightmare, and I'll be content to end my days never knowing a man's touch again.

Moving my hand across my stomach, I promise my child that I'll be everything he or she needs. It might be tough. I might not be able to provide a fraction of what I had growing up, but I'll make up for it with love. That I have in abundance.

I don't care who fathered it. My baby is mine, and nature be damned, my child will be shaped by his nurture, and I'm determined to do that right.

Weeks pass, but my fear that Duke won't stop looking for me never fades. I shop only when I need to, and apart from going to work, keep away from anyone who might want to make a record of me. Since coming to San Diego, I've not visited a doctor. I'm healthy, I don't need one, but as time passes, I do wonder about my child.

I'm five and a half months pregnant now, and I've got questions. Is he or she growing alright? Is it moving as much as it should? I've had none of the assurances normal moms get, not since I left the hospital, and that was still early.

I read pregnancy books by the bucketload and follow all the advice. But is it enough?

I know I need to make sure, and I long to find out what gender I'm carrying. I don't want it to be a surprise. I want to know whether I'm having a boy or a girl. Not that I've a preference for either sex, but I'd like to think of names and start to prepare.

I've been in San Diego three months, and Duke hasn't caught up with me. I must be safe, mustn't I? Veering between thinking it's a mistake, and knowing I have no choice, coming to a decision, I pick up the phone and make an appointment. Then, I sit back and smile, my hand rubbing my stomach.

Soon, baby, I'll know what you are. Then I can start planning our life together.

That done, I pick up a catalogue I got from a baby store, and start looking at cribs and other paraphernalia, a kernel of excitement bubbling inside me.

In three and a half months, I'll meet him or her.

I can't wait.

CHAPTER FIVE

Niran

I t had been an interesting discussion with Kink last night, not that I really got what he was talking about. Sex was sex, wasn't it? Some good, some so-so, but not very often bad—for men, at least, who normally get off, women, possibly not so much, if they go with the wrong man or mislead him by faking it.

I can understand why when you add love into the mix, fucking transcends casual sex. But love isn't what Kink's talking about. All that negotiating rubbish seems to take the spontaneity out of that shit. If you go to a sex club, don't you want to get fucked? If you wanted conversation, you'd go to a bar. Still, I suppose as I made do with my hand last night, any sex with another party might be good right now. I seem to be going through a dry spell. Maybe it's time to rectify that. Perhaps I need to go into town and see if I can connect with someone.

No chance today, though. I grin to myself as I walk out of the clubhouse to where Pennywise, Salem and Hard Token are waiting by their bikes. As had been planned after my chat with Kink, today we're just going to head out and see where the road takes us.

Can there ever be anything better than four guys out for a ride? Letting the wind blow away all thoughts other than how good our life is? Nah, not even sex.

Sunday passes in a whirl of pavement beneath our wheels, good food at a bar we find which we've never tried before, and great conversation when we park up and just enjoy the scenery and fresh air for a while.

I return to the clubhouse renewed and refreshed, my mind circling back to that conversation the night before. Who needs to jump out of a plane or control a sub to put their life back into balance? Riding my bike does exactly that.

Inside, the MC life just gets better. Patsy, the club's first old lady, has gotten the club girls under her thumb in the kitchen, and we're treated to a very passable pot roast. The evening is spent dissecting the day's ride, playing cards and losing a game of pool to Bones.

I'd enjoyed my time as a Marine, thought I'd never find anything to replace it, but joining the club has come a close second, and sometimes even tops it. Sure, I'm not flying halfway around the world at the drop of a hat, but neither am I risking my life for a war I care nothing about.

The ride out was good but tiring, and when I start to yawn and feel my prosthesis rub against the stump which is all that remains of my leg, I bid my goodnights and take myself up to my room.

Stripping off, I exchange my prothesis for my cane, and ease onto my mattress. Snuggling under the covers, I think I've got everything I need in my life. Of course, if I had my way, I'd have two flesh-and-blood legs, but I've moved on from regretting the loss of it.

But maybe there is one thing missing. Turning onto my side, I gaze at the empty side of the bed. What would it be like to find an old lady? Is there really someone out there for me? Someone who'd be there just for me, someone to come home to?

I don't want casual. I want to care about a woman and want her to care about me.

Once, I thought I would find someone, settle down, start a family like everyone else, but as it turns out, it wasn't to be. First my service career had gotten in the way. I was never home long enough to find anyone. Now, I'm a biker with an extra complication. While I may have come to terms with it, any woman I find has got to be okay with my missing leg. I'm already aware for some, it's a turnoff.

Still, if Grumbler can find a woman of his own, maybe there's hope for me yet.

Hopefully I won't have to wait as long as him.

In the darkness, I grin, moving into the centre of my king-sized bed, spreadeagling my arms and legs, happy that I can hog everything. Maybe there are benefits to sleeping alone. With that thought I turn over and stop thinking at all.

Monday dawns. I might love my job—working at the auto-shop owned by the club is like working for myself as I take a share of the profits we make—but like anyone else, I don't particularly like the start of the work week. At the weekends, I can do what I want and when. During the week, I'm at the beck and call of anyone who wants their work done.

Despite all the years I was a Marine, dragging myself out of bed at the crack of dawn is not my idea of fun. Even though I retain the ability to leap into action as soon as the alarm goes off, it doesn't mean I necessarily do so with good grace. Wiping sleep from my eyes, I reverse my bedtime routine—piss first, shower, then get myself dressed in some fresh clothes. Yawning widely, I descend the stairs.

Two of our prospects, Connor and Curtis, are in the kitchen doing their best to cook edible food. Seeing the bacon looks okay, the pancakes just this side of acceptable and the eggs are decidedly iffy, I help myself to a coffee and fill a plate deciding to leave the latter.

"Morning, Brother." Wrangler's greeting me but smirking at the prospects. Being one of their number until a few months back, he's still getting mileage from his elevated status. Unlike me, he voices his demand and accompanies it with a rap on the table. "Get me a coffee, Prospect."

Prospecting being not so far in my rearview, I know how much the pair will want to answer by raising a finger, but like any good recruit, Curtis, his expression remaining impassive, puts down his spatula and fills a cup.

"You're up early," I observe to the new brother.

"Yeah, Deuce has asked me to take stock at the bar. Thought I'd get it done early and go for a ride."

"Part-timer," I observe, tucking into my bacon. My comment not quite deserved as working with Deuce, Wrangler will often be there until late into the night.

"Yeah." He doesn't rise to my bait. "Deuce is worried some shit's going missing. Wants me to check."

I raise an eyebrow. If he's right, we could have problems with the civilian staff at the bar. Though that anyone would be crazy enough to steal from the Satan's Devils begs disbelief. "Let me know if you need help sorting it out."

Wrangler shrugs. "It's likely some of the stock's just got mixed up, but I'll let you know if I need anything. Thanks, Brother."

When Grumbler was laid up a year back, I'd temporarily taken over as sergeant-at-arms, a role I've semi-continued now that Grumbler's duties are divided between looking out for the club and caring for his pregnant old lady.

Wrangler gives me a final appreciative chin lift, then drains his coffee and walks out. Taking his lead, I swallow the last of my breakfast then down the remains of my cup. Patting my cut to ensure my keys and wallet are there, I head out to my bike.

Arriving at the shop, while I'm not late, Gibbs and Ross, a couple of our now-civilian but former-Marine mechanics are already checking through the books and assigning themselves tasks. Joining them, we divvy up the jobs, and soon have our heads down as we work.

"Grumbler not coming in?" Ross asks after a while, as the time for the man to put in an appearance has passed.

"You know that," Gibbs replies with a roll of his eyes. "He's gone to LA to pick up a part."

"He set off early," I remind them as Ross slams his hand against his forgetful head. "Mary's got an appointment this afternoon, and he never misses those."

"Your old brain injury playing up?" Gibbs asks, but his grin belies any concern.

"Fuck off," Ross responds good-naturedly. "I lost an arm, not my fuckin' mind."

I snort, then return to what I was doing.

Time marches on, and I begin to grow surprised Grumbler hasn't made it back. He'd planned to leave long before I'd gotten out of bed. Sure, the ride to Los Angeles takes a couple of hours, but he'd set out early enough to avoid the worst of the rush hour. As the hours tick past, I start to worry. *Where are you, old man?*

My phone ringing startles me, and I push myself out from under a car. The display shows me it's the man I was just thinking about calling.

"Hey, old man. You alright?"

"I'm good. Need to ask you a favour, Brother."

"Anything, Brother, you've got it." He doesn't even need to ask. I start making my way to the desk, thinking the store might have forgotten what part he'd ordered and gone to collect, and that Grumbler needs the serial number.

But that's not what he needs. "Got a nail in my tyre when I was heading back. Had to get roadside assistance to take me to a tyre place, but they didn't have the one I needed in stock. Gonna be stuck here a few more hours." I hear a sound in his throat that shows me he's not impressed. The reason clear as he adds, "Hate to ask this of you, but could you go with Mary to her appointment? I don't want her going alone."

Given the ages of Mary and Grumbler, the odds of them growing a healthy baby are stacked against them, and I hear the undertone in his voice. This isn't just a normal 'be there to make conversation to stop her getting bored', this is a 'be there in case she gets bad news' favour to him. Neither will want to put the appointment off, and under the circumstances, I whole-heartedly agree, Mary shouldn't be alone. While I don't relish the task in case the visit goes sour, to be honest, I'm honoured as fuck that he's asked me. Patsy, the prez's woman, would have gone like a shot, and she might be better to understand anything pregnancy related. It's a measure of his respect that he's made the request of me.

"Of course, I'll go, but all I can do is hold her hand."

"Not asking you to do more, Brother. She likes and respects you. She'll be good with you being there."

"I'll do it," I agree without hesitation.

"Great. I'll call Mary. You mind picking her up?"

That makes me smile. He hates her doing anything nowadays, even getting behind the wheel of a car. I know Mary finds it frustrating, but she tolerates his worrying because the concern comes from his heart. Grabbing a pen and paper, I jot down the details.

I decide to tease him. "Any particular kind of cotton wool I should take with me to wrap her in?"

"Fuck off, Brother," he growls. "And let me know anything she might not want to tell me."

How would I do that? Mary's hardly likely to share information with me that she wouldn't give him. I settle for reassuring him I'll let him know anything I find out.

"Shiny side up, Brother." I end the call.

By the time I've finished with the car I'm repairing, it's time to head out. Riding my bike back to the clubhouse, I swap it for the club's SUV, then make my way to Grumbler's house. As soon as I draw up, a figure runs out.

"Hey, Niran."

"Alicia." I pull Mary's teenage daughter in for a hug. "Shouldn't you be in school?"

"I am. I just popped home to pick some work up."

"She was bored and wanted an excuse to drive her car." Mary's waddling out, looking every bit the glowing pregnant woman that an ignoramus like me would expect. She's six months now and has a decided baby bump, slacker muscles due to her age and previous pregnancy, or so Grumbler had told me. Being a gentleman, I'd never ask.

"Well, I'm off." Alicia runs back to her mom and gives her a peck on the cheek. "Let me know how it goes."

"Kids!" Mary exclaims, but she's got a big smile on her face. "Sometimes I think I preferred it when I drove her everywhere, and when she wanted to come home, had to go and pick her up. Now she appears when I'm least expecting her."

I chuckle as I catch her gist. "That cause you and Grumbler problems?"

"It has." Mary laughs loudly. "Alicia has said she needed to bleach her eyes. Now if she comes back unexpectedly and finds his bike here, she sounds her horn to warn us."

The old man's obviously still got it in him. I start to wonder about the 'lunches' he pops home for. Guess it's more that he's working up an appetite rather than getting his hunger assuaged.

Mindful of the time and having had timeliness drummed into me by the Corps, I prompt her, "Are you ready to go?"

"Yeah. I've got my purse and all I need."

I like Mary, have from the first moment I met her. She's got a strength that comes from suddenly finding herself alone in the world and having to cope with bringing up a rebellious girl angry at the world after losing her father. I'd personally witnessed Alicia being more than a handful at first, but when Grumbler had pulled her out of a mess, she'd grown to respect her stepfather. Nowadays, I see a new maturity in her, and put it down to both Mary and Grumbler. It wasn't what I would have expected. Who would've thought a confirmed bachelor biker to take so well to being a dad?

As I help Mary into the SUV, I think how much Grumbler's looking forward to having his own child, even though they're both old enough to be grandparents. I sincerely hope that today's appointment is simply a confirmation that everything's heading in the right direction.

Mary settles into the seat with an oomph, and a rub of her hand over her stomach. She looks at me ruefully. "I don't remember it being this hard. Now I get worn out so easily." She waits until I've started the car before she adds, "I'm very grateful for the company, Niran, but I could have gone on my own. I'm sure you've got better things to do than cart a pregnant woman around."

"Hey, I'm just here to settle Grumbler's mind." I wave off her thanks as I get into gear, turn and pull away smoothly.

For a moment, we drive in silence, then a sideways glance shows her biting her lip.

"You alright?" *Am I driving too fast? Is she car sick?*

"I'm fine." She offers a brief smile. "These appointments are always worrying, just in case they find something wrong with the baby."

I'm an idiot. I should have guessed it was that. I try to be reassuring. "I'm sure they won't. You're doing everything right, aren't you? Eating well, resting and all that?"

She chuckles. "As if I could do anything else with Grumbler looking after me. He made me give up work, you know that? Still, I don't deny it's nice to not have to worry about things. Though I do get bored, it's good being able to take a nap whenever I want."

I know all that. I also know if she hadn't done it voluntarily,

Grumbler was going to speak to her boss. Once that man takes something on, he's all-in. He's determined to do everything he can for this pregnancy to have a healthy outcome, for both mother and child.

We fall back into a comfortable silence for a while, the only voice being the instructions uttered by the GPS. When we arrive at the hospital, Mary still seems concerned. When I've parked and helped her out, I offer her my arm.

"It's going to be fine," I try to impress on her.

Her squeeze on my bicep tells me she hopes that I'm right. So do I. Suddenly, the weight of responsibility settles on me. *What if there's a problem?* Grumbler should be here, not me. I now understand why he moves heaven and earth to be with her. *He would if he could.* But he can't, and I'll just have to be an adequate substitute. Straightening, I pull my broad shoulders back. *I got this. I can handle it.*

After she checks in, we go to a waiting room. Far from my fear I'd be the only man, most women seem to be accompanied. Mary picks up a magazine and starts to flick through it, while I settle back on a chair and surreptitiously eye the others waiting, occupying myself by wondering about their backstories. Some of the couples look lovey-dovey and excited, some look bored as if they've been through it all before. Of the unaccompanied woman, only one's showing a small baby bump. It would have gone unseen had she not looked so thin she could be undernourished. My eyes move on and then back, seeming to be drawn to her. Her hair is blonde and short, which seems at odds with the dark hue of her face. She's not tanned, but has a naturally deeper toned skin, brown eyes and almost black brows. I surmise her hair colour is due to dye, but is that advised during pregnancy? Well, what the fuck do I know? I'm hardly qualified to give advice or criticise.

I pull my eyes away, but soon they slide back again. She's not a young girl, thirty or so, perhaps? She's certainly not affluent. Her clothes are clean but cheap. Surreptitiously, I look but spy no ring on her finger.

She's sitting quietly, not reading, but her hands are smoothing over that baby bump as if reassuring the child inside. Her teeth worry her lip, and she keeps glancing toward the reception desk and looking nervous. As I watch, she takes out a tissue and dabs at her eyes.

I find myself wanting to know her story. Why's she here alone? Does her man not care about the baby? Or, is he not in the picture? Strangely, she pulls at something inside of me, making me want to hold her close. If a woman ever needed caring for, it's her.

Fanciful much? The excess of hormones must be getting to me. I laugh at myself, unable to believe I'm drawn to a pregnant woman. If I wanted a woman with a baby, I'd prefer to put one inside her myself.

"Ms Jones?"

The woman who caught my attention stands and follows the nurse. But still, after she disappears, I find myself thinking about her. *Has she a man? Has he abandoned her? Is she wanting for money?* I can't understand why, but something about her calls to me.

I'm still thinking about her when the nurse reappears.

"Mrs Winslow?"

Mary comes to attention by my side. Standing, I help her out of her chair, and then wait undecided, not knowing what's expected. *Should have asked her before if she wants me to go with her.*

As if she can read my mind, she tells me, "I'll be back shortly." She steps away, hesitates and turns back. "Would you like to come in and see the sonogram?"

Knowing Grumbler would kill me if I see any of Mary's feminine parts, I give a rapid shake of my head, raise my hands palms up in front of me, and say hurriedly, "That's okay."

She giggles as though she knows exactly what I'm thinking and what her man is like. "I'll be covered up, well, except for the bump and that's hardly sexy."

Yeah. I do a quick rethink. Perhaps I should be there. It's then they'll see if anything's wrong, isn't it? I'm here as my brother's proxy. It takes me a mere second to decide before I give her a sharp nod.

Before she disappears, she has a word with the nurse, who listens carefully, and then addresses me, "I'll come get you in a moment, Mr Simpson."

To entertain myself, I pick up the magazine that Mary had been reading. I start flicking through, not really focused on what I'm reading which seems to be all about fashion during pregnancy, but it bides the time until I hear my name being called.

I'm led into a doctor's office where Mary's lying on a bed, her top pulled up but decently covering her breast area, and a blanket over her hips. I stare at her pregnant stomach, unable to recall seeing one in reality, only in movies or photographs. With curiosity, I notice her skin is already stretched taut. When I realise there's a real baby in there, it takes my breath away. Of course, on one level I'd known and accepted it, on another, clearly not. I've never gotten up close and personal with a woman's ripe body before.

There's something beautiful about it, not sexy at all—this is my brother's wife—but I find myself envying Grumbler that this is all his. Up to now, the extent of my pregnancy knowledge has been how to avoid one by always using a condom.

Looking on, half-wondering how I'd be feeling if this was *my* woman and *my* baby, I watch as the technician places lube over her belly, then picks up a wand. As it connects with Mary's skin, a screen starts to display an image.

I need a bit of help, but once I can see the baby, its form becomes clearer. My hand seems to move of its own volition, sneaking over and touching Mary's. Mary grabs at it as though it's a lifeline.

"Is he okay?" *He?* My surprise must show on my face. Realising her mistake, Mary quickly recovers and explains, "Grumbler knows we're having a boy, but we're keeping it to ourselves for now."

"Your secret's safe with me." I grin. Grumbler must be over the moon. I'd bet good money he's already planning on buying motorcycle-themed shit for the nursery, and expect I'll be roped in to help put Harley decals on the walls.

"To answer your question, Mrs Winslow, everything looks good. He's a good size and all is where it needs to be."

I hear Mary's exhaled sigh and don't miss that the look she throws me is full of relief. I squeeze her hand.

"Your pregnancy is proceeding very nicely. Nothing to worry about here."

I'm transfixed on the screen. *That's Grumbler's boy in there. A recognisable child, who I'll hopefully meet in three months' time.* I feel overwhelmed and privileged to have seen him. My throat feels choked, and this time, it's Mary's hand tightening around mine.

CHAPTER SIX

Niran

Being a gentleman, I wait outside while Mary pulls some of her clothes up and the rest down and makes herself presentable. After a short period of hanging around while she sets up her next appointment, she's free to leave and we head toward the parking lot.

"That went well?" I raise my tone on the last word, making my statement into a question.

Mary elbows me gently in the side. "I know you'll report back to Grumbler, so here's the rundown. My blood pressure is normal, my blood count is what it should be. There's no protein in my urine, and I've put the right amount of weight on."

"Hang on." Scrambling in my pocket, I extract my phone. "Let me take notes." This time her elbow is sharper. I bark a laugh. "I'll just tell him baby's fine, and mom is as well."

She opens her mouth to respond, but my hand taking hold of her arm pulls her to a halt, and whatever she was going to say is forgotten as her eyes catch sight of what's caught my attention.

"Wait here," I tell her, then take off.

A Marine can never turn off his training. As I run to the clearly hurt or distressed woman leaning against a beat-up car, a vehicle I'm surprised to gather, only by the virtue that it must have driven her here, is roadworthy, I'm scanning the environment, checking for danger and wishing like fuck I was armed. As I draw close, I recognise she's the one who'd captured my attention in the waiting room earlier. She's propped up against the door as though needing it to hold her up, her head resting against the roof, and her whole body shaking. As I draw close, I can hear her sobbing, and then, to my horror, she sinks to the ground, her arms cradling her belly.

"Hey." Making my voice as gentle as possible, I crouch at her side, reluctant to touch her. "You alright?"

It's obvious she's not, but I don't know what else to say or ask. If it's a problem with her car, I can help her out. But as I came here with Mary with a dread of hearing the wrong news, considering she's just exited the hospital makes me fear the worst, and that her problem is one I'm not equipped to deal with.

She's sobbing as though she can't hear me, so I try again. "Darlin', can you talk to me? Tell me what's wrong and I'll see if I can help."

When she still doesn't respond, it worries me. Remembering Grumbler tries to prevent Mary getting the least bit upset, I'm getting concerned. She's pregnant, and such distress surely can't be good for the baby. Reaching out my hand, I touch her shoulder, wanting her to acknowledge me. Wanting to know if I should summon help from the building behind.

At my touch, she rears back, falls on her ass, and starts scrambling away.

"Hey!" I repeat, holding up my hands and getting back to my feet. I'm a big fucker standing at six foot three, and I'm Black. Even without wearing my cut, to some people, my colour and size are enough to label me as a threat. "I want to help, that's all."

"Niran? What's going on?" *Thank fuck, Mary didn't obey me and wait.* I could do with some feminine help. "Oh, honey."

Awkwardly, Mary covers the gap the woman has put between me and her. She manages to get herself down to the ground and holds out her arms, then hesitantly inches closer and pulls the woman to her. *Ms Jones*—that's all I know, courtesy of how she was addressed in the clinic—wails again and lets Grumbler's wife hold her. Mary's concerned eyes meet mine, but she simply lets her sob, rocking her like she was as much a baby as the infant she's carrying.

My gaze flicks over the parking lot, and then to the hospital entrance. "Should 1 get help?" I'm feeling more confident now that Mary's stepped in and has the look of a woman who's taking charge.

"Do you need medical help, honey? Is it the baby?"

Her enquiry makes the woman sob harder, but she shakes her head, and now her first words come out, wailed in utter anguish, "No one can help. There's nothing anyone can do now."

Mary and I exchange glances, both of us clearly thinking the same thing. Even if we're adding twos and twos together, we've got to be close to the right result. *Grumbler's going to kill me*, is my selfish initial thought. His old lady who's already preparing herself for her own bad news shouldn't be faced with a real example happening to somebody else. She shouldn't be getting distressed, even if it's on the other woman's behalf. But how can I tear her away? The woman clearly needs help, and there's no one else around to provide it, as evidenced by the way a happy young couple just walked past, hurrying their steps as though not wanting to get involved.

The woman is being wracked by violent shivers, even though the day isn't particularly cold, and the coat she's wearing should be more than adequate. Her face, pale as I noticed before, has whitened further, her eyes, red and raw, stand out in macabre contrast. Whatever news she's just heard must have been devastating. When I served, I'd seen the result of shock many times before, and she's showing classic symptoms. Enough to need medical help? I think so.

"I'm going to get someone," I say quietly to Mary. My job is to get Mary out of here and away from any angst, to get her home and back into that comfortable bubble that Grumbler wants to keep her in.

"No." Hearing me, the woman struggles to free herself from the comfort she's receiving. "I can't… not now. I just need to get away from here."

Becoming conscious the afternoon is darkening, I look up at the sky, seeing the ominous clouds gathering. Already I can scent rain in the air, and my biker instincts tell me this isn't going to be a polite gentle shower, but a downpour probably of biblical proportions.

"Mary, you comfortable with driving the SUV?" I need her out of here now. Grumbler would have my head if she caught a chill or got the slightest bit cold. As for the other woman, no good could come from her getting soaked.

"What are you thinking, Niran?"

I nod toward the woman. "That I'll drive her home."

The woman startles. "I'm not going home. I've got to get to work."

Jeez. That's the last place she should be going.

"No," Mary's no-nonsense voice addresses her, echoing my thoughts. "You're in no state to work. You need to look after yourself. Work can wait. They'll understand."

I hope Mary's right to be optimistic. I've worked for some assholes myself. But I wait to hear what Ms Jones thinks about it.

She considers Mary's words for a brief second, then shudders as she says, "You're right. I can't face going to the store." I think she already knew it herself, but someone else's confirmation has helped. Placing a hand against the ground, she attempts to push herself up. When she's standing, she sways slightly, and places her hand on the roof of her car to steady herself. She avoids talking to me but directs her comment to Mary. "I'm fine. I can drive."

I'm about to tell her she'll be a danger to herself let alone anyone else—hell, she's weak, hardly able to stand, and that pale skin shows me she's far from recovered from whatever caused the shock—but Mary gets in first.

"Honey, I don't think that's a good idea. How about I drive your car, and Niran can follow us, then after we drop you off, he can take me home?"

At that point, another couple passes us, the woman smiling widely and caressing her large pregnant stomach. Our woman utters a loud sob, closes her eyes, and a few more tears leak out. When she speaks, her word is barely more than a whisper, "Alright."

This is so not what Grumbler would want me to be doing, letting Mary out of my sight with a stranger. But neither would he want her out in the elements. With a resigned grimace, as the first of probably many raindrops starts to fall, I usher the two women into the car, knowing I'd lose any argument. I make sure Mary's been given the keys. When I ask if she's sure she can drive in her state, I'm subjected to a withering glance.

Doing what little I can, telling her to wait until I'm behind her, I go to the SUV, crossing my fingers that junker will make it to wherever it needs to go, and that I've not put Grumbler's old lady in danger.

In front of me, black smoke puffs from the exhaust, and the car seems to jerk each time we start off having been stopped at a light. I get a feeling of dread I've fucked up. I will Mary to drive safely, and for that engine to just keep going. *Grumbler would have my balls if anything happened to his wife.* Fuck, if it did, I'd chop my own balls off.

I should be relieved when we reach our destination, but I'm not feeling easier when ahead of me Mary brings the car to a halt and I pull up behind her. Hurrying to get out to be at her side, I lock the SUV and make a run for the car, scanning the area around me. This is one of the worst neighbourhoods I've seen in the city, or possibly anywhere in my life. The apartment block is shabby and uncared for, and under my feet I hear a discarded syringe crunch.

As I open the driver's side to extract Mary, my intention being to get her back to the SUV and out of here, I hear her saying, "Come on, Saffie, let's get you inside." She's obviously got at least a name out of her on the short journey.

Uh-uh, no way. "You got a husband or boyfriend waiting for you?" I snap, maybe a little too harshly.

Saffie looks shocked at the question, and her flinch makes me feel like an ass. "No. There's no one."

Mary releases the seat belt and starts to pull herself out. Automatically, I go to help her and then try to hold her back as her intention is clearly to go help Saffie.

"Go to the SUV, Mary."

She just glares at me. A glare that has me, a former Marine and biker, stepping back. I open my mouth to object, then see by her expression her mind is set, and the only option I have is to manhandle her and force her into the car which clearly, I can't. Cursing and mentally apologising to Grumbler, I throw up my hands in defeat.

I'd offer to stay with Saffie myself, and let Mary drive the SUV back home, but from her original reaction, I doubt Saffie would take kindly to me being the one helping her. My stomach rolls as I consider it's not the colour of my skin that might put her off, it could be my gender. Maybe her baby is a result of a rape? Fuck, I hope not. But the horrors I've seen don't allow me to rule it out. In any case, it's best if I keep my distance. One thing is for certain, I'm staying. I won't be leaving them alone.

Reluctantly, I allow Mary, pregnant herself, to put her arm around the devastated woman and follow them into an apartment building the likes of which Grumbler certainly wouldn't want his old lady to enter. Once inside, we find out Saffie lives on the fourth floor. *Of course, she fucking does.* And of course, the elevator is out of commission.

Fuck this. "Stay here, Mary, I'll take her up."

Without giving her a chance to protest, I sweep Saffie up into my arms and hold her tight so she can't escape. Then I'm tackling the stairs.

She's light, which is lucky as hell, though I'm still struggling, placing each step with care, and hoping like fuck my prosthetic leg can take the extra weight. Knowing I'll suffer for it later, I labour on. The exertion must show on my face, as when she stops writhing to get free, Saffie goes still in my arms.

"I'm too heavy."

"You're not," I refute.

"Your leg okay, Niran?" I curse as I hear Mary puffing her way up behind us, torn between wanting her to wait downstairs and not wanting her left on her own in this neighbourhood.

When Saffie's swollen red eyes pose a question, I don't hesitate with my answer. I've learned it's best to be upfront when directly challenged, rather than pretend to be the able-bodied man I'm not. "Lost half my leg. I wear a prosthesis. A fake limb."

Her eyes widen with surprise, but she doesn't say more, just holds on tight and seems to be making an effort not to unbalance me. I'm pleased as fuck when we reach a door which she says is hers. By this time, sweat is pouring off my forehead and my stump is screaming like a bitch.

Only now do I let her down and wait a moment for Mary to catch up. Mary's carrying Saffie's purse which it seems she'd forgotten. When she hands it over, Saffie takes a moment to find and extract her key, then attempts to place it in the lock. She's trembling so much it takes her a minute, but I don't take over. If my earlier thoughts are correct, I've got to stay back and from now on, touch her as little as possible.

When finally, she has the door open, she places a foot inside, then turns around. "Thank you for bringing me home." Her tone is dismissive and unable to misinterpret as anything other than she wants us gone, as she should. Why should anyone let two perfect strangers into her home?

"Honey, you don't want to be alone, not right now," Mary states, adamantly. "Is there someone I can call for you? Family, a neighbour or friend?"

"There's no one," Saffie replies, then corrects, "I don't need anyone."

The way she says it makes me believe the first statement was the only one which is right. She has no one to care for her. But my responsibility is to get Mary home and hope like hell Grumbler doesn't object to our detour today. My eyes continuously flit left and right, and my ears are pricked for any sounds I don't like. The hallway is full of rubbish I'd prefer not to examine too closely, music plays loudly from somewhere, and filtering down from the floor above are the sounds of angry voices shouting. While I don't like leaving any woman here alone, the overriding thought in my head tells me my duty is to get Mary out of here.

But Mary didn't survive bringing up a teenager without having a mind of her own. The expression on her face should have warned me she isn't the kind of person who'd just accept being told no, especially when she can see someone is hurting.

With a directness I wouldn't have employed, Grumbler's old lady takes the bull by the horns. "It's the baby, isn't it? Something's wrong."

It's as if up to that point, Saffie had been more focused on seeing us go than on the reason why we were here in the first place. Mary's brutal reminder has her falling apart in front of my eyes. She sobs, steps away from the door, lurches to a worn sofa and puts her hand on it. Without waiting for an invitation, Mary steps in, and what can I do, but follow her?

As Mary hugs the woman to her, rocking her in her arms just like she had in the parking lot, I step to one side and taking out my phone, place a call to Grumbler.

CHAPTER SEVEN

Saffie

Wave after wave of guilt goes through me as I shamelessly let myself be held by a woman who I don't know beyond the first names we'd exchanged on the way to my apartment. I'm crazy to be letting total strangers into my home, but right at this moment, that's the last thing that worries me. If they turned out to be serial killers it might be a mercy.

Mary holds me tight, rocking me without asking anything, seeming to know if she did, I'd be incapable of speaking right now. I'm lost in my own head, asking one overarching question.

What had I done wrong?

Just about everything, I answer myself.

The seed had been planted and I'd been pregnant long before I'd found out. In pain and hurting, and yes, seeking oblivion, I'd been doing what I could to take my mind off my misery—drinking and smoking weed. When Duke thought numbing my agony would make me easier to twist to his will, I hadn't protested when something else was injected into my veins.

Duke had hurt me. Who could blame me for taking whatever

painkillers had been offered to me? Internally wailing, I recall how I'd even relished the dreamy sensation that had taken my agony from me. *I should have known better than to placidly accept a cocktail of drugs.* But the thought of being pregnant had never occurred to me. If I'd even suspected, I'd have taken better care of myself and my baby.

The damage, however, has already been done. If it wasn't the drugs, it could have been the stress I was under. Living with the Crazy Wolves hadn't exactly been easy, and my blood pressure must have been through the roof. Then I'd witnessed Jude's killing, which led to the beating. *Maybe it happened then?*

Even after I got free, I lived daily on the edge, always looking behind and worried Duke might somehow find me. The fear hasn't dissipated even after three months. I never rest easy.

While the Freedom Trail had been amazing, I was anxious as hell, worried something would go wrong. Even with new papers, a new identity, accommodations and a job, I'd been terrified every minute on my journey, and live with the legacy of terror every day.

My life hasn't been easy, but it's not me who's suffering the consequences, it's my reason to get up and keep breathing each morning. It's my baby.

I'm not strong enough to bear the news I've just heard.

Hell, who is? What woman could cope with this under normal circumstances, let alone those I find myself in? I'm alone. I've no one to support me, no one to share the burden or the loss of my dream.

I cry and cry, totally unembarrassed or caring what these people think of me. *Nothing matters now.* If I could stop breathing, I'd welcome the release. When I think my tears will never stop, I must run out of energy, as my wails turn into sobs, and I become conscious of what's happening around me.

I hear Mary asking her companion to get me a drink. When

he comes back with just water, I have to suppress the scream that I'd prefer coffee, or whisky would be even better. To drink myself into oblivion sounds good right now. What further harm could it do? But I don't make the request. There remains that innate urge to protect the baby inside me.

He, who I now register Mary had called Niran, is too big and scary, too reminiscent of the men who liked to torture me. If I were in a different frame of mind, having him in my space would terrify me. As it is, when he hands me the glass and stares at me intently, I don't feel I've any option but to sip it to please him. *If I didn't, would he raise his hands to me?* Duke has me programmed to suspect all men are like him. As he continues to focus on me, my fingers tremble as I raise the glass to my lips a second time.

As I drink, I hear Mary and he have a quiet conversation.

"What did Grumbler say?"

I hear a soft snort, then, "He told me to tell you to get your ass back home. He's about half an hour away and wants you there before him."

Mary softly snorts. "Presumably with his dinner on the table ready and waiting."

"Hey, I'm only the messenger." Having glanced up in shock, I see Niran grinning at her.

Fuck no. Not her as well. I open my mouth to tell her she shouldn't stay in an abusive relationship, and that hers is one is what I'm hearing.

But she replies before I can open my mouth, "Grumbler's a pussy, Niran. I can handle him."

Niran grunts. "I know you can. I'm more worried about what he's going to do to *me*, woman. I should have taken you home."

Mary's peal of laughter is so at odds with my circumstances, it makes me sob, unwittingly regaining their attention.

"Oh, honey, I'm sorry." She looks at me in concern, and I know I look a mess—fresh and drying tears on my face, my eyes red and swollen. Heat burns my cheeks from my distress. She notices everything, making the suggestion now my crying has eased, "Why don't you go and wash your face?"

It's a sensible suggestion, but I immediately baulk at it. Why do I care how I look, or how I feel? Nothing could be an improvement.

Seriously, though, I do need the bathroom. That the baby is using my bladder as a trampoline hasn't changed. So, I give her a small nod, and Niran offers his hand to pull me to my feet. Avoiding him, I stand, pause to get my strength, then walk off on my own.

As I sit to do my business, I can't stop my hand running over my swollen belly. While I appreciate the strangers' concern, I don't want to talk to them, don't want to give voice to the words that echo around my head. Putting what's happened into words will make it real. If I don't admit the problem, I can still run from it, bury my head and continue as usual. I can get up in the morning, go to work—if they haven't sacked me for not turning up—and pretend everything's normal. That's a good plan, isn't it? Blot it out, forget it, concentrate on growing my baby.

Even if I wanted to talk to someone, it wouldn't be the kind and caring Mary. She's pregnant, maybe not as far along as me, and from her lack of distress, presumably the clinic told her that her baby is healthy. She'd never understand my situation, nor the choice I'm being asked to make. It's my problem, my decision, and I don't want to be influenced by anyone else.

Niran? He's a man. I wouldn't dream of involving him. He wouldn't want to hear about feminine weakness. I shudder. *He scares me.*

My best course of action is to get rid of them. For years I've been handling my problems alone. There's never been anyone there to offer advice, a shoulder to cry on, or just hear me out. I'm used to this. I can do this on my own. I prefer to.

Resolving to ask them to leave, I flush, then go to the sink to splash cold water on my burning eyes, wincing in the cracked glass at the image reflected at me. *I'm a mess.* Even my blonde wig has come awry, showing my naturally dark hair underneath. Automatically, I go to straighten it, while acknowledging I look like a stray dog uncared for and unfed. No wonder complete strangers were concerned about me.

Not all, I correct, recalling the happy couple that had just walked past as though my being distraught would taint them. *Not everyone would have stopped to help, nor seen me home safely.* Now I grimace, knowing full well where I live, and that they have walked into a shady apartment block that's surely beneath their station.

Get rid of them. Then I can grieve. I pull my shoulders back, determined to utter the words as soon as I go back out.

But when I do, it's to see Niran looking ridiculous, seated on my already sagging armchair obtained from Goodwill, and Mary sitting on the worn couch, staring at me entering the room with genuine concern in her eyes. Something breaks inside me, and all my good intentions about keeping my woes to myself come blurting out of my mouth without me meaning them to. "I have to decide whether to have an abortion." My voice starts strong, then cracks.

"Oh, honey." Mary manages to extract herself from the sofa and comes over to me. "I thought it was something like that. No one should have to make that decision on their own. I'm here for you."

Taking me by the hand, she encourages me to take the seat she just vacated and sits beside me. I'm already regretting telling them at all. The last thing I want is for anyone to try to influence me, whether they be 'all human life is precious and deserves to be born' or not. Despite what she's said, this *is* a decision I need to make for myself, as only I will have to live with it.

As though I've zipped my lips, I stay quiet.

Mary glances at Niran, then fills the silence. "I'm forty-eight," she begins. She's shocked me. I thought her younger than that. "My husband's ten years older. Both my eggs and his sperm have seen better days. I got pregnant by accident, certainly didn't expect to." She pauses, and again looks Niran's way. The Black man raises his chin as if to encourage her. I'm surprised there's no look of disinterest on his face. "We had the options explained when I first found out. My choices were, abortion, or continue, knowing there was a big risk that I might miscarry, or the baby wouldn't reach term, or that his development wouldn't proceed normally." She's got my attention, and I find myself staring her in the face. "We decided to leave it to fate and hope for the best."

Heavens. She's been living with this since the day she conceived. *She already knows she might not give birth to a healthy baby.* "He's okay now?" Her behaviour doesn't suggest she heard bad news today.

Mary grimaces before nodding. "I'm six months, and yes, all looks good now. But there's still a chance things could go wrong, which is why my man wraps me in bubble wrap."

She's someone who might understand. "If something did… if you find out he has severe developmental problems, would you terminate the pregnancy?"

Niran starts as though he wants to stop this conversation, but Mary waves him down. "It depends. If he couldn't survive, or if he was never going to live a normal life—by which I mean, not just a bit, but drastically, like he'd never talk, walk or think on his own—then yes, I think I would. Grumbler and I have discussed it. Of course, I'm not in that position, so I can't really say what I'd feel if I were." She pauses. "Yes, so far the pregnancy's going normally, but I still might not be able to carry him to term. I live with that thought daily."

At that point, my phone rings. In no mood to talk to anyone, I ignore it. So few people know my number, I can guess who it is, but I haven't got it in me to care. When the tone blares again, Niran gestures toward my purse.

"You want me to get the phone?" he asks in his deep, gruff voice.

I must nod, I'm not really aware, but he goes to my bag, extracts the device then shows me the screen. Yes, it's the store where I work and the caller's my boss who must be wondering why I haven't yet turned up.

"It's work," I respond, dismissively.

"Want me to deal with it?"

Again, I must indicate yes, as he slides his thumb across the screen and puts the phone to his ear.

"I'm sorry, but she's unwell... She won't be able to come in today... Yeah, it came on suddenly... She's seen a doctor and has been told to rest... Tomorrow?" He glances at me, and I nod my head. "Yeah, she'll try and get in... I'll tell her... Yeah." Putting the phone down on the side table, he now addresses me. "She sounds nice, your boss. Said she hopes you feel better soon, and just let her know if you can't go in."

It suddenly makes me realise how I'm surrounded by good people even if I think I'm alone. My boss, always friendly, didn't fire me on the spot. Mary's just shared her personal story with me, and Niran, who took charge, carrying me when I couldn't walk despite his disability. Guiltily, I register he's been rubbing just below his left knee the entire time he's been seated in the chair. A seat, I watch him now retake, sighing with relief as he takes the weight off his leg. Simply dressed in jeans and a clean t-shirt, he's just like any other man I might pass on the street. *He's not a biker.* He's normal. Perhaps I can trust him, despite his threatening size and those muscles of his.

These people aren't friends as such, but definitely friendly. And people who've done more for me in one afternoon than anyone else in the last five years. It's that that makes me give a little more to them. Not my complete story, of course. I'm too ashamed for a start and sharing too much would be dangerous.

"I haven't been to checkups before," I start, trying to telepathically transmit to them that I'd prefer not to tell them why. It must work, as there's no censure in their eyes, and no questions. "I'm twenty-three weeks pregnant, and I thought it was time to get myself and the baby checked out. So, I made an appointment."

"That was today? The first time you've seen a doctor?"

Checking carefully, I notice Mary's face carries no accusation at all, so I press my lips together, remembering the weekend I'd just been through. "No, last week was the first time." I have to swallow a couple of times. Mary passes me back the now topped-off water, and I guzzle it gratefully. "I thought everything was normal." But what do I know? I've not reached this stage before. I lost my previous baby much earlier in the pregnancy. I don't admit the truth that I was scared to show my face publicly, worried my new identity wouldn't stack up and terrified any official record might trigger something to enable Duke to find me.

"Go on," Mary gently encourages me.

As another rush of sadness floods through me, I cry out, "Last week they told me something was wrong with the baby, but they wanted to run more tests." I gulp, remembering how I'd spent the last few days unable to believe there was anything serious, despite the looks of sympathy the doctor had given to me. I sob, then take a fortifying breath, and tell them the rest. "The baby, *my son,* has anencephaly." They'd told me the sex at the same time as they'd identified the problem, making it a hundred times worse, as I started to think of him as a person.

Mary looks horrified, but I suspect with her history, she's been researching all that can go wrong. Niran looks puzzled, so it's for his benefit I tell him the dreadful facts, my voice breaking before I'm halfway through. "His brain isn't developing properly, a large proportion is outside his skull, rather than inside it."

"Oh, honey." Mary tries to hug me, but I pull away, wrapping my arms around myself. I don't deserve comfort or sympathy. *My fault. All my fault. Doesn't matter that things happened when I never even knew, but hell, on who else does the blame fall?*

"Is there treatment?" Niran asks, his voice probably sharper than he meant to sound.

After a moment to compose myself, I tell them, with a quiver in my voice, "None. If he's born alive, he won't have any functions. He won't be able to breathe on his own, eat, digest food, defecate or anything." That's all I can get out before I howl. Literally howl. Falling forward, my arms still hug my middle as if protecting my poor baby. While I bear most of the guilt inside, I also blame Duke. He'd kicked me so hard, it had to have caused damage. Or maybe it's down to the drugs he forced on me? *Forced? I took them willingly, but who wouldn't, given my state?*

I wish it were me bearing the consequences, but it's not. It's my poor baby, my child, who I already love more than my life.

Niran stands, crosses the couple of steps needed, then crouches at my feet and hovers his hands over my knees. "Look at me," he demands, so commandingly I have no option but to obey. When his hands lower, I realise he's touching me. For some reason, I don't protest. "Fuck, darlin', that's some hard shit for you to handle."

There's something in his eyes, sympathy as I'd have expected, but something more. A respect for the momentous decision that's been thrust on me. No censure, but then he doesn't know it's my fault. Despite my self-recriminations, my hands seem to move by themselves, uncurling from their position and reaching for him as if I deserve to take comfort. When he takes them in his, I squeeze tight, as though needing to hold on to something. He might be a man, but there's a protective vibe about him that doesn't scream I need to take caution. He's looking into my eyes, not my breasts, and not showing any signs of disrespect.

"The baby will suffer if he's born?" he asks.

"I don't know," I tell him honestly.

"Could he be suffering now?"

The thought makes me suck in a sharp breath, but again I tell him the truth, "I don't know. I don't think anyone can tell." The deformities described to me might mean he'd never feel anything at all—pleasure, pain, or anything in between.

Softly stroking the fingers he's holding, Niran gentles his voice. "What do you want to do, darlin'? What does your heart tell you?"

It was my stupid darn heart that got me into this mess in the first place. It may be the organ that keeps me alive, but it's the one I can't trust anymore, not after it let me fall for Duke. "That I should continue and hope they're wrong." I try to sound firm, but my voice trembles, and my body shakes.

Silence descends, neither of them telling me that's unlikely. Unlikely? Impossible. I've seen the scans for myself, and today the doctor had patiently explained them, along with the blood test results.

Niran moves again, but in a way that's completely non-threatening. He stands, pulls me up, then sinks down where I was sitting, pulling me onto his lap and letting his arms surround me. I should feel trapped, but I don't. When I start crying again, he smooths my hair, and just murmurs incomprehensible words to me. His hand lightly covers the back of my head, letting me sob into his shirt, uncaring of the mess I'm making.

I should be scared. I never wanted to get close to another man, knowing my sixth sense about them has led me so terribly wrong, but his touch is soothing, his concern genuine, and nothing about this is remotely sexual. Neither on my part nor his, as I can't feel any masculine stirring under my butt.

I hear Mary speaking quietly. "She shouldn't be alone, Niran. Not tonight."

"I know, I'll stay with her." I both feel and hear his words.

I'm surprised at how his pronouncement gives me strength. Instead of protesting I'm fine by myself, I realise I don't want to be alone. The mental pain is worse than anything physical Duke ever put me through, and I've no idea how I'll cope.

Until that moment, I hadn't recognised how alone I was, and how much I was dreading how to action any decision I make. If I take the sensible course and return to the hospital to voluntarily lose my baby, I'll be driving myself. Now I start wondering whether this angel in disguise might be able to take me.

I wouldn't ask much, just a continuation of the support he's shown so far, the assurance that there was one person, however remote and unconnected to me, who cares. In his arms, my brain starts to still, and begins to put the decision that's too hard to make on the shelf, if just for a little while.

"She can't stay here," Mary notes, primly.

Snapping my eyes open, I see her looking around with disdain. Sure, my place isn't one I'd have chosen, but beggars can't be choosers. San Diego isn't cheap, and this was all I could afford. So what if the paint's peeling off the walls, the stove looks like it should be condemned, and the furniture is worn? I've scrubbed the place from top to bottom. At least it's clean, and it's mine.

"I agree." Niran flinches as something heavy is dropped on the floor above. He shifts slightly, sitting me up and turning me to face him. "Why don't you come with us? We can take you somewhere more comfortable."

Oh no. I might have relaxed my guard with him, but I'm not stupid enough to go with anyone when I don't know them. Visions of my body lying dead in a ditch—which, actually under the circumstances might not be a bad result—or worse, returned to Duke, fill my head. I've only just met them. I'd be a fool to so easily give up my trust.

"I'm fine here." I put as much conviction into my voice as I'm able to. "Look, please, will you go?" I've had enough socialising. All I want to do is curl up in a ball and cry. Best all around if I were to go to sleep and never wake up. How can one woman cope with all the pain in my heart?

Please go, I repeat in my head.

CHAPTER EIGHT

Niran

This woman seated on my lap, barely holding herself together, is a complete stranger, and I shouldn't feel any sense of responsibility for her. Nevertheless, she's going through something terrible, something I wouldn't wish on my worst enemy, and my gut is screaming the last thing she needs is to be alone.

I hate that she's in this place. She should be somewhere safe, not in an environment that must be adding to her stress level and distress. But I can appreciate how it's far too soon to ask for her trust. There's only one option, I have to stay.

Taking out the keys to the SUV, I pass them to Mary. "You okay to drive yourself?"

For a response, I get a roll of her eyes, followed by her seeking confirmation I won't be leaving her new friend alone. "You're definitely staying?"

While Saffie looks at me in horror, I qualify to make her feel easier, "Just for a while. But Grumbler will be worrying himself senseless if you don't get home now."

With a worried look in my direction, and a more complex expression spared for Saffie, Mary stands, takes the keys out of my hand, then goes to lean over the woman sitting beside me. "Niran will give you my number. Anything you need, *anything,* you hear me? Just call, and I'll come around."

"You can both go," Saffie states, anxiously looking between me and Grumbler's old lady.

"No can do," I reply. "You shouldn't be on your own. Not right now. I'll just stay long enough to make sure you're okay. But first, I'm going to walk Mary down to the car."

"How will you get home?" she asks.

"Don't worry about me. One of my brothers can come collect me." Standing, I gesture Mary to hold back, as I walk to the door and open it.

Peering out, I check no one's shooting up in the hallway, and there's no sound of footsteps coming up the stairwell. *Sooner Mary's out of here the better.* Taking the lead, I walk slowly down the stairs, hoping Mary's following carefully.

Outside the apartment, I'm relieved to find the SUV unmolested. Ushering Mary toward it, I settle her in the driver's seat, pleased when with just one worried glance around, she adjusts the seat which had been pushed back for my long legs and starts the engine immediately. I watch until the taillights disappear around the corner, then, fortifying myself with a deep breath, attack those flights of stairs again.

Saffie's door is shut, as it should be. I bang on it and get no reply. Knowing she's in there, I don't give up.

"Open the door, Saffie. It's me, Niran."

"Go away," a small voice says.

"Nah. Let me in, or I'll stay right here." I eye the hallway critically, wishing I had my piece on me. There's no way in California I'd get a license to own a gun, let alone concealed carry, not with my affiliation to the MC. Being Black, I'm already at enough risk of being stopped as it is, being caught carrying could be a death sentence if I come up against a trigger-happy cop. Flexing my shoulders, I keep my eyes and ears open, ready to fight my way out if need be.

One moment passes, then another, then I hear the sound of bolts being drawn back, and the door opens a crack. It's all the invitation I need.

"I won't hurt you, Saffie," I tell her, carefully pushing the door wider, moving slowly so as to not scare her. I pause, then walk past her into her small living area.

"I don't understand why you're here." Her words are laced with suspicion.

Truth be told, neither do I. All I know is she's hurting, badly, and something inside me wants to ease her pain. I doubt I can fix her, that's beyond me, but to lend her my shoulder and do what I can to make this awful day easier, well, I hope I can go some way toward that.

In the end, there's not much I can do. She won't eat. She watches as I make a sandwich for myself hoping to tempt her, but it doesn't work. She won't drink anything other than the water I force on her, worried after all the crying she'll become dehydrated.

I sit on the worn sofa beside her. For a long while we sit in silence, then with a sigh of exhaled breath, as though tired of keeping herself together, she inches toward me, and I put a brotherly arm around her.

She might not be speaking, but I know her mind has to be whirring. I don't attempt to start a conversation. I'm so out of my league, I wouldn't know what to say.

Eventually, out of sheer exhaustion, she falls asleep. Gently, I lift her and carry her into the one bedroom, laying her fully dressed on the bed, only removing her shoes before sliding the sheet over her. Then, unable to stop myself, I lean down and plant a quick kiss to her forehead for no other reason than it seems the right thing to do.

"Sleep," I whisper, knowing she doesn't hear me.

I return to the sofa that's far too short for my height to stretch out but settling in as I don't want her to be alone tonight. Fuck knows why, she's not my responsibility. But she needs someone, and there seems to be no one else.

Knowing it's still relatively early and I've no inclination to settle in for what will be undoubtably be an uncomfortable and restless night, I take out my phone and start googling. I read up about the baby's condition and end up thinking she has only one route ahead. Medically, nothing can be done to help her baby. I don't believe in the power of prayer, especially not when the dice have already fallen. Her baby has zero chance to survive.

Will she live on hope? Put herself through the next few months which only a fucking miracle could end happily? The best she could hope for is a few minutes or hours with a dying child, and that's if she's lucky.

Is she strong enough to take the logical route?

How could I even begin to imagine what strength it would take to end the pregnancy, to close that door on hope. I'm a man, how could I ever understand?

While I'm a fixer, while I want to help, imposing my views on a woman I've just met would be a mistake of the highest proportions. Any views I have, I need to keep to myself, holding back, even if she asks my opinion.

What would I feel if I were the father?

Devastated, lost, raging at fate. For perhaps the first time, I truly understand Grumbler and Mary's concerns. Saffie appears to be in my age bracket, and this probably wasn't on her radar, or only as a minimal risk. Grumbler and Mary's eyes are wide open, and every day they live with the possibility that something will go wrong.

Fuck, what would it be like to lose a child? Even one that was only a promise as yet.

Saffie hasn't mentioned the father. As he should have been the one she'd contacted first, or been at the hospital to accompany her, I gather he's out of the picture. Does she know who he is? My initial impression of Saffie is that she's no bed-hopper, but even the best of us makes mistakes. A drunken one-night stand where no names were exchanged? Or was it conceived in a relationship that went sour? Did he throw her out as he didn't want to be a dad?

Glancing around the apartment, I wrinkle my nose in disgust. She's made the best of it, but there's only so much silk you can apply to a pig's ear. Nothing can disguise the unkempt nature of the building's fabric—shoddily thrown together with paper-thin walls. It makes me wonder how it's still standing.

Saffie must either be exhausted, or has learned to tune the sounds out, but I keep jumping as noises reach my ears—heavy footsteps overhead, the sound of a television from next door, and a loud argument with voices swearing loudly, and the shouting of someone who 'needs to score'.

Whoever the man is who's responsible for Saffie's predicament, if he knows his woman is living like this, he deserves a fucking beatdown.

When I start yawning, I quietly visit her tiny bathroom, wincing at the loudness of my stream of piss, but even that doesn't disturb her. Returning to the sofa, I take off my prothesis, snorting quietly when I start to lie down, finding amusement in that the couch is at least long enough for one of my legs.

As a Marine, I got used to sleeping anywhere. I employ the tricks I'd learned back in the day for snatching sleep whenever an opportunity presents itself. With my mind still whirring, it takes a while to work, but I drop off eventually.

I don't sleep easily, sounds continue from the building around me, startling me out of my rest. One such sound is Saffie's door opening.

Pulling myself upright, I realise it's the early morning, and despite my uncomfortable position, I've stayed the whole night.

As she moves to the bathroom, I strap on my prothesis, and

put my boot on my other foot. Then, thankful my hair is shorn short and needs only my palms to run over it, I go to her kitchen and get coffee started. It's decaf, as I expected. *Saffie's been trying to do everything right.*

"You're still here."

I turn around to greet her, disregarding the obvious. "Want coffee?" I ignore that she's not wearing what I knew was a wig. Her natural hair is dark, far more suited to her complexion.

Her mouth twists in distaste. "Water will do. I, er…"

I can see she's embarrassed and unsure how to greet a stranger in the morning. Assessing her quickly, I see her sleep has done little to refresh her. The shadows in her eyes show the hurt is, quite obviously, still there.

I don't ask how she's feeling, it's evident.

She comes closer, wrapping her arms around herself. "I keep thinking this is a nightmare, Niran. I want to wake up, but however much I pinch myself, when I open my eyes, it's still there." I go to speak, but she gets in before me, "I can't wish this away, and I have to deal with it myself. I have to come to a decision that's mine and mine alone."

"I can't tell you what to do." I'd come to that conclusion myself.

"I know." A brief, self-deprecating smile appears and fades just as quickly. "It would be easier if you, or anyone could."

"You going to be okay?"

"No," she replies honestly. "But I have to keep going. Maybe I'll just let nature take its course, or maybe not." She sits and puts her head into her hands, and then idly draws one down to caress her belly. "I don't know if I'm strong enough to do either."

"You are," I tell her, going to crouch in front of her, then taking hold of her hands. "You'll come to the right decision."

She looks at me as if she can't understand herself. "I didn't want you to stay but thank you for being here."

"I wish I could do more," I respond, earnestly. I wish I could wave a wand and solve her problems.

She shakes her head. "You're stopping me from freaking out. That's more than enough, Niran." Her eyes narrow, and she asks, "Am I right to trust you?"

It's an unusual question, but one I suppose is valid. "Again, I can't tell you what to do, Saffie. But I assure you, I've no evil intentions toward you. You need someone to support you and I'm willing to play that role."

"Why should that be you?"

I don't have an answer. "Who knows, Saffie? I've never been faced with this situation before. Who knows why I feel like I do? I just know if there's any help to be given, I want to be the one to provide it." Maybe there was something in what Kink said—I've an innate desire to fulfil a woman's needs, even if they aren't sexual. *Nah, he was talking out of his ass.*

She gives a half-smile. "And I don't know why I let you. But you being here, staying the night… I think you stopped me from going crazy."

At the back of my mind, I think I might have prevented her harming herself. At least, in that, I was successful. This morning her hurt is no less, but there's more of a determination about her.

"You going to be okay today?" Taking back my hands, I pinch the brow of my nose. I could take a day off, but that would set the guys behind. "I should go to work."

"Saying I'll be fine would be a lie," she admits. "But I can't give up. I've got to carry on, whatever the future will look like. You're not the only one who's got work, Niran."

"You sure you're up to it?"

She shakes her head. "No, but I have to be."

"Want me to come back later?" I'm prepared to catch her when she falls. After a day of pretending all's well in her world, Saffie's going to need someone to hold her. I don't need a crystal ball to know that.

She doesn't say yes, she doesn't say no. Instead, she warns me, "I work the late shift."

She hasn't eaten, and I doubt she had a restful sleep. I'm concerned she'll overdo it. "You sure you're up to going in?"

With a shrug, she tells me the facts of life. "I'm not ill, Niran. Whichever way I go, whatever my decision, I'll need to have money."

It's far too soon to offer to help her out. And why the fuck should I have to bite back the suggestion? She's nothing to me, just a woman I have the strangest desire to help.

"What time does your shift end?"

"I work four to midnight."

Late nights are no hardship for me. "I'll be here."

"Why should you?" she asks, her eyes widening. "Niran, I can't lead you on. I've nothing to offer a man."

"Fuck woman, I know that." There's nothing sexual between us. I don't even know if there would be if the circumstances were different. But she needs someone, and she's got no one else. "I don't want anything from you, but I can be here as a friend." While she's got all this shit going on, she doesn't need to be worrying about someone busting into her apartment, or a doped-up druggie trying to get into the wrong home.

She takes a moment, then says shyly, "I think I'd like that."

Which is why midnight sees me waiting anxiously for her car to turn into the apartment block, breathing a sigh of relief when I eventually see it. Only then do I step out of the club's SUV and go to greet her.

When I see the expression on her face, when I can tell that the effort of holding herself together has all but broken her, I hold out my arms. She comes into them and takes the comfort only another human being can offer.

It starts the pattern for the next few days. Saffie draws no closer to making a decision, and I don't hurry her. If she wants to talk, I listen, if she doesn't, I don't push. I bring food and am pleased as fuck when she eats some of it. I do what I can to help her relax—watching a movie before she goes to bed, or simply sitting in silence holding her.

While the question burns inside me, I don't question her about the baby's father because she still hasn't brought it up, and I don't want to cause her distress. Some men, I know, would be possessive about the baby she's carrying, and might want to influence her. I subscribe to the notion that even if I were the father, it's she who's carried the workload for the past months and it's her who'll be affected physically by what the future holds. If he were someone who'd support her in whatever decision she made, then yes, I'd want her to contact him, but she doesn't need more pressure. That she doesn't mention him is telling. Whatever relationship they had has ended now.

Perhaps he didn't want the baby and left her, or maybe it was a one-night stand. If she never told him, I respect the decision she's made, suspecting she had good reason.

While I don't ask for details, I spend our times of silence wondering about it. Little things come into my mind. Though she's got acclimated to me now, when I first met her, I remember how scared she'd seemed to be of me. Was it a general mistrust of my race, or that I'm male? Whatever it was, she seems to have gotten past it. But that it was there makes me wonder whether a man used his strength against her. Though I hate to think it, there's a strong possibility she could have been raped.

Knowing wouldn't help. I wouldn't be able to disguise my anger and my reaction would certainly scare her.

While she doesn't open up, I don't either. We share nothing personal. The most I glean from her is what food she likes, and what she doesn't, and which television programs can best distract her. Why should I burden her with my life? She's got enough on her plate. She doesn't even ask me how I lost my leg. It seems we're friends from this point forward, our pasts we keep to ourselves.

No sharing of history, no understanding of what drives us means for the past three nights, other than the companionable friendship that's growing between us, we remain little more than strangers. It seems to be what she wants.

But in that time, I start to value our bizarre relationship. I haven't asked to share her bed even innocently, and she hasn't offered it. For my second night, I came prepared with a sleeping bag and a soft mat and now sleep stretched out on her floor.

During the day, I work, then I stay at the clubhouse until it's time to set out for her apartment. A routine that doesn't go unnoticed by my brothers.

"You staying with that woman again tonight?" Kink asks, as I slowly sip a beer and wait for the time to leave to arrive. At my slight nod, he snorts. "Fuck, Brother, you've got it bad."

"I got nothing," I tell him, rounding on him furiously. "I'm there as a friend, helping her out."

Un-riled, he nudges me with his shoulder. "Us Doms, eh? Never can resist a sub in trouble."

"I'm no fuckin' Dom. I'm just watching out for her."

He shakes his head. "Dominant to a fuckin' fault."

Grabbing my keys, I slam the empty bottle down. "I'm out of here."

The next day at work, it's Grumbler who questions me, even calling me into the office to do it. "That woman of yours, she made her decision?"

"She's not my fuckin' woman." I shut that down fast. "She just needs someone to be there for her. Her situation couldn't be worse, Brother." I sit down on the chair on the opposite side of the desk. "What she does next is something she needs to decide for herself, and I can't stand the thought that I can't help her."

Grumbler's jaw clenches. "There but for the grace and all that. This could very well be me and Mary, you know?"

I do know, but if it were, they'd have each other to lean on.

Maybe that's why I'm driven to be something like that for her. Because I know the rock he'd be for his old lady.

He shakes his head. "Mary's worried as fuck."

"I'm sorry, Grumbler…" I know Saffie's situation has to have hit hard with them both. Are they thinking, *this could be us?*

Suddenly he sits forward. "I've tried to dissuade her, fuck knows that Saffie might not want a pregnant woman around right now, but Mary would like to go see her."

Grumbler's first instinct could well be right. Saffie might not want a glowing, happy, pregnant woman in her space. I start to dismiss it and hope he can dissuade her. Then I remember, Saffie already knows Mary is hypothetically grappling with similar issues, and it's just possible Mary's thoughts might help. I do what I can, but it's not the same as having another woman to speak to.

"Saffie's got the day off tomorrow," I tell him, coming to a decision. "I'll ask Saffie. If she's says it's okay, I'll take her with me. It's up to her, though." I add, warningly.

"If you take Mary, you fuckin' look after her," Grumbler growls, showing he'd rather I had turned the offer down. "She's told me about that apartment block—"

It's horrendous I know and hasn't improved by my increased familiarity. "Trust me," I interrupt.

"'Course I fuckin' trust you, Brother." Grumbler turns away and breathes deeply. When he turns back, his eyes plead with me. "Keep her safe. She's my fuckin' life, Niran."

I've seen them almost from the start of their relationship, been there through their highs and lows. I envy them for their happiness with each other. There's no need for him to explain.

CHAPTER NINE

Saffie

Is it wrong that I've grown to depend on Niran being here for the past few nights when I get off work?

That first night, I don't know what drove me to let him back in after he'd seen his companion out. I put it down to being at the lowest point in my life, and uncaring what happened to me. The news I received had been the worst. Nothing could hurt me more than that, not Duke's fists or anything else he'd done to me.

So I hadn't been cautious. While I knew it was far too early to trust Niran and some sense of self-preservation screamed I was doing wrong by letting him stay, I'd opened that door to him.

Niran is far stronger than me. He could overpower me easily. I wouldn't be able to physically throw him out. Balanced against that there was something about him though, a sense of caring which I'd never experienced from a man before—giving without thought of receiving.

He hadn't made a move on me. Well, of course not, I'm pregnant with another man's baby, and with a constantly tear-streaked face, hardly look my best. That first morning when I appeared without the wig I use as a disguise, he hadn't even noticed. If I needed more indication than that, he didn't really see me at all. There have been no lewd glances, no checking out of my body. I don't care if he regards me as unattractive, if I thought otherwise, he'd have been met with rejection. I certainly don't want him as a man, but as a friend who seems to want nothing from me? Yes, I was desperate for that.

Despite how caring he seemed, I'd expected him to reconsider. I hadn't expected him to be waiting for me that first day after work. But he was.

I'd had the worst day, battling to keep an insincere smile on my face, trying to deal with time-wasting customers, pretending all was well in my world when it was anything but. The act I'd kept up for eight hours immediately dropped the moment he put his strong arms around me.

I'd leaned on him, physically and emotionally, as though he was my rock, and he soaked it all up.

He didn't probe, didn't ask questions to which I wasn't prepared to give answers, and in return, I settled for what I got. I didn't need to know any more about him, other than he saw nothing wrong in me using him for a prop.

I've become used to him being here, used to just sitting without talking, giving me time to unwind and unpack my thoughts.

One moment, I think I've come to a decision, that I should take the sensible course and end what can have no future. Then, the doubts come into my head. *What if, despite the odds, the doctors are wrong?*

Perhaps I need to get a second opinion. But I keep putting that off. I know I've got to do something, but part of me prefers living in limbo, delaying the soul-destroying choice I must make.

When he tells me Mary wants to come visit, I hesitate at first. What good would it do to see someone in my situation, but unlike me, someone who's carrying a healthy baby? I'm not sure

I could cope. But then, I remember she's told me she's faced a similar question since she first knew of her pregnancy. While things are looking good now, she knows there's a chance she might end up like me.

Maybe it wouldn't hurt to get a female's perspective, to listen to someone else's thoughts. A bit reluctantly, knowing such a conversation would make me face things I'd rather not face, after some hesitation, I'd agreed.

Now it's like the first day again, both Mary and Niran in my space. At least this time I'm up to playing hostess. I place some cups in front of them. Decaf for her and me, the real stuff that Niran had bought and now resides in my kitchen cupboard, in front of him.

"How have you been?" Mary asks politely, trying to draw me out as she discreetly addresses the elephant in the room.

"I…"

But whatever I was about to say is interrupted by a commotion in the hallway outside my apartment. Loud voices, then a thump against my door, followed by fists hitting the wood gets Niran launching to his feet.

"What the fuck's going on here?" he yells, opening the door, then closing it behind him as he disappears.

My widened eyes stare at the closed door in horror. "Is he going to be okay?"

"Niran can look after himself," she tells me quickly, but I can sense her unease. "This really isn't a good place for you to live, Saffie."

I shrug, still concerned about my friend, but finding some solace in that nothing bad has happened to me. *Yet.* I keep my comings and goings to a minimum, my head down, and don't get involved in anything that I see. "I just stay out of everything, Mary. It's less dangerous than you'd believe." *But then no one had actually banged on my door before.* While I try to act nonchalant, inwardly I admit, that had scared me.

To my relief, when the door opens again, it's Niran using the key that I'd given to him. As if he heard what Mary was saying, he utters a warning himself.

"Hell, Saffie. That was a fuckin' drug deal gone south. A demented druggie was on the wrong floor, wanting to take it out on his dealer." He pinches the bridge of his nose in the way that he does and shakes his head. "I wish you didn't live here."

I don't much like it myself, but beggars don't get much choice. "I'm fine, Niran." I go to mention especially now he's staying with me, but I'm too well aware that he's sleeping on the floor, and that can't continue for long, so I keep my mouth shut. *To date, have I just been lucky? Is someone breaking in only a matter of when?* The incident has rattled me.

"You can't think straight here," Mary starts, her frowning face turning up at a thump and a roar of rage from directly overhead. Idly, I wonder whether that's where the drug-crazed person has found the right man to take it out on. She shudders, glances at Niran, then suggests, "Look, why don't you get away for a while? I'd love for you to stay with me and Grumbler. We've got a spare room."

I shake my head and try to refuse politely. It's the worst thing I can think of. I know Mary carries a worry that her pregnancy might also come to an end, but in the meantime, they'll be happy prospective parents. It would kill me to constantly compare their situation to mine. "I wouldn't dream of imposing, Mary."

"It wouldn't be an imposition—"

"Mary," Niran says sharply. "Perhaps staying with you isn't what she needs." He's right, how could I think straight when I see her preparing her nursery? For a moment, a wave of sadness rolls over me, and I almost miss what he says next. "Fuck, I wish that she could stay with me, but I haven't got my own place."

"There are spare rooms at the clubhouse." Mary's eyes gleam. "Maybe she could stay there? Then she'd be close to you,

Niran, and I could come around every day. And there's Eva..." For some reason she looks at him knowingly.

I start to consider whether changing location would help me decide when their actual words filter through to me. *Clubhouse?* My heart skips a beat. *Surely not.* It's too much of a coincidence. It's only my experience that makes me think of the only type of place that matches that description.

"What did you say?" I hold my breath, certain my mental leap must be wrong, but needing the confirmation.

"That here isn't the place for you, not right now," Niran says unhelpfully, looking like he's considering Mary's suggestion.

"No, the clubhouse," I prompt, hoping there's something wrong with my ears. Or if that's what they said, that it's not the type I was only too used to.

"The clubhouse?" He frowns in confusion and shrugs. "Sure, it's not ideal, but it's not *here*. It might not be quiet, but you're used to that." His eyes shoot to the ceiling in emphasis where some kind of argument is still going on. "But my brothers would treat you with respect."

Brothers? *What. The. Fuck?* Time stops. My blood chills in my veins, my heart misses a beat. My lungs cease taking in oxygen. *No, no,* I'm internally screaming. *They can't mean what I think they do.* Words come into my memory; *I'll get one of my brothers to pick me up.* At the time, I'd just assumed he has a big family. But brothers can have more than one meaning, in the context I'm used to, one that's chilling.

Shivering, still hoping I'm way off the mark, I enquire with trepidation, "What clubhouse?"

"Oh," Mary says airily. "My old man and Niran are in a motorcycle club. It's their clubhouse—"

I launch myself to my feet. *Why hadn't I seen this before? Why hadn't I guessed Grumbler was a road name?* Niran had never worn a cut and had always arrived in a truck. *He's been deceiving me.* "Get out of here, now!" I scream.

Both my unwelcome visitors stay where they are, looking shocked, exchanging worried glances with each other.

"Get out! Get out! Get out!" A loud banging comes at the paper-thin wall of my apartment, but that doesn't deter me. "Get out of my home, now." I'm shaking, my stomach's rolling with a fear so intense it makes me feel like I'm going to throw up. *Has Niran been playing me all this time?*

Stunned that they're not moving, and becoming more afraid, I glance for a weapon of some kind. Spying my phone, I snatch it up, key in the code, tap in three numbers and wave it threateningly. "I'm calling the cops."

"Whoa." Niran's on his feet now, looking worriedly at Mary then in utter consternation my way. "Saffie, listen to me." His hands are moving as though to soothe a spooked horse.

There's no pacifying me. "No, you listen to me!" I scream.

"Saffie—we're friends, aren't we?"

"No," I refute loudly, my voice showing I'm losing control of myself. "We're far from fucking friends. Give me your key and just leave!"

"Saffie…" He comes closer, and I take a step back, holding the phone out of his reach.

"Key!" My voice is shrill. *Why won't they leave?* If he tries to call my bluff, I'll dial 911. Surely, someone will be sent to help me?

He could overpower me, forcibly take my phone from me. I take another step back, increasing the distance between us, my finger hovering over the green button.

With a worried glance toward Mary, Niran shakes his head, takes my key out of his pocket and holds it out. When I don't move close enough to take it, he places it down on the table. "We'll leave, okay? Though there's really nothing for you to worry about. I swear to you, Saffie, no one in our club would hurt you." His calm voice has no effect on me.

Showing my finger is still over the keypad of my phone, I

give them one last warning. "Last chance. I mean it, I'll call the cops."

"Saffie," Mary pleads.

But if over the past few days Niran has learned to read me at all, it's to see when I'm serious. He reaches for her hand. "Come on, Mary."

Unwillingly, but seeing I'm set on the action I threatened if they don't walk through my door, her face falls and she steps up beside him. "Saffie…" She tries one last appeal. "Niran's given you my number. If you want anything, just call me."

"No." I don't want anything from her, or from anyone in a motorcycle club. They're all evil, twisted, demented. I'll never be safe from them.

They know where I live. *I'll have to move.* For all I know, they're associated with the Crazy Wolves and Niran's been here just waiting for Duke to come get me.

Duke might already be on his way.

Even as I have that thought, a voice inside me asks, *Why should I run? Why, when I've already lost everything worth living for? Why should I try to survive when all I want to do is die?*

I watch the door close behind them, not feeling any relief. If only they hadn't been connected to an MC, they'd both still be my friends. The woman I envy, and the man who was starting to mean something to me.

History's repeating itself. It's happening again. I thought I could trust him.

Why is it I keep getting in with the wrong people? What is it about me that makes the same mistakes over and over? Have I got a faulty gene which stops me reading people correctly?

What the hell does a biker want from me? And why did he hide what he was? He never arrived on his bike, never wore a cut, and never talked about his club with me.

We didn't talk much about anything.

I fall to the sofa, put my head in my hands, and howl out my sorrow and frustration as I let my thoughts flood through me.

When I learned I was pregnant for a second time, my initial reaction was how the hell even a small embryo could have survived me being beaten so badly. I hadn't been convinced it was real until I heard the cells vibrating against each other, that sound that people refer to as a heartbeat.

I knew immediately Duke must never find out.

I'd lain in the hospital bed thinking about the new life in my womb. It was alive despite all the odds. It was my duty to carry it to term. Despite who the father was, I was confident that with him out of the picture, I could bring my child up to be nothing like his sperm donor. It was a miracle, and I already loved him or her. Despite my best efforts to give my baby the best start in life, I'd failed. A baby I found out was a boy at the exact same time I discovered he had no chance.

This place has been okay up to now. I haven't been robbed and don't expect to be. I drive a junker which I pray for before starting each day, hoping it's not about to fall apart. No one in their right mind would expect to find anything worth stealing from someone who chooses to live here.

Now, there's even more to add to my plate. A member of a freaking MC has befriended me. I know I'd be wrong not to question why.

I'm not stupid. I know if Duke finds me my life won't be worth living. I ran, which is one black mark. I'll have earned another by keeping his son a secret. That there's something wrong with his development would again be down to me. It's not death I'm scared about, it's the manner in which he'll deliver it. Duke's honour will depend on how he dispatches me, and I've heard him boast how he can keep his victims alive for days.

If he doesn't kill me, I might end up wishing he'd stolen my final breath. *He could give me to his club brothers.* I know of a whore who was choked to death, and another disfigured for fun. I could be sentenced to years servicing the club.

It might be a bit of a stretch to immediately make the leap from meeting a stranger who admits he rides with a motorcycle club to think Duke will be given information about where to find me, but I've spent five years with a one-percenter club. I know there's often rivalry between MCs, but also some which are friendly to each other. If the tall, Black man called Niran belonged to one of the latter, befriending me might not have been accidental.

What do I do?

If I could, I'd curl up and die. How can the universe be so unkind to me? I've still not come to terms with the idea I've lost the chance of holding my newborn baby in my arms. Even if I decide to continue the pregnancy, if he's born alive, from his birth and for all of his short life he'll be hooked up to machines. I won't be there cheering on when he takes his first steps or holding his hand as he starts to toddle along. I won't need to equip him with life skills and eventually send him out into the world.

My son will never have a chance of any of that, and I won't play my part as his mom.

I feel like a mother already. From my first step on the Freedom Trail, I'd been doing everything for the baby. I hadn't even had a preference for what sex it would be.

Every decision I made was about what was best for him. My own wants and desires had come way down the list.

I'd weakened when I'd allowed Niran to comfort me.

There's only one conclusion I can come to as to why a biker has been keeping in such close proximity.

However unlikely, he has to have been working for Duke. It would be just like him to send someone I wouldn't suspect.

He was waiting for Duke to come and get me.

If that's the case, how long do I have?

CHAPTER TEN

Niran

Always conscious of my promise to Grumbler, I speed away from the neighbourhood that unsettles me and will admit to breathing a sigh of relief as we head into the more affluent area of the city. I might be a hardened biker and have faced more than a few bullets in my time as a Marine, so well used to the rougher side of life, but for the past hour or so I've been overly conscious that today I have Mary with me. Grumbler certainly wouldn't want her hanging around in an area full of druggies and criminals. Judgemental? Perhaps. But never naïve. That knock on Saffie's door had been a real eye-opener as to the risk she's in just staying there.

What if it hadn't been a lone intruder? What if a gang had appeared? Would they have taken my excuse that they were on the wrong floor? Damn it. Grumbler would rightly put my balls in a fucking vice if he knows I put Mary in danger, and that includes just a small rise to her heart rate.

Fuck, but it goes against the grain to know I'm leaving Saffie there, in a home I wouldn't want to house a stray dog. Those nights I'd stayed with her, I'd been aware of the potential for violence, but was lulled into a false sense of security when all that seemed to affect her had been noise. Today it had come far too close. That caller was so fucked up, he wouldn't have cared had she confronted him. Faced with an attractive woman, a junkie might have easily forgotten his beef with his dealer and taken something she hadn't been offering.

On top of that, I've left her alone and hurting, and that pains me deep in the gut.

But what could I do? Not only had she asked me to leave, she'd done the one thing guaranteed to make me go.

I glare out of the windshield, only half my attention on the road. Fuck, but I hate leaving Saffie alone.

"I want to go back," Mary says stubbornly, showing her thoughts are running along the same lines. "We shouldn't have left her there."

"Couldn't risk her calling the fuckin' cops." Especially not as she seems to have a deep-seated grievance against motorcycle clubs.

"Pah. What could she say?" Mary asks indignantly. "We weren't doing any harm."

"Mary," I start in exasperation. "Look at me." Taking one hand off the wheel, I gesture down at my body.

"So, you're big, but you're not a threat. I could have told them that."

Rolling my eyes, it appears I have to remind her, "I'm fuckin' Black."

Once I've put it so plainly, Mary sucks in a breath. "I didn't think of that," she says softly, reaching out and touching my thigh briefly. "I'm sorry, Niran."

So am I. I couldn't take the risk the cops turning up wouldn't ask questions first. It's likely I'd have been arrested, if not shot on the spot. I wonder if Saffie had realised the implications. Maybe she did, but whether done consciously, she'd made a threat that coming from a White woman, was strongest against a man with the colour of my skin.

Mary huffs and out of the side of my eye I see her twisting her hair. "She didn't give us a chance to explain about the type of club we are. We could be weekend warriors, fundraising, anything. She just assumed the worst."

"She was fuckin' terrified, Mary." I hadn't missed how the blood had drained from her face immediately after the facts had become known to her. "And I didn't only leave because of the threat of the cops, it was as much how our presence was upsetting her."

I have a dreadful feeling inside me that she's known a club which doesn't treat women kindly. As to what type of club we were, what could I have told her? If I were totally honest, I'd have had to explain that yes, we still wear the one-percenter patch. My qualification that nowadays that means we only occasionally step over the line, and not live on the other side of it, would probably have gone unheard.

Everything had been fine until the word 'clubhouse' was mentioned. A word that had such bad connotations in her head, it had triggered a severe reaction such that she was only one step away from a full-blown panic attack. It wasn't hard to immediately understand she had a fear of bikers, making me suspicious of what club she might have previously been associated with, or maybe simply had crossed their path. Of course, not all clubs were as family oriented as ours. Many are violent, many dealing in drugs, guns and heaven help us, women. We would never descend into such depths of depravity. I might be a Devil but I'm not selling my soul. Easy money? You can keep it.

I want to rant and rave. My protective instinct had been brought to the fore the moment I'd first seen her, only intensifying as I saw how distressed she was, knowing something serious had caused it. When I understood the pressure and sorrow she was under, my desire to hold her close hadn't been able to be denied. That's why I'd stayed, got to know that part of her that she allowed me to see, and in turn, kept back most of me. In not wanting to upset her, I'd lost my chance to be pre-armed for this situation. Goddamn it! I punch the steering wheel in frustration. *I should have demanded to know who the father was or why she was living in a pit only this side of hell.* I've only myself to blame by not pushing for answers.

Had I been glad the father was out of the picture? I think that's truer than I want to admit, let alone ponder on the reasons.

Now I'm being forced to leave her behind, and I don't fucking like it. It's like being asked to leave a Marine or brother. Her pain might be mental rather than physical, but it's abandonment just the same. Neither the Marine nor biker in me likes it.

Mary talks on, luckily satisfied with grunts for answers as my mind races as I drive, wondering how I can bring help to Saffie. She needs it, that's for certain.

I'd hated leaving her but there was no way we could have stayed, particularly having Mary with me. For one thing, our presence would have stressed her more, probably dangerously raising her blood pressure. As for another, even if the cops had stopped to ask questions, if my colour hadn't been enough, once they'd discovered my connection to the MC, I'd have spent the evening in lockup, and heaven forbid, if they wanted to go all out, Mary as well. Grumbler would have quite rightly killed me.

At the extreme, cops are always on the lookout for any excuse to bring down an MC, and the whole club could have possibly been dragged into it. Forcing our way into a woman's home and refusing to leave? Yeah, it might not be much to go on, but they'd have done their damndest to have built a tenuous case around it.

Fuck it. There must be some way to get Saffie to realise the last person she needs to fear is me, or the men in my club. Every one of them would drop everything to help her. I've no doubt of that.

But what can I fucking do? Right now, I've more questions than answers.

Driving up the track, I finally pull up outside Grumbler and Mary's house. The man himself, comes out to the car, wrenches the passenger door open, and helps his wife out. His eyes examine her carefully, taking her in from head to toe.

"You're back sooner than I expected." His eyes narrow. "You look pale. You alright?"

She smiles up at him, albeit a little wanly. "I'm good, but Saffie—"

"What the fuck's she done?" he interrupts.

"She threw us out," I input, as it turns out, unhelpfully, as it attracts his wrathful gaze.

"She's in a terrible situation, Grumbler." Mary sniffs loudly.

"Fuckin' hell, Niran. You said it would be alright to take my ol' lady there! And you bring her back fuckin' upset!" Grumbler roars, making me take a step back and hold up my hands, palms facing outward.

But Mary's fist hits him lightly in the stomach before his can swing. "Niran's got nothing to do with this. He was just doing what I wanted. But Grumbler, once she knew who we were, she didn't want us to stay. And I'm really okay. I'm just worried about her, and I don't understand why she made us leave."

"I want to hear this," he, well, grumbles. At first, I wonder whether he'd prefer to hear what had happened from me, but by the way he's focusing on his old lady's face, he needs her reassurance she's as okay as she'd have him believe.

And I've got things I want to do. "I'll head back to the clubhouse." I incline my head toward Mary. "Your ol' lady can fill you in on the deets. You know where to find me if you want me." I'm prepared to stand still if after hearing her out, he still wants to use his fists.

Grumbler lets me take a step, before he snaps, "This gonna be club business?"

On the face of it, no. Unless it's by accident at another of Mary and Saffie's hospital appointments coinciding, we may never bump into Saffie again. Or, not soon, in any event. She needs time and space. Maybe if she thinks about things for a moment, she'll realise whatever she has against bikers doesn't apply to me. If I have my way, I'll find some way to get back to her. But fuck it, somehow there's a connection, whatever it is, with another MC. Could I have unwittingly stepped into something as yet unknown? I can't rule out it might pit us up against a rival club. "It might," I answer him eventually. "It's a fucked-up situation, Grumbler. I don't feel right leaving it as it is."

Mary turns from her man to me, her face lighting up. "You're still going to help her?"

I gentle my tone. "Her situation upsets you, Mary, and it fuckin' upsets me too. It's clear to see she needs someone in her corner, so yeah, if I can figure out a way to put someone into it, I will." But I'm stumped as to how if she doesn't trust bikers.

Grumbler, noticing his woman's not quite as upset having been appeased that she's not the only one worrying, gives me a chin lift before putting his arm around her and leading her into their house. I watch them for a second, noticing how their love and respect is palpable, and wondering whether I'll ever find anything like that. *Could I have found that with Saffie?* Nah, no chance. Today has proven how little we know of each other.

Getting back into the driver's seat, I do a three-point turn and head to the club.

I'm a man on a mission when I arrive, with one thing on my mind and one thing only. Entering the clubhouse, I look around. I see Blaze, Dusty, Scribe—oh there's Kink, alone again tonight. Reboot and Keeper are deep in conversation. Alex is here with Tyler, her son, and Dart who's busy trying to corral Isla, their toddler who's running around seemingly intent on evading her father. Today I'm hard put to find a smile and the one man I'm seeking isn't in sight.

Striding across, just waving a hand at whoever tries to engage me in conversation, I head for the offices. Opening one door without knocking, I sigh with relief as I see Token behind his computer.

"Got a job…" My words trail off as I notice his head is rolled back, his face contorted, and under the desk I can see legs and a butt.

"Give me a moment," he rasps, unconcernedly. "Cindy, carry on. I'm close, girl. Oh fuck."

Rolling my head back on my neck, I half turn to give him some privacy. It's not more than a few seconds later that a long, satisfied groan shows he's reached completion, and when I turn around, Cindy's backing out, wiping her mouth.

"He's all yours," she tells me cheekily, and edging past me, goes out through the door. I might not partake of the club girls myself, but I'm not blind to the benefits for some by being in an MC.

Token's breathing heavily, a cocky, sated smile on his face when he at last looks up. His hands reach down, and his movements show he's tucking himself away and zipping up.

"Got a mouth like a goddamn Hoover that one." He gives me a lazy grin. "What can I do for you, Brother?"

I pull out a chair and sit down. My stump is throbbing, so I lean forward and rub the spot where my real leg ends. "Got a name for you. Can you look into it for me?" When he nods, I give it to him. "It's the woman I've been going to see. Saffie Jones." I add her address which I'd memorised and her place of work which I might have checked out one day when unbeknownst to her, I'd followed her. "I think she's in trouble, Toke, and maybe needs help."

"Trouble?" He sits up straighter. "I heard she's got fucked-up shit to do with her pregnancy. Women's stuff. There's no help I can be with that."

"She lives in a shithole and I don't feel she belongs there, for a start." When he gestures *give me more*, grimacing, I tell him, "I took Mary to see her. Jeez, Toke, we had an up-close-and-personal demonstration that place is the pits. There was an altercation while we were there between a junkie and a dealer—came right to her front door. Mary thought it was best to get her out of there, and I was on board, but as soon as the clubhouse was mentioned, she straight up asked if we were in a biker club and freaked at the answer."

Token's eyes sharpen, and his previously dilated pupils return to a more normal shape. "You think she's had a run-in with bikers and is scared of them?"

Scared? "Fuckin' terrified is more like it. As for the reason, I can't think of anything else." I shrug, adding a head shake to show I've put my mind to it.

Token deals with computers and data and spends a lot of time joining dots. I'm not surprised when he poses his next question. He eyes me seriously. "You like this bitch, Niran? Is it personal?"

Leaning forward, I clasp my hands between my knees and frown, not having it in me to lie and seeing no reason for it. "I wouldn't say I like 'like' her. I don't know her well enough, and I've far from seen her at her best. But we clicked. I call, called, her my friend. It hurts that I left her to deal with some heavy shit on her own." Again, I raise and lower my shoulders. "Can't say more than that, Brother."

Raising his chin, he responds, "Fair enough. I'll do some digging and let you know what I find out. In the meantime, Brother, are you going to try to try speak to her again?" His frown seems to question why the fuck I'm talking to him when I could be with her.

Grimacing, I explain, "She threatened to call the cops, Toke."

His head tilts, his eyebrow rises, then his mouth opens as he forms an 'O.'

Yeah. Welcome to my life, Brother.

"Best steer clear." Token shakes his head. "Unless you want one of us to try to approach her?"

"Nah, Toke." I brush my hand over my face. "I don't think she took my colour into account. I got no such vibe from her. Any biker's likely to upset her." Even if one of them went minus their cut, most have tats and look just what they are. Even if Dusty or Deuce could hide their ink, now she's on the lookout, I doubt even they would get past her. "Too risky, Bro. We'd risk her calling the cops on whoever turned up. Lost would fuckin' love that."

He would. Not. Prez would be furious if any of us garnered unwanted attention. Cops are always just one step away from getting a search warrant. They'd jump at any excuse.

Whichever way I look at it, I've got to put distance between Saffie and me. Maybe if Token can find something to explain her extreme reaction, I could take the risk of visiting her again, this time armed with arguments that would convince her I'd never hurt her. Until then, if I relish my life and freedom and that of my brothers, I'd do best to stay clear away. In any event, just my presence is likely to upset her, and she has far too much on her plate as it is.

I leave Token's office slightly pissed that I have no choice. Saffie needs help and support, and I very much doubt there's anyone else to give it. She, herself, had told me as much.

Who's there to hold her, who'll mop up her tears? Who'll make her that disgusting decaf when she gets in from work?

No one. That's who. *Not my fault,* I reason with myself. *She's the one who's irrationally scared of bikers, and who dismissed us without giving us a chance.*

What really bugs me is why she hadn't judged us on our behaviour but rather on a reputation she'd assumed. The only answer I can come up with is that she's once been badly burned, and still bears the scars from it. Irrationally, I'm irate at the unknown biker who's scared her so badly, and though I don't want to believe it, I doubt it's too much of a stretch to think maybe he raped her and bears responsibility for the situation she's in.

If that's the case, I'm determined to find out exactly who he is, then tear him apart limb by limb.

Until Token works his magic, there's nothing I can do. It's frustrating as hell. It's not like me to wait stagnant being unable to take any course of action.

I'm an extrovert. I possess the ability to mix with those from many different walks of life, and hence the type of person who likes people around. While I wouldn't describe myself as the life and soul of the party, I prefer to spend my free time in the club-room, enjoying making conversation and joining in with games of cards or pool. For me to keep to myself and be introspective is unusual enough that my silence and the 'leave me alone vibes' I'm giving off tonight doesn't pass without comment.

"What's up, Bro?" Kink comes over to the bar I'm seated at alone and purposefully at a distance from other brothers. Uninvited, he takes the stool next to me and places his beer in front of him.

I'm not in the mood for company, but my innate instinct isn't to be rude, though I do ask snidely, "No pets again tonight? Must be a record."

Kink laughs. "I've not been to the club. It's only open from Thursday through the weekend. Right now, I haven't taken even a temporary sub, so," he raises his hands, "I'm all yours."

"Now why does that thought send chills down my spine?" Exaggerating my gesture, I wince.

He chortles and slaps my back. "Not going to put a collar and leash on you, man. I don't give a damn what others do, but I'm not into dicks." His brow furrows then he grins. "But I can find you a nice cock and ball cage if you want to torture yourself."

No fucking way. My eyes widen in horror.

But Kink's teasing had been to serve a purpose, as he all but admits, "Now I've got you out of your head, what's got you so down in the fuckin' doldrums?" He picks up his drink, swallows a few times, and finishes it. "Or are you just itching to get back to your woman later, and the hours are passing too slow?"

Raising two fingers to Curtis who correctly interprets the gesture and appears with two fresh beers, I incline my head toward a table in the corner. Once seated and our throats have had the initial wetting, I proceed to tell him about my afternoon, finishing with, "So I won't be going to see her again."

His face grows gradually darker as I reveal the sad story.

"That's fucked up, Brother." Kink stares at the beers, shakes his head, then calls out a demand, "Two whiskys, Prospect." Turning to me, he adds, "This calls for the stronger stuff."

I wholeheartedly agree.

When two glasses and a bottle, yeah, Curtis has got a head on his shoulders, appear in front of us, Kink half closes his eyes. "That woman's suffering hurts the head of a Dominant."

"You've not even met her." I'm surprised he's feeling like that.

"I haven't and I'm not speaking about me. I'm talking about you."

My eyes crease. "I've told you before, I'm no Dominant."

"Aren't you?" He refills his whisky glass which I hadn't noticed he'd already emptied. "You've got all the traits, Niran. What officer position are you most suited for?" None is my initial response; I've not served enough time in the club. "You're the de facto sergeant-at-arms. Sure, Grumbler holds the title, but you've been playing the part for almost a year now. You've got an innate desire to protect and serve the club, as you previously did for your country." He shrugs. "The role suits you. If Grumbler ever steps down, I, for one, wouldn't hesitate to vote you in permanently."

Ignoring the compliment as I don't know how to take it, I chuckle. "You must be fuckin' crazy if you're implying the club's full of submissives I want to protect." Is it wrong I get a mental image of Salem and Pennywise naked and crawling around on their knees in front of me while I crack a whip? It so is. The vision makes me both want to bark a laugh and simultaneously vomit. Nah, I'd never want that.

"Dominance, the need to nurture and protect, isn't something that can be turned off," Kink says quite seriously.

"Then half the men in the club, at least, possibly all of them, are Dominant if that's your definition."

He nods. "Very true. But getting back to you. You met a woman, quite possibly submissive, who's in need of a fuck load of help. You saw that, stepped in, and tried to give your support until you were no longer in a position to provide it. That's what's tying you up into knots, Brother. Another man? He'd have walked away and simply said fuck it."

I don't agree. I think most men worth their salt would be worrying about her. "What about you, Kink?" I'm interested in what he would have done or would do in the same situation.

His eyes meet mine and hold them. "I'd be like you, Brother. I know I come off as a shallow bastard who exploits women to fuck them—"

"Not after our talk the other night," I interrupt, realising his activities now make sense. "Your ways might be bizarre, but you're looking out for them."

He winks. "And, getting my Dom kicks, don't forget that. Just as a sub has needs, Doms do too. If we don't have the chance to get into that headspace, it takes away part of what balances us."

My lips curve as I think I've caught him out. "So, if I'm a Dom, where do I get my kicks in the Saffie situation? As you said, I was giving support and not getting anything back."

He snorts and shakes his head, making his hair fly around him. "So fuckin' blind, you just can't see it. You got yours by knowing you were helping. That eased something inside you.

Which is why you're so fuckin' frustrated that you can't go back, and why you were sitting brooding by yourself."

I top off my own glass now and think about what he's said for a moment. While I've never considered myself dominant in Kink's way, it does bring my concerns about being unable to help a woman I don't really know into some kind of perspective. My desire to protect is being thwarted. I might not label it in the same way as Kink, but I do know whatever *this* is, I was born with it.

Suddenly, a hand drops onto my shoulder. I start, my Marine training must have forsaken me, as I hadn't been aware of anyone's approach.

"Lover, I know you're Dominant." Susie leans in close. "I'm up to games if that's what you enjoy. You can tie me up anytime or flog me."

"Fuckin' get lost, Susie." My rage rises fast. "Don't interrupt fuckin' private conversations." Or even listen to them. Even as a hangaround she should know that.

Kink adds in a growl and a glare.

Her hand rises and I'm so relieved at the loss of her touch, I barely resist brushing my shoulder to get the lingering sensation off. "If you want me, I'm over there." She points to where Cindy is standing, and then walks off to join her.

Good riddance. "I fuckin' hate that bitch," I snarl. "Why the fuck does she keep coming around? Does she want to be a sweet butt or something?"

Kink's eyes narrow as he watches her walk away. "More likely an ol' lady, and you, lucky fucker, are who's she's got her eyes on."

My gaze snaps to him quickly, but it's not jealously on his face but disgust. "Once, I went with her, Brother. And that was only when I was so fuckin' drunk I can't even remember."

"Some mistakes come back to haunt us," he says sagely, then

shakes himself and gets back on track. "Now, where were we? Ah yes, Saffie."

The concern in his eyes leads me to admit, "I can't stop thinking about her, Kink. What she's going through, how she got there—that she has no man with her makes me think the obvious —and the devastating decision she still has to make."

Kink leans back on his chair, tipping it up on two legs, and regards me thoughtfully. After a moment, he asks, "You making the assumption she was raped?" I lift my chin slightly, but also raise and lower my shoulders. I'm assuming, yes, but have no evidence one way or another. "What would your advice be in her situation? Abortion, or let nature play this shit out?"

My answer comes easily. "Not for me to say, Brother. I've got no iron in this fire. It's not what I think, even if my leaning was one way or another. What I'd like is to be there, maybe as a sounding block just to listen to her. It's she that's got to live with her choice. I just want to support her and make whatever route she chooses easier for her." I pause, then add, "If she was raped, you'd think the decision would be easier."

"Or maybe not." Kink's brow creases. "How it came into being isn't the kid's fault. Nor hers. Maybe she was making the best of it."

"She's strong, Kink." Then I contradict myself. "Nah, I know she seems weak as hell at the moment, but if I'm right in what I think, she's already made one torturous decision which as it turns out was all for nothing."

"She's one fuck load of complications. Can't you just walk away?" He's eyeing me curiously.

"No fuckin' way," I reply.

But why? I ask myself. *I don't even know her.* It's as though something inside her calls to me, making me arrogantly believe I should be the one to help her.

Kink brings his chair back down onto all four legs, and using his glass, salutes me. "Dominant to the fuckin' core," he pronounces, as if closing that subject completely.

His declaration unsettles me. I decide to put him right on a few facts. "I'm not attracted to her sexually. I mean, that shit wouldn't be right. She's more than five months pregnant with another man's kid."

"I rest my case." Kink grins widely. "Dominance isn't about sex. People think subs serve, but that's incorrect. As much as subs live to serve their Doms, Doms function best when they're providing a service to someone who needs it. You spent time as a fuckin' Marine, serving your country, Niran. You'd have given your life to make some unknown person's life safer, and sex certainly didn't come into that. Now, you're looking out for the club. It's the knowledge that you can help that makes you breathe easier, not any hard-on you might get. When you can't, it makes you feel helpless."

"I don't know what I can do, Kink." I'm not going to argue anymore. Too much of what he says makes sense. Another brother might have told me to move on and forget her, that by throwing me out, she'd made her own bed.

Kink shrugs. "You're already doing all you can, Niran. It's why you went to Token. Depending on what he comes back with, you'll work out another approach. Hell, there's a hundred ways this could play out. Token's a fuckin' genius when it comes to hacking. He can check into the hospital's database, see if she's made an appointment for a termination. Then, you could coincidently be there for her. If she doesn't want you, if she truly can do that shit by herself, that's on her. But it might just turn out that once again you're there when she most needs support."

Brightening, I finish my whisky. He's got a good point. If I were pushed to give my opinion, I'd say nothing was to be gained by her continuing the pregnancy. The only outcome would be that after another three months or so, she'd be burying a dead baby incapable of taking a first breath. If Saffie comes to the same conclusion, I'm sure, via Token, I can find out when, and, if she needs me, be there to offer a shoulder in support, or at least, to cry on.

While I'm still ruminating on what Kink's said, Pennywise calls out to get his attention. Soon, Kink's roped into a game of poker.

CHAPTER ELEVEN

Niran

Staring after Kink as he strides over to the table where cards are already laid out, I continue thinking. I might have some Dom traits, but I'm certainly not Dominant in the way that he is.

His previous description of his life sounds equally complicated and simple. Contracts and negotiations are things that belong in business, not in a relationship. Along with the concerns whether what you're doing is right, his method also takes away spontaneity and excitement. If you know what you're going to do before you do it, how can you push boundaries and discover what you both like?

I might like to take the reins in the bedroom, but surely that's the role that most women expect of a man? But should the woman want to turn the tables, I don't give a damn. Nah, while I'm idly interested in the games Kink plays, they're not for me.

Knowing it takes all sorts to make the world turn, I shake my head as I return to the bar and tap on it, attracting the prospect's attention again. There's been a shift change and now I'm served by our latest addition to the club. Fuck knows what the ex-hangaround's real name is. From the moment he appeared, he picked up the handle, Kid. Hell, he doesn't look old enough to shave, but is actually twenty-two. He's eager and keen, just like any new prospect should be.

The Satan's Devils are giving him a chance to turn his life around. He'd done a stint in juvie for hot-wiring a car, and during that time got into a gang. On getting out, he got dragged into some bad shit, and was picked up on a felony charge. This time, tried as an adult, he got sent to the penitentiary and served two years. Finding that no picnic, on getting out, he was determined never to go back.

Leaving a gang is never easy, and it helps if you have men at your back. Our MC's reputation trumps that of the kiddie gang he was in. In return for our protection, Kid's giving us his all. From what I've seen, he's going to be a good man to have at our backs.

"Beer?" Kid asks, respectfully.

I nod. "How's it going?"

"Fuckin' love it, man." Kid leans over as he places the beer in front of me. He runs a hand over his youthful face. "I'm not going to let you down."

I raise my chin to him, knowing that feeling. It had been my resolve not so long ago. Now, looking out for the club is ingrained in me. If it were not, I'd have called Saffie's bluff, let her call the cops and been done with it. But from fucking little seeds, acorns can grow, and before you know it, I could have been charged with assault or attempted kidnapping, or fuck knows what they'd make up. And worse, they could have investigated the club on trafficking grounds. Of course there would be nothing to find, but hell, there's always a chance they could use the opportunity to pin something on the club.

Now I'm at a loose end. My gut tells me Saffie needs me, while my head warns me, I'm the last person she wants. All because she's scared to death of men like me, a biker. Why the hell is she so terrified of any motorcycle club, and to the extent that just the mention sends her into a panic attack?

I've never denied I was one, thought somehow she'd assumed it. But then, not wanting to leave my motorcycle anywhere in the vicinity of her apartment, I'd always used the truck, and as I never wear my cut in it, hadn't bothered to take it along. There's also another good reason. In that area, wearing it without backup could well have invited an attack.

My phone vibrates in my pocket. I slide it out quickly, hoping it's Saffie and that she's reconsidered. *Maybe she's missing me by now.*

But it's not her. I frown, noticing two things. One, it's past midnight, and the second, the caller is my mom who I rarely hear from. The combination is worrying.

Leaving my beer, I stand and make my way hurriedly, pushing past brothers and club girls doing their thing, and moving around a card game, to head outside.

"Mom, hold on a sec while I get somewhere quieter." For her to be calling me this late, it must be serious. I want to be able to hear what she says.

A few more steps have me out in the night air, another few yards, and the loud music from the clubhouse fades. "Yeah, Mom, I'm okay now. Whatcha want?"

My mother and I don't have a normal son/parent bond, just a strained and awkward relationship. A dutiful son, I go back to my hometown from time to time, but never stay long.

It wasn't always that way. We might have been poor, but I grew up in a happy home. Dad worked hard to put food on our table and taught me how to be a man. However dire our straits became, he'd never countenance earning money other than doing it the hard way, and however Mom nagged, he'd never raised his hand. He taught me respect for women and those who couldn't look out for themselves, a love for my country and fellow man, and the ethics that you worked your balls off for anything worth having.

All was good until a drunk driver crossed over the centre line and took him away from us. At fourteen, I had to step up and become the man of the house. It had been hard; his life insurance couldn't even guarantee the meagre lifestyle that I'd known. But I'd remembered the lessons he'd taught me, and though my size and strength got me invited to join a gang, I'd resisted. Instead, I studied hard at school, and worked every free hour I had doing menial jobs, bringing in what money I could. Mom and I became extremely familiar with ramen noodles, a dish I can't stomach today.

But it was to no avail, my efforts weren't enough, and the woman whose skills had hitherto enabled her to keep house had to find a job for herself. With no education nor experience behind her, she became a minimum-wage cleaner.

Still, we jogged along okay, finding solace and support in each other until one of her cleaning contracts was to service a single businessman, ten years her senior. I'd like to say they clicked, but I'd always had suspicions that when he fell for my mother, it wasn't a love match for her, rather an escape from her circumstances. I didn't blame her, didn't resent her from moving on from my dad. A good son, I'd wanted the best for her.

I grew up as an only child, and still consider myself that.

Mom had been seventeen when she married the first time, just a year later she'd had me. Three years after my father had died, she'd gotten hitched again. While she'd found a replacement husband, I hadn't found a replacement dad. Grover was okay, but he wanted his own family and not one he'd inherited. Being thrust in the parental role, he'd gone into it too hard, automatically assuming a kid like me would need firm direction and a heavy guiding hand.

Having been the man of the house, I'd found his restrictions hard to accept. For Mom's sake, I'd put up with it, but as soon as

I turned eighteen, I joined the Marines. I had a new life, and knowing my mother was settled and as happy as she could be, I went out and lived it. I had no regrets, finding I relished my newfound freedom and the opportunity to make my own mistakes and my own triumphs. On visits home, Grover couldn't stop being heavy-handed. For my sake and my mom's happiness, I lessened the frequency, and fell into the pattern of returning only occasionally, and only ever for short periods of time.

She'd been just thirty-five when she'd met Grover, and while one baby had been sufficient for her and my dad, as though wanting to give her new husband everything that he asked for she quickly fell pregnant. In all, three kids—all girls—had appeared in rapid succession. They'd all been born after I'd left home, and I'd never felt they were siblings of mine.

I talk to my mom at Christmas and sometimes on my birthday. I haven't been home since I joined the Devils—I don't want to keep that secret, and me being a biker is something which my stepdad would not approve. All they know is that I'm a mechanic. I do know what Grover appreciates is that despite his wealth, I've never asked for handouts.

As memories flit through my head, I perch on a barrel and steel myself to hear bad news. *Had Grover met with an accident or died from an illness?* Hell, I hope not. Mom would never survive another such loss.

Mom doesn't take long to put me out of my misery. "Niran, it's your sister."

I suck in air, for a moment I'm trying to process what she's talking about. Oh, yeah, the three girls that I've never really felt were related to me because I've never been part of their lives. It puzzles me why she's calling me about any of them. "Who? And what the fuck's happened? What's going on, Mom?" The prospect of one of my siblings being injured or worse looms closer.

"It's Cynthia. She's gone."

Cyn, I remember, at twenty, is my oldest sister. I growl. "What the fuck do you mean she's gone?" *Dead?* Fuck I hope not.

"She's packed her bags and walked out."

"Is she missing? Have you checked around with her friends? What happened to make her leave?" And why talk to me?

"She's not missing as such," Mom shares mysteriously. "I, your stepdad, well, Grover, he was just being Grover. She's been such a handful, Niran, and Grover went too far." For the first time I hear real emotion as she unsuccessfully stifles a sob. "Her latest escapade upset him so much, he lost his temper."

Now my snarl is louder. *You never hit women, Son, however much you think they deserve it.* The voice of my dad echoes in my mind. "He ever hit you, Mom?" If I'd known Grover was violent, I'd have done more to check in on her and had a chat using my fists, man to man.

"No, Niran. Grover's not violent. He didn't hit her. He just lost his temper. It's Cynthia I'm worried about. She's been a handful the last few years. Sometimes, I don't think I know her. She's bullheaded and can't be made to see sense." Despite the circumstances, I grin. *Yeah, and I wonder where she gets that from.* Mom can be very single minded. Once she gets an idea in her head, it's firmly bedded in.

"Okay, let's break this down, Mom. Do you know where she's gone? Is she safe? And what can I do?" I don't even know her. When I do go home they treat me as an oddity, an interloper, and I'm just as distant as them.

I'm expecting her to say talk to her, but hell, Cyn might be my sister, but she's a stranger. She was a babe in arms when I first saw her, and on the few occasions when I've been back, apart from a blood bond, there'd been little connection between us.

"That's why I'm calling you. Grover, well..." Whatever Grover did or said, she stops that train of thought without enlightening me. "Cynthia's got it in her mind to come find her older brother, thinking you'd have sympathy for her. She emptied her college fund and is currently on a red-eye to San Diego."

What the fuck? I ignore the thought of a college fund which was a luxury I'd never had. "How the hell did she think she was going to find me?" I've always been vague about my address. Having never admitted to being a Satan's Devil, I'd been unable to share that I lived on the compound. I'd been a Marine so long, one room as my accommodation suits me well enough, and communal living was something that had attracted me to this life.

"I don't know, but it's Cynthia all around. I suspect she was going to visit all the auto-shops around."

I start to ask if she's any sense of how big San Diego is, when I realise it's *Cynthia*. It's all I need to know. Grover's first child had been spoiled from the day she was born and being daddy's girl had never wanted for anything. If she needed something, it would come her way. Now, apparently, she has for some unknown fucking reason, set her sights on me.

"When's the plane land?" I ask through gritted teeth, mentally counting the beers I'd had. Conducting a sobriety test on myself, I walk a crack in the pavement. Passing, as my feet move in a straight line, I decide I'm okay to drive.

Mom's done her homework and gives me the times of when the flight is likely to land and gives me the next one for good measure.

"I'll go meet her, turn her around, and get her back to you, Mom." How I'll persuade her, I've yet to come up with a plan.

"No, Niran," Mom almost shouts. "Please, can you keep her with you for a while? Maybe you can knock some sense into her?"

Me? I live on a fucking biker compound, hardly the place for my young sister. "Mom, I'm not set up to look after a kid."

"She's an adult, Niran. She just needs to learn some boundaries and a few of the facts of life. Please, just a few weeks."

"I haven't even a place of my own," I admit. "I live over my job, Mom." It's the closest description I feel I can give her.

"Maybe that's what she needs to see, Son. That life isn't always handed to you on a silver platter. Niran, both Grover and I respect you. I know you and he didn't always see eye to eye, but we were proud as fuck when you were a Marine, and how you've built a new life after losing your leg. You never came crawling back asking for help. We think you'll be a good influence on her."

I snort. Me, a good influence? I refrain from saying if she needs me to be that, she must really have gone off the rails.

Aware time's ticking, I reassure her, "I better get going if I don't want to miss her at the airport. I'll get her to call you, okay?"

"Grover thinks it's best if she stays away," Mom states, and I can hear her voice shaking. "Grover, well, Grover and I, and her sisters, we need some space, and Cynthia needs to get her priorities in order."

So this isn't going to be a case of a quick hello/goodbye and me sending her back to Michigan, which doesn't bode well for my future. But I've no time to waste, and no chance to protest being dragged into this shit.

It's not until the call is ended that I realise I didn't do the polite thing and ask about my other sisters. But hell, I'd left before they were born. All of them, even Cyn, are relatives on paper rather than in reality. My MC brothers are more my siblings then they'll ever be.

Taking one of the club's trucks, I realise I've got to put my foot down if I'm going to catch her. Half annoyed at the interruption to my life, and half intrigued at the out-of-the-blue request for help, I drive through the predawn quiet of San Diego and head for the airport. Annoyed at the extortionate short-term parking fee, I park the truck, then walk inside, immediately checking the information board. The flight from Detroit is on time and about to land.

As a Marine, my base had been Camp Pendleton. I'd come to prefer the climate of Southern California to that of Michigan, able to ride all year around, so even when I'd lost my leg and was medically retired, I'd found my place in San Diego and stayed. Home is where the heart is, as they say, and for me the heart went out of my hometown when my father had died. For a while I'd drifted, wanting something, not knowing what, but had no desire to return to my roots. The universe moves in strange ways, pointing me in the right decision and influencing the choices I'd made. It led me to where I needed to be. The Satan's Devils are more than a club, they're my family.

Blood might be thicker than water, but it's engine oil that unites us more. I feel a pang of sympathy for the sister I barely know. Has she run in a fit of pique, or is there really nothing left for her at home? And last but not least, what the fuck did Grover say or do to her?

Not knowing whether I'm waiting to greet a girl barely out of her teens and with all the angst that age brings, or a young woman determined to find her own future, I wait where the passengers will exit the terminal, hoping like hell I recognise her. It's been three years since I saw her last.

There she is. Tugging along a flight bag on wheels, her face set, her head tilted down as though she doesn't want to attract attention, she's following the other travellers and hasn't yet glanced my way. *She's not expecting anyone to meet her.* She can't have guessed Mom would have contacted me.

She's not grown taller, but then girls stop growing earlier, don't they? They shoot up, towering over boys in their early teens, being fast overtaken later. She's filled out though. Even wrapped in a thick fur coat, far too warm for our southern climate, there's no mistaking she's got a big chest on her. She sports long, sleek dark hair which had me fooled for a moment. I clench my teeth, realising she's fallen into the trap of repressing her heritage. Black hair is beautiful, why cover it up? *Because of the society we live in.* Alternatively, it could be a disguise, but it's not working well, as despite the length of time since I've seen her, I recognise her easily.

Still looking down, she moves to go around me when I step into her path.

"Cyn?"

She startles and looks up. A gleam appears in her eyes as she recognises me. "Niran!"

There are no hugs, no kisses, neither offered on my part nor initiated on hers. It makes me realise how little I know her, and that we're half-brother and sister means nothing.

"Mom called me." I explain my presence to her.

She grimaces. "I expect she told you everything."

"No," I contradict. "She told me fuckin' nothing. Only that you'd taken off with some hare-brained scheme to come find me. How the fuck did you expect to do that?"

Shrugging, she snippily states, "Well, you're here, aren't you? Now can we get out of here?"

Give me patience. "Cyn, I've no house to take you to. We're going to need to find a hotel for the night. We'll find something and talk, then you'll have to get a flight home tomorrow." I'm tempted to book her one right now but decide to give her a chance to cool down and to talk to me as her big brother as that seems to be what she's after.

"You've no home?"

"I live in one room, Cyn. That's enough for what I need and want." And it's in a motorcycle club where I've no intention of taking her.

"I thought you were doing well for yourself." I think I am. I'm living the life that I love and which suits me. Courtesy of my free accommodation, the money I earn from the club, and my military pension, I've amassed a respectable amount of savings, and I've nothing to be ashamed of. What more can a man ask for? But it's not a life conducive to entertaining a sister. She's regarding me carefully, then after a moment, sighs. "Oh well, a hotel will have to do for now. But I'm not going home, Niran. I'll have to find somewhere to live."

"San Diego is fuckin' expensive," I warn her. "You got a job lined up?"

Her eyes fill with horror, and she actually shudders. "A job?"

Of course she hasn't. She's here on impulse. I start to get an inkling of what Mom might have been alluding too. She's been spoiled, waited on hand and foot, and now she expects me to step up and do that for her.

I want to say one night and then she's on her own, but fuck it, how can I? We share blood if nothing else.

In some states, she'd be young enough to legally be my daughter. Breathing out a heavy breath, I lead her out of the terminal, knowing that if she insists on not going back to Detroit, I'm going to be stuck with her. How could I allow a girl of her age to wander the streets of San Diego? I can be an asshole at times, but not one as bad as that.

I head for a hotel I'd stayed in a few days after being released from rehab. It's not changed much in the intervening years. It's still basic, but clean and cheap. Cyn looks around with disdain as we walk to our room, but she keeps her mouth shut and doesn't suggest she was expecting better.

If Cyn's thinking of moving here permanently, I'll help her to find a suitable place, but won't change my lifestyle for her. I could easily afford a house, but I've never felt inclined to buy one. First in the Marines, now in the club, I've grown used to having people around me. Why run the risk of being lonely and having to cook all my meals for myself?

For Saffie perhaps, yeah. If we got together, I'd buy her a house. Fuck, why is my mind going there? I'll be lucky if Saffie ever gives me the time of day again. Besides, we weren't even headed that way. We were friends. There's nothing to suggest we'd have developed any other relationship.

I force my thoughts to the woman entering the room with me, wondering why she's here, and whether, hopefully, she just needs some space between her and her parents temporarily, for tempers to cool and such.

"You tired?" I ask, sitting my ass on one of the queen beds.

"Not really." She glances at me and shrugs, pulling her case to the other bed.

She's probably too hyped to sleep. Well, if she wants to stay awake, perhaps she'll start talking. As soon as I know why she's here, I can determine a way forward.

"So tell me, why are you here, Cyn?" Leaning back on the bed, I link my hands behind my head, and study her.

Shooting a look my way, she has an abrupt change of heart. "Perhaps I will try to get some sleep."

"Uh-uh, Cyn. You've got to tell me sooner or later, so you might as well spill the beans." I compose my features into a big brother's frown and focus my eyes on her. "You're not staying without telling me what the fuck's going on."

She huffs and sits herself down, her arms folded over her chest. "Dad's a control freak."

Yeah, I get that. It's why I had to get out—curfews aimed to keep me on the straight and narrow when I hadn't needed them, chores demanded that I'd have done in any event. Everything had to be to his timescale and by his inexperienced methods of raising another man's son. Strangely, I'd been jealous of the freedom awarded to my sisters, another reason I'd stayed away, putting it down either to their gender, or that he'd grown into the father role having known them since they were born.

I suppress my *you don't know the half of it* retort, and settle instead for, "In what way?"

Her shoulders rise and fall again. "I had a boyfriend, he chased him off."

Rolling my eyes, I realise I'm not equipped to deal with problems of the heart. But assuming Grover had some basis for doing so, I ask, "Why did he do that?"

She grimaces. "I love him, Niran. I was living with him. Then when I went home to visit, Dad saw him and scared him off."

So much about that doesn't make sense. "Why didn't your dad like him?"

She gives a rise and fall of her shoulders as if she doesn't have a clue. But there's a slight guilt there.

"Come on, Cyn. You want my help? Well, that comes at a price. Your honesty. I want the truth. I can call Mom tomorrow—"

"Alright, alright." Pleading eyes meet mine. "Hester's a good man. He just likes things done his way. I know I pushed him. I deserved the slap."

He fucking hit her? I get to my feet fast, wobbling as I hit my false leg wrong and need a moment to get my balance. I might not have seen eye to eye with Grover in the past, but like him, this is something I won't stand for.

"He fuckin' what?" I growl.

"He didn't mean to hurt me." Unconsciously her fingers touch her eye which now that I look carefully, I can see is slightly swollen. Other things now come to my attention—the redness and the bruising that had been disguised by the darkness of her skin and which I'd put down to tiredness before. Before I can exclaim, she's speaking again. "Dad got some of his buddies to beat him up, and Hester told me we were over. I love him, Niran. Dad's got no right to interfere in my life."

Grover's got buddies capable of beating a man up? I'd never have expected that. But he does go up in my estimation for dealing with it in the same way I would.

"What fuckin' life?" I rasp. "A life where you're a punching bag? No man hits a woman, Cyn."

"I love him," she cries.

"Was that the first time he'd hit you?" I manage to get out.

Her shrug tells me everything.

I might not know Cyn, but I know she's worth more than a life with an abusive fuck. If Grover hadn't taken care of him, I'd have done it myself.

"You don't know Hester," she cries. "All my friends were jealous when he picked me. He's got money, drives a nice car. He apologises... *apologised,*" she stresses rapidly, correcting herself, making my jaw clench. "When he lost his temper, he bought me flowers and everything. He promised he'd never do it again, and I believe him. But Dad... Dad flipped when he saw what he'd done."

I don't blame him. I'm certain this wasn't the first time, but maybe the first where he'd left visible marks. I revise my view of my spoiled sister, and my brain makes some connections. She moved in with this man, probably the first proper relationship she's ever had, not surprising if Grover kept her on a tight rein. Probably an act of rebellion to move out, and she ended up with an abusive fuck just because he showed her some attention.

I also rapidly review my idea about keeping her away from the club. Maybe it's time she had an education on how real men treat their women, and that no fists are involved when it comes to true love.

I have to know. "Cyn, what did you do to upset him?" No reason would be good enough to justify this asshole's actions, but I'm interested in seeing what excuses she'll make.

She bites her lip, looks down at her hands, and then admits, "I'd arranged to go out with my friends. He objected to what I was wearing, and thought I was going out on the prowl, looking for someone to replace him."

She'd taken off her heavy coat as soon as we'd gotten into

the truck, and as her clothes were the last thing on my mind, it's only now I look at them, seeing she's dressed quite conservatively—smart pants, not jeans, and a blouse buttoned up. She looks more middle-aged than twenty.

"You lived with him?"

She nods. "Just for a few months. Dad didn't want me to move in with him, but I'm an adult now. Mom didn't mind, and she persuaded him."

She's over eighteen, but her naivety shows. She jumped at the first man to show her attention, left her family and jumped into his life. What the fuck was my mom thinking? All of a sudden, I want to give her back her youth which she seems desperate to leave behind.

Life is for living for oneself, not for family and definitely not for an abusive boyfriend.

"Cyn," I say gently, as I sit back down. "Mom doesn't know this, and it's up to you if you tell her. It's true I'm a mechanic, but I'm also a member of a motorcycle club. I live at the clubhouse." While I'd kept my life to myself, it's not something of which I'm ashamed. If Cyn can't keep secrets to herself, it's past time they came out.

"You're a biker?" Her eyes widen, then glance down to my prosthetic leg hidden under my jeans. "I didn't think you could ride a bike."

Shaking my head, I appraise her of the fact that I sure can.

"Are you a gang member?" Strangely my revelation has her animated. She's brightened and is leaning forward as if eager to hear more.

"We're a club, not a gang. In fact," I wipe my hand over my face, wondering whether my hastily decided course of action is indeed the right one, "I'd like you to meet the other club members. You want to come stay at the club for a while?"

"Niran!" For the first time tonight, a genuine smile lights her face. "You'd introduce me to your friends?" Coming over, she leans down and gives me an awkward hug, which I return after a moment. "I knew I was right to come see my big brother."

Hell, it might work for her, but now I've taken on responsibility for my young sister, I'm having doubts. Doing so is something I never expected and am far from certain that's what I want, especially with another woman occupying my mind.

Dom traits? That's what Kink thinks I have? Nah, he's wrong. I want to be there for Saffie, but I'd gladly walk away from my sister if I had the choice.

As Cyn goes to the bathroom and does whatever women do to get ready for the night, I lie back on my bed.

Why is it I think of Cyn as a burden? I never saw Saffie that way. From the moment I'd first seen her crying, all my instincts were to protect, help and do what I could to make her life better.

Cyn's my fucking sister, yet if she agreed to go back to Michigan tomorrow, I couldn't be happier.

One woman's compliant when I don't want her to be, the other anything but.

Fuck my life.

CHAPTER TWELVE

Niran

With Cyn seeming happy her immediate future is sorted, and me wondering how much I'll regret it later, we settle down for what remains of the night. Trying to keep my tossing and turning to a minimum so as not to disturb her, I can't switch my mind off.

Why did Cyn want to stay with an abusive partner? I really don't understand. Does she really think that's all she's worth, or as it was her first boyfriend, all she thought she could settle for? Is she misinterpreting his controlling nature for love? If so, she's sorely mistaken.

Was Saffie's missing baby daddy abusive? Was that why she'd run? While I try to concentrate on the woman I'm supposed to care for, I can't help but think about the woman I have no blood connection to. If that's Saffie's situation, she was wise to get herself free. That could be why she's in such a shit apartment. Cyn, though, she wants to go back to the fucker. How the hell do I deal with that?

I've met abusive assholes before, and never had time for them. I'd met some of their wives and had wondered why the fuck they stayed with them. I'm hopeful when Cyn sees examples of Lost, Dart and Grumbler with their wives that she'll come around to the view that men can be protective and loving without taking over their women's lives. Even Tits, Cindy and Pearl have more of an idea of their self-worth, and wouldn't stay if the brothers were violent toward them. As for Eva, I wouldn't want to be the man who tried anything with her. With her medical knowledge, I think she could be quite inventive.

Yes, hopefully taking Cyn to the clubhouse will be an education.

I wish I could have persuaded Saffie to come there.

I must doze a little, as my thoughts become merged, and I find myself thinking of the discussion I'd had with Kink. Had Cyn had a satisfying relationship? Not that I, as a brother wanted to know, but maybe it was so good it compensated for his other failings?

My thoughts start to jumble, wondering where control begins and ends. Kink restricts his dominance to the bedroom; Hester used his to take over Cyn's life. There must be a middle ground. *Was Saffie hit, just like her?* My fists itch to punch something— Saffie's ex first, followed quickly after by Hester.

My final thought before I give in to sleep is that I should keep Kink and Cyn far apart. If she's, in his terms, submissive, and I think that she is, she'll scream to the Dominant in him. Or, conversely, he might be able to give me insight into what makes her tick.

Waking from dreams, or nightmares to be exact, where my naked sister is crawling around the club, I first rouse myself and then her.

What I should have been thinking about is how exactly to introduce her to the club, and what I'm going to say when my mom gets wind of what I do and where I really work, all while I can't stop wishing it were Saffie I was bringing to the club.

Seeing Cyn's dropped back asleep despite my shake to her shoulder, I take my phone and quietly make my way outside. Once there, I breathe in the fresh air, then place my call.

"You got Lost."

As always, I bite back my desire to respond by asking for directions, knowing it would go down like a ton of lead. "Prez. I gotta problem. Need to ask the club for help."

"Speak to me, Brother. This about the woman who kicked you out?"

I take another lungful of air. Shit has gotten around fast. Not that I expected Token to keep his mouth shut, he lives on information and likes to share—with brothers, of course, no one else. "Not her, no. Prez, I know I don't talk much about my family, but one of my sisters turned up. She's left home and needs a temporary place to stay."

"She okay?"

I sigh. "Long and short is, she was made to leave an abusive ex. I think my folks took the right path, but she's still cut up about it."

"He still breathing?" Lost growls.

"Unfortunately, as far as I know, yeah. It's got her all twisted up. She's only twenty, Lost."

"Still a kid," he observes. After a moment, he adds, "Why you, Niran? You close?"

"About as far from it as half-siblings can get. I know it's an ask, Prez. I don't really know her, but if I turn her loose, I don't know where she'll end up. She seems pretty adamant she's not going home."

"She's family, Brother. She's welcome to bunk down with us for a spell. We've got plenty of room. Doubt we'll even notice she's here."

Grateful as I am, he deserves a warning. "I can't vouch for her, Prez."

"Kid like that? Can't see she'll cause trouble for us." He chuckles softly. "For you, perhaps."

"Thanks, Prez," I respond drily, then end the call.

A peek back inside shows me Cyn's not stirred. Stepping away once again, I place another call.

"Mom, it's Niran. Cyn's here. I got her." I'd messaged last night, but a verbal confirmation always helps.

"Oh, thank the Lord. Is she okay?"

"Yeah. She's sleeping right now. One question, Mom. This Hester, he get sorted out?"

There's a pause, then, "She told you? And yeah, Grover got some of his ex-Army pals to have a chat." I'm sure I hear disapproval in her voice, but then Mom was never into violence.

"Is he going to be a problem?"

"You mean, will he take it out on her?" After I respond with a nod that she can't see, and an audible yes to back it up, she continues, "Not according to Grover, no."

"What do you think?"

"On my part, I liked him, Niran. I didn't expect him to do that. I do wonder if it's all been blown out of proportion."

Well, she's no damn help. "Mom, I'm asking if he's likely to come after her. I want to be prepared. Or if she comes back, will he be waiting for her?"

Again she replies, "Not according to Grover."

I'm not so sure. Abusers are often bullies who don't like their marks to get away. One thing's for certain, when she does go back to Michigan, I'll be going along with her, and having a few words with Hester myself. Knowing my brothers, I wouldn't be surprised if one or more of them wanted to tag along. Maybe even finish the job Grover's buddies had started.

After waking Cyn and stopping off to get us both some breakfast, I make my way to the compound. Casting a sideways glance at the woman beside me, I notice she's acting like a kid, bouncing on the seat in excitement. Not for the first time, I wonder what type of life she had before she made a disastrous start on her own. Loving, no doubt, but from my memory of Grover, probably restrictive, making her easy pickings for a guy like Hester.

"What was it like at home?" I ask, as we pull up at a red light.

She looks at me quickly, her browed furrowed. "Okay, I guess."

"Your dad let you have boyfriends?" I hazard a guess he did not, and that Hester was the first man she'd met.

She snorts. "I'm his precious daughter, what do you think?" Her mouth forms a pout. "Claud and Caro were given more freedom than I." I grin. Our parents insisted on calling all their kids by their full names. Cyn's obviously used to shortening them. My smile fades as I realise I barely know the seventeen-year-old Claudia, or Caroline, at just fifteen. My dad had been traditional, wanting me to have a name reflecting my heritage, which I've worn proudly. Grover, though, had wanted his all-American kids to fit in.

"Why were you treated differently?" I wonder aloud.

"Because I'm 'difficult.'" She snorts as she puts the word in air quotes, while I wonder if our parents know better than I, and what I might have gotten myself into.

"Like how?" The light changes to green, and I pull forward.

A shrug, then, "Claud's got a car, mine was taken away."

"Why?" I prompt when she offers no explanation.

Another rise and fall of her shoulders. "I stayed out beyond my curfew more than once."

Yeah, that's something Grover wouldn't have appreciated. I remember that myself. Being in by ten pm had been restrictive to me as a teen. I have some sympathy for her.

"How did you meet Hester?"

She huffs in air, puffs out her cheeks, then explains, "I joined a gym. I was going for dance lessons, but Dad thought I wanted to get fit. He encouraged it."

"How many classes did you actually attend?" I indicate left, then make the turn.

"Loads of them."

But my sideways glance catches her wide grin. "And they were?"

"Weightlifting." She snorts again. "And some MMA."

"Watching Hester," I surmise, not needing the dip and raise of her chin to confirm it.

"Dad used to drop me at the gym, and Hester and I would take off for a few hours. We fell in love, he asked me to move in, end of story."

End of story? Seems like she's left out one hell of a lot, including the reception she'd gotten from our mom and her dad. "And Mom and Grover just accepted that?"

"I was nineteen, Niran," she states, as though there's nothing more to add. "And Mom approved of him. I mean really approved. She was on my side against Dad."

Really? Their relationship must have changed over the years. I park that to ponder on later. "How long were you together?"

She stares at her fingers, wiggling one after the other as though adding them up. "Ten months?" Why she poses it as a question, I can't fathom. It's she who's got the information, not me. She then adds to qualify, "We were living together for eight weeks."

It can't hurt to casually drop my next question in. "How often did he raise his hand to you?"

Yup. I've caught her off guard. "Not often. Only when I deserved it. And it was mostly a smack, barely anything."

My jaw clenches, and I ask through gritted teeth, "What the fuck did you do to deserve it?"

She shifts in her seat, her body as uncomfortable as it seems she is with the explanation, as if she's given it before and knows what my reaction will be. "I've never been responsible for a house before, so I often did things wrong. Dinner was late or burned. I stayed out too long, shit like that."

"You did nothing fuckin' wrong, Cyn." But my words slide off like water from the back of the proverbial duck. I think for a moment. "You see Mom and Dad often?"

"No," she states. "Dad made it clear he didn't like Hester, and Hester didn't like me going around their house without him."

So how did they... "How did they know that he'd hit you?"

The disused airfield where we have our compound starts to come into sight. I slow to make the final turn, catching sight of her biting her lip as I turn my head.

"I ran home to see them." She glances my way, a pleading in her eyes, begging me to understand.

Which I do, only too well. Hester's slaps had turned into more, and like a frightened animal, she'd run to the only sanctuary she'd had.

In a small voice she adds, "I made a mistake, I wanted to go back to him, but Dad wouldn't let me. Then, after Dad spoke to Hester, he ghosted me. I couldn't stay with them, so… I came to you."

Lucky me. And lucky that we've reached our destination and can end this awkward conversation. Cyn sits forward on her seat, bouncing in anticipation as I drive past a row of bikes and park the truck behind the clubhouse.

"Do those bikes belong to your friends? Will they take me riding? I can't wait to see inside, Ni. Is this really where you live?" She glances around again, then frowns. "It's not as I pictured it from watching *Sons of Anarchy*."

Oh shit. That's all I need, my sister thinking I'm living a life as portrayed in the television show. What the hell have I led her to expect? "My name's Niran," I tell her shortly, knowing her preference for shortening names. "And one word of warning, bikers don't take women on their bikes. Not unless they've become special to them. There are things you should know, Cyn. Never, ever touch a man's ride without permission, and don't touch his cut. That's the leather vest we all wear."

"You're not wearing one," she observes.

"That's because I'm driving a car. I'll put mine on when we get inside."

"Jeez, all these rules make you sound like Dad." She opens the car door without waiting, and throws one last parting comment inside, "I thought bikers lived free from all regulations."

"We live on respect," I tell her, warningly. Then I too get out and go around to her side. "And you'd do well to make that something you never forget."

What have I gotten myself into? I muse, as I lead her up to the front door, trying to work my sister out. In many ways she's naïve, though from what I'd heard, I thought she excelled at school. She obviously sucks at relationships and doesn't know what to expect. And now, she's my responsibility. I promised Prez. Fuck.

Hoping she doesn't like it here, and soon wants to go back, I open the clubhouse door and let her precede me inside.

"Well now, who have we got here?" Dart, our VP, is first to notice the newcomer. He looks from me to her, and frowns slightly.

Realising I should have expected them to make the mental leap which, up to now, hadn't occurred to me, I quickly correct his assumption this is Saffie, and far younger than I led them to believe, and get the introduction over fast. "Dart, meet Cyn, my little *sister.* Cyn, meet Dart. He's the VP."

Cyn's eyes widen as she takes in his serious face, his tattoos and his cut. She moves backward into me.

Dart's face, though, has relaxed. "Sister? Well, hell. Nice to meet you, Cyn. You come for a visit?"

"Just for a bit," I put in, before she gets any ideas about staying. "Needs a place to clear her head."

Dart smiles at her, but his eyebrows rise toward me. Yeah, I've not spoken much about my family, but now's not the time to let him know he's no more surprised than me that she's here.

"Sister?" Dusty appears as if by magic, his eyes assessing Cyn, and his lips curve in a wide, lascivious grin.

Glancing down, I see Cyn fluttering her eyelids. Unseen by her, I make a slashing motion across my neck, letting him know if he lays one finger on her, he'll be dead.

"Sister," he repeats, this time with a different emphasis. "Got it, Brother." Losing interest, he steps away.

Cyn pouts but shakes off her disappointment and looks around the room. "Who's that?" she asks in a too-loud whisper.

Both Dart and I glance to where she's looking, and Dart grins, then beckons. As Alex comes over, he introduces her. "This is Alex, my wife. Alex, meet Cyn, Niran's sister."

"Hey, Cyn. You visiting?"

I notice Cyn's looking between her and Dart, her eyes flaring with interest.

"Staying for a little while," I explain, answering on her behalf, then take my opportunity. "You know if there's a room I can put her in? I didn't get much notice."

Alex isn't at all fazed. "Sure. You want me to get her settled in?"

I breathe out a sigh of relief. "That would be great, if you don't mind."

When I check, Cyn seems happy enough to go with her and walks off in her wake.

As Dart turns to me, I pre-empt him. "I barely know her, Dart. She's had a bust-up with her parents and for some fuckin' reason ran to me. The bust-up was that they didn't want her to go back to an abusive motherfucker."

"What the fuck?" He turns to look in the direction she's gone. "Perhaps Alex can tell her a thing or two about that."

What he's alluding to happened shortly before I joined the club, but I know the story. Alex's abusive ex had tried to kill her. In the end, it had been he who'd been taken out by an impressive shot from Pennywise, our resident sniper.

"Couldn't hurt her speaking to Cyn." I think it would do her some good, to understand once that behaviour starts, it's only going to get worse.

"You don't want her here," Dart observes sagely.

"I just don't know what to do with her." I shrug. "She's all but a stranger." And, unfortunately, not the stranger I'd prefer to have here in my domain. "I honestly don't know what to do with her, Dart. I've got to work, and I can't just leave her hanging around here." Who knows what fucking mischief she'd get into, or how many people she might upset?

"Hey, Salem?" Dart calls out to the man just entering, then when he approaches, asks, "You still thinking about hiring a receptionist?"

Salem seems taken aback and takes a moment to get his thoughts on Dart's track. "I thought we'd dismissed it? Sure, it would be good, but one of the prospects can handle it, maybe the new one, Kid? The custom build place is on the compound, and I don't want a civilian with open access to it."

Dart grins widely. "Niran's sister's going to be staying a while at the club. If all it involves is answering phones and shit, why not give her a try?" As I stand open mouthed, he adds to me, "Gives her something to do so you don't need to be here to entertain her."

Well fuck. I grin at him. "Sounds fuckin' good, Brother. She'd get bored as hell sitting around here doing nothing."

"Suits me," Salem agrees.

And while Cyn might object to doing a good day's work, Salem won't let her get away with shit. As enforcer, he'll lay down those rules she's not keen on. Might be a sure-fire way to get her heading back out.

"Niran?" I swing round, and my heart rate speeds up.

"Toke, you got something for me?"

"Not that you'll like," he warns. "Did a search on Saffie Jones. Her background is solid and uninteresting. Parents dead, clean record. Got her GED but didn't go to college. Has worked several low-skilled jobs and moved to San Diego from Los Angeles a few months back. Never been married and no associations with any MCs that I could find. No reports about abuse or any attack made to the police. In summary, I found zilch."

I tap my fingers against my chin. Of course, being scared of bikers and MCs could mean she was raped by a man wearing a cut. Devastating enough, but I'd suspected with her severe reaction she'd had it would go deeper. She was downright terrified to find out what I was. I can think of nothing else to explain it.

What is it, Saffie? What am I missing? Why did you suddenly become so scared of me?

That Token has found no police reports means shit. If she'd been raped, she might not have reported it. She could have been embarrassed or didn't want to make a victim of herself, especially if the rapist was backed up by his club. She'd been spooked enough to move to a different city.

"You're staying away from her, yes?" Token asks, looking concerned. "Just because I found nothing, doesn't mean there's not something there. If she's spooked about clubs, she could bring trouble down on us."

Of course I've thought about going back to see her, but what right have I got? I'm not her man. "Don't see what choice I've got. I don't want to distress her further. She's got my number if she comes around."

"From her extreme reaction, I think that's right, Brother." Token slaps me on the back, and then starts to walk off.

"Toke?" When he turns around, I ask. "Keep an eye on the

hospital appointments for me. Let me know if she books herself in for an operation."

He gives me a thumbs up and walks off.

That's as much as I can do for now. Standing, I brush my hands over my head, thinking about the results of Token's research. Saffie seems to have an unremarkable past, nothing out of the ordinary. So why is my gut telling me that Token's not dug deep enough?

"Why not?" comes a shrill shout, breaking into my thoughts. "You're younger than me."

I swing around, hearing Cyn's voice, seeing her at the bar confronting Kid, who for once is on this side and not serving.

"What's going on?" I snap, stepping up.

"He's drinking," she glares at Kid, "and he," she turns that death stare on Connor, "won't serve me."

"Kid's twenty-two," I explain, sending a look of apology toward the prospect. "You're only twenty and too young to drink."

"In an MC?" she asks, incredulously.

She's right, here in our home, we couldn't give a shit about citizen rules, but a drunk Cyn is something I don't have a yearning to see.

"In an MC," I confirm, my eyes conveying my message to Connor. "Make sure everyone knows it."

"Sure." Connor grins and mock-salutes.

"Huh!" Cyn states angrily. "I should have stayed home."

"You can fly out tomorrow if you want." *Please say yes. I've too much on my plate.* There's another woman I'd prefer to worry about.

For an answer, she pouts, then seeing I'm not going to be moved, flicks her hair over her shoulder, looks around, and goes to watch Pennywise and Salem playing pool. I don't fail to notice the exaggerated swing of her hips as she crosses the room.

Give me strength.

The next couple of days I give her time to settle in, two days in which I start to learn about my sister. She's overly confident, talks to anyone, and is so oblivious to nuances going on around her, I reckon I'd have to remind her to look both ways before crossing a street.

She seems thrilled to be living with an MC, something that apparently she'll get street cred for. Too happy, it seems to me, as if she's been dropped into a fantasy.

She's airheaded and tends to think only of herself. Too often, I'm following her and apologising when she asks pointedly about the meaning of road names, if she can see brothers' weapons—yeah, double entendre intended—and begs for rides on the back of their bikes.

Alex, luckily, she seems to respect, as well as Patsy and Mary, being polite and minding her language. The club girls? Well, she seems to side with them. I grow worried she'd like to become one of their number.

When I'd seen Cindy, Tits and Pearl gathered in a group around her, I'd rushed up, but stopped dead and hid my grin when I heard them handing her ass to her, metaphorically, of course. Seems like she was looking for sympathy at having had her boyfriend chased away and was told in no uncertain terms not one of them would have put up with abuse. I'd backed off, thinking there was something she could learn from them, as long as she didn't emulate their style of clothes or express a yearning to join their ranks.

To top all joy of joys, she takes to being a receptionist like a fucking duck to water. It's all because of the *hot* bikers, she informs me.

After that particular conversation, I'd approached Salem, and stated in a hiss, "I thought you were going to make her life hell."

He chuckles and shrugs. "What can I say? She's actually good on the phone. Customers seem to like her."

"Only because she's an outright flirt," I retort. "Can't you stick her with boring paperwork?"

He slaps my back. "Tried that, Brother. Actually, she's got a good head on her shoulders. She's been ordering parts and keeping records in order. Came up with a new filing system to boot."

She's never going to fucking leave at this rate.

If I were a man who liked to get my dick wet on the regular, I'd be severely compromised by her presence, as every evening she monopolises my time when the others have gotten fed up with her, wanting me to play pool or stand at the games machine while she plies it with tokens.

Wishing I was elsewhere, I try to enjoy getting to know my little sister, but it's hard. The schools she went to aren't the same as those I remember, and her friends aren't mine. Having money courtesy of Grover, she'd grown up in a different lifestyle. While at her age I was in the hell of the sand pit facing enemy gunfire, she was choosing which series to binge next on Netflix.

Truth is, we share nothing in common except for a mother. My main issue is that she's already showing signs of getting too comfortable here.

I don't mind my style being cramped for a while, but long-term? Hell no. My life is more than being a big brother.

Though Cyn occupies far too much of my time, my thoughts keep returning to Saffie, wondering how she is and what she's doing, and whether she's come to a decision. I hate thinking about her in that apartment block, even if she didn't have the problems she has.

She doesn't call, and as the days pass, I realise it's been longer since she chased me away than the time I'd actually spent with her.

When it's been a week, I tell myself to stop thinking about her. All I'm doing is driving myself crazy. When I weaken and want to say to hell with it, and go visit, all I have to do is remember her sheer terror when she found out I belonged to a club.

I've gone from friend to someone who scares her. It should be no surprise she doesn't make contact.

The ball is in her court and there's no sense me trying to retrieve it. She knows how to get in touch.

I'll just have to deal with the fact that me being a biker is too big an obstacle for her to get over.

CHAPTER THIRTEEN

Niran

"You persuaded her then?" Pennywise yells out.

Shaking my head despairingly, I walk toward the group of my brothers waiting by their bikes. "Eventually. With Alex's help."

For the past week, Cyn's taken more of my time than I'd expected, playing the little sister card far too often for my liking.

She doesn't need me as much as she thinks. She's fine to be left alone in the clubhouse. The old ladies are happy to take her under their wings, and even the club girls make time for her though the jury's still out on what I think about that. My brothers treat her with the respect she deserves, sometimes taking the time to entertain her so I can have a moment to myself. I mean, a man's got to take a piss sometimes. But even then, she seeks my attention.

"Niran, did you see that shot?"

"Niran, come look, see what I've done."

"Niran, what card would you play?"

She's no closer to leaving than she was a week back, and not having expected her to make an appearance in my life, I'm starting to feel suffocated.

It's got to the extent my brothers are feeling sorry for me. Last night, Salem suggested we head out and see where the road takes us as we had a week or so back—just us boys and our bikes out on the road for a while. The problem being Cyn expected to come with us.

It had been when I told her she couldn't I'd gotten an inkling of what my mom had meant when she'd described her as 'difficult', and that word was an understatement. Gone was the simpering girl idolising her big brother when she'd thrown a tantrum, including tears and much stomping of feet, and then pulling out the *nobody loves me* card.

I'd tried to reason with her, in the end resorting to pointing out in no uncertain terms, what I'd tried to tell her more gently before—I never wanted a woman on the back of my motorcycle and sister or not she wasn't going. Adding that, fuck it, while I was her brother, I needed some time to myself.

It wasn't my argument that ended her tirade, it was when Alex had suggested they have a girls' outing and that she'd take her shopping and to get manicures or some shit. I'll be owing Dart my marker for that.

Alex's suggestion had Cyn preening as if she'd gotten one over on me. She hadn't, of course, she'd simply made me resolve to call Mom again and see how quickly we could persuade her to go home.

It's not that I never want to be a family man, I just want one of my own making. Is it wrong to say that Cyn might carry fifty percent of the same blood, but the jury's still out on whether I like her, let alone feel any type of sibling love? She's hard work, and definitely an acquired flavour.

Instead of taking my mind off Saffie, Cyn makes me think of her more. Before she'd known I was a biker, Saffie had accepted my help, albeit reluctantly, as if the world owed her no favours. Her, I want to support and help. Cyn who demands it as a due, I do not.

The day is sunny and warm with a gentle breeze blowing. I shake my head again, clearing my head. I'm determined for the next few hours to think of nothing but the pavement beneath my wheels and the wind in my hair, where the only decision I have to make is whether to change gears up or down.

It works to some extent. The day stays fine, the company's good, and the food when we stop off may not be the most satisfying, but critiquing it occupies our minds, as does the overt advances of one of the waitstaff who simpers and seems overly entranced with our quintet of bikers.

"She's looking at you." Salem nudges Pennywise. "Reckon you've got a chance to tap that."

"Nah, it's you," Pennywise informs Dusty. "If you want to take her up on it, we'll wait." He pauses, winks, then adds, "We've got time. I mean, what's your average? A couple of minutes tops? Oomph!"

The last is in response to Dusty's sharp jab to his ribs.

"You're wrong," Snips informs us, gumming the soft pasta he'd ordered. "Clear as fuck it's me she wants."

"Keep on dreaming," Salem retorts.

"Maybe it's Black meat she's after?" Dusty suggests with a grin in my direction.

I know it's cruel, but I can't stop myself pointing out, "It would help us work out who if both her eyes looked in the same direction."

Pennywise collapses over the table, dropping his head into his hand. His shoulders are shaking.

What? I just voiced what everyone else must have thought.

When she comes back to suggest she's due a break about the time we'd be finished with our meals, we're still no nearer to discerning exactly who she wants, or maybe it's us all?

She can count me out. A quick fuck in a roadside stop is certainly not something I have on my bucket list.

When she leaves again, I point my fork at the blond biker

seated opposite. "You should take one for the team. We might have to wait the two minutes but at least it won't keep us off the road for too long."

Dusty, quick as a flash, retorts, "See, now you're just projecting your problems onto me, Niran. A real man takes longer than that."

Yeah, I probably walked straight into that. I shrug.

"No fuckin' work ethic." Salem gets in on the act. "If you do a job, you should do it properly."

I can't let them have it all their own way. "Yeah, but if you have a Black dick, the bitches can't take it for long."

Now it's Salem who snorts so loud, his exhaled air pushes food off his fork.

"Oh fuck, she's coming back," Pennywise hisses.

"So, boys, what can I do for you?"

"The check, please, ma'am," Snips requests with a wide grin that shows all his missing teeth. "Then I'll meet you outside if you like." He waggles his tongue in emphasis.

Her eyes widen and she runs off like a scalded cat.

Having paid the waitress who refused to meet any of our eyes, we exit the restaurant laughing and with arms slapping each other's backs.

I return to the clubhouse renewed and refreshed, pleased to find Cyn smiling. When she drags me up to her room to show me the clothes she'd bought, my only concern is how she could afford them.

Her answer comes fast. "I've still got some money left from my college fund. And Dad gives me an allowance on top."

Of course he does. I had to make my own way, but then I wasn't of *his* blood, just a kid he had to adopt. Believing I'm a better man for it, I admire them, glad to see Alex has contained her excessive tendencies, and that she hadn't gone shopping with the club girls. Her clothes, unlike those she arrived in, are fashionable and well suited to her age without being overly revealing. Not that I subscribe to the notion that women are responsible for encouraging the excesses of men, women should be able to wear whatever they want without having to face repercussions. But I do firmly believe there are some parts of the human body that should be reserved for the eyes of a partner, and not anyone else.

Her good mood continues through dinner and into the evening, leaving me in one too. I'm enjoying a drink and a chat with Scribe, relishing for once not having an eavesdropper sitting beside me, until suddenly I spin around to find the reason for the burst of childish giggles which reaches my ears.

Fuck my life.

Cyn's with the club girls, cavorting on the pole. When they see I notice, my brothers quickly avert their eyes.

"Cyn! Get down here, now!" I roar, noticing, like the whores, she's stripped down to her bra and panties. *Girl's got no fucking sense.* While I trust my brothers to look but not touch, more than one I notice is adjusting themselves.

I make my way across, only to be told, "I'm having fun."

"Put your fuckin' clothes on," I snarl, trying to shield her body. Her bra's so sheer I get a glimpse of nipples before I avert my eyes.

She comes off the stage, approaching me with her middle finger pointed my way and stabs it into my chest. "You sound like Dad."

That's one insult too many. Taking her elbow, and with the other hand catching the clothes Kink has retrieved and thrown at me, I lead her away, taking her to the far corner of the room where we can speak undisturbed. When I let her go, she rubs her arm ruefully. I roll my eyes. My grip was firm, but it wouldn't have hurt. Thrusting her clothes into her hands, I wait with arms folded while she puts them on.

"Cyn," I start, choosing my words carefully. "Have some

fuckin' self-respect. You've got every man here eye-fucking you. Is that what you want?"

"I was having fun," she repeats, sticking out her lower lip. "I was doing it for me, not them. And they…" she jerks her head to where Cindy, Pearl and Tits are standing, staring across the room, looking slightly anxious as if I'll berate them next. I won't. They might have encouraged her to dance, but I doubt they'd have been behind her stripping.

"Cyn, it's not the cavorting around the pole I object to, it's the time and the place. Alex will gladly give you lessons if you ask." *During the day, when Dart's chased everyone else away.* "You know why Cindy, Tits and Pearl dance on the pole?"

"Well, duh. It's exercise. They enjoy it."

Is she that naïve?

"Cyn, they're not dancing for themselves. It's for the benefit of the men. Men who get off watching, or, who use it to choose who to go with that night. You get my meaning?"

"I wasn't doing it for that!"

"I know you weren't." Or I fucking hope I do. Nothing would surprise me. But while I might not trust her, I trust my brothers. "But that's the effect you were having. As for stripping off—"

"Cindy's not even wearing a bra. At least I kept mine on."

Thank fuck for small mercies is all I can think. "Cyn, your behaviour reflects on me. Believe me when I say it was wrong. Dance during the day when no one's around, but for heaven's sake, not in the evenings."

"Your brothers weren't complaining."

The stubborn twist of her mouth gets to me. "Is that what you want, Cyn? For men to see you as nothing more than a body?"

Her shrug reminds me this was the girl who professes to still love the only man who ever looked twice at her, despite him being abusive. Could she be so desperate for attention that she'll take it in any way she can get it? *Difficult*, Mom had warned me. I'd just had no idea how true that was.

If she needs help, I'm not qualified to give it.

Fuck me. I don't deserve this. I might be worried about Saffie, but that's my choice. Cyn, well, I know just as little about what makes her tick, and what I'm learning, I don't find attractive.

Tempering my voice, I ask, "You had any thoughts about going home?" It seems the best solution all around.

Her eyes widen. "I want to stay here."

I sigh. "This is only temporary, remember?"

She looks disconcerted, and then a sly smile comes over her face. "Salem says I'm indispensable. He won't want me to leave."

Damn the man. What initially seemed like a good idea is coming back to bite me in the ass. For a moment, I don't have a response.

"There are conditions to you staying, Cyn. The first is that you don't embarrass me. Something like this happens again, I'll be buying you a one-way ticket to Michigan."

She opens her mouth and wisely closes it, then gives an exaggerated sigh as she senses I'm in no mood to hear the retort she wishes to utter. "I'm going to bed." Without saying anything more, she gets up and leaves.

My eyes watch her until she disappears up the stairs.

"That your sister?" A woman comes over and sits herself in Cyn's vacated chair. She jerks her head back toward the pole. "She's got some good moves." Winking, she adds, "It must run in the family."

"Susie," I growl in warning.

Ignoring me, she continues, "You look like you could do with some stress relief. Why don't you and I hit the sheets?"

I'm in no mood to be diplomatic. All the good vibes I brought back from the ride out earlier today have disappeared.

Leaning forward, I make myself clear. "Once was a fuckin' mistake, Susie. Been there, done that, not going there again. You feel me?"

"No need to be like that, Niran." She pouts, and fuck me, she inches herself forward so our heads are all but touching. "You sure you want to rob me of that big Black dick of yours?"

"Fuckin' certain."

Seeing there'll be no reasoning with her, I get to my feet and stomp across the clubroom, heading toward the stairs. I could have done with another drink, but my mood has soured, and I want to be alone and away from the company of fucking women.

Closing my bedroom door, I stand with my back against it. Perhaps it's for the best Saffie doesn't want to see me. I've too much going on. Susie, for starters, who seems to think her vagina has some hold over me, and Cyn, who's becoming a pain in my ass. Why did my sister have to come find me? It's not like we've ever been close. If she wasn't related, I wouldn't even like her. Similar to Susie, she's the kind of woman who turns me right off.

Cyn's a complication and a responsibility I never asked for. Problem is, Mom doesn't seem to want her back either. The whole thing's a mess.

A mess I'd have been wrong to bring Saffie into.

If she saw me treating Susie as badly as I had, but little more than she deserved, I reckon I'd become the epitome of a biker in her head.

I know, though, by now, Susie's probably already warming someone else's bed.

Morning arrives and I'm still in a foul mood. Cyn wouldn't speak to me at breakfast which should have been a pleasurable result but being made out to be the one who'd done wrong doesn't settle with me. Hell, maybe I'm not good brother material, but I didn't ask for this role. All I'm asking for is a little respect. Not for me, but for Cyn to have some for herself. Otherwise, she'll continue to make the same mistakes over and over, and probably replace Hester with a man of the same ilk.

Another day has passed and Saffie still hasn't reached out to me. Not that I expect her to, but today that seems harder to accept. Instead of absence making her fade from my mind, it gets worse by the day. How is she, and has she come to a decision? If so, which way has she decided to go? *Is she still safe in that apartment of hers?* Damn, I wish I were able to be there to protect her. Anything could have happened, and I'd never know about it.

She's just a friend. Yeah, but that doesn't stop me from worrying.

Having dealt with Susie and Cyn the previous night, and being unable to turn my thoughts from Saffie, I'm in a foul mood this morning. I snap at Ross when his only crime was to ask to borrow a wrench, and damn near take Gibbs' head off when he gets too close and jostles me. Snips nearly gets my fist in his throat when he makes a joke about Black dicks.

"Niran!" Grumbler's voice is sharp. "A word?"

Tossing down the tools I was using, I follow him into the office.

"This can't go on," he states. "You're upsetting everybody. Fuck, Brother. I know this woman's got your head in a spin, but you've got to forget her. She's fuckin' terrified of bikers, and unless you want to turn in your patch, you haven't got a chance with her."

I know that. If it weren't for that strength of feeling, I'd have confronted her again, but leaving the club is something I can't countenance. "It's not just her, Grumbler. It's fuckin' Cyn as well, and Susie doesn't fuckin' help."

He grins. "Yeah, I heard your sister put on quite a show last night."

Sighing, I rub my nose. "I don't know what to do with her."

"Send her home?"

"I would, but it's the last thing she wants. And her parents seem to think they're well rid of her." I hold out both hands as if asking, *what can I do?*

"She reminds me of Alicia when I first met her." Grumbler refers to his eighteen-year-old stepdaughter. "At war with the world."

"At war with authority," I correct. "I'm not sure what's the best way to be done with her. At least Alicia has some darn self-respect."

As if realising there's no advice he can give, Grumbler reverts to the first topic again. "Mary and I were wondering if she decided to keep the baby." He says it conversationally, as if it's of little consequence. He can't know how much my ignorance on the subject is eating me up.

I realise I've never asked his opinion before. "What would you do? If that happened to you and Mary?"

Grumbler winces. "Don't be putting the hex on us, Brother," he rasps back. "We're too well aware of the problems in pregnancy. But yeah, we've spoken about it. Neither Mary nor I could see the point in continuing if there was to be no hope at the end."

"Really?"

He shrugs. "Why prolong the agony for the baby or mom? Some things can't be saved. Don't mistake me, hell, it would break us to make that decision, but when all hope is gone, what's left?"

His view coincides with mine. I wonder if Saffie's come around to thinking the same way. Of course, at first, she'd hope the doctors were wrong, but the prognosis can't be denied—a baby so badly formed as hers has no chance at life. It's heartwrenchingly sad, but that's the way of it.

"Anyway," Grumbler continues, "it's a decision only the parents, or in this case, the mom, can make. It's she who's going to have to live with the choice. Mary's worried about Saffie. Whatever she decides, she'll need support."

I'd give anything to be able to give it. "She wants nothing to do with us, Grumbler. That day Mary and I went around, she was this close," I put my finger and thumb so there's barely a gap between them, "to calling the cops. Black man unwanted in a White woman's apartment, what d'you think they're going to make of that?"

He presses his lips together, before offering, "Shoot first?"

"Happens far too fuckin' often, Brother."

His face falls with sympathy. "Then you'll have to move on. Look, I understand how this is fuckin' with your head, but you can't take it out on the civilians."

He's right. "I'll apologise to Ross and Gibbs." Snips though, he can go hang. He knew what he was doing.

"They don't want your fuckin' apology. They want you to get your head back in the game. Just like I do."

Raising my chin, I exit the office, determined to pull myself together, while wondering how long it will be before I'm smiling again. I'm plagued by two women with two different problems. One won't admit she needs my support, the other demands only what I can offer unwillingly. Three, if you count Susie who only wants me for my damn cock.

I do make an effort. By the time lunchtime comes around, the atmosphere which could have earlier been cut with a knife has lightened. I even attempt a laugh at one of Snips' lame jokes, which, of course, encourages him to embark on another.

Before he can reach the punchline, my phone rings, and I step aside to take it.

CHAPTER FOURTEEN

Saffie

After the door closed behind Niran and Mary I collapsed down on the couch, giving in to the wave of dizziness that I'd only just managed to keep at bay until they'd gone. My body was violently shaking, and there was a rushing sound in my ears which almost blocked out the sounds from the overloud television next door. My vision was blurry and my stomach roiled. For a moment I thought the nausea would overtake me, but gradually the impulse to throw up began to recede.

I felt drained, completely exhausted, as though all fight in me had gone. Nervously I raised my eyes to the closed door knowing if they came back again, I'd be in no state to take anyone on, even to mentally challenge them.

But I'd done it. I got them to leave.

It had been easier than I'd expected. My threat to call the cops had been the only thing I could think of, and it had worked with the results that I wanted. I wondered whether Niran's got something to hide, and whether he's a wanted man. *Of course he is. He's a biker.* A member of the criminal underworld I knew only too well.

Just when I started to think I'd got my body under control, the shakes started again. *Bikers know bikers.* They have meets, mingle and mix. They run drug and weapon lines together, and as for women, well, I knew Duke used an underground railroad. It was not too much of a stretch to think Niran's club could be involved.

But Niran had known where I was for a couple of weeks now. If he'd let Duke know, why hadn't he come to collect his property? I would have expected him to come immediately. But then, I'd been gone for so long, perhaps a few days more was neither here nor there. Maybe if he was hatching business deals with his prez, at that moment, I took low priority. Nevertheless, I was certain there'd shortly be a knock on the door. The question was, how much time did I have?

Knock on the door? I scoffed at myself. Duke would just bust it down, and in this apartment block, the likelihood is no one would even notice.

My panic attack returned at full blast as images in my brain turned imagination into fact. This time I did vomit, only making it to the bathroom just in time. I was trembling so much I could barely splash water on my face, and sank to the floor, with my head in my hands, almost deafened by the thumping of blood rushing through my veins.

A body was not built to have so much adrenalin rush through it. Even after my breathing returned to something approaching normal, it was as though I was working through fog that filled my head. I worried about the effect on my baby. All this stress couldn't be good.

Half of me thought I should pack as much as I could carry, pick up my keys and just leave. Then the sense of urgency started my heart racing again, and I ended up doing nothing at all. I felt like a guillotine victim, just waiting for the blade to drop. I was damned one way or another. If I ran, the problem of what to do about my baby stayed with me. What's a pregnant woman to do while on the run without a place to stay or much money? If I left, I risked Duke catching up with me. If I stayed, he'd find me in any event. It would just speed up the inevitable.

As night approached, the darkness which hides monsters descended and my thoughts grew worse. Like a wave crashing into the shore, my predicament had hit me once more. I might be pregnant, but my baby probably won't be born, or at least alive. No blow from Duke could have hurt me more, no insult hurled, no abuse.

Nothing else mattered. Not my own safety, not Duke, I realised as I collapsed on my bed, in my head hearing once again the fateful words the doctor had delivered as if she were here in the room.

With Niran here, his presence had kept me grounded. My problem was still there, of course, but somehow, he'd prevented me totally losing it. Now on my own, the pressure becomes too intense.

It couldn't be true. The doctors must have made a mistake. But why would they have told me otherwise? Why talk to me with such sadness in their eyes if it was a lie?

Why the hell am I worried about Duke? Let him come to me. I deserve worse.

For that night and the next morning, I didn't move, didn't eat, didn't get showered or put on fresh clothes, wavering between imagining things could be different, and crying out in utter distress knowing they wouldn't change. My thoughts kept coming back to the fact that in another life, in another world where I could have looked after my baby better, maybe he'd have had a chance at a normal life.

Uncaring of myself, I waited for that knock on the door. What have I got to live for? What punishment could be bad enough for a mother who'd failed to care for their child?

If not Duke, I was expecting Niran or Mary to knock at the

door, coming to entice me once again to their lair. *Nothing good would come of being associated with bikers.*

Waiting in limbo, lost in my devastation, I neglect to go to work. But by design or by accident, there Niran had helped. My boss assumed I'd had a reoccurrence of what had ailed me before.

The second night, when Duke still hadn't appeared, my common sense began to vie with my distress as I began to wonder whether I might have read the situation wrong. Both my visitors had seemed concerned about my less-than-ideal living arrangements. They'd offered sanctuary, and once I'd refused, they hadn't come back. Maybe they had no connection to the man who haunts not just my nightmares, but every moment of my life. But Niran's a biker, and that can't be ignored.

I've got his number on my phone, but I don't call. I can't take the risk that he knows Duke, or of him. And being a biker, I'm pretty certain I know what he'd say if I admitted to being another's property. Hell, I'm still married to the man. Niran might think his obligations are to another man wearing a cut rather than a woman who means nothing to him.

Even if Niran's got nothing to do with Duke, the manner in which I sent him away was embarrassing. How could I see him again without offering an explanation? Especially one I'm not prepared to give. My past is something that happened to Sapphire Marshall, not to Saffie Jones.

As I don't call Niran, he doesn't contact me. Why should he? If he knows Duke, he has all he needs, if he doesn't, he's clearly washed his hands of me, and who would blame him?

Abandoned to my fate, I feel very alone. For some reason, although I've been that way for months, it hits harder now. More than anything, I want someone to tell me what to do, what action, or inaction to take. Is carrying this baby for a further three months a punishment I feel I deserve to inflict on myself?

That night I still can't sleep, can't eat. Semi-delirious, I dream of a future with a happy, healthy son, and then have waking nightmares about giving birth to my child who'd have only minutes, if that, to live.

The next days follow the same pattern. I ring work, telling them I've got a serious virus, and begging for a few days off. My boss's best wishes and instructions to look after myself don't help one iota. I'm not too concerned about losing my job, in the scheme of things it would be the least of my worries, but I doubt there's too much risk of that. I don't qualify for sick leave and otherwise fully staffed, she can afford to be magnanimous.

I'm left with far too much time on my hands. Time in which to think.

Do babies feel pain in the womb? Some people say yes, some no. *What if he does and he's suffering now? Would it be fair to allow him to suffer for three more months, and all for nothing? What if for now he can't feel anything, but birthing him would cause immense suffering? Or would it have no effect on him at all?*

As for myself, I don't know what would be best for me. Ending my pregnancy now would allow me to start healing, if that's even possible, which I doubt. But if I continue, am I just delaying the inevitable? Simply putting off the pain for another day?

He's alive now, I can feel fluttering. Is he moving like a normal baby? *How would I know?* For him, continuing will only result in a death sentence. Am I selfish wanting to hold him in my arms if only for a minute?

I love him with every fibre of my being. I just don't know what to do for the best. If I continue this pregnancy, my thinking about what's in store for him will gradually drive me crazy. But if I end it, how will I cope?

Sometimes in the night when I fall into an exhausted sleep, I dream of a sweet little boy, his arms reaching out for me calling *Mommy, Mommy,* but in my dream he's drifting away. I run with my feet stuck in quicksand. I pull one foot free, only to have the other sink in deep. All the while he's getting further and further from me. I can't get to him, and I scream and jerk awake.

I can't go on like this, day after day, torturing myself, not knowing for certain whether I'm torturing him, the most important being in my life.

That final day, I wake shaking and crying in total anguish, knowing there's only one decision I can make. I can't take the risk my baby's already in pain, making him endure that for the next three months just to give me the chance of holding him. I can't think only of myself; I've got to let him go.

Before my resolution fades, I ring early, insisting on speaking to the doctor who'd given me the prognosis, and hear her assure me once again, *"No, Ms Jones. From the sonogram and the other tests we've done, there is no hope. A large part of his skull is missing. He won't survive."*

Not allowing myself second thoughts, I arrange the appointment.

The time between that phone call and leaving for the hospital passes with me in a kind of trance. I spend it talking to my baby, explaining how much I love him, how I'd have given him the best life I could. How sorry I am for whatever I did to lead us to this place, and that there'll always be a part of me that's died along with him. The truth is, without him, I don't know how I'll survive, nor whether I want to.

How I drive safely to the hospital I'll never know. But I do. I was given two options—a local or general anaesthetic. I took the latter, knowing I'd lose the last vestiges of my sanity were I to be awake.

Internally screaming *I can't do this,* I let them put me to sleep.

When I wake, feeling sick and disorientated, I already feel empty. I'm barely aware of what anyone is saying to me, except for the warnings that I will continue to bleed. Symptoms of what to look out for that may be a problem go right over my head. At that moment, I truly don't care what happens to me.

I feel like a murderer.

After a period of time monitoring me, they say I'm okay to leave. When they check whether I've got someone with me, I lie and say I have a friend waiting outside.

I stumble across the car park, unsure whether what I'm feeling is more mental than physical, but I'm dizzy, my head aches, my stomach feels sore, and as for my heart, it's smashed into pieces. I head for my car thinking I'll sit for a bit before starting to drive. If I was sensible, I'd call for a cab. Maybe I will, but I need some time to pull myself together first. I might not care about my life, but I won't be a danger to others.

Everything inside me is screaming that I've made a mistake. What do doctors know, they could have been wrong? Why did I come here today? Why hadn't I carried on and pretended everything was normal?

Now there's nothing left.

No baby.

No hope.

I might as well be dead.

I shouldn't have done it.

CHAPTER FIFTEEN

Niran

Staring at a carburettor as if it could talk and tell me what was wrong, I'm distracted by my phone vibrating in my pocket. "What can I do for you, Token?"

"Got some info for you. I've been keeping tabs on your woman. Thought you'd like to know Saffie's booked herself into the hospital. She went in first thing this morning. From the notes I managed to get into, it looks like she's going through with the termination."

Oh, Saffie. I pull the phone away for a moment and swallow hard, trying to dislodge the lump that comes into my throat. While I support her choice, I can't imagine how hard this will be for her. I know she'll be devastated.

"You said she went in. Is she still there?" I appreciate that Token had given me a moment.

"I don't know. I'm sorry, I've only just found out."

"Gotcha. Thanks, Brother." I end the call.

Shouting to let Grumbler know I'm heading out, I head straight for my bike. Whatever reason she wanted rid of me, the colour of my skin or the fact I wear a cut be damned. Something tells me she's going to need someone, and all she's got is me, so it's me she's going to get.

I don't even think about it. All I know is that Saffie's alone and going through one of, or even maybe the worst thing that can happen to a woman in her life. The loss of a child.

If she went to the hospital early, then she might already be home. Or do they keep women going through procedures like her in? I wish I knew more, but it's her apartment where I go first. Privacy be damned or not, when there's no answer to my knock, I pick the lock, and a quick check around shows me she's not here.

Locking up after me, it's back on my bike, and the hospital where I go next. I find the right department, but of course they won't give me any information about her—if she's here or whether she's already been and gone. But they do answer my query—for a procedure as I've described, it's unlikely she'll need to be kept in.

Banging myself on the head, I realise I should have checked the parking lot first. I walk out, and there, at the back of the lot as if ashamed to be in the company of far newer and less scruffy cars, is hers.

I lean against the door, fold my arms across my chest, and settle in to wait, dismissing the notion of going back into the waiting room. If there's to be a confrontation, I'd rather it was in private. With nothing else to occupy my time, I take out my phone and start playing a mindless game.

I've run out of lives and am just debating whether to waste some cash when I catch movement out of the side of my eye.

It's Saffie. She's a complete mess, her face red and blotchy. She's holding her stomach and walking, or more correctly stumbling and lurching slowly across the parking lot, her uncaring progress making it seem like her world's been completely shattered. My heart breaks, and my feet spring into action as I run over to join her.

In the depths of her misery, she doesn't notice me at first. When she does, she looks up, then catches sight of my cut, and her face pales more.

"Saffie," I start, imploringly. "Yeah, I'm a biker. Yeah, I'm in a club. But I'm no threat to you. I want to be there for you. You fuckin' need *someone,* sweetheart."

She turns away and starts to walk off. It's as though anywhere away from me will do, as she's already taken a few steps in the opposite direction of her car.

"Saffie," I call after her, using my long legs to quickly catch up and move in front to impede her progress. "Please, Saffie, hear me out."

Her eyes close, and her face turns downward. "Did Duke send you?" The question is voiced in a tone of surrender, as if she's expecting a positive, but unwelcome, response.

"What?" I shake my head in confusion. "Duke? Who the fuck's Duke?" My eyes narrow and my nostrils flare. "He a biker who hurt you, Saffie? Is that what this is all about?" I place my hand over my heart. "I swear on all I hold dear, on my family's and my brothers' lives, I have never met nor come across a man named Duke. Not in any MC." I think for a moment, then add, "Or out of it to my recollection."

Raising her face, her eyes open again. "You swear you don't know Duke?"

"I swear." I put my hand over my heart. I don't know what more I can do or say to convince her. "Let me in, Saffie. Let me care for you."

She looks so damn tired as her hands raise as if in surrender. She seems to slump, as though the reality of what she's been through begins to overcome her fear of the cut that I wear, and whether she can trust my denial of knowing the asshole she seems to think I've got connections to. Tearful eyes rise to meet mine, a moment while she seems to have an internal battle, then after just one further slight hesitation, she's in my arms, sobbing as though her world's come to an end.

I hold her tight, trying to imbibe her with my strength. "It's alright. You're alright. Cry it out, darlin'." For a moment or two, she rests against me, giving me almost her full weight as though her legs will no longer support her. I just hold her tight and repeat my meaningless words. I rock back and forth, as though comforting a child.

After a while, I ask, concerned, "Are you hurting?"

"Not really," she replies through her sobs. "They… they gave me something. I still feel a bit woozy from the anaesthetic."

The truth is, I have no clue what she's gone through, what care she needs, or how to comfort her, but I can see she's in no fucking state to drive.

"I'll take you home."

Again between heartbreaking intakes of air which exhale as sniffles, she gives a slight push and tells me, "I've got my car."

I don't allow her to break free but loosen my hold so she doesn't feel trapped. "That's good, as I'm on my bike. We'll take your car. Saffie, you can't drive. Surely the hospital warned you? If the anaesthetic hasn't completely worn off—"

"I told them I was being collected."

"And you are." I give her a small smile, cupping her face and turning it up to face me. "By me."

She stiffens slightly, but then sighs, completely defeated. "I want to go home."

"Car keys?"

In answer, she holds out her purse to me. Opening it, I peer in, then gingerly stretch out my hand. After fumbling around, touching things I can't even name, I eventually find them at the bottom of the bag. How women find keys in an emergency I'll never understand.

Wasting no time, I need to almost fully support her as we

move closer to her car, as if she's mentally and physically given up. Once there, I open the passenger door and help her inside, leaning over to fasten her seatbelt. Then somehow, I manage to get my large form into the tiny driver's space, pushing the seat back as far as it can go.

Once I'm in gear and pulling out of the parking lot, I reach for her hand and squeeze it tight. I don't ask questions, just let her be.

The journey continues in silence, broken only by the distraught weeping at my side. It's not loud but sounds like thunder to my ears. I'd give anything for the audible evidence of her distress to cease, it's simply increasing my sense of uselessness. What the fuck do I say to her? I can hardly tell her everything's going to be alright. There are literally no words which would help.

I can see in the rearview that her car still belches smoke, but I drive gamely on. At least we keep moving, until suddenly, the engine splutters and dies and we slow to an unplanned halt.

Fuck.

I coast to the side of the road and put it in park. A glance to my side shows me she's barely registered the unplanned stop. Her nod is barely perceptible when I tell her, "I'll check under the hood." I pull the lever, then get out.

Like any male by the side of a broken-down car, I stand, looking down at the engine without a clue as to what's gone wrong. Even with my mechanic's eyes, seeing the state it's in, it could be anything. It all looks so old. It could have just reached the end of its line. Without tools and stripping it completely, there's no easy fix to be done.

I take out my phone and place a call.

"Grumbler? I'm with Saffie…" Pulling my phone away from my ear, I ignore his *what the fuck* and the *where the fuck have you been,* and the accusatory *you just walked out,* instead silencing him with my next words. "Saffie, well, she's no longer pregnant." After I listen to a few more, but this time understanding, *oh fucks,* I continue, "I picked her up from the hospital, but we've broken down… yeah, her car, not my bike. Can you send the tow truck out?" When he gets my location, I add another request. "I also need the prospects to collect my bike. I left it in the hospital parking lot… Sure, I'll give them the key when they come to collect the car. I can't leave her." Grumbler, full of sincere but unhelpful apologies for the way everything's turned out, tells me he understands.

I go back to sit beside her, leaving the hood open and the hazard lights on, so anyone can tell we've broken down. I'm thankful for small mercies, the battery is still good, the emergency lights are flashing, and at least we're not on the highway. I've managed to get it far enough to the side that cars passing should be able to do so safely enough.

Thank fuck I was here. Saffie, in her state, on her own… I don't even want to think about what would have happened, or whether she could have coped.

"What's wrong with it?" she asks disinterestedly, holding a sodden tissue to try to mop the tears continuously streaming from her eyes. The state of her car is clearly an inconvenience and the last thing on her mind.

I answer her anyway. "Fuck knows. Could be any one of a number of things." *Or all of them combined.* "I'm getting the boys to come tow it in. Your engine looks fucked, Saffie."

She shrugs as if it doesn't bother her, and I doubt it does. Not now, not in the scheme of things.

We don't talk, just sit, waiting. She uses tissue after tissue, but even when the tears begin to dry, she still gives a far too regular sniff and a sob. Luckily, it isn't long before the tow truck arrives driven by Ross with Kid sitting beside him, along with Curtis and Wrangler behind in the crash truck sent to take back my bike. I notice with relief, and as should be the case, as they're in cages, none of them are wearing cuts.

"I want to go home." Saffie seems to only just realise her plans have been interrupted.

"I'll get you home," I promise.

Aware she's probably sore, as well as full of regret or wishes about what might have been, I think for a moment how best to do this, then get out of the car.

After shaking Ross's hand, I thank him for getting here so fast, then issue my instructions. "You and Kid hook up the car and tow it to the shop, will you?" After he nods, I turn to the prospect and brother who've just stepped out of the crash truck and joined us. "Wrangler, can you and Curtis drive Saffie and me back to her apartment, then go get my bike?" When my brother gives a raise and dip of his chin, I pass him my key and tell him where I left it.

All four men spring into action, Curtis helping Ross even though the one-handed man knows exactly what he's doing having picked up a tow a hundred times, and Kid looking on watching how they do stuff. I wait with Saffie, who's standing, clutching her purse to her. I want to hold her and comfort her, but now she's giving off *stay away from me* vibes, so I just stand next to her. Her face is expressionless, but her eyes, they're so full of pain I'd give my other leg if it would save her this anguish. But knowing there's nothing to be said or done, I just give silent support.

As Ross and Kid leave, she watches her car start to move away behind the tow truck as though it's just one more blow that's been sent to hurt her.

When Curtis signals he's ready to leave, I ask her, "You feeling okay, Saffie? Want my help to the truck?"

Like an automaton, she starts walking forward, her movements jerky. Her hands are again wrapped around her stomach, suggesting it's both mental and physical pain she's feeling.

The truck's built for men, not a petite woman. I help her up, my hand on her ass just there to give her a boost, but she jerks away and heaves herself in, the sudden movement being too much for her, and her wince betrays the strain. When I reach for the seat belt, she takes it herself. When I slide in beside her, she moves away.

As I lean forward and give Curtis instructions on how to get to her place, I hear her let out a relieved sigh. *Did she expect me to kidnap her and not take her home?* Another sign of how little she trusts bikers.

Approaching the block where her apartment is, I don't miss the way the prospect's jaw tightens nor the quick backward incredulous glance that he gives me, or the way his eyes meet Wrangler's.

"You want your bike brought *here*?" Wrangler's voice is tight.

I shudder inwardly, knowing what he's thinking. *Definitely not.* "Nah, take it back. When I need a lift home, I'll call you."

My words seem to sink in to Saffie's head. "You're not… you're not coming in, Niran."

I take a deep breath. I'm prepared to fight to the end on this. "Darlin', you need someone with you. I'm not leaving you alone. Either I keep you company for a bit, or you come back to the clubhouse." Turning, I see her stiffen at my ultimatum, but I'm relentless. "Which is it to be, Saffie?"

As if realising it would be too easy to kidnap her, outnumbered as she is, she shudders, then says, "I don't seem to have a choice. You can come in." The words are all but spat at me.

Curtis pulls up and parks, and stays sitting in the cab, Wrangler, taking his cue, also stays put while I help Saffie out. They wait until we reach the main door of the apartment building. When I turn and give them a dismissive wave, Wrangler shakes his head, then Curtis drives off.

Seeing Saffie eyeing the stairs with trepidation, I gather the fucking lift is still not working. Inwardly groaning that I'm going to again put strain on my leg, I sweep her in my arms and carry her. I swear she's lost weight even in the short time I've known her. Then, I want to smack myself in the head for the thought.

Of course she has. She's lost her baby.

CHAPTER SIXTEEN

Saffie

I ended my pregnancy.

Now I'm staring at the same front door I walked out of hours earlier, but everything's different. I'm not the same person who left. I feel so damn empty.

I'd walked into the hospital knowing my life was about to change, and not for the better. I'd thought I'd made the right decision. I thought I could be strong. But when it was over, I had nothing but regrets, and an overwhelming sense that what I'd done was wrong.

I stand on the threshold of my apartment, fearing stepping inside. Frightened of the person I'll find in there, and I'm not talking about the man at my side, it's me, who I don't recognise.

I'd left the hospital surprised when the skies didn't open and a bolt of lightning hadn't come down to strike me. How could a woman do what I had done?

Distraught, I'd headed in the general direction where I'd left my car, tears blurring my vision. I didn't care when a figure came close, only hoping they'd leave me alone. It's only when he drew nearer that I realised who was there.

My worst nightmare. A biker. It didn't help that I recognised it was Niran, it was his cut that I saw at first. Fear blasted into me, and I followed my initial instinct to run.

He stopped me and spoke. I couldn't tell you the words that were uttered or whether either he or I made sense. Maybe it was my desperation, maybe it was because I knew I'd nothing more to lose, or that any punishment dealt I'd deserve, but my resolve crumbled and I took the only comfort on offer, that I could find in Niran's arms.

I heard his voice, calming like the trickling of a brook, telling me for this moment, I wasn't alone. Selfishly, I lapped up all that he was giving me. How my heart was still beating, I'd never know, but somehow, in this man's arms, I found some strength to go on, or at least the will to get myself home.

And thank God he'd been there as it turned out. When my car broke down, I was incapable of doing anything other than letting him take charge. Will I see my car again? I strongly suspect it was men from his club who'd come so fast, and they can steal it and break it for parts for all that I care.

"Are we going in?" Niran's voice breaks into my reverie.

I startle. While I'd been daydreaming, he'd opened my door. *How?* My keys are on the same fob as that for my car, and those were taken with the vehicle. I glance at him suspiciously, then realise the key is in his hand, and he had the forethought to remove it.

"Come on." He puts his hand to my back so gently, I'm only just aware of his touch encouraging me forward.

There's my Kindle on the table, just where I'd left it. A glass I'd used for water last night is still on the side. The curtains are open, just as I'd drawn them earlier. My home is the same, but it's not. I feel like I've walked into another person's house.

I take one step, then another. Then like a wave crashing into the shore, anguish hits me like a physical wall. A wail bursts out of me, and I sink to the floor, curling in a fetal position as I start to bawl. I rock back and forth, the pain so devastating, so debilitating, I can't see how I'll ever survive.

Crouching beside me, his hands reach out then withdraw as his eyes search my face. "What do you need, Saffie? Do you need to lie down? Something to eat or drink? Painkillers?"

I want my baby back. But he's lost to me now. I gasp in air as the brutal reality hits me. *My child is gone.* Niran wants to comfort me, but there's nothing he, or anyone can do now.

I wail once more, unable to do anything to stop sobbing.

A hand rests on my shoulder, but he says nothing more. He just positions his legs more comfortably and settles beside me on the floor.

I cry until I've no tears to cry anymore, and all the while those fingers so gently touching my shoulder seem like an anchor, keeping me from breaking completely.

Thoughts of him being a biker flee. If his hand can ground me, I want more.

"Will you just hold me?" I try to tell myself I'd take advantage of anyone, but have to admit for some unknown reason it's Niran who keeps me drawing breath in.

Though even in the state I'm in, I question my sanity, forcing myself to look at the cut he's laid down so carefully. *Any port in a storm. That's all this is.* I deserve everything that's coming to me. If bringing Niran back into my life brings Duke to me, so be it.

Without a word, Niran gets to his feet, bends, then lifts me, moving me over to the sofa, then sits beside me. His strong arms surround me, pulling my head against his chest. There we sit in silence, me selfishly enjoying this temporary closeness of another human being.

We could have sat for minutes, or maybe an hour, I couldn't say precisely, but Niran seems to understand I need time. I feel numb, as though my mind doesn't want to acknowledge what I've done. I could have stayed there forever, but when Niran's phone rings, he gently pulls his arms away and stands up.

His face is puzzled as if he's being called from an unknown number and doesn't know who the caller is. Then he frowns, suggesting the voice on the phone isn't welcome.

"Yeah?" At first, he starts off gently. "I'm sorry, Cyn, I won't be back." Then as the call continues, his impatience begins to show, until he says very firmly, "Fuck, Cyn. I've got something to do. I can't be there tonight, okay? You've got friends... Don't give me that. Play pool with Pennywise or someone... No, Cyn, I won't be home this evening. I've already fuckin' told you that." He ends the call while I'm still hearing strains of a tinny sounding voice on the line. He sighs heavily, and his jaw is clenched.

Has he got a woman, an old lady? A handsome man like him probably wouldn't be lonely, but the way he spoke to her... I'm puzzled. His dismissive attitude is reminiscent of Duke. If it is his woman, he has no respect for her.

He pulls in air, expanding his cheeks, and then huffs it out. Then, in an abrupt mood change, he looks down and gives a small smile.

I have to ask. My voice full of censure I'm direct. "Was... was that your old lady?"

He cocks an eyebrow my way. "You know the lingo?" He seems to think on that for a moment. I don't enlighten him on how I know or admit that technically, I'm still one myself. After a pause, as if he's wondering how much to say, he explains, "Cyn's my sister."

Ah. As an only child, I can only guess at a sibling relationship. But the way he spoke to her still grates. "Are you close?"

He harrumphs. "About as distant as a half-brother and half-sister can be." A shadow falls over his face, and he shakes his head. "Enough about me. Is there anything I can get you now that I'm up?"

Feeling bereft now he's taken those comforting arms from me, I grab for a cushion and hold it instead. For a response, I move my head side to side.

Niran sits back on the couch, but this time doesn't get close to me. His thighs are splayed wide, his elbows on his knees with his hands clasped between them. With his eyes focused on a dirty mark on the opposite wall, he starts, "If it helps, I think you've done the right thing."

As at the moment I'm not certain I have, I'm surprised he's expressed an opinion. "Why?"

"The baby didn't have a chance, and you knew that, Saffie. Why put you both through hell for another few months when no other outcome could come of it."

Deep down I know that, but it doesn't prevent me from beginning to sob again. "I feel so guilty. It's all my fault. I didn't give him a good start in life."

"Nah." He now turns his eyes on me. "Listen to me. I was here, I watched you, you were doing the best that you could, but sometimes nature has to have its own way. Sometimes things aren't meant to be. Take Mary and Grumbler. They've doing all they can to ensure their baby's healthy, but at the end of the day, it might not be enough. It wasn't anything you did, Saffie."

But it was. It was the beating I had from Duke, the drugs I'd imbibed albeit unwillingly. It was the stress of taking my chance to leave. I turn away, knowing he won't understand unless I explain, and not wanting to share such information about me.

Instead, I turn the tables on him. "Tell me about your sister." Despite him being a biker, he's never seemed anything but kind, but that phone call had showed him in a new light. Before I trust him with my sorrow, I want to know why.

He gives me a concerned glance, then shrugs. "My dad died, and my mom married again three years later when I was seventeen. She got pregnant straight away, and Cyn was born just before I joined the Marines. My stepdad and I didn't see eye to eye, so except for a few short visits, I didn't go home again. Cyn and her two younger sisters are virtually strangers as far as I'm concerned." He pauses to rub his hands over his face. "She ran away, and for some fucked-up reason, she came to me."

"How old is she?"

"Twenty, going on twelve." He shakes his head and his mouth quirks, but it's not fondly. "The only thing on which I and her dad agree is that she couldn't stay with an abusive asshole of an ex."

My ears prick up. If Niran's against abuse, he wouldn't condone what happened to me. "Abusive?"

"Yeah. Her father ran him off when he blackened her eye. Cyn thought she'd been treated unfairly, so ran. Luckily, I suppose, she didn't take off blindly, but came to find me."

"Treated unfairly? By the ex you mean?"

He snorts. "No, in her mind it was by her fuckin' family who kept her from him."

I turn my head to the side, *oh how I wish someone had saved me.*

"Saffie." Niran's hand comes under my chin and turns me to face him. "I might sound rough about Cyn, but her arriving out of the blue took me by shock. Especially when I've been worried as fuck about you." *He worried about me?* "She's safe. My brothers won't touch her, won't give in to her games. They've given her a job… No, no sweetheart, I can see where your mind's going. They've not put her to work on her back." He snorts, as if considering that a joke, then rolls his eyes. "She's a receptionist in our custom-bike workshop."

"But she wanted you to go back. You say she's safe, perhaps she doesn't feel it." I do know how blind men can be.

Again he snorts. "If anything, it's my brothers who I should be worried about. Cyn's fine, but she clings to me. It's not a refuge she's seeking in my company, but a sort of possessive vibe. She wants her big brother all to herself."

I can kind of see why. If Niran were my brother, I'd want him for myself too. That thought means I must view him positively despite his affiliations which surprises me.

"Shouldn't you go to her?"

He turns his earnest black-as-night eyes on me. "Nah, here's where I want to be."

"Why? Look at me, Niran. I'm a fucked-up mess," I cry. I'm a murderer. I just killed my baby.

"Saffie, Cyn just needs to get her head on straight, and I'm doing what I can to help her. You, though? You're going through something no woman ever should. Where I want to be is here with you."

"I've nothing to offer you, Niran."

"Don't want fuck from you, Saffie. I just want to comfort you."

"Sounds to me like you should be with your sister," I snap, waspishly.

Niran shakes his head. "She thinks she needs me, but she doesn't. Me not being there will give her a chance to stand on her own two feet, but with a safety net around her. You, though, you've not got anyone else. I might not be much, but while you need me, I'm all yours."

CHAPTER SEVENTEEN

Niran

For a while, talking about Cyn with Saffie had distracted her, but then she'd grown quiet, and the tears had started falling again. Having no words to comfort her, I'd just held her, letting her cry in my arms. It's clear Saffie is exhausted, and no wonder given what she's been through today.

I do think she'd made the right decision. Her baby had no chance of life. Religious folks might have opted to wait for a miracle, but even if God exists, those are in short supply. Myself? I prefer to rely on the word of the experts which doesn't make me a non-believer. After all, God had given us both science and free choice.

You don't need to believe in an unseen being to know however much I could tell her she'd done what was right, Saffie's doubting her choice. I wouldn't expect any different. We're human. Hope is hard to give up. I suspect today's events will play on Saffie's mind until the day she dies, maybe getting easier to deal with, but never disappearing.

I'm not qualified to discuss it. I'm a man, I'll never carry a baby, so what the fuck do I know about how she's feeling? I stay quiet on the topic, knowing it's her who's got to come to terms with it.

It hadn't escaped me that even given her fears about bikers, she'd grabbed at me like a lifeline. Probably I could have been anyone with a friendly face and supporting arms. However much or little she thinks of me, I'm not leaving this apartment. She needs someone, whether or not she admits it, and part of me is afraid of what she might do if she's left on her own. Cyn's problems fade in comparison. I know my brothers and the old ladies will look out for her. It's one of the benefits of having a family I can trust.

As Saffie settles back and sheer exhaustion makes her close her eyes, I wonder at myself and why I feel this strong desire to help her.

Even though I've not seen her at her best, we've not even kissed, yet alone fucked, something about her makes me wonder how it would feel to claim her. Something about her keeps drawing me back. Despite that I've seen her crying more often than not, even tears can't detract from the fact that she's pretty. Perhaps not in the classical magazine cover beauty, but she's got big eyes, a generous mouth, and on those few occasions I've seen her smile, her expression could light up a room. *Is that it? Am I attracted to her?* If so, it hasn't started the way I'd have predicted. No girl meets boy and falls in love stuff. I've seen her at her worst. Which poses the question, at her best, would I still want her? Of course, none of our interactions have been about sex or even the acknowledgement of any attraction between us, which makes any idea of making her my old lady a complete nonstarter. Though something tells me I certainly would be proud to have her on my arm, or riding at my back. Of course, that would only be if she could get over her fear of bikers.

Sitting quietly, I try to analyse the reasons why I'm here and not running hell for leather and trying to extract myself from her mess. Saffie needs me, and I know inherently I could be good for her. Maybe Kink did see something in me. Maybe that's all it is. A broken bird I think I can fix, much like a car that's been brought in after a fender bender.

Whatever drives me, I want to be her friend, want to have her back and support her. Whether it would ever go further than that has a big question mark over it. She's still not explained who got her pregnant, and if she were raped, as I expect, it would take a fucking lot for her to consider trusting any man in her bed. And who could fucking blame her? My fists clench as I think of all the ways I want to make that man hurt and the hundreds of painful means by which he could die.

My thoughts are interrupted when Saffie groans and rests her hands on her stomach.

"You sore?" She opens her eyes as if she'd forgotten I was still here. Her grimace shows she indeed is. "You got some painkillers?"

"I'm okay." It's a lie, but I don't call her out on it.

"You hungry? Want me to rustle up some food? Or order in? Just tell me what you'd like."

Her face contorts with disgust. "I couldn't eat a thing." Awkwardly, she stands, then wraps her arms around herself. "You should go. I'm going to lie down."

Emphatically, I shake my head. "No can do, darlin'. I'm not leaving you alone. You go ahead and get some rest, but I'll be staying right here."

She looks like she wants to argue but lacks the energy to find the words. I settle back and watch her go, then hear her enter her small bathroom. When she exits, instead of going to her room, she comes back into the living area instead.

"Er, Niran?" Her brow creases and she hangs her head.

"Whatcha want?" I'll do anything but go.

Her mouth twists. "I should have stopped by the store."

I raise and lower my shoulders. "Anything you need, I can get."

Now her face reddens, twin crimson patches highlighted in the otherwise pale of her skin. "I need to go myself."

"Nah. You need to rest. I can get whatever you want." One phone call and it will be here.

She blushes again, showing her discomfort, and I've an inkling what it might be about, and absolve her from having to say it aloud. "Tell you what, why don't you write me a list? Leave it with me, then go get some sleep. I'll have everything you need by the time you wake up."

Her head lifts slightly, suggesting she's accepted my compromise. Turning, she shuffles off. Within moments, she returns and places a folded note in my hands.

"I'll understand if—" She speaks without meeting my eyes.

"I'll get whatever you need, darlin'. Now go and have a nap. When you wake up, we'll see about getting some food."

Waiting only until she's closed her bedroom door behind her, I unfold the note and smirk. Just as I thought, she's requested some feminine products and some painkillers. I add a few extra requirements of my own, then take my phone out of my pocket.

"You got Grumbler."

"How you doing, old man?" I grin as I imagine the expression on his face.

But Grumbler isn't in the mood for levity. "Hell, Niran, is Saffie doing okay?"

Though he can't see me, I shake my head. "No, she's not, Brother. I don't want to leave her, so I need a favour."

"Just ask."

"Is there a prospect around? I need him to pick up a few items for her if someone's free."

"Kid's not busy. Text me a list and I'll see that he gets it." Grumbler pauses. "You sure you're the right person to be there? I can check how Eva's fixed."

"She's probably working," I tell him, reluctant to be replaced, even by a qualified nurse. "And," I grimace hearing noises from the floor above, "it's not a good area for any woman to be here."

Putting away my phone, I go into the kitchen and take stock of the food reserves. She's running low on everything, but with the problems she's had to think about, groceries probably didn't come first. I can't blame her. We'll get takeout later, if I can get her to eat, that is. Even if she isn't hungry, I'll order in for myself, making sure I've got extra. Maybe that will tempt her.

Back on the couch, I switch on the television, keeping the sound low. There's nothing much on to interest me, in fact, the yelling and screaming from the apartment next door is far more entertaining. Apparently, Joe had been caught with his pants down, and his woman isn't accepting his lame excuse. *You tell him, girl.* I grin to myself.

An hour later, there's a knock at the door. I go to open it and find Kid. He's carrying a grocery sack as though it's going to turn around and bite him any moment.

"Got everything?"

"Yeah." He hands the bag over to me quickly.

"Wait a sec," I demand, as I open the bag, having to roll my eyes at the contents. "You'll have to go back." I extract a box of tampons. "These aren't what she wanted. I asked you for pads."

His face is so red it amuses me. "They're women's shit, aren't they? Won't they fuckin' do?"

I'd take bets he just went to that aisle and grabbed the first thing that came to hand. "No, they're no fuckin' good." I might not know the mechanics but can imagine her pussy's been mucked around enough as it is today.

"How the fuck am I going to know what pads are?"

I shrug. "Ask?"

The red on his cheeks darkens and there's a look of horror in his eyes.

Taking pity on him, I take out my phone which is now

showing a red bar and Google. Tapping an image, I turn it to show him. "This is what she needs."

He looks down, then up to meet my eyes. "Sometimes I wonder whether getting this fuckin' patch is worth it."

"Whoa," I say sharply. "With an attitude like that, you're not going to go far."

"Sorry, man." His face falls. "Grumbler had me out searching for a left-handed hammer for Ross today. The store gave me shit, saying they had to order one in. I thought Grumbler was going to tear me a new one for returning empty-handed before he cracked up."

Par for the course. And I've been through hazing twice, once in the Marines, and then for the Devils. Kid's got to grow thicker skin.

Seeing my total lack of sympathy, he eyes the image again, then straightens his shoulders. "I'll be right back."

True to his word, in half an hour he returns, this time with everything she requires. He's also brought a few beers, which restores some of my faith in him.

"Need anything more, just call me."

As I nod, I have a thought. "Come back first thing in the morning, Kid. We might need more errands run."

"Sure thing." He mock-salutes me, turns around and leaves.

A flushing toilet tells me Saffie is awake. Holding the bag, I turn, but before I can call out, I hear her bedroom door closing again. Going over, I knock gently. When she calls out "Come in," I enter, then I wave what's in my hand.

"Your supplies, ma'am."

She sighs with relief and holds out her hand. "Thank you so much. What do I owe you?"

"Don't worry about it." I hadn't paid Kid yet, but doubt it cost a lot. "I'm about to order some food. Want anything?"

"I still feel a bit nauseous from the anaesthetic. I think I'll just try and sleep some more."

Sleep a little, maybe. Recriminate with herself, yeah, I suspect she'll be doing that a lot.

"You want to talk, or just be held, you call out for me, you hear?"

She gives a tired nod and turns away but then back almost immediately. "Just for the record, Niran, I'm glad you're here."

"Saffie," I start. "I know it's hard. I know it will take forever to get over. I know it must have fuckin' hurt and I can't begin to imagine the pain. But as I told you before, I don't think you had a choice."

She stares at me for a moment, then her chin raises a little. "Thank you, Niran. That helps. I know some people would think I should have carried on and waited to see what happened, but it would have just been torturing the both of us. It's just going to take me some time to get over. I—" she breaks off, sobs, then covers her mouth as though to stop more following. "I just don't know where to start. I miss him already."

"He'll always be here," I tell her as firmly as I can, hovering my hand just over her heart, not touching her, but leaving her in no doubt of my meaning. "But he's at peace now. He won't have a world of hurt to look forward to. As a mother, you made one of the hardest decisions in the world, but it was his best interests you had at heart, not yours."

Words can do nothing to heal a soul. She needs time to come to terms with her loss. She'll go through different phases before she gets anywhere close to normal again—sorrow, anger, regret, and finally acceptance. I might only have lost a leg, but I know that only too well.

But she'll get there. I'll be right there beside her to make sure of it.

CHAPTER EIGHTEEN

Saffie

Niran says all the right words, but I don't deserve to hear them. I feel so damn empty, a shell of my former self. So full of guilt for whatever I'd done to cause my child such harm and the one thing I couldn't do, give him life.

I don't want to eat. I don't want to talk. All I want to do is curl up and mourn. I feel so alone. For no reason other than needing company to take me out of my head just for a moment, I go back to the living room, but stop when Niran takes out his phone. I wait while he places an order for pizza.

I note he's ordered a lot, far too much even for a man his size, probably hoping it will tempt my appetite, but food is the last thing on my mind.

When he ends the call, he frowns at the device in his hand. "You got a charger?" he asks.

"Not one for that." I point at the model he's holding that's a competitor to mine.

He mumbles to himself something about the *prospect, tomorrow,* and *fucking companies slowing old phones down,* then focuses on me again. "You look done in, darlin'."

"I can't sleep."

He stands, approaches me, but without my say so, he doesn't attempt to get close. "Whatcha need?"

There's nothing I can ask for. No one will give me my baby back. My nightmare isn't over but just beginning. I shrug.

"You go back and lie down, sweetheart. Try to get some rest. If you need anything, call me, okay? If you get hungry, I can bring you some pizza."

Lying down doesn't help, but I don't call Niran, and don't go out to see him again.

My body aches and so does my soul. I'm bleeding just as I was told to expect and will be for quite some days. Surprisingly, I was told I don't need a checkup unless things don't seem to be proceeding well. Even at the stage I was at, the procedure was simple with few complications. I'd rather have a huge visible scar to match the one in my heart.

Will I ever forgive myself? Not for having the termination, I can't see I had any choice, but for damaging my baby in the first place.

I can't fully sleep, but I must doze, waking with a start. That's when my mind starts working overtime all over again. Gradually, once more I drift off, veering between dreams where I'm holding a healthy baby in my arms, and nightmares where he's born hideously deformed. The night passes torturously slow. When dawn comes, I'm lying awake, only not stirring because of the man who's currently asleep in my living room.

Suddenly conscious I'd offered him nothing, no blanket or pillow to ease his sleep, I'm embarrassed to go out and see him. But needs must, my bladder's demands are insistent, so finally I rise, dressing before heading to the bathroom.

As I pass the living room, I see Niran's awake—well, he probably didn't get much rest, he's too big to lie on my couch— and is wolfing down a piece of cold pizza that must have been left over from last night.

He nods at me as I indicate the bathroom, and after taking a few more minutes of reprieve, I go out to meet him.

"Sleep okay?"

For an answer, I shrug. Terribly is the answer, but probably better than he had.

"The prospect will be here shortly. You gonna want something to eat? He'll go out and get anything we want." He pauses, then adds, "You need any more supplies?"

Despite myself, my lips quirk. "You made him buy that stuff, didn't you? Is a big man like you afraid of going yourself?"

Niran snorts. "Babe, takes more than a few feminine products to embarrass me. I wanted to make sure you had someone with you, that's why I stayed. And if you hadn't noticed, I've got no transport. But yeah, I'll admit, I did enjoy yanking Kid's chain." He chuckles to himself.

Carefully, I sit myself on a chair, easing myself down as my stomach is hurting similar to having terrible period pain.

Niran stares at me. He'd noticed my grimace, and his head tilts as if he's not too sure whether I'm hurting, or whether it's something he's said. "Don't worry about Kid, Saffie. We give all the prospects shit, giving them bum jobs and running them off their feet as a test. They need to prove their loyalty before they patch in, and if Kid can't handle a bit of embarrassment, then he's not the man I want at my back."

Once again, I wonder about the Satan's Devils MC. If making their prospects feel awkward is the most hazing they do, they're not like the Crazy Wolves. Prospects with the Wolves don't have it easy. Once, a tall gangly lad was forced to fight Slit. The sergeant-at-arms was twice his size, and his weight all muscle. It was an uneven fight, and the result was guaranteed from the time the scared youngster had bravely held up his fists. He had escaped with his life, but his back was broken and would never be fixed.

If you got patched into the Crazy Wolves, you had to prove

you were one of them. Prepared to fight literally to the death for a chance to wear their patch, or to commit murder, kidnap, and torture on their behalf.

A knock on the door pulls me from my thoughts. As Niran's posture is relaxed when he peers out the peephole, I gather it's probably who he's expecting. He opens the door and in steps who I assume is the expected prospect as he's wearing a cut.

Ushering him in, Niran closes the door and locks it.

"Saffie, this is Kid. Kid, Saffie."

I raise my chin. I don't think I've ever been introduced to a prospect so politely before. On his part, Kid offers me a wide grin.

"Any news from the clubhouse?" Niran asks.

Kid shrugs and looks sheepish. "I, er, didn't stay there last night. Came straight from…" When his voice trails off and Niran rolls his eyes, I can guess what he was going to allude to was some female's bed.

"What do you want to eat?" Niran turns his body slightly to face me. "Kid will go out and collect something."

I thought I'd never want food again, but at that point, my stomach rumbles. I might want to give up, but the gnawing pains in my gut tell me I'll have a fight with my body.

"There's a breakfast place close by that delivers. Why don't we just order from there?"

Niran glances at me, looks at Kid, then inclines his head. "Nah. Kid can go collect it."

Armed with our orders, the prospect, who doesn't seem at all put out, leaves again.

Niran's a rock that first day. I'm numb, I can't think of anything. While I sit in a daze, unable to believe I'm no longer pregnant, Kid, after delivering breakfast, is sent off grocery shopping, then he and Niran put it away. I have no appetite but pick at food that's put in front of me. At some point, Niran leaves as he's got some business he needs doing. *Club business,* I think to myself, not that I let on that I already know were I to ask, he wouldn't tell me. Kid stays with me, but plays on his phone, keeping quiet and out of the way.

Initially, I cast him in the role of prison guard, then realised my past was influencing me. Kid gives off no vibe he'd stop me if I wanted to leave. In fact, I even tested him, saying I was going out to see a neighbour, then when he nodded, I said I'd changed my mind.

Kid's okay, I decide. Unassuming, fading into the background, not commenting when I disappear into my bedroom when the next bout of immense despair hits. I am mindful, though, not to talk to him. *I can't risk another Jude.*

Niran returns that evening, quickly dismissing the prospect. He comes prepared, bringing a new sleeping bag with him to replace the one I'd given to the homeless man living on the street outside.

I appreciate the company more than I expect. Alone, I'd just relive everything over and over again. I can't even put on the television as all I seem to see are babies and happy moms, or ads for toys and equipment.

Niran doesn't expect anything from me. If I want to talk, he's there. If I don't, he does whatever I indicate I need, holding me or just sitting in opposite chairs keeping silent.

Our pattern goes on for a few days. Slowly, it grows on me how much I appreciate him being there. Each morning, Niran leaves for work, but after the first day seems to trust that I'm safe to be left alone, as Kid doesn't make a reappearance.

When he comes in, I've taken to asking about his sister, and become used to hearing the shit she's got up to that day. As I hear more about her, I start to understand why a male can't get inside her head, and begin to feel sorry, not just for her, but for him.

Growing up as I had, I've always had one regret. "I wish I had a sister," I tell him one night.

"You can have mine," he retorts.

For the first time in days, my lips start to curve. Then I voice the question I've been meaning to ask him for days. "Why don't you wear your cut when you come here?" He'd had it that first day, but not since then.

He barks a short laugh. "Because I drive a truck. Don't want to leave my bike parked in this area." His raised eyebrow speaks volumes.

"Oh."

That's sensible, but he'd rather ride. I know that. The discussion about transport reminds me.

"What's happened to my car?" I wait to hear that it's been scrapped. It's so far gone, I doubt it would be able to be fixed. How I'll get around is just one more problem I'll have to deal with, but far down my list right now. Practical things are way too much for me to handle. I've enough issue remembering to breathe oxygen in.

Now both his eyebrows rise. "Your car's outside."

I tilt my head in surprise, then slump. Of course it is. It will be up to me to scrap it. He'd have overstepped if he'd taken that on himself.

It seems he can read my mind. "Don't look like that, Saffie. It's still an old junker, but it's been fixed for now. Not sure how long it will keep running, but for short journeys A to B, it should be fine."

My eyes widen. "How much do I owe you?"

"Fuck all. It wasn't much." His expression challenges me to question him, but I stay quiet.

I'm sure it took more than a new set of spark plugs to get it running again, but I don't care enough to argue, or worry I'm beholden to him. I'm mobile again, that's all that matters.

The next day I return to my job, and gradually normal daily actions get easier to go through. My heart still aches, and I don't think I'll ever be able to feel whole again, but I'm starting to think I'll be able to exist in a world without my baby, even if I never forget him for a moment.

I've only one problem, and that's that I'm starting to depend on Niran. I find I'm watching the clock, anxious for the time when the end of my shift comes around, knowing he'll be waiting for me at home, being there to share my burden, hold me, let me cry, or put food in front of me.

It's not fair I only appreciate him when I forget he's a biker.

It's been a week now since that fateful day when I made the decision to say goodbye to my baby. Not long enough for the wounds to heal, or even for my body to stop bleeding. But putting one foot in front of the other has started to become habit again.

I know Niran's only here because he thinks I need him.

My worries that he'll bring Duke to my door have at least subsided, but he's a biker, though it's been all too easy to forget that. Outside our bubble of my apartment, I wouldn't want anything to do with him. There'd never be a time where I'd be comfortable meeting his club or being a part of whatever is his life.

I'm grateful that he's been here at a time I didn't think I'd be able to carry on, but in the real world, he and I would never have a chance, and it's not fair to mislead him. My fears of motorcycle clubs are just too entrenched.

That night, I confront him.

"Niran." I approach and sit down next to him. When he goes to put his arm around me, I pull away. "I think I need to do this on my own now."

He glances at me sharply. "What do you mean?"

My shoulders rise and lower. "You coming around, being here when I get home, I'm leaning on you when I should start to stand on my own two feet."

He looks taken aback. "But you don't have to. I'm happy being here for you."

I place my hand on his, squeezing gently. "You're a good man, Niran. But how long is this going to last? How long will you keep coming around?"

He turns his hand over, now his is trapping mine. "For as long as you want me to. It ain't no hardship, darlin'."

He's crazy. He's got a life of his own and a sister who needs him. "And if that's forever?" I challenge.

"Then I'll be here," he says firmly.

I shake my head. "That's not friendship, Niran, that's a relationship. And I'm far from ready for that yet. Maybe I'll never be." And certainly never with a biker.

"Why label it, Saffie? Who the fuck knows what's between us and who cares? You may not believe me, but I get something from helping you. I get a sense of worth."

"What about getting that helping your sister?"

He moves his hand, using it to wipe down his face instead. "She doesn't need me like you do."

I do need him. But. "I feel I need to wean myself off you." When he looks at me, perplexed, I try to put my unformed thoughts into words. "At some point, you'll want a woman in your life. I doubt you've signed up to be a monk. I can't see a point in the future when I never want sex again."

"I can control my urges. And, babe, there's nothing wrong with my hand."

I stare at him sadly. "I've changed, Niran. I don't even know who I am. First, I was a woman who thought she knew what she wanted, then…" I can't go there, so finish more lamely, "I saw myself as a mother, and that was taken from me. I can't imagine what it's like to feel aroused, to want someone for more than comfort." I don't tell him it's not just the loss of the baby, but it's down to all those years I spent with Duke. "I can't keep you hanging around, waiting for something that might not happen."

"Maybe I don't want you for sex," he throws at me. I raise an eyebrow at him. He gives a self-deprecating grin and shrugs. "I like you, Saffie. But if I ever want a woman in my bed, maybe it won't be you, and we'll stay friends."

That thought hurts me. I might not want all of him in that way, but I'd be jealous of another woman. I want him, even though I'll never be able to give him that.

As I feel the green flame burn inside me, I know I can't hold on to him, letting him wait for what I'll never be able to give. A good man like him deserves happiness, and a willing woman in his bed.

Standing, wrapping my arms around myself, I decide there's nothing for it now but the truth. "Even if I did want you like that, Niran, it wouldn't work." Taking a deep breath, I know I've got to tell him everything, or at least as much as I'm prepared to say. "I was raped by a biker."

"Duke," he states, his mouth twisting in distaste, showing there's nothing wrong with his memory. "Where is the fucker, Saffie? What club does he ride with? I'm going to fuckin' dismember him with my bare hands."

It's the most bikerish expression I've ever heard from him, and I'm not surprised, but I've got to stamp that down. "He's not important." I brush his statement away, not wanting to give him the information that I know he's going to request. The Crazy Wolves would kill him before he got close. While vengeance would taste good, it can't be at the cost of my only friend. I have to offer another explanation. "Because of what happened, I freak at the sight of a cut, at the sound of a motorbike or when I see bikers passing. I'll never get over that, and I can't string you along that I might."

"Saffie, tell me about him." he starts with a growl, his mind still clearly on Duke.

I hold up my hand. "It happened, Niran. Killing him won't sort anything. It won't make me feel better. Please, it's not about him, it's about you and me. Continuing this would be wrong. My fears are too deep seated. Unless you gave up being a biker—"

"I can't do that." The admission's wrenched from him. His soulful eyes full of emotion show me how much being a biker means to him. "I don't know what club Duke was associated with, nor anything about them. All I know is the club I belong to. Saffie, I was a Marine, then I wasn't anymore. I had nowhere to go, a family who wouldn't have welcomed me. All my friends were Marines like myself, and hell, I felt jealous of them still being able to do what I couldn't anymore. I was floundering in civilian life when I met the Devils. They fuckin' saved me, Saffie. Fuck knows where I'd be now if I didn't have them."

"Perhaps they're a crutch you no longer need."

He goes quiet, and I can see him thinking seriously. "I work at the shop that we own, Saffie. Which means I'm like my own boss. How could I exist as a civilian? I tried that, and it didn't work. More than that, the Devils are my family. I can't leave them."

"Not even if you find a woman you love?"

His jaw clenches and he takes a while to respond. "I don't think I could. Leaving the club would destroy me. I wouldn't be the man she fell in love with."

There we have it. I couldn't be with a biker, and he can't be anything but.

"Your telling me this makes me feel it's right that we should call a halt to whatever this is now."

His eyes narrow and he vigorously shakes his head. "You can't fool me, Saffie. You need me. Or at least, someone to lean on. And I'm the only person you have."

"Maybe it's me using you as my crutch." I shrug and wipe an errant tear away. "Niran, I appreciate all that you've done for me, but only I can fix myself. While I may never come to terms with what I've done, I've got to forge a new persona for myself. I came to San Diego to make a fresh start for me and my baby. But now..." I place my hands over my empty stomach and try to summon the strength to go on. "Now, he's not there anymore, and I have to start living for me. If you stay around, propping me up, I'll never know what I might achieve."

"Is me staying extending your misery?"

I think about his words, and partly agree. "It means I'm not having to deal with the pain and perhaps delaying my moving on."

He's quiet, thoughtful. Then at last, he speaks. "Maybe I've been selfish. As Kink would say, I'm fulfilling my own need. My desire to be helpful. I might have been wrong or too damn arrogant thinking this was something I could fix." When he glances at me, I can't tell him he's mistaken. "Me being a biker is the final nail in the coffin, isn't it?"

It's the crux of the matter, so all I can do is nod my head. There's no future for us, probably not even as friends. There's no point in prolonging this.

"I think you should go now, Niran."

He stands. Pacing, he goes to the wall and leans his head against it, then bangs his fist gently on the plaster. "I want more for you, Saffie. I want you out of this shithole of an apartment. I can set you up with a place if you want, and I want to be there beside you." When I make a sound, he turns and holds up his hands. "And my wants don't end there. I'd also want you to meet my family, my friends. And in time, I'd probably ask you to be my old lady."

As firmly as I can, I state, "That's not what *I* want."

He grimaces, takes out his key ring, and once again is handing me back the key it had seemed easier to give him. "Anytime, Saffie. Any fuckin' time, day or night. If you need me, you call. If you want to talk to me, I'll be there on the end of the line."

"I need to not need you." Inside, I'm breaking. Inside, I don't want to be on my own. But as I suspected, he'd mentioned me as an old lady, and as I'm determined never to be property again, I've got to cut all strings. Otherwise, he'll destroy me. "Don't ring, don't check up on me, Niran. If... if I do break and need saving, I promise I'll call you, okay?"

He sounds anguished. "You're asking too much of me."

Not as much as I'm asking of myself. Bowing my head, I wipe the tears away. He waits in silence.

"A month," I suddenly say, as a vision of life without Niran in it flits through my head. It's not a nice picture. "I'll call you in a month, or if I don't, you can ring me. I'll have my head on straighter." *And what? He'll still be a biker, and I'll still be me.*

"One month," he reluctantly agrees. His eyes shutter. "But Saffie, I'll still be a biker." He echoes my thoughts exactly. "Hell, I never thought the day would come when I hate my fuckin' cut. It's part of me, though, every bit as much as my prosthesis. Maybe you're right and it is a crutch, but I'd fall without it."

The hurt in his eyes makes me want to take my words back, but I can't influence how he lives his life, just as he can't force me to accept it.

What does giving us a month help? Nothing will change. I won't get over my total fear of bikers. Sure, Niran's great, but the rest of his brothers? Nothing he can say would reassure me they weren't the same as Duke and the rest of the Crazy Wolves' rejects from civilised society. Niran's the exception, not the rule.

"A month." He states it as if the timeframe is the only reason he'll leave today.

He glances around the room, then goes into the bathroom and collects the few items he'd brought over. Finally, he walks across to me.

"I fuckin' hate this, Saffie. But you're in the driver's seat." Gently, carefully, he leans down, and his lips caress my forehead. When he straightens, he pulls his shoulders back and steps to the door.

"You want to take that?" I call out, spying the sleeping bag he'd forgotten.

He swings back, his eyes going to where I'm pointing, then a half-grin settles on his face.

"Nah, I'm sure you'll find another needy homeless person."

Nothing gets past him, does it?

The small upward curve his parting words had brought to my lips turns downward immediately after he closes the door. The apartment is quiet, and emptier than it was before.

What have I done?

I stand, pacing, with my hands clenching then opening.

What choice have I got?

Niran has no idea how much Duke hurt me. It wasn't one rape, it was constant, horrendous abuse for five long years. I doubt there's enough therapy in the world that could repair me. Duke had completely destroyed my faith in men, and especially those who ride motorcycles.

If Niran had any other occupation, then I'd have held on to him with both hands. But he's a biker, and that's a complete no-no for me.

I couldn't allow myself to be stupid for a second time. Once was enough. *More than fucking enough.*

CHAPTER NINETEEN

Saffie

FIVE YEARS AGO

"When are you going to introduce me to your friends?" I ask, bouncing on my tiptoes, hardly able to contain my happiness as I admire the impressive new ring on my finger when we step out of the courthouse. The diamond flashes almost blindingly in the brilliant summer sunlight. The sight makes me feel excited and light, and not because it had cost a fortune. I had no idea nor cared whether it had or had not, my delight was because it had been chosen by the man at my side and represented my future.

I'd neither expected nor wanted to marry again. When my previous husband had cheated on me, I'd left his sorry ass. With hindsight, I should have known far earlier than I had. The signs had been there, but at the time, blinded by love, I'd missed them. Gradually, though, doubts came into my mind. Were his excuses just a little too smooth? When concerns about him had crept up on me, I'd spoken to my mom. Her only response was to tell me in no uncertain terms that I was expecting too much, and it was obvious Clive was a man in love.

Whatever she said, and she'd said a lot, I couldn't rid myself of my suspicions that Clive was being unfaithful.

When I had the proof in front of my eyes, I wasn't happy to be proved right.

I'm sure my mom had known all along, and I suspected my own dad had been unfaithful, but marriage vows apparently trump all. Even when confronted with concrete evidence that my suspicions had proved correct, she'd told me to be adult about it.

You can't get divorced, Sapphire. Just think of the shame it would bring.

But even if sticking in a relationship built on deceit was expected, I couldn't do it. Not when I realised Mom had been partly right. Clive was indeed a man in love, but with the other woman and not with me.

I'd left, bringing disgrace on our family. As Clive had been quite happy to carry on with the sham, all the blame for the dissolution of our marriage had fallen on me. Divorce in our family wasn't the done thing.

Burned, I wasn't sure I'd trust anyone again, so I set out to prove I could be happy on my own, and had been busy trying to live for me, and not revolving my life around a man. In that I'd been successful. I made friends. I was happy. I grew as a person. For the first time in my life, I no longer needed to be a wife or a daughter, I became me. I was happier for it.

Then Duke entered my life, and I was knocked off my feet. He was everything my ex hadn't been. Charming, and from the start, making it clear he only had eyes for me. He was handsome, tall, a man who obviously worked out. His body was covered in tattoos which I'd found both naughty and at the same time delicious. I was proud to have snagged his attention, aware that other women spared him more than one glance, but it was me he was with. Duke was generous to a fault. I only had to indicate there was something I wanted, and the next day, or sooner, it would be in my hand. As for the sex, it was out of this world. He was so considerate, gentle and loving.

I loved Clive once, I trusted him. I wasn't going to fall into the same trap again. Duke, though, was persistent. While I just wanted to date, he wanted something more permanent.

Still, I held back. Being bitten once, this time I was determined to be shy. I wasn't going to rush into anything.

My parents were rich with old money. Clive had been an investment banker of whom they'd approved, to the extent they couldn't understand why I hadn't been able to overlook the 'little issues' in our marriage. Duke, a man who owned a motorcycle shop, they hated on sight. Maybe it was some kind of delayed rebellious stage, but the more they put obstacles between us, the more they pushed me Duke's way. It was after one particular row with my father, when he declared if I continued to see Duke he'd no longer recognise me as his daughter, that focused my mind. When Duke had next proposed, I'd overcome my own objections to things moving too fast, and I'd accepted.

I was an adult, a grown woman. I could make up my own mind.

As I stand in the sunlight admiring my ring, coming to grips with the thought that once again I'm married, but this time it's to the man of my dreams. Sure, I'd sacrificed my family, but Duke is the one who makes my world turn. I turn to him with a beaming smile. He doesn't disappoint, planting a scorching, possessive kiss on my lips.

I'm his 'little socialite' as he fondly calls me. I think that's sweet. Sure, there's a world of difference in our backgrounds, but that doesn't affect anything between him and me.

Having come from money, I'd been cautious enough, doing my own due diligence until I was certain Duke didn't want anything from me. At the start, I'd been prepared for Duke to make monetary demands, but those demands never came. He would pay for everything, as though determined to show me he was a successful businessman in his own way. Duke was a proud man. I had nothing to worry about him.

Although I'd been burned once by a man who cheated on me, because it was *Duke,* I accepted the many times away and trips out of town as requirements of his business. He needed to source parts, or check on a bargain, or go give advice. Each time he returned, it was with a generous and thoughtful present, proving it was me who'd been on his mind. That he also stayed a number of nights in his own home was logically explained by his garage being full of expensive bikes, and the need for him to watch over them.

It might sound strange now I'm his wife to admit I've never seen his garage or where he lives. At first, because it was a bachelor mess he was too embarrassed to invite me to visit, then it became a project to turn it into the home of my dreams. I can't count the evenings when he'd bring home catalogues, wanting my advice on furniture and fittings to set it up just how I wanted, though the final unveiling was to be a surprise on our wedding day.

Soon, I'll see the home he's designed for me.

It follows that due to his business, Duke has many friends, all of whom seem to own motorcycles, and who take up a lot of his time. I've asked before when I can meet them, but on every occasion, he'd brush me off with kisses and loving, telling me he wanted me all to himself for now. Now that we're married, it seems more imperative I should know everyone important in his life.

"You want to meet my friends, Sapphire?" There's a glint in his eyes as he turns to me, then, raising my hand, admires the wedding band as it sparkles in the light.

"I do." Going on tiptoe, I kiss his cheek. "I'm your wife."

"You are, aren't you, my little socialite. You've given up everything for me."

I have, and I don't regret it. But there was something in his tone that put me on edge, just like your mood can momentarily sour when a cloud moves over the sun. I shake that feeling off. This is the happiest day of my life. What care have I my parents hadn't been there to witness it? I have Duke, he is my future, they're in my past.

Suddenly Duke grins. "As it happens, my friends want to meet you too, Sapphire. In fact, they're throwing us a party."

"A wedding reception?" Over the past few months, I'd lost contact with many of the friends that I had. Arrangements to meet had fallen apart when Duke had been free that same night. Others had taken my parents side and had tried to dissuade me from seeing the man who was so perfect for me. As old friendships had drifted apart, I hadn't thought anyone would have wanted to join us in celebrating our matrimony. That his friends do makes me want to dance on the spot.

"Of sorts," he says, mysteriously, reaching again for my hand and this time curling his fingers around it. "Come on. We'll go to the club, and then I'll show you the home I've made for you." Before he moves, he lowers his head, taking my lips in a scorching kiss. "Only for you, Sapphire. You're mine now."

Oh yes, I'm his, you can bet on it. I'm positively glowing with the emotions his statement brings forth.

In my specially bought pure-white figure-hugging dress that flares from my hips, I walk at his side as we approach his car.

"Gotta get you some bike wear, pretty thing," he says, unlocking the passenger door. "You'll be riding on my bike from now on."

That causes another flare of excitement to go through me, that illicit pleasure Duke had kept to himself up to now. *I'm special, I'm his wife*, I think to myself.

As we drive away, I'm wondering what club he'll take me to. I love to dance, to let down my hair and drink cocktails. I muse they must have arranged a special opening as it's only mid-afternoon. Settling back, I smile. Oh, the lengths this man will go to please me. I've won the jackpot.

I'm slightly surprised as we head out of town and drive into the desert. I've never heard of a club out this way. But what do I know? There's probably some I haven't frequented before now, though I'm sure I've experienced the best in town. Fidgeting, eager to arrive, I sit forward on my seat, looking forward to charming his friends and celebrating the start of our married life. I have no fear of meeting strangers. My parents had me attending their business parties since I was old enough to be polite. I know how to socialise and can hold a conversation with the best of them, having met many people from all walks of life.

When Duke makes a turn, I'm slightly surprised. The steel industrial-type fencing looks ominous, and as we drive on, when it comes into sight, the worn ranch house surrounded by barns and an oversized garage doesn't look particularly hopeful. But the number of motorcycles parked outside makes me realise this must be the right place. As the car pulls up, loud heavy metal music floods out from inside. *Not exactly dance music.* I suppress a pout.

For once, instead of coming around to help me out, Duke just waits in front of the car, casting an impatient look behind him. So, being quite capable and shrugging off the slight, I open my door and step out, almost twisting my ankle as my high heels meet the rough ground. The place where we've parked is the worst in the lot, the pavement only extends so far as where they've parked the motorcycles.

Teetering carefully to Duke's side, I reach for his hand. Instead of taking it, he pushes me in front of him, then steers me with his palm on the small of my back. Little signs that should give me pause, but I think nothing of them.

The doorway looks foreboding, and over the top is a sign, *Crazy Wolves Motorcycle Club.* I grimace, knowing now it's not the type of club I was expecting, and explains why Duke's is the only car in the parking lot. It looks like I'm about to meet bikers, and a lot of them.

Mentally, I shrug. Duke rides a motorcycle, and I already knew all his friends all have bikes, that's why I hadn't been surprised to see them. I'm amused that I expected any different and begin to doubt there'll be a dance floor and cocktails inside. *It's our wedding day,* I remind myself. *His friends want to celebrate with us.* That automatically gives them a place in my book, even if I'd anticipated somewhere very different. *This is my new life. By Duke's side.* I'll draw on all my experience to make sure I don't disappoint him. I know I can cope.

With one hand around my waist, Duke snakes out his other and opens the door, then, with me tight to his front, pushes me inside.

The interior is gloomy, and I can't immediately make much out, except for wall-to-wall leather, and a strong odour of cigarette smoke, stale beer and male sweat. A flicker of doubt makes me wonder just what I've stepped into. *Duke's brought me here. I trust him implicitly. Everything will be alright.*

Focusing on trying not to let my nose wrinkle or outwardly show my disgust, I smile brightly as Duke raises his hand. He must make some kind of signal, as the music is cut off. For a second, there's silence. As my eyes adjust to the level of light, I notice the leather-clad men have turned and are all facing us.

"This is Sapphire," Duke calls out loudly. "She's my ol' lady."

My wait for cries of congratulations is unrewarded. Instead, only one man, wearing a patch that says sergeant-at-arms, steps forward. Expecting a greeting, I'm taken aback when far from offering an outstretched hand or a warm welcome, his eyes roam over me, pausing at my breasts, before heading south, then rising once more to my face. The leer he's sporting makes me feel cheap. I tense, expecting Duke to say something. This isn't respect, it's far from it.

"Nice looking bitch. Gonna share, VP?"

The title VP barely registers. Holding my breath, I wait for Duke to punch the man, but instead he laughs. "Once I've broken her in, maybe." Then he raises his voice. "Got a welcome, brothers, for your new piece of club property?"

Cheers and shouts come from all directions, but these aren't the congratulatory ones I'd anticipated, loaded as they are with lewd suggestions, and accompanied by quite a few rude gestures with men's hands grabbing at the front of their pants. Duke pulls me tighter in front of him, and I lean back against him for protection, then freeze as he ominously announces, "She's mine, for now."

"Duke," I hiss, taking a tight hold on the sides of his shirt. "I don't want to stay." It's an understatement, I want to run for my life.

His hand goes to my head, tangles in my hair and pulls it painfully. When I look up and back at him, it's into a face I don't recognise. With tight lips and a hard voice, he replies, "Oh you're staying, Sapphire. There's no doubt about that. Welcome to your new home."

Letting go of my hair, he pries away my hands and steps to the side. "Who's got my fuckin' cut? I'm naked without it."

A man runs up and hands him a leather vest. When Duke shrugs it on and settles it on his shoulders, it fits him like a glove and turns the man I thought I knew into someone else. Someone who immediately scares me.

"Now let's get this fuckin' party started. Where's that phone?" he calls out.

While the men start flooding to what I now recognise is a bar, the one wearing the sergeant-at-arms patch passes him a device. "Burner," he tells Duke.

My *husband*—God, how many women start regretting their marriage in such a short time?—taps in a number. With the phone to his ear and his eyes pinning me in place, he waits for an answer.

"Ah, Winston." Over the noise I can't hear the other party, but only Duke's side of the conversation. "Yeah, I got who I want. Nice to speak to you, Winston Bartell."

My brow furrows. *That's my dad.* Why is Duke ringing him, and why now, when it's only been two hours since we exchanged vows?

"Yeah. It's Duke Marshall. Sapphire's mine now, you lost, old man. I warned you not to cross me—" He pulls his phone away from his ear, and chuckles. After a moment, he moves it back. "You finished? Yeah, I'll tell you why I'm certain. I've got my ring on her finger. It's all legal… Sure, go ahead, you check it out. She's Sapphire Marshall now… Nah, it's too late. Nothing you can do. You lost your chance… See, you should have made that investment." He barks a laugh. "Cops won't lift a fuckin' finger, she's my *wife*. Don't you get it? I warned you I'd retaliate… Sure, I'll treat her right. She's a great addition to our club-house… Oh, no, I wouldn't do that if I were you. I get one sniff of the cops or any interference and Sapphire will meet with a nasty, fatal accident. And that you can take to the bank and store along with my investment I never had." Another removal of the phone, and this time I can hear my father screaming. "Let's be clear. Sapphire's dead to you now, and you can spend the rest of her life wondering how your little girl's being treated… Oh, you disown her? Like I give a fuck about that… Yeah, this is what I want. You meet my demands, and I'll keep giving you proof of life. Sounds like a fuckin' good deal as long as you keep your end of it."

He ends the call, tosses me a disdainful look, then shouts out, "I need a bitch."

As if it's expected, the men, all holding drinks now, part, and a girl is pushed through. I see fear in her eyes, but she pulls back her shoulders and puts on a tremulous smile. It's about all that she's wearing—apart from a thong, she's naked.

"VP?" her quivering voice asks.

Duke waves down to his groin. "Need you to suck me off, honey, and do your fuckin' best. Show my cunt of a wife how a real girl gets to work."

No, no, no, and no. I've been cheated on before, but not like this. Not right in front of me, or not deliberately. Not by a man so totally oblivious to my feelings. At least my ex had been discreet until I'd been in the wrong place at the wrong time. Duke knows my history. He knows how much this will hurt me.

All this goes through my head in one split second and I've only one thought, to get out of there. I spin on my heels to the door that's still just behind us, only to find another leather-clad body there. A man standing, arms folded, blocking the doorway.

"Entertainment's that way, ma'am," he tells me, mockingly polite, and jerking his head behind me.

"Yeah, Sapphire." Duke's voice, now sounding lazy, makes me reluctantly turn. "Watch and learn."

I do, and immediately regret it. Duke's thrusting his hips, his cock disappearing deep into the clearly reluctant girl's mouth, making her gag and her eyes water. She gasps frantically for air each time he pulls out. I turn away, but the man behind me is there, clasping me tightly. His painful hold on my chin forces my face forward. I close my eyes, wanting to block out the sight.

"Open your fuckin' eyes," Duke snaps. "Take notes as it will be your turn later. If you don't get it right, you'll have to practice on my brothers." He waits for a beat before adding, "*All* of them."

The man holding me in place lowers his lips to my ears and chuckles softly. "Guess you're going to have a sore jaw tonight. And a sore cunt if I've got anything to say about it. The VP's made a good choice, I'll give him that. I wonder if he'll let me take your ass."

Duke overhears, grins and snorts a laugh. "Her face, you fuckin' see that, Brothers?" Then he adjusts his eyes to glare around the room. "She's mine, for now." He shifts his gaze back to me. "You do what I say, Sapphire. You belong to me, you got me? You can't run, there's nowhere for you to go. Even your cunt of a father doesn't want you, and wherever you go, I'll bring you back. You treat me good? Then I'll keep my brothers away. You disobey or disrespect me, and you'll be theirs. *All* of theirs. You fuckin' feel me?"

I feel sick. I'm shaking. I go hot, and cold. *This can't be happening.*

"Answer me!" Duke snaps, then pauses as he thrusts a couple more times, then groans loudly. He pulls out, leaving his cum dripping down the woman's mouth, sighing in satisfaction, then stalks toward me while tucking himself away. He repeats his demand. "You get what I'm saying, little socialite?"

It's the stranger behind me who answers on my behalf. Still having a firm hold of my head, he forces me to nod violently.

Duke snorts, then says sarcastically, "Good girl."

CHAPTER TWENTY

Niran

I fucking hated leaving Saffie, but she was the one calling the shots. I'd known she was starting to depend upon me, her welcome each night when she'd return showed me that. On my part, my feelings toward her hadn't diminished, they had been growing. Was she feeling the same and was that what frightened her? That she was becoming too invested in a biker.

What the fuck had happened to her to make her so scared of bikers, to tar all of us with the same brush? Being raped is an awful crime and not easy to recover from, I'm not dismissing that. I can understand her being wary, not wanting to repeat any mistake she might think she made. But to have such an irrational fear of all members of all clubs suggests I don't know the half of it yet.

As I exit her apartment block, pushing my way past an obvious drug dealer, making his mark jump out of the way and ignoring the prostitute and her pimp exiting her apartment, I make my way to my truck uncaring who I'm upsetting, knowing I'm more than a match for any man in the temper I'm in.

I'm annoyed at myself, not at her. Never at Saffie. My only beef with her was she had come too close to the truth. Yes, I'd harboured hopes that as she recovered, we'd grow closer. While far too soon to make promises, I had been thinking in terms of making her my old lady. I'd entertained dreams of introducing her to my brothers. I'd brushed over that her fears were so deep seated and were something she'd never be able to get over.

She was raped. Terrible, heartbreaking, the thought makes me see red. But why did that taint all men who ride motorcycles?

Hell, if being the type of man who takes women without consent defines bikers, I'd want to pull the cut off my back and shred it myself. *We're not all like that.* I'm not so naïve as not to know there are some clubs which don't treat women with respect, clubs which share their old ladies, or change them like they do underwear. Some keep sex slaves or run prostitution rings.

But that's not the Devils. Even our sweet butts aren't pressed if they're not in the mood.

My rage won't be satisfied until I find this Duke myself and remove him from the land of the living. But I've got to find him first, and that might prove a challenge. Duke can't be an uncommon handle. *I should have asked her where she'd moved from.*

I know why she hadn't given me details; she knew I was set on murder.

It's three in the morning when I arrive back at the compound. Kid's wearily mopping the bar, but there's no one else to be seen.

"Whisky. The bottle," I demand as I approach him.

"How's Saffie?" he inquires, innocently, as he reaches for the bottle behind him. "She doing better?"

"She is," I growl, my tone menacing enough that he doesn't ask for more details. She's so much fucking better she's decided she can do without me. That will get around soon enough, no need for me to enlighten him.

I take the bottle, ignore the offered glass, and make my way up to my bedroom. Passing along the hallway, I hear a moaning coming from one of the rooms. *Sweet butts are still awake and working.*

It makes me realise just how long it's been since I last got laid, and again, Saffie was right. I can wait, would wait a fuck of a long time, but I'd never be able to resign myself to a sexless existence. I'd have banked on that she wouldn't either. But maybe waiting for a day that might not come, or heaven forbid, until she found someone else who could better arouse her, maybe wasn't the best course of action.

I open my door—I never bother to lock it. If I can't trust my brothers, who the fuck could I? I switch on the light and come to a full stop.

There, lying in the middle of my bed, is Cyn. My fucking sister.

"What the fuck?"

The light had made her startle, my roar made her leap up and almost out of the bed. "Niran!" she shouts, delightedly. "You're home."

Ignoring her welcome, I go for the pertinent information. "What the fuck are you doing in my bed?"

I'll be fucked if her bottom lip doesn't tremble, and she wipes at her eyes as if to dab at what to me are invisible tears. "I've missed you, Niran. You're never here. I've been feeling so lonely."

Lonely in a club full of bikers? It suddenly occurs to me that while I think she's got more than adequate company, maybe that's my view and not hers. What has she in common with the men I ride with?

Though I've given time to her in the evenings before I'd gone to see Saffie, I've often left at ten, wanting to make sure her apartment is tidy, and that there was food ready for when she came in.

I've been spending the nights with Saffie, even though not, as others might think, in her bed, while the sister who apparently needs me has been crying in mine. All of a sudden, I feel like an asshole.

Cyn apparently needs me, and while I doubt I have much to give her, maybe now Saffie has sent me away, I should focus my attention on her instead.

"Are you going to ask me to leave?"

Taking it she means from my bed, and not from San Diego, I shake my head. "Nah, you can stay here tonight if you want to."

I sit on the opposite side of the bed to which she's occupying, and shrug out of my jeans, knowing my boxers will preserve my dignity, and start to unstrap my leg. Behind me, the bed dips as Cyn moves over, puts her hand on my shoulder, and leans in to watch.

"Ew. I've never seen your stump before. Does it hurt? It looks disgusting."

Yes, little sister, I'm only too well aware that the scars from the surgery aren't pretty, nor is the redness caused by a long day wearing my prothesis. Grimacing, I reach for my cane, and stand. "It's not meant to be pretty." Turning my back, I hop away to the bathroom where I do what's necessary, before lighting a bedside lamp, turning off the main one, and coming back to bed.

"Shift over," I tell her. "Give me some space."

I'm tired as fuck, upset about Saffie and now worried about Cyn and how she's really doing. Maybe her bravado is all an act, and underneath she's just a frightened child.

One month, Saffie had asked for. Four weeks during which I should give her space. Perhaps instead of moping around, I should use the time positively and focus on Cyn. If I can get her head on straight, there's a chance she could return to her parents and get out of my space.

Sharing my bed with my sister? Hell, I could never have predicted that. While my head knows the warm feminine body beside me is that of my sibling, I'm worried as fuck that in my sleep, my hands might wander. Anchoring them under my head,

I force myself to stay still. Each time I drop off, I wake, disturbed by the presence of another person, when normally I sleep by myself, or with a woman I am allowed to snuggle with.

When daylight finally breaks the tortuous night, Cyn isn't impressed.

"You toss and turn a lot. And you snore."

Do I? I've never heard myself. Still, my restless night is easily explained by everything I've got on my mind. Despite my promise to give Saffie time, she's the first thing I think of as I wake this morning. *Is she okay? Is she eating? Did she sleep?* I just fucking hope those bastards living in the other apartments or hanging around waiting to score hadn't bothered her.

I don't apologise for Cyn's disturbed sleep. "You've got your own room, Cyn."

Ignoring my response, she grins at me. "It's a lovely day. Will you take me out on your bike, Niran? Please?" She flutters her eyelids as she begs.

Is it wrong I really don't want her there? The only arms I want around me are those which right now, wouldn't give me the time of day. "I've got to work, Cyn. And so have you," I remind her. When she grimaces, I raise an eyebrow. "I thought you like working for Salem?"

"Salem's fine," she admits grumpily, then raises wide eyes to mine. "But Kid's there today, and he gives me the creeps."

Bristling, I question her further, my voice deep and growling. "He upset you?"

She shrugs. "He makes me feel uneasy."

I'll have words with the fucking prospect later. As my sister, Cyn's higher in the pecking order than a darn prospect who can be sent away, but I need to know more about what I'm dealing with. "In what way, Cyn?"

She gives another rise and lower of her shoulders. "He just does."

Has he made a move on her? Fucking prospect should know

she's out of bounds. For now and forever. Even if he was patched in, she's another member's sister.

Adding talking to him to my mental list of things to do, I go into the bathroom. When I come out, Cyn's disappeared. To get dressed I expect, in her own room.

My mind keeps whirling. She was in my bed. *For company or protection?* Had she been scared fucking Kid would go to hers?

By the time I've put on my prothesis, a clean pair of jeans and a fresh t-shirt, I'm in a foul mood. My brain's in a mess about something I can do nothing about, so I'm channelling my anger into something I can. Getting more enraged by the second, I stomp down the stairs as I search for my target, my eyes zooming in when I find him.

"Prospect!" I yell, then have to send waves of stand down toward Connor and Curtis, and even Wrangler who'd jumped at the tone of my voice.

I point to my eyes, then to Kid. "You and me, Kid. Outside now."

Kid's expression is almost comical. He swallows hard, making his Adam's apple bob. With a stiff posture but a steady gait, he goes to the door of the clubhouse and exits. I follow straight after.

Grabbing his shoulder, I swing him around and plant my fist in his face.

"What the fuck, Niran?" Dart's voice sounds behind me, as ruefully, Kid rubs his jaw.

I toss a reply to the VP over my shoulder. "Prospect's been making my sister uncomfortable, and I fuckin' want to know why."

"That true, Kid?" Dart growls as he comes up alongside me.

The prospect's eyes are wild, flicking from me to Dart, and then back again. Another rapid swallow, then he opens his mouth. "I don't know what you're talking about."

"You don't, huh?" As my fist clenches, Dart's hand steadies my arm. I give him a sharp look, but recognising his warning, continue to use words. For now. "Cyn came to my room last night as she was too frightened to stay in hers. Was that because you threatened to fuckin' visit?"

Loudly, Dart sucks in air and again, but this time more forcibly asks, "Is this true, Prospect?"

Kid holds his hands in a gesture of surrender and cries out, "No, I swear it's not. I don't know what you're talking about. I only spoke to her for a moment."

Taking a step closer, I crowd him. "What did you fuckin' say to her?"

He looks past me to Dart, then his worried eyes come back to my face. He slumps in front of me as he admits, "I told her she needs to have some fuckin' self-respect. She came on to me, man, not the other way around."

She wouldn't do that. She might be naïve as fuck, innocent for all that she'd lived with that fucker Hester, but she wouldn't make a move on a member of the club.

"You fuckin' liar." I advance on him.

"Niran?" an anxious voice calls out, and Curtis, brave that he is, comes running up and steps between us. Prospect he may be, but like me, he'd been in the Marines. Showing that backbone that he needed to serve, he places one hand on my chest and pushes firmly, keeping in position between me and Kid.

"I was fuckin' there," he says, his voice full of scorn. "Kid's right. She was flirting with him all night, trying to get him to give her a drink, then inviting him up to her room. Sounds to me like she had second thoughts and might have gotten worried he'd take her up on the offer. Kid did nothing to encourage her."

"I wouldn't, Niran." Now Kid speaks for himself. "Even if I wasn't after my patch, I wouldn't go after a bitch like her."

"Why the fuck not?" I find myself asking. "'Cos she's Black?"

Curtis snorts and at the same time Kid's eyes go wide.

"Because she's too fuckin' young—maybe not by the calendar, but fuck, Niran, hate saying this seeing as she's your sister, but that girl would be hard work."

"Man's got a point, Niran," Dart exclaims by my side.

Turning, I shoot him a look, still undecided as to who to believe. My sister, or the prospects. If she'd accused another member who'd already proved his loyalty to the club, I wouldn't have hesitated for a moment. But these aren't yet members. They both still need to earn our trust.

It's hard to discount the word of Curtis, he'll soon be patched in, and has proved his worth. But Kid? He's too new and yet has to show his true colours.

And my problem is, if I believe him, and not her, it doesn't bode well for her continuing to stay at the club. Pitting brother against brother, or even brother against prospect, isn't going to go down well.

As Dart confirms with his next words. "A word, Brother?" When he jerks his head, I follow him a discreet distance away. He leans in and speaks quietly. "Kid's got one thing right. Cyn's been hard work. I know you've been tied up with Saffie, but that's left her running wild around the club. I believe Kid, I'm afraid. I think she's trying to stir up trouble."

Pinching the brow of my nose, I take in a deep breath, wait for a second, then breathe it out. As I do, some of my rage and bad temper leaves me. "Why, Dart?"

I don't expect him to have an answer, but he does. "Because she wants your undivided attention, which you can't give, spending half your time at work, and the nights with your woman."

I have an immense amount of respect for Dart. It was he who'd originally approached me three years back, and it was his suggestion I should join the Devils. At the time, I'd been wary of joining what was clearly an all-White club, but he'd read the situation correctly, and knew the brothers wouldn't give a damn about the colour of my skin. I have tremendous respect for his judgement. Which leads me to wonder, is he right, now? I grimace, knowing I have to at least give his theory merit.

"You know what will happen if she does anything like this again, don't you?" He poses it as a question, but I hear the unspoken threat within.

I nod, knowing only too well. No woman, family or not, can cause trouble amongst the members. Or prospective ones, come to that.

She's apparently made an unfounded accusation. Surely, she knew I wouldn't leave it like that? I'd already punched Kid, for fuck's sake, and was prepared to do far worse to him.

Damn it!

"I'll speak to her, Dart." I start to turn away, then turn back. "For your information, I'll be here more now. Saffie and I have decided to cool things for a while. Kid?" I call out to the prospect, gaining his wary attention. Nodding my head toward his face, I instruct, "Best get some ice on that."

His sharp look is penetrating, but I don't give him more. Instead, I stomp my way back into the clubhouse, roaring Cyn's name.

"She left a while back with Salem," Snips informs me. His head tilts. "Problems?"

I don't waste my breath explaining, just turn on my heel and stride through the clubhouse, exiting through the kitchen and taking the fastest route to the second hangar where Salem has his customisation business.

Sure enough, Cyn's seated at the front desk. She's shuffling paperwork. Hearing me approach, she looks up.

Placing my hands on the desk, I loom over her. "Never, ever, fuckin' lie to me again."

She rears back, and her eyes go wide and innocent.

So close I know she can feel my heated breath on her face, I expand, "I've spoken to Kid. It was all you, not him."

"He's the liar," she fires back, her cheeks reddening.

"Got a witness that says otherwise, Cyn."

"You believe the prospects more than your sister?" Her wide-eyed look of pretend innocence doesn't fool me at all.

Rolling my eyes when she all but admits she knew Curtis was there by her use of the plural, I tell her through gritted teeth, knowing now that I'm convinced and I mean it, "Yes."

Her mouth snaps shut, she looks down, then to the side, anywhere it seems rather than to meet my eyes. Then she shrugs. "Maybe I misunderstood what he was saying."

Just like that my rage is back with a vengeance. "You're fuckin' lucky you're not packing your bags this morning. That shit won't fly here, darlin'. You got that?"

"Niran, I…" Her voice trails off.

Salem appears from the back. "You ordered those parts yet, Cyn?" He gives me a chin lift then narrows his eyes. "What the fuck is going on?"

Shaking my head, my accusing gaze still on my sister, I give him an honest reply. "I don't have a fuckin' clue, Brother. But you keep an eye on her. She's fuckin' trouble."

I need to get out of here. Need to think on this shit. Think about what more Cyn expects from me. Do I owe her? Fuck no. I should I get her to pack up and leave.

Difficult? Mom didn't tell me the half of it.

I'm not cut out to be a blood brother. And, after Saffie's dismissal last night, I'm not qualified to be a friend.

CHAPTER TWENTY-ONE

Niran

Time drags when you want it to pass. Like when you're a kid waiting for Christmas which never seems to speed up and come. Four weeks feels like a fucking long time.

For the first few days, I'm hopeful Saffie will come around. Then I start accepting this time apart will only give her space to do what she needed to do, to come to terms with the tragedy that had happened to her, for her to learn how to wear the cloak of her sadness without it overwhelming her. By finding herself on her own, she might be learning how to cope. If I give her some time, she might accept me back in her life.

My missing leg will never heal, I still use a crutch from time to time. Saffie, though, she can mend and not need to be propped up anymore. While I would have stood beside her, there was too much between us that was wrong. And for her, already trying to deal with her grief, the differences were insurmountable.

On the other hand, leaving her alone might not make her miss me, it may only make her more determined to cut me out of her life. As time goes on, it's this latter premise I settle on, and I start to have no expectation I'll be hearing from her when the month is up.

I miss her more than I expected. My life which seemed so perfect before isn't anymore. My brothers who once were my everything, can't completely fill the hole that she left. But it's all I have, because, if as I suspect, the weeks will pass with no contact from her, I'll know her decision without having to ask her. *I'll have no place in her life.*

It's a bitter pill to swallow. She'd come to mean more to me than I'd anticipated.

I could wallow in misery, or, in preparation for the worst, throw myself back into the world that stops me from being a part of hers.

To that end, and no longer with a reason to be distracted, I look to deal with my other problem, Cyn.

After the stunt she pulled with Kid, I placed a call home. It wasn't fair on my brothers for her to stay longer.

Instead of Mom, I got Grover. It was, to say the least, a strange phone call.

"It's Niran. Mom there?"

"I'd like to talk to you myself, Niran." There's the sound of footsteps as though he's moving to another room. My suspicion is confirmed when I hear a door firmly being closed. "How are you doing? You still with the club?"

Pulling my phone away from my ear, I stare at it in consternation. Not knowing how else to respond, I say simply, "Yeah."

He chuckles. "I've known all along, Niran. For your mother's sake, I've kept eyes on you. I kind of know why you hid it from us, and your mom still doesn't have a clue. But, Niran, I'm ex-Army. One or two of my cohorts did the same as you—joined clubs when they got back."

You could have knocked me down with a fucking feather. "And you still sent Cyn to me, knowing my life?"

"Could have done worse." He sounds unrepentant. *"You know Peg? He's in Tucson."* I've heard of the man, and I tell him so. *"Yeah, well, one of my friends who stayed in longer, he was in the same unit as Ron Rinter as he was known then. Was impressed as fuck with the man and kept up with him. He's assured me the Satan's Devils are an okay club."*

So blown away that he knows, and that he has no issue with it, it takes me a moment to remember the reason why I called. *"Cyn's stirring up trouble, Grover. She needs to go home."*

Another laugh, but this time there's no mirth in it. *"Rather she didn't do that. Her, your mother, well, just let's say, her mother and I don't see eye to eye on some things."*

"Like what?" I tense at the suggestion there are issues in their marriage.

"Like whether Cyn should get back with Hester again."

What the fuck? *"You want her to go back to that abusive fucker?"*

"No, no," he refutes fast. *"But your mom's not quite of the same opinion."*

"Why the fuck would she even consider that?"

There's quiet for a moment, then, *"It's complicated, Son."*

Once again, I move the phone from my ear and shake my head in confusion. It's the first time in my life and far too late he's indicated any relationship other than duty between us. I get suspicious why he's now claiming it.

"Complicated is what's at my end," I rasp at him when I next speak.

"Please, Niran. Keep her with you a while longer. Until I can make sure Hester's staying away."

Flabbergasted by several elements of the call, still not understanding why in his view, Cyn's in the best place, after a few more unsatisfactory exchanges, I find myself reluctantly agreeing.

Seeing as I'm stuck with her for the present, I determine to make the best of it. To that end, I've worked hard at cultivating a better relationship with Cyn. I've given her my time, both in the evenings and during the days at weekends. She's never come to my room again, nor made any more accusations against any of my brothers or prospects.

I've taken her to the world-famous zoo in San Diego, spent a day with her at SeaWorld, driven across the Coronado Bridge, and had actually enjoyed being a tourist for a while as together we explored the Old Town and sought out new restaurants to try. I find out much about her, though not anything of importance. She likes creatures with fur, not so much those with scales and has a particular dislike for snakes. She loves ice cream and stuffing her face with junk food like hotdogs and burgers. She gasped when the view we had from Coronado showed the planes picking their way through the skyscrapers, and she giggled like an excited child when we watched the seals lazily basking on the beach at La Jolla. To my surprise, seeing old sights through her fresh eyes, our outings didn't prove too much of a chore, even if I kept wishing it were another woman by my side.

The only blight in the new relationship between us is that the one thing I haven't done is have her ride on my bike. Even when the club had a beach barbeque, she'd gone in the truck with the club girls when I'd resorted to using the excuse that with a prosthetic leg, I was worried her extra weight might unbalance the bike. I don't think she accepted it, but to her credit, she didn't complain too much.

Have I developed a love for my sister? The stark truth I have to admit is that I have not. I've come to a begrudging acceptance of her, and while I acknowledge the blood relationship, she wouldn't be my friend out of choice. Our views are often one hundred and eighty degrees apart. For instance, however much I try to talk to her, she still believes she was the victim when Grover chased her boyfriend off.

"Hey, Cyn. Can you give us a moment? I want to talk to your brother."

Looking up at Kink, Cyn pouts, waiting for me to tell her she can stay, but when I keep my mouth shut, she gets up and walks off in a huff.

Kink's eyes follow her as she reaches the bar, then turns to me. "She's cramping your style, Brother."

I snort. "You noticed?"

"Yeah. Pretty damn obvious when you're spending every moment with her. Don't you think it's time she went home?"

"I'm working on it," I tell him. And I am. Trouble is, Cyn's spun Grover and Mom a cock and bull story about having a great job and how she's paying her way. Only fifty percent of that is correct, but she's got them fooled. Mom's over the moon thinking she's taken responsibility for herself at last, and even congratulated me on the good job I was doing. Despite what Grover had said, she'd seemed in no hurry for her to get on a plane and return to Michigan. It seemed at odds with what Grover had been saying. I made a mental note to try to speak to him again soon.

"When was the last time you got your dick wet?"

Through lowered eyelashes, I raise my gaze. "What dick? Darn thing probably fell off."

It's his turn to snort. Lifting a hand, he signals to the bar, holding up two fingers. The prospect comes across, rather cautiously.

"Thanks," I tell Kid, as he places my beer down. I've gone out of my way to go easy on him since I'd punched him for no reason.

Kid shrugs my thanks off, and sidles away again.

"He's a good kid," Kink observes, staring after him.

"Fuckin' know that." And for putting that doubt in my head, I've still not quite forgiven Cyn.

Kink raises his beer, swallows a few times, then puts it down. "You heard anything from Saffie? Your month's almost up, isn't it?"

My mouth twists. "It is. But I'm thinking I'll leave it there. If she wants me, she's got my number. She can get in touch." I know she's still in the land of the living. I've had Curtis go to the store where she works a few times, minus his cut, of course. When he reported he'd gotten a smile out of her, I knew she was on the mend.

"Yeah. She had a real thing about bikers." Kink knows, this isn't the first time we've had a chat. Those early days after she first banished me, he'd caught me off guard and extracted exactly what had gone down. A bottle of whisky may have been involved at the time.

But there was no reason to keep that a secret. When I'd returned from that final visit to Saffie, I came back vowing to move heaven and earth until I found the man who was responsible for stifling a relationship between us before it started.

None of my brothers like that she'd been raped, by anyone, let alone a biker.

Of course, I'd involved Token, but looking for a biker named Duke was like searching the proverbial haystack and turning up pins galore without knowing which was the right one. Still, he'd kept his searches going, looking for reports on bikers gone rogue, or any named Duke that had a connection to a woman named Saffie. A big stumbling block was that she'd never filed a rape report.

Kink frowns. "I'm sorry, Niran. I know you liked her—" He breaks off, then continues with, "Hey, what's she up to now?" He's got an amused grin on his face.

I turn to see where he's looking. Cyn's standing with the club girls, her hands on her hips, she's clearly remonstrating with them.

"Think she's applying for a job?" he asks with a wink.

I emit a growl. *Fuck me.* I wouldn't put it past her. Abruptly, I stand and go across just in time to hear Cindy round on her.

"Have some fuckin' self-respect, girl."

Cyn's eyes are blazing, and a job interview is certainly not what I've interrupted, to my utmost relief. "You fuck the men. You let them do anything to you. Right here in the clubhouse. I've seen you."

What the hell's she talking about? She can't tell the girls what to do. I open my mouth to draw attention to my presence, but Pearl gets in first.

"Sure, Cyn. I fuck anyone and anybody. Man after man, I'm happy for them to use me. Why? Because I get pleasure in return. What I'd never allow is a man to hit me." She flicks her long curly hair over her shoulders as though making a point.

"I didn't allow him too," Cyn cries out.

"You didn't fuckin' stop him." Tits gets in on the act now. "And here you are, telling us how wonderful a boyfriend you've got, and how you're going to get back with him."

Oh no, she's not. It says something when whores have more self-respect than my sister.

"Yeah, get lost, Cyn." Eva leans toward her. "You think you can upset us by telling us you've got a boyfriend which none of us have?" She waves her hand around her. "We've got more than enough cock to satisfy us, sweetheart. And right now, it seems you have none."

"Okay, okay," I step in, getting between my sister and the girls. "Cyn, it's late. Go to bed."

"I'm not a fucking child."

Taking her arm, I pull her away from the group. "What have I told you about causing trouble in the club?" I snarl. "I'd think very carefully if I were you, Cyn. And for the record, you haven't a fuckin' boyfriend. That fucker's long gone."

She looks like the cat that got the cream when she retorts, "That's where you're wrong. He's been calling me."

He what? First thing I'd done was replaced her phone.

"Who the fuck gave him your number?"

Her face reddens, but her mouth stays shut. Assuming she'd memorised his number, I move on. "Does he know where you are? Is he coming for you?" I half hope he is.

She rolls her eyes. "Duh, no. You'd kill him."

At least she's got that right. "Keep it that way, Cyn. And next time he calls you, tell him to get fuckin' lost, you hear me?"

She huffs. "You think you're such an example to look up to. I know what you did to *her*." Her pointing finger leads my eye in another direction.

Fuck me, it's Susie. *Cyn's been talking to her?*

"What's that c—woman been telling you?" My eyes narrow as they land back on my sister.

"That you fucked her and promised she'd be your old lady, then you turned your back and walked away. You broke her heart, Niran."

"Hell, Cyn. I never said anything to her about being my old lady. She knew the score. And for your information, I was drunk as fuck and barely remember it." I know I never made any commitment. Drunk or sober, my recall would be perfect on that. Those are words you don't utter, or even think lightly.

"You used her," she accuses. "She thought she was going to be yours."

Hell, I wish I could remember what drove me to take her to bed. "She's sorely mistaken if she thought that would be the outcome."

Cyn's eyes watch me accusingly. "So, big brother. You're not so perfect, are you? Get a woman's hopes up and then ignore her."

That wasn't the way of it, but instead of arguing further, I decide to let it go. Throwing up my hands, acknowledging there's no reasoning with my sister, I stomp off in Salem's direction.

He swings around when I approach him. "What's up?"

"Fuckin' Susie. Telling sob stories to Cyn who believes them. She's put it in her head I promised she'd be my old lady."

Salem's eyes become slits. "She's not even a particularly good fuck, Brother. Wouldn't be any hardship to lose her. I'll give her her marching orders if you want."

I raise my chin. Yeah, that's exactly what I want. She's only a hangaround here. While Cyn got a pass after causing trouble, it's because she's my sister. Susie's here on sufferance, and once banned will stay gone.

Salem gives me a return chin lift. "Leave it with me, Brother. I'll get her out of your hair."

I toss him a sharp grateful nod, knowing it would have done no good for me to approach Susie myself. As enforcer, Salem can impress on her that her face is no longer welcome here.

He doesn't waste time. Even above the music, I can hear the indignant screech, followed by a slap. Turning fast, I see Salem rubbing his cheek, then Susie being dragged out by Pennywise and Bones. Luckily, they got her away. If Salem had chosen to hit back, she'd have been laid out on the floor.

He comes back to me, his hand still scrubbing the reddening mark. "She's fuckin' lucky I don't hit bitches. Bitch thought she had a right to be here. I told her otherwise, Niran."

"Sorry, Brother."

He shrugs. "Comes with the territory of being the enforcer. Next time, though, Niran, can you get a male to have you in your sights? Then I can hit back." He grins.

"Ain't turning gay for you or anyone." My own lips curve.

Loud kissing sounds come from behind, and Dusty's tattooed arms come around me. "Not even for me?" He purses his lips and smacks them again loudly.

"Get the fuck off," I reply, with a laugh. Then when he hangs on, I brace my arms, then flex and break his hold. "Fuckin' comedian."

But his antics have brightened my mood, reminding me that I'm among brothers, who'll have my back when I need them to, and pick me up when I fall.

It's just a fucking pity Saffie couldn't comprehend what we really stand for.

It's only later, as I make myself ready for bed, I realise I'd gotten distracted and had never asked Cyn why her ex, to my mind, boyfriend in hers, was contacting her? I'll have to find out.

But by the next morning, it doesn't seem urgent. I get up, dress, go to work. I've got my head under the hood of a Mustang, concentrating on a tricky job, when a voice makes me jump so hard, I bang my head when I stand up.

"What the fuck?" Grumbler laughs, and expertly dodges my playful fist. "Whatcha want?" I snarl, a little ungraciously, rubbing my scalp.

"Hey, just wanted to give you an update." He passes a sonogram picture across. "Mary had another ultrasound yesterday. All's going well."

Taking it, I examine it, comparing it to the memory of that time weeks ago when I saw the baby on the screen for myself. It's certainly grown and is looking more like a recognisable baby now. It's even sucking its thumb. Cute little thing.

I grin as I hand it back. "I've been meaning to talk to you, Brother. Something I noticed when I went to the hospital with Mary, and that," I point to the picture he's holding, "confirms it now." I force myself to look serious. "Hate to tell you, ol' man, but I don't think that kid is yours."

His eyes go wide. His brow furrows. Then he growls, "What the actual fuck are you talking about?"

Raising and lowering my shoulders, then bringing them level once more, I shake my head. "Look at the sonogram, Grumbler.

That darn kid has no tattoos. No way can it be the fruit of your loins."

Grumbler blinks, then launches forward. "Ass!" He holds up his fists. I go to block him, and we trade a few playful shots.

By the time we finish dancing around each other, he snorts, barely holding back his laughter. "Guess you need to learn some facts of life. Tattoos aren't fuckin' genetic."

Again, I shrug, but try hard to keep the grin off my face. "Giving the amount you've got, I kinda expected some of the ink to seep through."

"Jeez." Beside us, Ross snorts. "Ain't that a thought? A baby Grumbler being born, complete with tats."

"Would save a shitload of money," Gibbs, also having entered, agrees. "And put Blaze out of a job."

Ross, with one hand rubbing the stump where his prosthesis attaches to his other arm, furrows his brow. "Imagine if that was a thing. What if the kid hated the tats they're born with?"

"Be like having an ugly birthmark," Gibbs replies. "And would they be miniature like, and grow with the kid? Or stretch out of proportion?"

Grumbler and I just glance at each other, then we both crack up. It wasn't that funny, but both of us are able to use that moment of light relief. When at last we can look at each other without laughing, he slaps Ross on his back, and toward me, jerks his head.

I follow him into the office, noting he closes the door, indicating this is personal or he wants words about the club.

He doesn't keep me waiting. "You still not heard from Saffie? Mary always asks about her. She'd like to know how she's doing." His mouth twists, probably because Saffie's circumstances hit too close to home, and aren't far removed from what they could be facing.

"That ship's sailed, Brother. I doubt I'll hear from her again."

I shrug, then admit, "It's a shame Mary met her. Must have put thoughts in her head."

"It fuckin' did." His tone makes me brace myself, but then his tight jaw relaxes. "My ol' lady's stubborn as a fuckin' mule, as well as pragmatic. She and I both know what might be coming without any reminder, though all the tests look positive so far. Hope to fuck it doesn't of course, but we're as prepared as we can be." He pauses a moment. "Mary's concerned as she's got more than her fair share of compassion. She's gutted that girl is dealing with everything on her own." He closes his eyes momentarily. "You don't get over ending a pregnancy in a minute. Mary understands that only too well. If it happens to us, we've got each other for support. Saffie's got no one. It's been all I can do to stop her driving over to see her."

"Saffie made her decision, Grumbler. She wants nothing to do with me or the club. Hate to say this but tell Mary visiting won't help her. It might make things worse."

Grumbler grimaces. "That's what I thought. Saffie's clearly had some dealings with an MC, dealings that didn't settle with her. I told Mary she could do more harm than good. Saffie knows I'm her old man and an MC member."

I raise and dip my head. "That's why I'm abiding by her wishes. I can't leave the club."

Grumbler's stare and shake of his head shows he's surprised I'd even consider it.

"She was raped, Grumbler." He already knows it. "What I don't know is if it was by one, or a number of members."

"Jesus," Grumbler breathes out. "If more than one was involved, no wonder she doesn't like bikers." He picks up some paperwork, preparing to get back to work, but has time to add, "That poor little girl."

To me, Saffie's all woman, to him, she's young enough to be his daughter and then some.

"I'll get back to the Mustang." I'm turning to go when Grumbler suddenly barks a laugh.

"What now?"

"Just had an idea brother. I'm gonna get me some fake tattoos and stick them on the baby once it's born. Bring him in to see Ross and Gibbs' faces."

"Yeah?" I raise an amused eyebrow. "Whatcha think Mary's going to say about that?"

His mirth disappears immediately. Guess he hadn't thought that far. Grumbler might be our sergeant-at-arms, but behind closed doors, he's putty in his old lady's hands.

I get back to work, fighting with screws that don't want to be turned, and bolts which have fused in their casings. I'm deep in concentration when, for the second time this morning, I'm interrupted. This time it's the vibration of my phone alerting me I've received a message. Dismissing it as unimportant and can probably wait, I ignore it.

Only a few minutes later, I hear my name.

"Niran?"

Sighing, I pull my head from under the hood again. "Whatcha want, ol' man?"

Grumbler's standing right in front of me. "For you to fuckin' read your text. Prez has called both of us in for a meeting."

That does come under the heading of important. Within seconds, I'm wiping oil off my hands, and questioning the sergeant-at-arms with my eyes. As he shakes his head, I realise he knows nothing. Only pausing to take off our overalls and to instruct Snips that he's now in charge, we head out to our rides.

The parking lot at the clubhouse is relatively empty, only a few bikes occupying spaces; Lost's and the VP's, Bone's, Token's and Brakes'. The latter is understandable, he runs our strip club, and works late into the night. Apart from the members we left at the auto-shop, I know Salem and Pennywise will be working next door in the recently renovated hangar doing their customisation work. Blaze will be at the tattoo parlour, Deuce setting up the bar for tonight, and Keeper will be at our motorcycle apparel shop. All the rest will be dotted around our businesses. Bones' presence is explained as he has his office here and will be working through our books.

I'm in the lead as we enter, wondering why Grumbler and I have been called back. Lost doesn't interrupt a workday unless it's important.

Lost's door is open. Taking it as an invitation I walk straight in, noting the presence of both the VP and the computer expert. Extra chairs have been brought in, so at a wave from the prez, I take a seat.

"You took your fuckin' time." Dart's infectious smile takes the sting out of his words.

Grumbler just harrumphs, ignores him, and turns his attention to Lost. "What do you want, Prez?"

Lost's eyes are on me, and I get the feeling whatever this is, I'm in the thick of it. *What the fuck has Cyn done now?* He waits for a beat before speaking. When he does, he waves to the man seated next to the VP. "Toke brought something to me just now. Seems the searches he set into motion a while back, searches initiated by you, Niran, triggered some red flags."

Immediately, I sit straighter. Red flags can only mean one thing. And recently there's only been one piece of information that I asked Token for. *Duke.* Full of anticipation, I sit forward eagerly. "You found Duke? You got the man who raped Saffie?" My fists clench and my breathing speeds up as I imagine getting revenge for her.

"Nah, the hits I got were on Saffie."

Saffie?

Now noticing the look of concern on his face, my gut starts to churn. Damn it. Have I made this woman's life worse just by asking about her? She's the innocent, isn't she? Who could be looking for her?

"Saffie?" I ask, my gut clenching at his firm confirmatory nod. "What flags?" I follow up with tightly.

Prez waves his hand. "Back track. Remind me again what you know about Saffie Jones, how you came across her, and what the fuck made you involve us? And Grumbler, before you ask why you're here, Token tells me Mary was in the thick of it too."

Grumbler jerks, growls, and asks, his voice full of concern, "She in trouble that could fall on my old lady?"

"That's what we're here to find out, Brother," the VP replies reasonably.

As Grumbler shoots a death glare at me that would have any other man quaking, his unspoken words threatening unmistakeably, *if you've put my old lady in danger, I'm gutting you,* I clear my throat and begin speaking.

"I think you've heard what little I know already." I brush my fingers down my face. "Saffie was raped by a biker. She relocated to San Diego to bring up her baby. Unfortunately, that didn't go as planned. I tried to get close to her, but her fear of bikers is deep seated. All I know of the man who raped her is that his handle is Duke. And that's about all I can tell you."

Lost's face is full of sympathy, and Token thumps his fist on the desktop.

"Fuck," Lost breathes out, exchanging a glance with his VP. "I had hoped you'd know more." He sits forward. "Token?"

"Yeah. Well, you know I was digging for info about a man called Duke and his links to Saffie Jones. Well, I kept those searches running in case anything else turned up. Forgot all about them if I'm honest. Woke up this morning and had two enquiries. One was an offer for information as to the whereabouts of one Sapphire Marshall with money attached. The other was from one of our brothers in Utah who asked what the fuck I thought I was doing."

Utah? I shake my head. As for the other puzzling thing, I state, "I know fuck all about any Sapphire Marshall."

"Saffie could be a shortening of Sapphire," Dart suggests. *Could it?*

"People on the run often use names similar to their true ones as its less hard for them to fuck up." Lost gives the information knowingly. Patsy, his wife, initially came to San Diego under witness protection, so he speaks from experience.

Token raises his chin. "Saffie's not been in San Diego long, we know that. It sounds to me like she might have changed her name to get her rapist off her trail, but more than that, assumed a new identity as well. It was a fuckin' good job. All her back history checked out as genuine. I never had any doubts about it."

It takes a second for my brain to compute what he's suggesting. Could Saffie be on the run? That might explain why she has no one to turn to. But that makes the suggestion anyone is trying to track her down extremely worrying. "Who was the fucker offering the money to find her?"

Token grimaces. "No fuckin' idea, Brother. Anonymous contact."

Lost taps the desk. "And leaving that aside, what we should be asking is why Utah's got their panties in knots about us seeking info on her."

Token snorts. "Other than the feds, Utah's the only people I know who could construct a background which would stand up. I've got a gut feel they might have had a hand in moving her."

"You made contact?" Grumbler asks Prez.

"No." Lost shakes his head. "I wanted to know more on what we knew about her before I spoke to them. You know they sometimes work on government shit, and I wasn't willing to give her up if we didn't need to."

"From what I've heard, the last thing that woman wants is the fuckin' law on her back," the VP says furiously. "She's got enough to deal with as it is. I don't give a shit what she might have done."

"I tend to agree," Prez states, then his eyes meet Grumbler's. "Which is why I like to know what I'm dealing with before diving in."

It's a good reminder of how Lost works. He never does shit on impulse and always thinks first. Sometimes his level of planning drives us crazy, but it has saved our asses before.

But Utah knows something, and I want to get a hold on what. "I want to find out what info they have on her." I fix my eyes on Prez. That she might have the law or other trouble after her could mean she needs my protection even more. "She's scared of MCs. I don't think *she* has done anything wrong, but it is possible that the law might want her to testify or some such shit. Did she report her rape? Have they now found her rapist?" I know Token hadn't found anything under the name we knew, but now we know that's a fake one.

"She wasn't moved by the feds," Token stresses. "Else they'd know where to find her for her day in court."

I doubt Saffie would want to face this Duke, not even across a courtroom. Not that she'd have the chance, as soon as I've eyes on the fucker, he's dead. Even locked up, I'd find a way.

"Makes sense Utah's involved with getting her relocated," Dart states. "And why else would they make contact?"

Nodding, Lost takes the phone Token's holding out to him, and places it on the table. "Guess it's time we find out."

"Prez." I raise my hand, wiggling it frantically, making him pause from tapping in the number. "Don't give her away. Not even to Utah."

He shoots me a *who the fuck do you think I am?* look, then continues entering the digits.

Yeah, he'll be cautious. He's using a burner phone for a start, one that Token must have ensured is clean and can't be traced or hacked into. Utah will soon know who he is and already know where we are, but not any other fucker. The alien number does mean the recipient doesn't recognise the caller.

"Yeah?" a gruff, cautious, voice answers.

I've only met two of Utah's members, Swift, their brother without a dick as we often refer to her, and Bolt, who's got the most amazing prosthetic hand I've ever seen in my life and, as a fellow amputee, one which I'm jealous of. As such, I don't recognise who's picked up, but would place a bet this is a chat Prez to Prez.

"Lost here."

"Lost, Brother. I've been waiting for you to get in touch. Seems that your man Token has touched on a nerve."

With his eyes focused on me, Lost states, "Don't understand how, Snatcher."

"Hang on. Let me get Stormy in here. He's the one dealing with this."

Stormy? Hell, the last time his name was mentioned at church it was during discussions about whether we should kill him on sight. I'd heard he'd wrangled his way back into Utah's good books, even getting the mother chapter prez, Drummer, to wipe the slate clean. A slate that had gotten very dirty in San Diego, when Stormy had taken the kill shot that should have been Lost's, and which had erased an opportunity to find out whether his old lady, Patsy, was free from whoever was after her. It had all been fucked up. Our chapter has no love for Stormy.

Grumbler's shooting Lost a look of disgust, but Lost shakes his head, holding up a finger, signalling we should wait before passing judgement.

"Right." Snatcher comes back on the line. "I've got Stormy with me."

"Your end clean?" Stormy asks without preamble.

"As a fuckin' whistle," Token growls. "What about yours?"

For an answer, there's a chuckle, followed with, "I was

impressed with the searches you set off, Token. Just a shame you didn't close them all down."

Shrugging off the patronising compliment, Token responds, "Clearly, I didn't find anything of importance."

"Thank fuck you didn't. If you had, Snatcher would be offering you my job." There's more than a touch of arrogance in Stormy's voice.

Lost snarls, "Fuckin' get on with it, Stormy."

There's a murmuring of voices in the background, then Stormy's voice comes back on. "Swift and Bolt tell me San Diego's solid. I, well, I kind of have trust issues, but I'm working on that. But under the circumstances, I need to know why you're looking for info on Saffie Jones. You asking for you, or for someone else?"

"Lack of trust goes both ways, Stormy," Lost coolly states. "But this might help. You're not the only party interested. Token's searches were picked up by someone else. Interestingly, they breezed over the name we were seeking, and asked about a Sapphire Marshall instead. They want to know any info we have, and there are dollars attached."

"Fuck." The other end of the phone goes quiet for a moment. "Okay." When he comes back on, Stormy's voice is firmer. "She's not your problem. Leave it with us, and we'll move her on."

"Uh-uh. No can do…" I can't say the word *brother*, it doesn't slip off my tongue. "She's in no state to move on as you'd have it." And I'm not ready to have her disappear from my life.

"She's hurt?" There's an urgent note of concern in his voice.

"Nah," I reassure him, but don't want to say more.

"What is she now, six months? Has she had the baby prematurely?"

He knows she was pregnant? Lost sees me bristling, and waves me down. "How about you tell us how you know so much about her? We're fencing around here, Brother, without anyone getting in any strikes. Ain't no one going to get anywhere until one of us comes clean. I think you owe it to us to go first."

There's another brief period where no one speaks, then Snatcher takes over. "We're Satan's Devils, Lost. All of us wear the same patch. None of us tolerate violence toward women. But Stormy here, he's seen some shit, and his lack of trust isn't always unwarranted. He needs your reassurance that you've got Saffie's best interests at heart and won't put her in danger."

"I can give that assurance," I answer for my prez. Personally, if the club doesn't want to get involved.

Lost's mouth quirks, and then adds his reinforcement, "This club doesn't make money from spilling info on a bitch who's better off staying lost. You should know that more than anyone, Stormy."

At his obvious reference to Patsy, Stormy exhales a breath, his sigh of capitulation audible over the line. "Okay. Here it is. Are you aware that we're part of a pipeline, a network that helps abused women escape their abusers? Well, we are. Saffie was brought to the attention of the Freedom Trail by a nurse in a hospital in Nevada." He pauses, before continuing. "If this is news to you, then it's going to be hard hearing." He lets that sink in before proceeding again. I take the opportunity to steel myself. It turns out, I need to. "Saffie was in bad shape. She'd been kept by an MC for five years, and there was evidence of multiple previous injuries, but no medical records, suggesting they treated her in house. This time, they'd gone too far, and the damage they'd inflicted was too much for them to handle. Not wanting her dead, reluctantly they had to get her help, and thank fuck for that. A nurse treating her recognised the signs of abuse, got in contact with the Freedom Trail, and Saffie, having just learned she was pregnant, jumped at the chance to escape."

Fuck!

For a moment I forget to breathe. I'd known it had to have been bad, but this? As my head fills with sorrow at the horrors

Saffie's suffered—so much more than I could ever imagine—a quick glance around shows Dart, Lost and Token are also letting the dreadful facts sink in, Stormy continues, "Saffie's a pet name, one by which her family called her. Once she became a teenager, she'd ditched it as being too childish. But it's familiar, and one she has no problem answering to, so we resurrected it for her fake identity."

"She was kept as a club whore?" I ask, re-evaluating what I'd thought I'd seen in her, and comparing her to Pearl, Tits and Cindy. She hadn't seemed like a person who'd flaunt her sex, so probably wouldn't have gone willingly. Stormy had said kept, which implies she was imprisoned and forced. *Fuck.*

"She wasn't a whore." Stormy contradicts what I've just been thinking. "The MC might not have worried so much if she was. At the time of her disappearance, she was Sapphire Marshall, that was the name she was known by to the club—her surname courtesy of the VP, Duke—real, not road name—to whom she was, and still technically is, married."

What the actual fuck? She'd never given any inkling of that.

At first, I bristle that I'd almost entered a relationship with a woman who was taken, then abruptly come to my senses. Duke is the asshole she's terrified of and was probably responsible for almost killing her. Marriage licence or not, she owes him nothing, and certainly not her fidelity.

She wasn't a club whore but a wife. *Duke's wife.* Whatever claim he had, legal or not, doesn't apply now. He's going to become separated from his wife voluntarily or not if I have anything to do with it.

"The VP's property," Lost states, his jaw locked, making me glance up. He's right. A fucking abuser who'd put his wife in the hospital would see her exactly as that—something he owned, and not as the Satan's Devils do, property to be loved and cherished.

"Got it in one, Brother." Stormy growls, adding coldly, "He wants her back, if only to save face, but seeing the lengths he's going to trying to find her, it could well be other reasons." There's a pause, then he adds, so chillingly I almost shiver, "If he finds her, I doubt she'll stay long breathing, or if he keeps her alive, that her life will be a living hell. He'll make an example of her. Duke doesn't have a good reputation."

"He know about the baby?" I ask, still not saying it doesn't exist anymore. No one likes putting all their cards on the table.

I can hear Stormy's deep intake of breath over the phone. "The nurse who helped her escape was found dead a few months ago, not long after Sapphire left. She was tortured, so it seems likely."

Fuck. This man obviously doesn't play around.

"What are the Utah rules on custody?" Dart asks, his brow creasing.

Stormy's answer comes quickly. "Fucker would only lose custody and visitation rights if he were convicted for rape. Duke's her husband, it's her word against his." Snatcher says something in the background. "Yeah, he put her in the hospital, but she lied to the cops about why she was there. Coerced, probably, of course, but it would be hard to bring up a rape accusation now given that history."

"That's one thing we don't have to worry about." I decide to come clean. "Saffie, well, she's lost the baby."

Stormy sighs. "Fuck, that's hard on her. But in some ways that makes it easier."

Fucking easier? The man doesn't know what he's talking about. I recall her abject misery, those first few days when she could barely drag herself out of bed.

Lost raps his fingers. "What's the club, and has this Duke got club backing to find her?"

It's Snatcher's voice now. "The Crazy Wolves based in Nevada, and we presume so. Someone's sanctioned the use of club assets to find her. Though we can't discount, as he's VP, he might be directing it by himself."

As he's VP, he'll have men who'll follow him, maybe even without the sanction of their prez. As an old lady, Saffie's club property, and some clubs would go to the ends of the earth to hold on to that. It's a matter of respect.

Jesus, Saffie. What have you gotten yourself into?

She's his fucking wife! And under the circumstances, it's impossible for her to ask for a divorce.

I may have thought I wanted to protect her before, but now that streak inside me leaps to hitherto unknown levels. One way or another, this man's going to exit this marriage and if it's by my hand, so much the better.

Grumbler can keep quiet no longer. "His full name's Duke Marshall?"

Without hesitation, Stormy replies, "That's him."

The four of us exchange glances and shrug. That name's a new one to us.

"How close do you think he is to finding her, Stormy? Any suggestions on how to play this?" My distrust of the man has been put into the background. To save Saffie, I'll take answers whatever heritage they have. Except for having them relocate her again. If he's found her once, he might do so again, and next time she wouldn't have me.

Stormy doesn't hesitate. "Too close if he picked up on Token's searches. Token, can you mirror an IP address with a location in another state? Throw them off the trail for now."

Our computer guy nods in answer, then states, "That I can do. It might deaden the scent for a while. They're suspicious and looking. I already deleted all my files, closed down the server and moved them to an independent one."

"What implications are there for us?" Lost asks sharply. Token's ability to keep his eyes on the underworld has paid dividends before now. Deleting info doesn't sound good.

Both the voice on the phone and Token chuckle. "I copied

them first and stored them securely, and I've got multiple access points," he explains calmly. "I can afford to burn one."

It's Snatcher's gruff tones we hear now. "Sounds like you've got your info buttoned down. As for the woman herself, I'd feel happier if you could bring her under your protection, Lost, while we figure shit out and how close he's got. All we know for certain is that he knows what name she's now going by. However, that they were able to hit on Token's enquiry makes me worry they've got access to shit we don't know about. I have no idea of their IT capabilities, but we have to assume the worst."

"Prez, if they've found the ID she's using," Stormy points out, "she'll have left footprints in San Diego. We have to relocate her."

Yeah, she will have. Her job, her apartment, and the hospital records.

"And this time with a fuckin' watertight ID," Snatcher growls. "And where no bugger will try to trace her." It's a poke at us, me and Token. "Jeez, what a mess. We need time to sort something out. My request stands, Lost, for you to extend your hospitality."

Having been party to this discussion, I want nothing more than to bring her under our wing. But there's a problem, which I share. "That won't be as easy as it sounds. Quite rightly, from what I've just heard, she's fuckin' terrified of MCs." Now I know, I'm not surprised, at last able to understand why she never quite trusted me, seeing the patch and not the man. I could tell her clubs were different until the cows come home, her extreme experience would lead her to believe otherwise. *Not just one rape, but five years of abuse.* Fuck, that must have felt like a lifetime.

Lost's brow is creased, and he rubs at his temples. Suddenly he smiles. "Your railroad, Snatcher. You ever use any kind of password to help folks along? So they know the contact is genuine?"

"Sure do," Snatcher says. "It changes all the time, but the one Saffie knows is…" there's a brief pause followed by, "thanks, Storm… 'Did you lose your purse? I found one with X dollars in it.'"

"What's X?" Lost frowns.

"An increment of the last number she'd been given. We just need a moment to figure that out, then we'll get back to you. Why, what you thinking, Brother?"

"I'm thinking I could send my ol' lady to check up on her, purportedly sent from the Freedom Trail. As they've not met before, she's likely to trust her if she presents the correct credentials. Patsy could befriend her."

"Your woman sound?"

Lost snorts. "Sometimes I think she's got a better head on her shoulder than I have, and not only that, as you know, she's been under witness protection herself."

"What's siccing a fuckin' bitch on her going to do to help?"

Lost's face goes apoplectic, but Snatcher's taken it on himself to call Stormy out. "Have some fuckin' respect, Storm."

To my surprise, Stormy backs down. "Sorry, Lost. I sometimes slip back into my old ways." He sighs. "All I remember is Patsy running off to take the heat off her kids and the club. But that shows she's got spunk, and if that's half what my own old lady has got, it's a good call and she'll do the job."

Lost states firmly, "She trusts the club and can vouch for us, and I can vouch for her. Patsy's not only my ol' lady, but her son is a prospect, her daughter's married to Ink from Colorado, and they've just had a child. She's club through and through. Once she's gained Saffie's confidence, she can bring her into the fold. I've no doubt she can do it."

It's a good idea. I harbour no hesitation about the first old lady's abilities. And if she fails, I'll drag Saffie back here myself.

Force her to see we're different. *Yeah, like that's not going to confirm her view of what an MC is.* While I'd rather it was me dealing with Saffie, I have to admit, Lost's idea has benefits, and once she's here and has an insight into how we run our club, maybe I can take over.

"Right," Snatcher starts. "You deal with Saffie and get her under your protection. Token will make contact and try and get them off the trail. We'll keep digging and see how they figured her alias out and how close they've got. You keep her undercover while we get new papers and ID sorted, then plug whatever the fuck hole we've got somewhere."

"Sure," Token answers quickly. "Er, I'm confident in my skills, but this is a matter of life and death. Stormy, any problem with me keeping in contact, and picking your brain?"

"No problem, Brother. I'll set up a closed comms channel between the both of us."

Token grins. "You gonna tell me how I can send messages direct to your screen?"

It had been a bone of contention for a while, when Stormy had managed to get under Token's more than adequate defences and do just that. I wonder how the other man will answer.

"Share trade secrets? Why the hell not? We all bleed Devils' blood."

As Lost, Dart and I exchange glances, I note I'm not the only one surprised. Token though, well he's beaming as if he'd just won the lottery.

On that positive note, the call is ended.

I leave the meeting, my head spinning with all I'd heard. When I allow myself to dwell on the things Saffie must have suffered, I rush to the heads, only just making them before I vomit.

Saffie. Fuck. *Five years.* How could I have ever thought I could fix her? How much time does it take to get over something like that? And top of which, she's just lost her baby.

I'm impressed as fuck that she keeps on breathing.

I splash my face, rinse out my mouth, then stare at my face in the mirror.

Saffie has very good reason to be wary of anyone wearing an MC cut and I don't see how she'll ever get over it.

Would she ever see beyond the patch on my back? Would she accept we're trying to help?

And lastly, however much I want to personally keep her safe, she might not give me a chance.

And who could fucking blame her?

CHAPTER TWENTY-TWO

Saffie

It's been almost a month since I ended my baby's life. A lonely month with nothing growing inside me. I feel empty, wondering what's worth living for.

Each day, I regret having to make the decision I had, but I don't doubt it was the right one. Time's a healer they say, but I'm not so sure. I'll never forget the dream I once held within me. If it were possible, I hate Duke more and more. Vying with my own guilty feelings, I'm convinced he caused the harm to my baby, before I even knew it was growing inside me.

It's also a month since I last saw Niran. *I miss him.* Why, oh why did he have to be a biker? Why did he have to be so wedded to his club? More times than I can count, I go to pick up the phone, then pull back my hand, knowing he won't change, and I can't.

I'm lonely, longing to hear a friendly voice. When I'm not at work, I stay in the apartment, living my life through the sounds of my neighbours—a new couple has moved in next door, newlyweds who have sex a lot, while I lie in my bed, knowing I'm no longer a fully functioning woman and unknowing whether I ever will be again.

Sex is a weapon. Duke used it to hurt me. Sex with my previous ex was pleasant at first but ended up being just a chore.

I wonder what sex would be like with Niran? I'll never know, and am not even sure if given the chance, I'd want to find out.

Something died within me that day I lost my baby.

I go through the motions of life—going to work, coming home, doing laundry, eating only to keep myself going. I've no pleasure in anything anymore.

Call Niran. What does it matter that he's a biker?

No, the devil on my shoulder replies, *he's Duke in disguise, or if not him, one of his brothers will be. Women are property.* Nothing more.

Today is just like any other. I sleep late as I've nothing to get up for. I tidy the apartment though it barely needs it, wincing as a cockroach runs across the floor. Perhaps I should look for somewhere better, there's nothing to save my money for now. The thought brings those never far away tears to my eyes. Just a few short weeks ago, I had a future to look forward to, me and my child. Now there's nothing, and no one.

Not that I deserve anyone to make my life easier, not after what I've done.

Duke's fault, not mine, I try to tell myself. But I can't absolve myself of all the responsibility. If I'd been wiser, and never been with Duke at all, any baby of mine would have had a different father.

When I've done all that I can to the apartment, which is only the equivalent of polishing a turd, I slump on the couch, and once again my mind relives my history. The ever-present question in the fore of my mind, *how was I ever sucked in by Duke?* Quickly followed by, *will I ever be free of him, or is he still searching for me?*

About mid-afternoon, a knock on the door startles me. My heart rate speeds up. I've no family and have made no friends who would visit me. Although it's almost been a month since I last saw him, I'm certain Niran would call, and wouldn't just turn up at my door.

Or would he?

I'm surprised my heart beats faster, and not just in fear. *Could it really be him?*

He'd certainly be the least of all evils.

No one knows my address. I didn't tell work that I'd moved, and I've been so terrified in case Duke was tracking me down, I haven't wanted to get close to anybody for fear that they would learn enough of my story to inadvertently sell me out.

No one brings up my mail, not that I really have any, no one pops in to ask for a cup of sugar or see whether I have spare eggs. In the few months that I've lived here, there's never been anyone knocking—except for that one occasion when the addict came to the wrong floor, something that's luckily never been repeated.

Except, maybe up to now. It could be a drug dealer out there.

At least it wouldn't be Duke. He wouldn't wait to be let in; he'd kick the door down. But he could have sent someone else to check up on me. My recurring nightmare is that it's only a matter of time before he finds me. I'd be naïve to think he'd give up. I'm still his property, and his wife in the eyes of the law.

When the rapping comes again, overly cautious and silently, not giving away that there's someone home, I tiptoe toward the door and use the peephole to look out.

It's a woman. The lines on her face suggest she's older than me, but attractive in a mature looking way. Her face looks open and friendly. She's wearing subtly applied makeup, a flowery blouse, and a light jacket over a pair of well-fitting jeans. I'd put her down as someone who might be collecting for charity, but if so, she's come to the wrong apartment block.

She doesn't look dangerous in any way, but she's a complete

stranger to me. I'm not in the mood for company and she'll have nothing I would either want or need.

But as she stands there, alone and vulnerable, I know she's in danger just by being there and wonder how the hell she doesn't know. That she's made it to the fourth floor without being robbed is a miracle. If she knocked on a wrong door, she might get more than she bargained for. I start feeling sorry for her and think I should warn her to get out of here fast. Even a do-gooder should be given a chance.

Another glance out and she's still there, staring at the door expectantly. While I watch, her expression turns into a frown.

I take a breath. I can tell her to go away politely enough, and if I'm right about her purpose, explain she won't get any response from my neighbours. Checking the chain is on, I open the door a crack.

"I'm sorry to bother you," she says, as soon as I give her the chance. "But did you lose your purse? Because I've just found one with nine dollars in it."

The password. And she's got it right. The last contact is etched on my memory, and the amount was eight dollars at that point.

Smothering my gasp, I drop my voice. "Why are you here?"

Equally quiet, she responds, "It's just a routine check to make sure you're alright, and no one's been bothering you. You moved from your original accommodation."

I suppose it's not surprising they'd kept tabs on me and found out where I'd gone though I've no idea how. I suppose I should have questioned it more, but that password only known by the Freedom Trail literally opened the door.

I do think, clearly, I'm low priority, as my move was more than three months back, so why bother checking up now?

"I'm fine," I manage to get out without choking on the lie.

The woman doesn't look convinced. "Could I come in and have a chat?"

"I'd rather not."

"Please?" She looks left and right and lowers her voice conspiratorially. "I don't feel comfortable standing here in the hallway."

I can understand that. Especially as I hear the heavy clump of boots coming up the stairwell. Who knows who is going to appear? My neighbours might know I have no money, but her? While she's not overdressed, her understated clothing is smart. Easy pickings for a mugging.

As I don't want someone from the Freedom Trail who'd helped me so much being stolen from or hurt, I close the door, undo the chain, then open it again.

She hurries in as if only too well aware of the threat she's leaving outside.

"Thank you," she breathes out relieved. "Do you mind if I sit down?"

Still in my pjs—I only get dressed before I leave for work— and all too conscious I must look the world's worst mess, I want to object, but innate politeness makes me nod. She doesn't comment or even raise an eyebrow at my appearance. If she'd challenged me, told me I hadn't been rescued just to allow myself to go to the dogs, I probably would have reacted snappily. Instead, I wave my hand toward a chair.

Maybe tolerating her presence will force me out of my head for a while. It's been a very long time since I last had company.

"I'm Patsy," she says, sitting neatly with her hands folded in her lap. "And I moved to San Diego under witness protection, so I know what it's like starting over in a new town."

It falls into place, why she's been sent to me. She'll understand what it's like to cut ties with friends and family and move to a different state. Not that after Duke chased them away I had any of the former, and the latter has disowned me. Still, the principle is there.

"Where were you from?" I ask to be polite and with little interest. "And how long have you been here?"

"Colorado. And, oh, about a year now. It's hard, isn't it?" She grimaces. "I had to leave my daughter and follow my son. Beth was doing okay, she'd settled down with her man, but Connor, my son, had fallen in with bad company, and even at twenty-two needed his mom to keep him on the right track. I made a rational decision to leave Beth, but absence doesn't just make the heart grow fonder, it makes it positively ache."

There wasn't anyone in particular who I'd regretted having to leave. Duke had isolated me years back, and there wasn't one member of his club I missed. But I suspect I'd feel the same in her place. Never having friends in the first place doesn't make the loneliness any less. *I miss Niran,* I remind myself. Even if it was my fault he left. But my phobia of bikers is real, and always present. We could never have gotten past that.

I force myself to be friendly, an alien action for me. "It must be awful not knowing what your daughter's doing and how she's getting on. Have you anyway of getting news about her?"

Patsy smiles warmly. "Yeah, now I do. I talk to her and we visit each other. I'm a grandma now."

Good for her, I think bitterly. But I'm also intrigued. "How did you manage to do that? Isn't it forbidden or dangerous?"

"I was lucky enough to fall in with a good crowd, and the threat was removed. The man my son and I were hiding from is dead."

How I wish the same fate for Duke. I should feel bad for wishing him six feet under, but that man hasn't a redeeming bone in his body. As long as I live, he'll feel I belong to him. I'm even permanently marked with his name and property patch on my body.

"You *were* lucky," I agree, wondering who the crowd is she's referring to, and whether they would do the same deed for me. Assassins for hire? What am I even thinking about? It's not

Duke's demise that would bother me, it's knowing I'd never be able to pay them. My savings wouldn't stretch to that.

"Was it expensive?" I still find myself asking, intrigued. Then correct myself, feeling my cheeks burn red. "Oh, I'm sorry. You're probably talking about the cops." I flush with embarrassment, knowing my original thought was because I'd been around bikers for too long.

"What?" Then she laughs, seeming to find my erroneous mental leap amusing rather than something to question. "It cost me nothing. What they did, they did because it was right."

My eyes widen, then narrow suspiciously. *That doesn't sound like the cops.* It sounds more like my initial reaction was correct.

But if so, who does something for nothing? Not in my experience they don't. A thought triggers more suspicions. Our discussion has verged into dangerous territory. Those words spoken to the wrong person could bring a heap of trouble down on her head. And why is she divulging so much about *her* when she said she's here to talk about *me*?

I rub at my eyes which are red and sore from my habitual sorry-for-myself crying jag this morning, noting she's not commented on the state she's found me in. I'm obviously distressed and not coping which was what she came to check. *Maybe it's obvious?* The Freedom Trail knew I was pregnant, but my baby bump has now gone. Except for some stretch marks only visible under my clothes, you'd not know I'd been with child at all. Any weight gained had been lost through me not eating properly over the past few weeks. That she's ignoring the topic makes me suspicious and wonder if she already knows.

Could the Freedom Trail have gotten into the hospital's databases? But why would they check? They'd done what they promised, got me to a new town, set me up with enough to get me started, and never said they'd keep tabs on me. I'm just one in a long line of people they've helped. I was given a new chance in life. What I do with it is up to me.

I begin to wonder whether Patsy really is from them?

How else would she have known the password?

All my misgivings rush to the fore. My trembling hands and shaking voice betray my fear as the words tumble out. "Why are you really here, Patsy?"

CHAPTER TWENTY-THREE

Saffie

Patsy's kind-looking eyes gentle, though instead of answering me, she poses a question. "You've had a bad experience with an MC, haven't you?"

Abruptly, I stand. I should have shut her out, shouldn't have let her in and shouldn't have given a damn what would happen to her in this apartment block. Now I'm tolerating a stranger's presence in my home, and one who's broached the one topic guaranteed to send terror shooting through me. "I'd like you to leave."

"Saffie, I'm here to help," she says, imploringly.

"No, you haven't offered a word of help or asked about me." *Except for that worrying reference to an MC.* "I'm not telling you anything. It's best you just go."

Patsy's eyes sharpen slightly. Good, I'm getting her riled, but she makes no move to vacate her seat.

"Have you heard of the Satan's Devils MC?"

My hands curl into fists. Yes. That's Niran's club. But I choose to lie. "No and I don't need to. Motorcycle clubs are all the same. They're outlaws and threats to normal people like me. If you're after information, take my advice and leave them well alone."

She chuckles softly. "I'm afraid it's far too late for that. You see, I'm very happily married to the president of the San Diego chapter of the Satan's Devils."

She's what? The words take a second to resonate, then I realise she's an old lady, *just like me.* "Get out!" I shout, feeling all the blood rushing from my face. I won't listen to a lecture about how I'm still a man's property. *Duke must have sent her,* although, admittedly, sending a woman to do a man's work isn't his normal approach.

"Saffie, you need to listen to me."

"Get out now. I'll call the cops if you don't." That threat had worked on Niran and Mary, I've no doubt it will work on her.

But she proves a more difficult nut to crack.

"And say what?" She scoffs, obviously unimpressed. "That a middle-aged woman is trying to have a conversation with you? Have I threatened you, pressured you? Pulled a gun on you? No. Unfortunately for you, I'm not Black." She crosses her legs and folds her arms. "Until you listen to me, I'm staying right where I am."

She's not Black? Very belatedly, I realise why the threat had worked so well on Niran, and at the same time realise it has no power on the woman in front of me now. I had more ground to stand on when there was an actual biker in my living room. It makes me slightly ashamed that calling the cops and adding the words Black and threat would have had them here in no time, and him taken out in cuffs if not worse. They'd laugh if I called Patsy a danger to me.

Neither would my neighbours look kindly on me calling the police to the apartment block. So, it seems like unless she leaves of her own accord, she's staying.

Shaking, thinking the whole world's against me, I wonder what her purpose is. *Is she here to persuade me to go back to Duke?*

It seems though, I have little option but to hear her out. *If she mentions Duke, just once, I'm calling the cops and to hell with it.* If she confirms a relationship with him, hell be damned, I'll base my accusation on her association with an MC which I suspect has a high chance of not being legit.

Forcing my voice to sound a lot firmer than I feel, I demand, "Just spit out what you're here to say."

Patsy's eyes soften, and she keeps her voice calm as she begins, "I knew of the Satan's Devils before I moved here. My daughter got friendly with one of the Colorado members. That's who she's married to now."

I'd told myself I'd only pretend to listen, but it's hard to block out her words. *Poor girl* comes into my head. I wouldn't wish it on anyone to marry a biker. Hold up, but Patsy said she's married to one as well, and to the president to boot. But she seems happy enough and doesn't look abused. *Bruises don't need to show.* There's nothing to say she wasn't coerced into coming here but it's the why I don't understand. Are the Satan's Devils in league with the Crazy Wolves? If so, I'm on borrowed time.

I know what bikers think about property. In their eyes, I'm Duke's. Is she here to persuade me to return to him? Or does he already know where I am? My legs threaten to not support me, but I don't want to sit down. Seated, I'd feel more vulnerable.

My baby's gone but I'm alive. Suddenly, I know I want to live, and not a living death that Duke would impose on me.

"My son, Connor, is now a prospect for the Devils too," Patsy continues. "He'd gone off the rails. What happened to him showed him the seedy side of life and taught him it was something to steer clear of. The Satan's Devils have put him on the right track. He's now going to college, and learning a trade, all paid for by them."

What? Duke would have laughed in anyone's face if they suggested he sponsor a prospect to go to college. A prospect for the patched Wolves was patched in *if* they got through their probation period alive.

Noticing my confusion, Patsy seizes her chance. "Not all MCs are the same." She pauses, "Saffie, you might not know, but your escape was aided by an MC. They're part of the Freedom Trail. How else do you think I knew the password that would give me access to you?"

Her words take a moment to compute. When they do, I flop down on the chair. *An MC works with the Freedom Trail?* That was totally unexpected. "Why? How?"

"In cases like yours, they work in the background, make the arrangements, get new identities, alter databases to give you a history which stands up, get any tickets required to you and organise the people who help."

"Why an MC?" It's the first thing I ask. In my experience, MC members are only out for themselves. "Do they get paid?" If so, by whom? I hadn't been asked for a cent, which is lucky. I'd left with nothing and had still been wearing my hospital gown.

"They do it because they're good men and they want to help women like you get free and have a chance at a new life. Why an MC? Well, they straddle the line between right and wrong." I open my mouth to snark that it's the wrong side of the line most of the time, but she doesn't give me chance. "My new ID was set up by the feds as I was legitimately in witness protection. In a case like yours, the cops wouldn't have helped. Oh, they might have arrested the man who put you in the hospital, but you'd have to have appeared in court, and whether or not he was given a sentence is a matter of your word against his." When my eyes widen in horror, she nods. "That's bad enough when it's just one abusive ex, but when that one has an MC behind them, it would have been signing your death warrant."

"But I've got a new ID." I hadn't thought where it had come from and that it might not be legit. *Would it stand up to scrutiny?* I'd always had that fear at the back of my mind, now I'll have to be extra careful.

She smiles, and her next statement alleviates my concerns

somewhat. "You have. And it will be at least as good as anything the feds would have produced." She chuckles softly. "They'll have used the same databases and taken the same steps to concoct a history for you. Not that the feds would know of course." She pauses again as though for emphasis. "People determined to stay on the right side of the law wouldn't have helped you as much as they have, their hands would have been tied. I suppose the question is, can you condone some illegality if it's done for the right reason?"

My brow creases as I think. In my case, I certainly would, and apparently already have. "I suppose so," I eventually reply, as long as it steered clear of the things that were done by Duke. Those weren't in a grey area, they were positively black.

"I can't give you details on who they are. It's not that I don't trust you, Saffie, but if they're to help others like you, they need to stay under the radar. But I think you can tell they're good at what they do."

I'll give her that. I nod. It's been months since I ran, and Duke's not caught up. *So far.*

Looking down at her hands, she shakes her head. "You heard the phrase *club business* before?" The roll of my eyes gives her the answer she's looking for. *Every fucking day.* "I'm not normally involved in the business of the club, but Lost, my husband, wanted to get information to you, and using me seemed the best way. It's the first time I've heard of the Freedom Trail, and I've got to admit, I'm proud of the men who help women like you escape."

"Was it the Satan's Devils?"

She doesn't say yes, but she doesn't say no. I don't push. When something comes under the heading of being the business of the club, they mean it's the province of the members. Women are better off not knowing and keeping their life can depend on knowing when not to ask. Or at least, that's so in the Crazy Wolves.

So I focus on what else she's said. "What information does… Lost?" She nods, a slight smile appearing at my rendition of the strange name. "What does Lost want me to know?"

"Okay." Again, she leans forward. "Niran, who I believe you know, is a member of our club. He's an outstanding guy. He served with the Marines before he lost his leg, you know about that?" I'd known he'd lost a leg, but nothing more, so I shrug. "He's a really good man." She tries to impress his virtues on me again. "It hurt him when you pushed him away."

Is she here to plead his case? Knowing Niran, I'd have expected him to come himself.

Deep down I know what she says is the truth, but there's one massive strike against him. "He's a member of an MC—"

"Saffie, we've established not all MCs are the same. Look at me. Do you think I'd be associated with thugs and criminals?"

Shrugging is my only response. I could have said, *hey, look at me. Do you think I'd want to be associated with violence and murder? Yet here I am.* But I keep my mouth shut.

"Niran was worried about you. He knew you'd been raped and wanted to find out by whom for his own reasons."

To take revenge. It was what I'd feared, and why I'd given him no information. *Is she here to tell me Niran killed Duke, and now I'm free of him?* My heart leaps. Oh, please. Let that be what she's getting around to saying.

"And?" I prompt, impatiently.

"We've got our own intelligence guy, and he, well, he started looking into your background."

And? That shouldn't matter. Who would link Saffie Jones from San Diego with Sapphire Marshall from Nevada? My manufactured past, I'd been assured, was watertight. It's ironic, but it appears to have something to do with this woman's husband's club.

When Patsy grimaces, some of my optimism leaves me. "He found nothing except what was left for him, your new identity.

But his search triggered another party to question," Patsy pauses, not for effect, but by the way her face is twisting, to delay causing me pain, "where Sapphire Marshall is?"

What? There's my confirmation that anything to do with an MC is bad news, well-intentioned or not. "Did he tell them?" I hiss, my heart threatening to jump out of my chest.

"Of course not." She snorts. "Token's leading them on a wild goose chase, so they can't even locate where his initial enquiry came from. He's covered his tracks. But Lost is worried the Crazy Wolves have got technical skills you might not have considered or maybe not have been aware of. But if they've found out your new identity, it's only a matter of time before they catch up with you."

Jesus. My heart beats so fast I think it's going to jump out of my chest.

"You know Duke's from the Crazy Wolves?" I manage to stammer out.

"We know all the information given to the Freedom Trail."

So Niran knows. Yet he hasn't come to see me. Does he know all that happened to me? Everything I'd admitted confidentially? Is that why he sent her and didn't come himself? Is he disgusted that I've been used and abused, not just by Duke, but by everyone?

I feel faint. My palms sweat, and nausea floods through me.

Duke's never stopped looking for me. How could he have found my new name?

Grit. Damn it. I must have underestimated him. Duke boasted about his abilities, but I never knew their extent.

But if it's him and he's come close to finding me, what can I do? Options flit through my mind, but there's only one that makes sense. "I need a new identity. I need to disappear again."

"Yes," Patsy says gently. "You will, I'm sorry. You'll again have to leave your friends and start over. I'm sorry to be the bearer of such bad news."

The thought of going through relocating all over again, this time without the thought of a baby to sustain me, is terrifying. Supportive friends sound nice, but she's overlooking that I haven't got any.

On that I can set her mind at ease. "I've no one to help me, Patsy. I'll be alone whether I stay or go." Maybe I should just stay put and not try to run anymore. I'm not enjoying life at the moment, so if Duke finds me and kills me, problem solved. *Or he takes me back and tortures me.* I shudder. *I've got to go.*

"You have, Saffie. You met Mary, who's fast become one of my best friends, and there's Alex, the VP's old lady who you've not yet met. Alex is actually the club's lawyer. You'll like her, I know." The club lawyer? A woman? As my eyes widen, Patsy continues, "We're all worried about you. And you've got Niran, and all his brothers. I know you'll be wary, but I assure you, they're not like the Crazy Wolves. They'd give their lives to protect friends and family."

Even if I accept there might be people who would keep popping around to visit me, what happens when I'm alone? I can't have someone here twenty-four seven.

"Duke's the type to break doors down and doesn't give a fuck who hears him," I tell her, also knowing the kicking in of the door wouldn't raise an eyebrow in this block. "If there's a chance that he's learned who I am, I can't waste a minute before leaving this apartment." I'd be better off taking my chances living rough.

Patsy smiles. "But you won't be here, that's what I'm trying to explain. While your new paperwork is getting sorted, you'll be staying with us. Lost wants you to move to our clubhouse, temporarily of course." As my mouth drops open, she adds, "It will give you a chance to decide what you want to do, and for us to know what support you need. Your new ID and background will take time to construct to ensure it's going to stand up this time." She looks around and can't hide her shudder. "And, in the meantime, you'll have a more appropriate place for you to live."

If the situation wasn't so dire and I wasn't scared sick about an imminent visit from Duke, I'd have laughed out loud at her definition of somewhere more appropriate. Accepting a visit from a woman involved with a club is one thing, but moving to their clubhouse? That sounds like a case involving a pan and the fire. Putting my head into a den of iniquity that bikers call home? There's no way I can do that. I've already been someone's property, still am as far as I know. Once I'm there, just like in Nevada, I'll be trapped, and they'll prevent me from leaving. What can I say but no?

"I can't come to a biker compound." My voice isn't strong, but I'm adamant. Never again. The thought alone is enough to raise hives.

"Yes, you can," she insists, waving her hand as though wiping away my concerns. "I'll give you my own promise that you'll be safe there. Lost, my husband, would never let anything happen to you. The members are respectful." Her brow furrows as though she's trying to think, then she chuckles softly. "The VP's wife, Alex, well, she does pole dancing, to keep fit, you know? There's a pole in the clubhouse for her to practice on. When she does, all the members make themselves absent, as they respect her, and the wishes of Dart, her husband."

Yeah, I knew all about that. There were times when Duke had become possessive about me. He'd use his fists on a man who dared to look at me even fully clothed and in those moods, certainly wouldn't countenance anyone leering if I'd ever done such a thing as cavorting on a pole. If one of the brothers had looked at me wrongly, I'd feel those fists on me for giving what he'd described as a show. Subsequently, other times, he wouldn't hesitate to share me. I could never judge which way it would go.

My face softens in sympathy. "Does he abuse her as well?"

"What the hell?" Patsy looks stunned. "No, he does not. He

might come over as a possessive caveman, but truly it's because he's thinking of Alex's dignity and self-respect. Some of those poses can be quite sexual." She chuckles again. "I know, she's tried to teach me a few moves. Not that I'm any good, but I wouldn't want men looking on either except, of course, for my man." I notice she blushes and that it looks cute on the older woman. Then she smiles. "It's because he loves her, wants her to be happy, that he protects her by giving her space."

I suppose that's one way of looking at it, but I'm not sure I'm convinced. Could I be wrong about all MCs? I'd rather not put it to the test.

Sure, the VP sounds different to Duke, and Niran I've already met. Lost, she's also vouched for. But how many more men have they got? And can she speak for them?

But Duke's closing in. A new ID, a new name, a re-creation of the person I am or who I want to be will take time, as it will need to be even more watertight. After considering it for a moment, I ask, "Tell me about the other members."

Patsy grins as though she's got me hooked. She settles back and begins, "Where do I start? Hmm. Well, I've told you about Lost and Dart, then there's Salem…"

CHAPTER TWENTY-FOUR

Saffie

I would have said nothing could have persuaded me to voluntarily step into an MC clubhouse again, but Patsy proved a force to be reckoned with. As she'd described her husband's club to me, finding a counter argument to all my objections, I'd soon come to realise I'd never want to go up against her in any negotiation as it fast became clear I was on the losing end.

She settles in with only a slight flinch and a glare sent upward to a loud noise that comes from the floor above my apartment, and gives me a rundown of presumably all the members in their chapter of the Satan's Devils MC. She offers so much detail that some of them I think I'd recognise as soon as I meet them. Bones with his sniffing habit which came from snorting too much cocaine in days gone past, and Dusty, an attractive man whose claim to fame had been catching her bouquet at her wedding. She rattles off names so quickly they seem to run together, but each one she sings the praises of. Neither is she shy on the bad points, though, of those, there aren't many to name, and everything tamer than what I'd witnessed with the Crazy Wolves.

The Arizona Chapter, she tells me, has a different vibe, the majority of the men there have settled down and the compound is overrun with kids. In that aspect, San Diego was only just starting out. Their VP was the first to get his old lady, followed by Lost and herself, and more recently with Grumbler and Mary. In her view it wasn't that the men liked their single lives, but that they hadn't yet found the right woman. I think she's being overly romantic. Easy pussy comes with no strings and no sense of being tied down. Freedom-loving bikers are unlikely to want mates.

That there were only a couple of kids I'd be likely to come across in the clubhouse was actually a bonus. I'm weak, but the sight of what I'd hoped to have but instead lost, makes me envious of anyone else's baby.

I don't take her words at face value. I ask probing questions, hoping to catch her out, suspecting she's giving me the good parts, and glossing over the bad. But her honesty shines through, and I have to concede, if there are reprobates in the Devils, she's obviously kept in the dark. She's even open about the club girls, but tries to assure me they aren't forced, and able to come and go freely of their own accord. This I certainly take with a huge pinch of salt. *Who'd service bikers voluntarily?* The idea has me shuddering.

Patsy is patient, happy to tell me about the Devils for as long as it takes to persuade me. In all, she must speak for a good couple of hours. I soon get the impression that she isn't going to leave until she's got the answer she wants.

Despite myself, she makes me smile at some of her anecdotes, recalled so fondly, as if she were talking about her kids rather than hard-core members of a motorcycle club. Every word out of her mouth seems so genuine, that I begin to lay aside my misgivings and start to trust her.

When Patsy finally relates the story of how she came to meet Lost, a man with apparently so many virtues I've lost count of them, she's well on her way to convincing me to give them a chance. As though trying to prove it hasn't always been unicorns and rainbows, she adds an abridged history of the club, about Snake, the ex-president, who'd gone loco and nearly brought everyone down.

Lost, she told me, had had his work cut out to keep the club going after Snake and eight others had defected. He'd had to rebuild trust between the members who were left. After a rocky ride, with their bad apples gone, he's succeeded in reuniting the club. I wonder, of course, whether there were any left still hidden in the barrel, and how he can be sure he's emptied it.

When I query their finances, or where their money comes from, I know she won't know about their illegal activities. But she seems genuinely convinced their money is earned legitimately, and they aren't about making bank the illegal way. With a quick glance around her as if anyone could be listening, lowering her voice, and sitting forward, she tells how women had been rescued just a few months back from a slave trafficker, and how the club never sought or wanted credit for it.

As a final attempt at persuading me, she broadens my mind when she lists all the different types of motorcycle clubs that exist. Having been blinded by the Crazy Wolves, the only example I'd had experience of, I'd thought them all much the same. But apparently there are riding clubs, men and women who join purely for the enjoyment of riding their bikes and who meet at weekends just to ride out together. I hear there are women's only clubs, gay clubs, and even those for people with a religious slant.

She gets me to the point where I question why I'm automatically painting them all with the same brush. Despite my fears, some of the men seemed to be such characters, I start leaning toward wanting to meet them. Her words make me think of Niran in a new light, rather than dismissing him because he's a biker, and to wonder whether the man I saw without the cut was no different to who he is once he's wearing it.

She wears me down, one sentence after another, one paragraph after the next. When she sees me weakening, she plays on my fears. That Duke is searching for me was a certainty. That he might have the ability to hone in on where I am, a strong possibility. It's a matter of when, rather than if he catches up with me.

I feel physically sick at the reminder he's waiting in the wings to come reclaim his property, and that he clearly hasn't, as I'd hoped, given up.

When she sees me falter in my objections, she acts fast, instructing me to pack a bag of necessities, and I find myself doing exactly that, such is the force of her personality.

Her suggestion, though, that I follow her in my own car rather than ride in hers, I welcome. That alone had reassured me, having the advantage, I won't be trapped and could leave under my own steam if I don't like what I find. Unless my car falls apart, which is far from unlikely, even after Niran had had it fixed. It had only been given a reprieve, not a new lease on life.

Being faced with Patsy's powerful personality and persuasive techniques was one thing, but alone in my car, following her through the streets of San Diego, I begin to have second thoughts. Third ones and fourth soon follow as she takes a turn and starts heading out in the direction of the mountains.

Duke had driven me to their isolated clubhouse. Hell, he'd persuaded me I was going to my wedding reception. And I, gullible fool, had fallen for his lies. He'd groomed me for months and still I couldn't tell what an asshole he was. An afternoon chat with Patsy has me similarly throwing caution to the wind.

Am I destined to repeat the same mistakes over and over?

Maybe I'm stupid, but somehow, even though a large part of me wants to yank the wheel and zoom off in a different direction,

I keep driving in the wake of the Satan's Devils' president's old lady as if I were being towed by an unbreakable thread.

I want so much to believe her. I've been on my own for so long and have been through so much that I'm tired and want someone to guide me. Since I'd lost my baby, I've been adrift, just going through the motions, and not thinking about my wants and needs. Misery and depression have settled over me like a brain fog. Someone pointing out a direction to me is almost refreshing.

Duke told me what to do. So did his brothers. What makes me think this club would be different?

I've no way of knowing, but still, despite all my doubts, I continue to follow Patsy's car.

Am I that desperate I'll do anything just to have friendly faces around me? No, of course I'm not. But people affiliated with this club have apparently proved they can set up my new identity, and from what Patsy said, are already setting out to do so again. This time, knowing the Wolves' capabilities, maybe they'll do so more carefully.

But how were there holes in their plan? What led Duke to me?

How can I trust the Devils? It could be a trick. Even now Duke could be waiting for me, laughing like a loon that I'm driving to him, delivering myself on a platter.

What if I enter their clubhouse to find he's wormed his way in there? I know how charming he can be, he could have gotten them onside by fooling them.

I whimper, realising there's a huge risk Patsy has been lying to me. That this MC will turn out to resemble the one from which I'd escaped, and all I'm doing is letting myself be ensnared and returned to the man I've been free of for months. They could be working for him, even if Patsy herself is innocent. Bikers don't keep women in the know.

I should turn off, disappear. Go where no one would be able to find me.

My sweaty hands clutch at the steering wheel, my heart beating so fast I can hear the thumping of blood in my head. If I turned this car, where would I go, what would I do? I haven't enough money to start somewhere new. The only ID I have is in the name of Saffie Jones, and Patsy's told me Duke knows my alias.

My parents?

God, I hadn't contacted them for years, not my choice of course, but Duke's. I haven't a clue what Duke had wanted from them, what benefit he'd gained by marrying me, only that it probably came down to money. If he'd used me to extort funds from my father, I doubt he'd have ever forgiven me. By ignoring the warnings of my parents, I brought it all down on my own head. My father might turn me away from his door. I couldn't take the chance he wouldn't nor cope with the disappointment if he did.

Would Mom be able to see past the fact that I'd left my legal husband? I'm sure she'd known all along that my first husband was unfaithful to me, but in her eyes, marriage vows mean for better or worse, never mind how bad the latter can be. Would that still apply, even though they had no love for the man whose ring I used to wear before I threw it away, and who I promised to love forever? Would it apply when he didn't, and never had, loved me?

At the worst, they might tell Duke where I am if only to reunite husband and wife. I can't risk it.

No, I laugh mirthlessly at myself, *instead, I'm putting my faith in a club full of bikers.* I wonder if I need my head examined. Probably.

Before Duke, I'd been a sociable woman with a wide circle of girlfriends. Some had taken themselves off once they'd seen the man I'd hitched my wagon to. *The joke's on them,* I'd thought at the time, convincing myself I'd seen deeper depths to Duke than they had. Any friends that remained, Duke had chased off.

I have no idea where any of them are now, whether they have their own families or what they're doing. I can't call on friends out of the blue when I've not seen or spoken to them for five years, and I certainly can't depend on them.

My loneliness, together with my lack of options, keeps me following the car in front of me, while acknowledging to myself, if I were in a better place mentally, if I hadn't had such a recent and devastating experience, possibly I'd never have accepted Patsy's invitation. But in my current state, the thought of anyone being there to help with my problems is too tempting to ignore.

One last moment when I could drive straight on instead of turning where Patsy indicates, but instead of taking that route, I blindly follow as she enters through gates guarding what looks like an old airfield. It's seeing the gate sliding shut behind me and the steel fencing reminiscent of the Crazy Wolves' compound that starts my brain screaming, *what have I done?*

I should never have come.

My car barely runs, it's certainly not capable of ramming through metal gates. I've lost my chance. All I can do is pull up beside Patsy's car. I'm trembling, my fingers fumble as I try to take the key out of the ignition. I feel sick and delay so long getting out, that in the end she has to come coax me.

"I don't think this is a good idea." My hands, hell, my whole body is shaking. In front, there are a few bikes parked neatly in a row, not many, but enough to invoke bad memories. *There's a door.* My eyes are glued to it. In my head, it morphs into that fateful entrance into the Crazy Wolves' clubhouse. My palms sweat, my stomach roils, and my whole body shrieks *flight* as adrenaline floods through it.

She regards me with a concerned look, and says reassuringly, "It will be fine. Anyway, you're here now. Might as well come in and meet everybody." Her eyes scan the parking lot outside the clubhouse. "Well, whoever's here that is." As if realising I need further cajoling, she adds, "If you don't like it, you can leave. All I'm asking is that you give us a chance."

Having noticed the small number of bikes myself, unless the Satan's Devils MC has only a few members and from the names Patsy had told me, there's certainly more, the rest are probably out doing the legit jobs Patsy had spoken about. *Or running drugs, guns or women.* But at least I won't be faced with the whole club at once. That though, does nothing to slow my racing heart. Flashbacks, one after another, keep returning to me. My mind stuck in the past keeps me rooted to the seat of my car.

When Duke had at last invited me to the clubhouse, I'd been excited to see where he spent his time and to meet his friends. What a fool I'd been, so naïve. I'd never expected anything like I'd walked into. That doorway ahead is so reminiscent, I could be entering hell once again.

"Come on, Saffie. You'll get a warm welcome, I promise you."

A warm welcome was what I'd hoped for when I'd first walked into the Crazy Wolves' clubhouse. I suppose that was what I'd got. They'd been like a pack of lions being brought fresh meat. I would never have gotten within a hundred miles of that clubhouse if I'd had an inkling of what to expect, but Duke had deliberately deceived me.

Patsy reaches out her hand, and I take it, allowing her to pull me from the car. I bounce on my tiptoes, my keys firmly grasped in my hand. The only thing stopping me from making a run for it is the vain hope that Patsy's right. Here I could find support and people who'd help me move forward. People like her and Mary.

And Niran. Heaven help me, but I want to see him again.

Urging me forward, Patsy walks me through the parked bikes, then, once at the building, leans around me, and taking a firm grip on the handle and pressing it downward, she pushes the door open.

Unlike when I entered the lair of the Crazy Wolves, I don't need to wait for my eyes to become accustomed to the darkness. The inside is bright, flooded with sunlight. Nothing is hidden from my eyes.

There's a child. There were no kids in the Crazy Wolves' clubhouse. Not that I doubt the members sired them or thought their fathers purposefully kept them away from the depravity. It was more that the men there wouldn't have given a damn whether they had offspring or cared what became of them. My eyes widening, I watch as the little girl runs too quickly for her stubby legs to carry her, and crashes into a table. Her scream is heartwrenching.

Oh no. Kid, be quiet, I scream internally, covering my mouth with my hand as a big burly biker, with overalls shrugged down on his hips, rushes over to her, his face set and tight. Terrified on her behalf, I suck air into my lungs and hold it.

"You got a boo boo, kid?" The rough biker's now holding her, and the expression I thought was anger, I now interpret as concern. After he's run his hands over her, dispassionately akin to a medical way, not anything sexual or predatory, he pronounces, "I think you'll live. That was a naughty table to hurt you, wasn't it?" Leaning over, his fist hits the offending object, and he growls, "Bad table."

A pretty, curvaceous, but short Black woman rushes over to her, and tries to take what I presume is her daughter from the biker. But he swings the kid up in his arms, holding her out of her reach. *Give her back,* I internally scream.

"Momma doesn't understand, does she, kid?" the biker, says, looking like he's fighting to keep his face straight. "That table has it in for all of us. I've bumped into it myself more than once after a few too many drinks."

Though she looks too young to understand half of what he's

said, and hopefully nothing at all about the effect alcohol has, the little girl cups her hands around his face and plants a sloppy kiss right on his lips. Then she leans backward and kicks, in the way children do having absolute confidence that the adult won't let them fall. Interpreting her desires, the biker carefully puts her on her feet, steadying her until she gets her balance.

"Bad table." The toddler copies her saviour, doling out a punishment of her own on the innocent tabletop. Her screams have now abated, and when her actions cause chuckles to burst out around her, she giggles and joins in.

"Hey, little monster. You done causing damage?" Another biker leans down, making sure himself that she's now upright and steady.

"Da-Da." The child stamps her foot and tries to get out of the grasp of who I gather is her father.

Another, who's already got an older boy climbing all over him, casually stretches out a hand, makes a beckoning gesture, and calls out, "Come over here, kid. Let your mom and dad have some peace for a bit."

The interaction between the bikers and the children is a real eye-opener, and not a chilling one. I feel something loosen inside me. It had been around the same time of day when I'd entered the clubhouse of the Crazy Wolves, and the air had been rampant with sex and depravity. Here, it's totally different.

Maybe it's going to be alright.

A roar of bikes approaching the clubhouse reaches my ears, and my heart starts racing again. *I knew there would be more to come.*

"Come on," Patsy encourages. "I'll introduce you."

"Ah…" My voice comes out as a squeak as I half turn, assessing my chances of escape.

But before I can move, I catch movement out of the corner of my eye and looking back see a large and familiar man moving toward me.

He looks as good as he ever did, if not even better. He's got an air of self-confidence on his home turf that was missing in my apartment. He's wearing a tight black t-shirt which hugs his impressive muscles, and his cut, that piece of leather which I so detest, settles on his shoulders as if it was always meant to be there.

I've not put on makeup and know my eyes are red rimmed and bloodshot. Though I'm beyond crying all the time, tears still come daily at times when I least expect them. I've lost weight, and my clothes hang off me.

As he nears me, I see his jaw tighten. Then his judgemental expression disappears to be replaced by a welcoming smile.

"It's good to see you, Saffie," Niran states. He waves to indicate another man over to join him and slings his arm over his shoulders. "This here is Grumbler. He's Mary's old man."

"Heard a lot about you," Grumbler states, stretching out his hand and ducking out from under Niran's arm. "Welcome to the clubhouse, Saffie." His voice is gruff, and immediately scary, but the smile on his face looks genuine, and not in the least predatory. But as my eyes drop, I notice he's the sergeant-at-arms, just as Slit had been. And Slit was definitely an enemy. *I'd never guessed Mary was married to the sergeant-at-arms.* She'd seemed so, well, normal.

The Crazy Wolves' sergeant-at-arms had certainly not been a friend of mine. More than once when I'd transgressed, Duke left it to him to punish me while he looked on, raising a drink and encouraging him. In full view of the man whose ring I wore, Slit had violently raped me and more than once. With my eyes focused on the patch Grumbler is wearing, memories slam back into me as if I've run into a physical wall.

Niran's eyes miss nothing. In a light voice, he offers me something about the man. "Grumbler's a fuckin' amazing guitarist and singer. He and his band often play here."

For a second, the blood rushing through my ears drowns out

what Niran had been telling me, but slowly it sinks in. *Grumbler's a singer and guitarist?*

Still half in flight mode, I try to concentrate on my breathing, taking in deep breaths through my nose and breathing them out through my mouth. Slowly, my panic subsides to a manageable level and I feel slightly embarrassed that both Niran and Grumbler are patiently waiting, giving me time. I belatedly realise Grumbler had dropped his hand when he realised I wasn't going to shake it. But he gives no sign he's been slighted.

Instead, tossing me a quick grin, and continuing as if I hadn't just had a minor breakdown, Grumbler asks, "You got any favourite songs, darlin'? You just let me know, and I'll try to work them in."

"Yeah, the older that shit is the better." The man who'd picked up the child has now joined us. "Grumbler's band tends to focus on the classics. I'm Salem, by the way, as no one's fuckin' bothering to introduce us."

He takes care to respect my personal space and doesn't hold out his hand, probably having noticed my treatment of his brother, but gives me a respectful raise of his chin.

I've heard many biker handles; indeed Patsy had already spoken about his merits, but not why he'd been named. Suddenly I wonder how he'd come by it. I'm not rude enough to ask, but he seems able to read my mind as my brow furrows.

Salem indicates behind him to the man who still has two kids crawling all over him, their childish voices and giggles seeming so out of place in a clubhouse. "That there is Pennywise. You wondering about the handles, darlin'?" He snorts a laugh. "Unfortunately, our old prez was a Stephen King fan. I'm just pleased he didn't call me IT."

"Would have suited you, clown face," Grumbler snarks.

Salem's arm snakes out and goes around his brother's neck, pulling him into him, making the sergeant-at-arms growl and bat him away. "And you got the handle that fits. Saffie, would you believe this man's always fuckin' moaning? I have no fuckin' idea what Mary sees in him."

"Oi! What's the hold up?" An impatient voice sounds from behind me. "Are you fuckers going out, coming in, or just taking up residence in the doorway?"

The loud voice makes me startle, and I feel like a rabbit trapped in the headlights, frozen to the spot and unable to move. Niran's eyes focus on me so intently, I stare at them as though they're a lifeline. "Your decision, Saffie. No one will stop you if you want to leave, but if you come in, you'll be safe. I promise no one here will lay a finger on you."

"Too fuckin' right," Grumbler snarls. He taps his patch. "If they so much as look at you wrong, I'll be on them quicker than they can blink."

"Same goes for me, sweetheart. And I enforce the rules around here." For that, Salem gets an appreciative raise of Niran's chin.

Without making a sudden movement, Niran holds out his hand, leaving it hanging in the air, and the decision up to me. "I swear I won't let anyone hurt you, Saffie. You've got my personal assurance on that." His voice drips with conviction.

I continue to stare at his face, then drop my eyes to his leather. I shudder, then slowly, feeling like I'm jerking like a puppet on strings, my hand rises to rest in his.

He closes his fingers, but only a smidgeon, allowing me to know I can pull away at any time. As he tugs gently, I allow him to encourage me away from the doorway.

As the bikers I was holding up walk in, I draw closer to him, as though he's my protector, innately trusting him to keep his brothers away.

A few seconds later, the final arrival just barges in, shouting loudly, "What's for fuckin' dinner? It better be something I can eat!"

Hearing his voice, a woman emerges from the kitchen. "I've pureed yours just like I have Isla's," she yells back.

"Yeah, yeah. Very fuckin' funny," the newcomer calls out to her, revealing a mouthful of missing and crooked teeth.

"Snips has got problems with his teeth," Niran tells me, quietly. "And he's scared stupid of seeing a dentist."

Grumbler grins. "Last time we had to sedate him to get him there."

The aforesaid Snips turns sharply, suggesting there's nothing wrong with his ears, and catches sight of me for the first time. His eyes meet Niran's before descending to me still holding his hand. He compresses his lips, then pouts and says in a whine, "See how these fuckers are cruel to me? You'll be on my side, darlin', won't you? You won't let them cart me off to the dentist again."

What would I have to do with it? The Crazy Wolves wouldn't put up with a woman telling them what to do, or even making a suggestion. Hell, most of the time they didn't talk to me. I don't know what to answer, or whether I'm even allowed.

Seeing my difficulty though he won't be able to guess the reason for it, Niran steps in and replies on my behalf, "Saffie's got more than enough problems without worrying about your sorry ass, Snips."

And to my utter astonishment, Snips looks chastised, and goes so far as to apologise, with a wink, though, which loses some of the effect.

Dental hygiene had been the least of the Crazy Wolves' worries, and if anyone had pointed missing teeth out, there would have been a few more gaps in the mouth of the person who'd mentioned it. But Snips seems to take it in stride, instead, he'd played on my sympathy. He's more like a big kid than a scary biker, and I have to fight back an actual smile.

I realise no one's checking me out. No one's leering or eyeing me up like a lamb to the slaughter. They're all being respectful. They're teasing each other good-naturedly without the use of fists to settle scores, and no one's trying to be top dog. To top it all, Niran's not claimed me.

Maybe Satan's Devils are different?

But still, I don't dare speak. I know a woman's place in a clubhouse. I only do so when Niran asks a question of me directly. *Hungry?* Hell no. The loss of my baby coupled with the fear of what I've stepped into trumps any desire to eat. But when Niran tugs at my hand, I go with him.

CHAPTER TWENTY-FIVE

Niran

Saffie's here. In my house.

Only an hour earlier I'd been minding my own business, not daring to hope Prez's old lady would be able to persuade her to face her greatest fear. I still can't believe it.

"Patsy's fuckin' worked her magic." Grumbler approached me, locked thumbs and pulled me in for a man hug.

My eyes went wide. Well I'll be fucked if I was interpreting his words correctly. "Saffie's coming to the compound?"

The sergeant-at-arms grinned. "Should be arriving any moment now."

Hell, I hadn't expected that. It was great fucking news. Hastily, I looked around, seeing the place as if through her eyes. There weren't too many brothers around as most were at their jobs or had gone for a ride. Salem was here, obviously having just come over from the adjacent hangar. He still wore his paint-stained overalls which showed his desperation for an after-work beer. They actually softened the appearance of the tall, rugged and often vicious-looking enforcer. His sidekick, Pennywise, was already seated on one of the sofas, his head rested back, and eyes closed. Relaxed, he looked deceptively harmless, but I knew within one second, he could leap into action mysteriously armed to the teeth.

Bones was here too, sniffing loudly as normal, and deep in conversation with Kink. Apart from Reboot, and one of the prospects, that was all the men who were around.

Shaking my head, I pondered, I'd never looked at my brothers in terms of how threatening they appeared before. Features that appealed to me, in that they're the men who I trusted to have my back, would be off-putting to Saffie. Did we resemble who she was running from? We're bikers, we wear cuts. Wincing slightly, I suspected there were far too many similarities, and hoped that she wouldn't appear, just to turn tail and flee.

As if I was expecting an important guest, I ran through, other than the men, who else was in the clubhouse. Patsy, obviously, was out. Mary was resting at home. Eva was in the kitchen organising the rest of the sweet butts and they had dinner under control. Enticing aromas were already filling the clubroom, which should be a plus. On the negative side, none of the club girls seemed to own presentable clothes. I've gotten used to the way they're attired, but to Saffie, it would scream that they were here for only one reason. Could I get them to go? Nah, the rest of the brothers would kill me if I turned them out. Apart from the obvious, the prospects couldn't cook for shit, and that would be who we'd be left with. Cyn, I noticed, wasn't in sight. Still, my sister wouldn't come as any surprise to Saffie, we'd talked about her a lot. Except, perhaps, for the fact she was still here.

Anxious, just like a man anticipating a visit from his girl-friend's fussy parents, I eyed the clubhouse in ways I wouldn't normally, noticing the rings on the tables, and was that dust I saw on the shelf?

My inspection came to an abrupt end when the clubroom door opened. Expectantly, I'd swung around, and swallowed my disappointment when I saw who was entering. It was the VP with Alex, his adopted son, Tyler, and their daughter, Isla in tow. Tyler scanned the room as though he was much older than his nine years, spied Pennywise, and ignoring that the man was clearly resting, ran over and launched himself, landing next to him on the couch making the piece of furniture bounce.

Pennywise startled, pivoted, then seeing the boy, put away his knife that had magically appeared like a magician's rabbit out of a hat, and proceeded to tackle and tickle him.

Isla, hating to be left out, tore her hand out of that of her father's and toddled over to her brother as fast as her little legs would go. Unfortunately, the momentum of her drunken stagger had her falling straight into the leg of a table. Bouncing off, she crashed to the floor, and let out an ear-piercing wail.

As did a number of others, I took a step forward, but Alex was already making a beeline for her. Salem was there first. Crouching down, he righted her, then teased, "What's all this fuss about?"

At that moment, there was a gasp from behind me. Turning fast, I saw Saffie standing in the doorway with Patsy just behind her. As though she was a magnet, I couldn't draw my eyes from her. Wincing, I noticed her face was as pale as I'd ever seen it, apart from the flush on her cheeks. Her hand was over her heart, and the way her chest was heaving, she was hyperventilating. She was terrified, I realised, then following her line of sight, realised it wasn't just on her behalf. She was staring at the screaming child, her eyes flicking between Isla and the big biker looming over her, and her hand covered her mouth.

Oh fuck no. She was going to turn and run.

She wasn't to know we all had a fuckin' soft spot for that child and would do nothing to harm her. And as Salem comforted the sobbing child, Saffie's fear was partly replaced by surprise.

I made every move with care as I approached and started to introduce her to my brothers, touching her hand as though it was made of fragile glass. I felt I was taming a wild animal which could spook at any moment.

She was quiet, I noted, not speaking even when spoken to which made me wonder about the Crazy Wolves, and what her relationship had been with their members. Were any of them her friends or on her side? Probably not, if they'd condoned the treatment Duke had doled out. When Snips asked a direct question of her, I took it on myself to answer on her behalf.

It's still hard to process, but she's here. In my domain. By my side. And I'm going to do everything I can to keep her that way, and vow to look after her. I'm impressed as fuck that she'd been able to set some of her fear aside.

"Dinner's ready if any of you want it," Eva calls out, then steps back to stop herself from being run over.

"You hungry?" I ask the woman at my side.

"Not particularly," she replies, quietly.

"Well, I am. Come and keep me company. Hey, Grumbler!" I shout out as the sergeant-at-arms hurries off, "Save us a couple of seats, will you?"

His hand wave in the air is my answer. Tightening my fingers just a little, I pull her with me as we cross the clubroom. Hungry buggers they might be, but many of my brothers are hanging back, mindful of the need to not crowd her. I give them grateful chin lifts as I walk past.

Our kitchen is large and equipped with industrial scale appliances. In the middle of the room is a long table that's able to seat a dozen of us. First comers get a place to sit, stragglers take loaded plates into the clubroom itself. I could have sat Saffie down in a quiet corner and brought her something to eat, but I'd decided on a baptism of fire.

Patsy's come in behind us, and Kink vacates the chair he was using, allowing her to sit. I notice how Saffie's eyes widen at that. Grumbler is standing behind one, his hands splayed over two more, and he nods when we enter.

"Fried chicken, or beef casserole," Eva calls out. "Grab

plates and help yourselves." She nudges Cindy who comes over just as I'm getting Saffie sat down.

The sweet butt hurries across. "I'll get you your plates. What do you both want?" *Christ, I wish the sweet butts spent more on their wardrobes.* Fashion be darned, some shorts that cover her ass cheeks would be appreciated right now.

Saffie looks extremely uncomfortable and fidgets. Ignoring Cindy, she leans into me. "Shouldn't I stand?" Bemused, I raise my eyebrow at her. "The club's for members, isn't it?"

At that moment, Dart comes in. "Hey, who's going to let my old lady sit down?"

Quick as a flash, Reboot stands. "Here, VP."

Alex ushers Tyler in, pulls up a highchair and places it next to the vacated seat then proceeds to settle Isla in. All this Saffie watches with her eyes wide open.

Cindy's still hovering. "I'll have the chicken," I tell her, then turn to Saffie. "What do you want?"

She starts shaking her head, but I narrow my eyes, knowing she's got to at least attempt to eat. She's lost so much weight it worries me.

Seeing my expression, she says quietly, "Beef."

I notice Cindy's looking at her curiously, and hope she'll keep her claws drawn in. Club girls can get possessive over their bikers, but as I'm making it clear Saffie's with me, and I never partake of their services, hopefully she and the others won't see her as competition.

While Cindy's getting our food, Saffie's attention is caught by Isla shoving her fingers in a bowl of food while Alex is patiently trying to get her to hold a spoon. My gut twists as I realise such scenes will not be in Saffie's immediate future. Maybe I should have taken her straight to the room that's been prepared for her, instead of shoving kids in her face.

As if she feels Saffie's eyes on her, Alex offers a friendly smile her way but doesn't say anything. What could she? Nothing could make the situation easier.

"Hey, there's a piece of shit car outside," Dusty walks in. "We got a visitor?"

Saffie blushes bright red.

"It's Saffie's," I tell him. "Needs a good service. While she's here, I'll have a look at it in the shop." I'd had my brothers change the plugs and replace the filters the day we broke down, but I wouldn't be surprised if it needed a total engine and gearbox refit. Or sent to be scrapped if she'd let me replace it.

"You don't have to do that," she hisses at me. "I can't afford to pay."

"Club friends don't pay," Grumbler rasps, overhearing.

Patsy nods in approval and states, "I saw in my rearview mirror it was belching smoke on the way here."

Again? I was right, it hadn't been fixed. I raise my chin to her. "Then that's settled. I'll take it down tomorrow."

"I'll put Ross on it. He's handy with that model."

Snips, slurping his stew from a spoon, looks up and snorts.

"You could choose your words better," I admonish Grumbler.

He shrugs and grins, and is about to retort, when Pearl, as scantily clad as her fellow sweet butts, drops a plate. She crouches to pick it up, and jumps back with an ouch, cradling her hand while exclaiming, "Son of a fuckin' bitch."

Saffie flinches and presses herself back in her seat.

"Here, let me take a look." Eva grabs a clean towel and steps over to the injured sweet butt. Pearl looks away while Eva gently opens her hand. "You'll live," she pronounces. "Doesn't even need stitches. Just keep it wrapped up for now."

"Hey, Pearl? I got something that will make you feel better later." Snips gestures down to his groin and thrusts his hips suggestively.

I feel like bashing him over the head, especially when Saffie seems to shrink back into herself. "What is it?" I bend my head and speak quietly to her.

She turns, and says so softly, it's hard for me to hear, but I get the gist. "Isn't she going to get hit?"

"What?" I frown. "Pearl? For breaking a plate and cutting herself?" I jerk my head to indicate where Kink's now kneeling down, handling a dustpan and brush like an expert sweeping up the bits of broken plate off the ground. Her eyes widen as I point the sight out. "Guess we're kinda different to the Crazy Wolves, huh?"

She stares at a patched member doing the work we could have summoned a prospect for, or perhaps instructed Pearl to clear up the damage she caused. Slowly, her body begins to relax, and she sits up straighter. For the first time since she entered the clubhouse, the lines on her forehead start to smooth out. "You are." She picks up her fork and puts a small piece of beef into her mouth. I grin, taking it her eating has to be a good fucking sign.

"Saffie, isn't it?" Lost bellows as he appears from the clubroom. He bends his head and takes Patsy's mouth in a scorching kiss before looking back up. "Welcome to the Satan's Devils MC."

I nudge her. "That's our prez."

For a second, her fork hovers midair, then drops to her plate.

"Hey, Prez. You can sit here." Keeper stands and takes his plate to the sink where he rinses it off.

Taking the seat he vacated, Lost focuses on Saffie again. "These assholes been treating you okay?"

Again, looking as scared as potential roadkill, Saffie can't seem to get a word out. Again, I find myself answering for her.

"I think we compare favourably to the Crazy Wolves, or at least so far." I give her a wink.

"I fuckin' hope we do." Lost frowns. "Saffie, my ol' lady's

going to get you settled in after you've finished eating. Let me assure you, you're safe here."

"No one's going to get to you on this compound, sweetheart." The VP backs him up.

"Trust us." I take hold of her hand that's lying on the tabletop and squeeze it.

Saffie doesn't know whether to resume eating, or whether we expect her to speak. After a second, she decides on the latter. "Thank you," she addresses Prez. "But I won't be here long. Patsy said you'd help me get a new ID and relocate." The last is said hopefully.

"That's the plan," Lost confirms, then with a glance my way adds, "If that's what you want."

It's not top of my list of things I want to do, but it seems to satisfy her, and she settles back to eat.

A figure appears in the doorway. It's Cyn. As I raise my chin in greeting, I see her eyes narrow, her mouth form a pout, then watch as she makes a beeline for me.

Standing too close to the woman at my side, she sneers down at her. "That's my seat."

"Cyn!" I say, sharply. "Where are your manners? Saffie's eating."

"Saffie? Who the fuck's she?"

"She's my fuckin' friend," I tell her, my eyes blazing, and my jaw clenched. I force myself to sound more normal, and I glance to my side. "Saffie, this is my sister, Cyn."

I swear I see a pent-up breath leave her body as Saffie gives a little nod. I'm certain that's a look of relief as I remind her who this is.

"I always sit next to you, Niran." Cyn places her hands on her hips and glares at Saffie.

She does if there's a seat beside me and we're eating at the same time, but that's just circumstance, isn't it? It hasn't become a thing.

"I've finished." Saffie puts aside her almost untouched plate.

"Stay right where you are," I growl. "Cyn can sit somewhere else."

She does, taking Grumbler's chair now he's stopped eating and has stood up. Conversations that had been flowing around us cease as her ill-contained ire puts a damper on the mood. I deliberately keep putting my fork to my mouth, but Saffie has ceased to eat.

I try to signal to Cyn that I'm going to kill her later, but she refuses to look at me. At Saffie, yes. She keeps shooting looks of disgust her way.

It becomes a battle between brother and sister. Stubbornly, I refuse to have her think she's chased us away. So for possibly longer than necessary, I stay at the table, and, of course, Saffie stays with me.

Thank fuck for Patsy who, for a second time, saves the day. The first, of course, being by getting Saffie here.

"Well, Saffie, if you've had enough to eat, I'll show you your room," she says as she gets out of her chair.

It's almost comical how fast Saffie's on her feet and picking up her plate. "I'm ready," she says overly brightly.

CHAPTER TWENTY-SIX

Niran

"Cyn!" I call out, rushing to catch up with my sister who had quickly stopped eating and hurried away when she'd finally noticed the black mood I'm in once Saffie had left the table.

She stops mid-clubroom, and swings on her heel. "What?" she tries in an innocent tone.

"Saffie's a guest here and you fuckin' disrespected her."

Her hands go to her hips and she challenges, "So am I."

Guest? I see her more as an intruder. At least Saffie was invited to stay. Moving closer, I grasp her chin with my fingers, and raise her head so she's forced to meet my eyes.

"Get this straight. Saffie's fuckin' important to me, and you make sure you're polite to her."

"But Niran…" she whines.

I realise for the last few weeks she's had it all her own way, and my—except for club business—undivided attention.

"You play nice, Cyn, or you'll be out of here so fast your head will be spinning."

Her mouth opens and shuts, stubborn lines appear on her face, but showing for once she's not stupid, she recognises the determination in my expression. In a pure Cyn way, she shrugs. "Whatever."

"Niran?" Lost's voice barks.

Begrudgingly lowering my hand, I turn away from my sister, not totally satisfied with the way our discussion had ended.

"Toke's got something to share." Lost, with Dart standing beside him, jerks his head toward his office.

Moments later, I'm seated opposite his desk and handing a tablet back to Token with a scowl on my face, and a burning in my gut. Raising my eyes to Lost's, I shake my head. "I can't believe Saffie even fuckin' entered the clubhouse."

What I've just read makes me feel sick. It's a report from Utah that has given us a rundown of the Crazy Wolves MC and all they were up to—the headlines being, prostitution, extortion, trafficking, gun running and drugs. Whatever crime they could commit, they appear to be into. Bile rises into my stomach as I realise I don't know the half of what Saffie had suffered.

"Girl's got spirit," Dart offers, stretching out his long legs. "She wouldn't be here otherwise."

"Girl's got no fuckin' choice," Token observes. "Patsy told her their VP knew her fake ID. What options did that leave her?"

He's right. I don't like it. The four of us take a moment to digest the information Stormy's just fed us. I stare at the Satan's Devils flag hanging behind Lost's desk. Memories come back to me. I'd once pledged my soul to the stars and stripes, after prospecting, I'd had no reservations swearing allegiance to the band of brothers I now ride with.

Like Saffie, at first, I'd been cautious, and like her, I was unwilling to take things at face value. That first meeting at the party down at the beach, I'd been encouraged by the camaraderie I'd witnessed, but I'd held back, caution in the back of my mind repeating a warning, MCs are gangs who choose motorcycles as a mode of transportation.

Alone and adrift, again, not unlike Saffie, they'd been the

first people who'd tempted me in. When they invited me to prospect, I'd gone along with it, a chance to discover what they were about, and for them to see whether I'd fit in. We'd clicked. There was no other word for it.

If I'd had one sniff they were into anything like what the Crazy Wolves were known for, I'd have run a mile. Who would throw in their lot with an MC like that?

"Any idea how Saffie got mixed up with them in the first place?" Lost questions, wiping a weary hand over his head. "How the fuck did she get mixed up with Duke, let alone married to the motherfucker?"

Token nods. "Yeah, some. Stormy gave me details on that. Saffie comes from an ultra-rich family and is their only child. Seems her dad crossed Duke somehow, and he stole her away from them. He couldn't tell whether or not she went willingly, but that he put a ring on her finger suggests she didn't protest."

She can't have known what she was getting into. "The parents never tried to get her back?" I sit up straight. Loaded might mean enough money to buy a personal fucking army, and the question is, why they did not?

The computer guru's eyes meet mine, and the lines on his forehead suggest I won't like what he's going to tell me. "It looks like the Crazy Wolves may have had some hold over the father. He never raised hell or fuck, Niran, he never even reported her missing. They fuckin' disowned her for running off with a man of whom they didn't approve. She apparently brought disgrace on the family."

"Did she try to go back?" Dart asks.

"I'd say it was more likely she never had a chance. She was kept a fuckin' prisoner," Token snarls. "I've also seen medical notes of the injuries that put her in the hospital. Brother, they all but killed her. And from scars and evidence of previously healed bones, that wasn't the first time."

I take a shuddering breath in an effort to stop myself from

smashing something. Each statement I'm hearing makes Saffie's ordeal worse. It's a second or two before I'm composed enough to ask a rational question. "You said they may have had something to hold over the family?" I can't believe her parents could have turned their backs on such a lovely woman.

Token shrugs. "Rich doesn't mean folks that toe the straight and narrow. It's possible, Duke forced their hand."

"She must know," Lost states. "She clearly doesn't trust them. If they've got money, they could buy protection for her. Yet it wasn't to them she ran."

So Saffie didn't believe the people who should love her would raise a finger to help her. Placing my head in my hands, I rub my temples.

"Stormy also suggests," Token picks up the thread once more, "that losing Saffie might have lost Duke any power he had over her father. That could be why he's so determined to get her back now."

Fuck. But that makes sense. Sure, losing property is a low blow to a biker, but losing money could better explain why he hasn't given up searching for her after all these months. It could also mean that she's important not just to him, but to the whole club. Noticing Dart's set face, and Lost's eyes glazing as though he's deep in thought, makes me suspect I'm not the only one leaping to such conclusions.

Dart all but confirms it when he asks, "How big is the fuckin' club?"

"Good question, VP." Lost raises his chin to Dart. "Whatcha know, Toke?"

"Twenty at their base in Nevada. They also have support clubs. Stormy reckons they can muster about fifty altogether."

"Whatcha thinking, Brother?" Lost queries the VP again.

Dart shrugs. "If they find out we're sheltering her, there might be trouble heading for us."

Prez grimaces. "That could be a problem for us."

"Not with the other chapters," I state. Their numbers are nothing to our manpower if we pulled in other brothers.

"And why would they ride to us? For a woman who's not club?" Lost moves his head side to side. "At least Nevada's a fuckin' long way from San Diego. We should get warning if they start riding toward us, especially in numbers."

Head-on, prepared and on our own doorstep, I've no doubt we could take them. Though there could well be damage to us.

"It's just for a few days," Lost reminds us. "Utah only wants us to keep her under guard until they've got a new place sorted for her."

Dart brings his legs back under his chair and sits forward. "Hopefully, it won't be longer than that, and not long enough for them to get organised." I frown, the VP's desires are at odds with my own. If I had my way, Saffie would be here forever. But Dart sends me a glance and carries on, "We've got more worries than just Saffie. We now know they don't give a shit about hurting women, that they're into trafficking proves that. I've got a wife and two kids. Grumbler's woman is pregnant. Hell, even the club girls I wouldn't want to see hurt. There's a fuckin' risk keeping her here."

Token nods and takes over. "They must have a fuckin' ace computer expert somewhere as they found out her identity. I've checked Utah's shit, and that club knows it's stuff. Right now, I wouldn't put anything past them. The moment they link her to us, every one of us is a target."

"You suggesting we turn her out?" The words leave my mouth on a snarl. "And how the fuck would they link her to us?"

Token widens his eyes and starts a lecture. "You wanna know how I would do it? That nurse who was tortured and killed knew she was pregnant. Pregnant women make hospital visits. With her identity, it would be fuckin' easy to find which clinic she's attending, then I'd hack into the security footage at the hospital to prove it was her. Were you ever with her, Niran?"

He makes it sound too damn easy. I shrug. "Only in the parking lot."

"Yeah. Where the cameras were probably filming. All they'd have to do is run facial recognition and… voilà."

For the first time, my lips curve. "I'm Black, Toke. Not so easy for cameras to make me." It's probably the first time my skin has acted in my favour.

"You want to bank on it?" Lost asks. "You want to risk the safety of the club? Were you wearing your cut?" I grimace. That last time I was. He pauses, then continues without waiting for an answer. "It's a long shot they'd connect you to her, and hence to us. But for the reasons Dart's just listed, it's a risk I'm not willing to take. The sooner Saffie's moved on, the better."

"You too?" I'm incensed. "They found her once, what's to stop them finding her again? You risk literally throwing her to the fuckin' Wolves. You seriously suggesting that?"

"Not for a fuckin' moment." Dart's angry eyes meet mine. "But we've got to be careful as fuck. The longer she stays, the greater the risk. Some of us have a lot to lose, Brother."

"I'll get Stormy to hurry up on getting new paperwork for her. He was talking about setting up a few false trails in case the Crazy Wolves IT skills are more than we expect." Token opens his laptop.

"How long does he need?" Lost asks.

Token shrugs. "A few days. A week perhaps? Then she'll be out of here."

"So, we wait it out," Dart states, and rubs at his brow. "I can live with that."

Lost is tapping his fingers against the table. "I wish it were that easy, VP."

I slant my eyes as I look at the prez. "The fuck you mean?"

Lost's jaw tightens. "As Dart said, we've three ol' ladies in this club, one pregnant and one with two kids. We've got club girls who are ours to protect. There's also your sister, Niran, not to mention brothers who've earned the right to sleep soundly in their beds." My eyes widen as he continues, "*I* agreed to bring her in, but we've not had a club vote on it. As a favour to Utah, we've got her out of her apartment, but I thought from here she'd immediately move on, not be here for a fuckin' week when we don't know what the Wolves are doing. I had my concerns even before we thought of a motive. She means more to the club then we previously thought."

"They've been searching for her for months," I almost yell at him. "I can't see there's much risk them closing in now."

"No?" Lost raises an eyebrow. "For months she kept under the radar, no one knew where she had gone. Then they caught Token's chatter, and who knows what they were able to pull from that. You really think they'll sit on their asses and wait for her to come back to them? Nah, if it were me, I'd immediately start pulling out all the stops. My view? She's not got much time."

I brace and open my mouth, but he waves me down. "Not suggesting we cut her loose on her own, brother. While we're waiting for a watertight ID, maybe we can secrete her somewhere she'd be safe, and so would the club. It might be an idea to send her to Utah."

No fucking way. Not on my watch. "I don't like that." I don't like it at all. "I don't fuckin' trust Utah. And what about how she gets there? Without our eyes on her, she could be picked up at any time." Putting my head in my hands, I examine the thought that comes into my mind. It's the only option. I add, "But if that's the solution, I'll go with her."

"No can do, Niran," Dart says reasonably, jerking his head toward Token. "If they've got your identity, it will be the two of you they'll be looking for."

"Or she could stay, until her new ID gets sorted out," Token offers, sensibly. "A few days, a week. What would that hurt?"

Lost turns to him. "My reading is that if the Crazy Wolves find out we're helping, or fuck it, even helped her, they'll come straight for us without giving us time to get organised. If they caught sight of Niran's patch, d'you think the Crazy Wolves would leave us alone? If nothing else, they'll think we've got information. With the women and kids, we can't risk it."

I slam down my fist. "Moving her on without her safety net in place just leaves her as easy pickings."

"She's not one of ours, Niran," Prez reminds me in his sharp *don't mess with me* voice. "I can't ask the brothers to go into a war they're not part of. And we're not throwing her to the Wolves. Where we put her will be as safe as we can make it."

"Utah asked us to take her in," I say stubbornly. "That makes her club."

"Like we owe so much to Utah." Lost rolls his eyes. "You think this club will fight on just Utah's say so? If they're so damn concerned, they can come down here and collect her themselves."

"No way!" I stand so abruptly my chair topples over.

"Sit, Niran!" Lost barks. It takes a lot to rile the prez, but I seem to have done it now.

Fuming, I right my seat, and plonk my ass on it so hard I'm surprised it doesn't break.

"We can't take on a fight that's not ours," Lost offers more mildly. "It's not fair to the brothers."

"No?" I sit forward and slam my hand on the table. "And isn't that what we did for your ol' lady? We took on a fuckin' slave trafficker as I remember."

"Patsy's my ol' lady," Lost says, deceptively calmly. "Saffie has no connection with us."

"So what was that all about then in the kitchen?" I shout. "You said she was safe here, and that we'd protect her."

"And she is safe here while she stays. I wanted to reassure her about that. None of our members will touch her. At the time I thought getting a new identity in place would be quicker."

I thought these men were my brothers. I'd expected them to

step up and take pity on the woman just as I'd done. I can't believe they're talking about sending her away to sort her problems out by herself. I won't let them do it.

"I don't fuckin' believe this." I shake my head, letting the sheer disgust and disappointment in them shine through my eyes.

Dart grimaces, looks at Lost, then suggests, "There's one way out of this. If someone steps up and claims her, that immediately makes her part of the Satan's Devils MC. She'd be protected by us, and have the backing of all the other chapters."

If someone claims her? My eyes widen. "What the fuck, VP? That woman was claimed by a man in another MC, and look how that fuckin' worked for her. You think she'd ever put herself in that position again? Claim her?" I snort. "She'd be exactly what she feared she'd be. Property traded between clubs."

"I don't know about that," Lost says mildly. "It would be up to the man who stepped up to show her the benefits of wearing our patch."

Token's looking from one of us to another. He holds up his hands as if to ward something off. "Who the fuck are you thinking of, Prez? And don't look at me. I don't want a bitch, particularly one with the baggage that she comes with."

"Snips is quite harmless," Dart suggests.

I gaze at him in horror. *Fuckin' Snips?* Again, I rise to my feet, but this time my chair remains standing. I start to pace. Claiming her keeps her in the club and under our protection. Claiming her gives her support. Claiming her means the brother doing the claiming might never get his dick wet again due to the horrors she's experienced and what she's just been through.

I hear them murmuring behind me, *fuck them—they're going through names.* Kink? I snort. Not fuckin' likely. She'd run away from him fast.

If anyone's doing any claiming, it will be me.

Creasing my brow and staring down at my hands, I think about it. Sure, from what I've seen of Saffie, I like her. I'd hate for harm to come to her. But a lifetime commitment where I'd be tied to someone who, as Token rightly suggested, comes with more baggage than an airport's baggage claim carousel after a flight's just landed, I'm not ready for that or qualified to fight her demons.

Perhaps she should leave the club.

That thought doesn't settle with me either. She'd be alone living with the aftermath of the decision she had make. It hurt me enough over this last month when I couldn't see her, but at least she had my number and could call on me for help.

I rake my hands over my head, then do it again. I pace to one side of Lost's office, and then back again. *Claiming her makes her my old lady.* But only in name. It doesn't need to be permanent. It's a ruse to get my brothers to bring her under the full protection of the club, for as long as she remains tied to me. Yeah, that will work.

Before I quite understand what I'm saying, I swing around. "I'll claim her."

"Bout fuckin' time, Brother." When Lost holds out his hand, Dart slaps a ten dollar note into it.

Closing my eyes, I realise the trap they'd set and that I'd walked right into it. Giving a loud snort, followed by a wry smile, I again sit down. "There's one condition, and everyone needs to sign up to this."

"Name it, Brother."

I meet Lost's eyes. "I tell her she's mine in my own time. No one else can breathe a word to her." I'm fully aware that day might not come.

"Deal," Prez answers. "We'll tell everyone at church. Niran, I know you can see the drawbacks, but the one plus is, not one fucker from ours, or any other chapter, will say a single word against protecting her. You've just given the Devils a green light, up to and including, going to war."

"You set me up," I observe. *Fucking assholes.*

While a grin spreads across the face of the VP, Lost doesn't look quite so happy about it. "Don't want to force you into anything, Niran. But Patsy's already all but adopted the woman from the looks of it, and she'd have my guts if I didn't step up."

"No." I raise my hand to get him to stop. "You're right. This is the best way to handle it. Cuts short any discussion about who she is and why we're prepared to risk our lives for her. I understand." Brushing my hand down my chin, I add, "I'm just not sure how the fuck I can work this."

Lost stands. As he moves out from behind his desk and squeezes past Token, he pauses with his hand on my shoulder. "Just play it by ear, Brother. All you need is to be there for her."

The VP stands and follows the prez out through the door. Token stares at me for a moment before closing his laptop and rises to his feet. When he too has left the room, I stay seated, staring at the Satan's Devils insignia.

How the fuck did it come to this? I've got an old lady. And one who would run a mile if she knew that I'd claimed her.

Staring, thinking, doesn't give me any ideas about how I should approach her. Answers won't come if I avoid her. Eventually I stand, and without a fucking clue of what I'm doing, I go out into the clubhouse to find her.

CHAPTER TWENTY-SEVEN

Saffie

While the prospects were tasked with keeping the brothers' rooms clean and tidy at the clubhouse of the Crazy Wolves MC, they did so with little grace and far less aptitude. If it hadn't been for me, Duke's room would have been like the rest, filthy with dust, dirt and cobwebs, and sheets that were never changed on the beds.

I hadn't given much thought to where I'd be staying, so when Patsy leads me up the stairs, I've expectations I'll be walking into much of the same. The thought isn't particularly enticing. As we reach the hallway at the top, she turns to me.

"We've a few empty rooms. I thought this one would suit you." She pauses by a door that's ajar. When she steps back, I precede her into it.

The first thing I notice is that it's clean. Well, maybe it wouldn't be spotless if I purposefully hunted for dust, but on first glance, it's a one hundred percent improvement on any I was used to in the only other clubhouse I have for comparison. The floors are bare wood, with an unblemished rug by one side of the bed. The bed is unmade, and the mattress looks clean and, thank God for small mercies, unstained. There's a television, a desk, a chair, and a view out of the window. Intrigued, I step up to it. It looks out over the gate of the compound, and as the land drops away, gives me a view of the distant Pacific… and is that the famous Coronado Bridge? I think it is.

"I'll send a prospect up to get the bed made."

I turn quickly, my hands held facing her palms up. With memories of Jude coming into my head, I don't want any prospects putting themselves out for me. Though it's unlikely anyone here would care as I don't belong to anybody. I still remember that living nightmare clearly, and I won't take unnecessary risks.

"If you can bring me some sheets, I'll make the bed up." I turn and walk to the door, my experience warning me to check. There's no lock on the outside, no way for anyone to imprison me. But nothing to secure it on my side either, I'd be unable to keep anyone out. I've met a number of the bikers so far, and though they seemed okay, they're men. And there might be more I've not met and not gotten the measure of yet. Anyone could walk in here. I turn around in consternation.

Patsy's eyes have been following me and must notice my look of dismay as I place my hand against the door. Shrewdly, she interprets it immediately. "I'll get a prospect to pick up a lock and we'll get it sorted. But Saffie, no one's going to be anything other than respectful here. You've got your privacy, lock or not."

It's evening now. While I know stores are open at all hours, the likelihood is that even if the promised lock is collected, it's unlikely to be fitted tonight. While the bikers I've met seem pleasant enough and so different from their Crazy Wolves' counterparts, drinks flow freely in clubhouses. Who's to say they won't revert to form when they're drunk? I doubt I'll have a wink of sleep tonight, and as soon as Patsy's gone, will search for something with which to defend myself and jam the chair under the door handle.

My hands start trembling. At least most times the only violence and abuse I had to fear was from Duke himself. Though etched on my memory, it was only on rare occasions he'd share me. Here I belong to no one, and my MC knowledge tells me, an unattached woman is fair game.

"Have you got everything you need?" Patsy's shown me the attached small bathroom, which is adequate if not anything fancy, and I've brought with me the stuff that I use.

The one thing I'm lacking is a suit of armour, a chastity belt and a gun for protection, but I keep that to myself. "Yes, I've got everything. Thank you."

The older woman regards me with sympathy. "I know you've had so much thrown at you at once, Saffie, hopefully you'll be able to get some sleep. Try not to worry too much."

Patsy's old enough to be my mom, and she's got her own daughter. Her advice is that which would come from a mother. I'm mentally drained, and appreciate she understands.

"So," Patsy glances around. "You've got juice, water and snacks. It looks like you're fixed. Lost and I are staying here tonight. We're the furthest door at the end of the hallway. If you want anything, come and find me. I'll leave you my son's number. He's a prospect so he's used to being at anyone's beck and call at all hours. If you need more water and don't want to go down to the kitchen, just give him a shout and he'll bring whatever you need up."

I allow her to program his number in my phone but know I won't be calling him however dire the situation. Again, visions of Jude being beaten to death go through my head, and I turn away to swallow back my tears, vowing again, I won't put another prospect in danger.

"I'll be fine, Patsy. Thank you." As long as no biker comes to bother me. Oh, how I wish there was a lock on the door. Not that it would keep anyone determined out, but they'd make a racket breaking in, and maybe someone would hear and come to save me.

"Saffie," Patsy says, hesitantly. "Er, I'd say you're welcome to go back down to the clubroom, but—" She breaks off, then stretches out her hands and shrugs. "Well, there will be sights that maybe you don't want to see. As I told you, most of the brothers are single."

Yeah, I know exactly what she's talking about. Bikers getting drunk and rowdy, forcing the club girls to meet their deviant needs. Though she hasn't stated it in those terms, maybe there's a chance by showing my face I'd risk being treated like a whore. I've no standing here, no reason for them to give me sanctuary. Maybe they'll be expecting payment in other ways than thanks or money.

"I'll stay up here." I try a half-smile, knowing it looks weak.

There's a knock at the door. Patsy goes to open it.

"Curtis. Thank you." She takes a bundle of bedding from the Black man wearing a prospect patch, closes the door behind him, and places the fresh-looking sheets and comforter on the bed.

As she starts to unfold them, I go over to help. Within moments, we've got the bed made. Patsy gives a satisfied nod then comes over, stands in front of me for a moment, then reaches out her arms in invitation. When I step into them, she gives me a quick hug and a peck on my cheek.

"We'll catch up in the morning, Saffie. You try and get some rest."

"Goodnight, Patsy. And, thank you." I add the last belatedly, and though I hope it sounded sincere, a little half-heartedly. Right now, I'd prefer to be back in my apartment all alone and not in this nest of biker iniquity.

I shiver when Patsy leaves me alone. Though there's a television on the wall, and I brought my tablet and e-reader with me, I know I won't be able to occupy myself with frivolous activities.

So far today, my mind's been engaged on survival, now it circles back to the constant regret in my head.

Does Patsy know I aborted my baby? If she does, would she blame me?

How could she not? I blame myself. If I hadn't been taken in by Duke, then maybe instead, I'd by now be married to a good man and be raising my family. If I hadn't been exposed to the Crazy Wolves, I wouldn't be so scared, and would be taking the Satan's Devils at face value, trusting them as the good men they appear to be.

But having had the experiences I have, trusting them is far from easy. I'm frightened to relax my guard, worrying doing so would prove I was being blind all over again. My caution of bikers I wrap like a protective cloak around me.

I pick up my e-reader hoping to lose myself in a fictional world, but of course it doesn't work. Placing it back down, I lie on the bed, thoughts of how I move forward from here vie with fears of the bikers downstairs.

The music has grown louder, and the odd shout filters up, suggesting that alcohol has started to do its work, making me all too conscious I'm in a clubhouse full of men and no way of stopping any of them coming in. *I need to find a weapon.*

When the drawers and closet offer nothing to me, I look under the bed. I don't know what I expect to discover, but as no one had conveniently left a gun, knife or baseball bat behind, I've come up with zilch.

I'm never going to be able to sleep.

A check in the bathroom finds there's no lock on that door either. Desperate for a pee, I quickly use the facilities but don't even consider the shower. As for undressing for the night, nope, I'm going to sleep in my clothes.

My heart is beating far too fast as my mind throws me back to how this would play out in the Crazy Wolves' clubhouse. An unclaimed female wouldn't just be molested by one, she'd have them all queued up outside all night, and probably more than one in the room together.

Patsy and Lost are just up the hall. Surely, they'd hear me if I screamed out?

My car's still outside. Could I escape and go back to my home? Or will I be stopped on my way out?

Sitting on my bed, I rock with my arms wrapped around my stomach. My whole life is a mess, and I've no idea what to do for the best.

Suddenly there's a sharp double tap on the door. I breathe in deep and hold it. But whoever's outside doesn't enter. Instead, they knock again.

Maybe it's Patsy come back to check on me?

At least whoever's there is prepared to wait for me to answer. Before the knock can come again, I get to my feet, wipe the ever-present tears from my eyes, and shuffle my way toward the door. Reluctantly, I open it just a crack, enough to recognise the man who's standing outside.

It's Niran. I swallow rapidly. He looks even bigger than he had in my house. My mouth's so dry I try to summon enough saliva to speak, but before I do, offering a weak grin, he holds up a pack containing a lock in one hand, and with the other raises a toolbox.

"I know it's late but thought you'd sleep easier if I fastened the lock straight away." He holds up his hand holding the new lock, and I see something else. "I've also got a sturdy bolt you can use from the inside just for extra peace of mind."

Bolts in the Crazy Wolves' clubhouse had been on the outside, designed to keep people in. For a second, his offer makes my eyes widen in surprise.

At last, I find my voice. "Thank you, Niran. Are you sure it's not too late to fit it now?"

"Nah. Most members are still downstairs. Anyone already in bed will understand." He waves his hand. "May I?"

He means to come in. Of course he has to if he's to complete the work. Stepping back, I allow him to enter.

The drill sounds overly loud, and I wince on behalf of Patsy who I suspect is trying to sleep just up the hall, but Niran seems to know what he's doing. In no time at all, I have keys in my hand, and to my joy, knowing how MC members often have lock picking skills, a sturdy bolt on the inside of my door. Niran disappears for a moment, then returns with a Hoover and soon cleans up the mess he's just made. Then he steps back and seems to eye me critically.

"You doing okay, Saffie?"

CHAPTER TWENTY-EIGHT

Niran

When I ask if she's doing okay, Saffie's tired eyes meet mine. A moment passes, then she admits, "No."

It's confirmation that at least once, we were friends. With me, she doesn't need to keep up a pretence.

When I'd bumped into Connor on his return from the store, I gave mental thanks to Patsy for watching out for her. Of course she needed the control of who she let in through her door.

I'd hoped she'd feel safer once I'd attached the lock, and sure, there was an expression of relief on her face, but not enough. Fuck, her experience of bikers was so fuckin' bad, she must have been terrified to think anyone could walk in, even a flimsy lock wouldn't keep a determined man out. How can I reassure her no one is like that around here? That she's as safe—safer—than she could be anywhere.

Bikers drink, we get rowdy, I admit I'm no exception. It's far from unusual to hear raised voices and the sound of bodies banging into walls and doors late into the night. Without her door secured, it's easy to imagine her lying awake worried. And hell, she wouldn't have been wrong to, even if the only intruder would be someone mistaking hers for his room. Only last week I'd had a visit from an inebriated Pennywise who'd been convinced my room was his. I'd only just managed to persuade him otherwise before he'd joined me in bed. I shudder just thinking about it, and where his meaty paws might have roamed in his drunken sleep.

I'd hoped she'd relax with the lock keeping people from coming in, and the bolt that gives her the security that visitors are hers to decide whether to admit. But her answer to my casual enquiry as to whether she's alright, I feel like a blow to my gut.

Of course she isn't. She's lost a baby and has a bastard of a husband after her. I fucking wish I could refer to him as her ex, but in the eyes of the law, he's very much in the present. On top of all that, she was faced with children tonight, a reminder, at least in the short term, of what she's not going to have.

I wish there was some way I could take her pain from her, but I don't know how.

"You want to go to sleep? Or would you like to talk?" My presence is the only thing I can offer her. Perhaps I've got some ideas about her not needing to get a divorce—dead men don't tend to have much influence in their widows' lives, but something like that will need to be considered carefully, and a death sentence time to be carried out. Her other issues, now I've fixed her lock, I've no idea how to deal with.

She hangs her head like a dog which has just been kicked. "Coming here was a mistake. I'd like to go home."

In my view that's the biggest error she could make. Firstly, we've no idea how close Duke is to finding her location and secondly, I've already let her spend far too much time alone. The state she was in when she arrived testifies to that. Without me looking out for her, she's not been taking care of herself.

Purposefully leaving the door ajar, I step further into the room. "If you really want to leave, no one will stop you. You're not a prisoner here. But Saffie, it is best you stay. That way, I, we, can protect you and give you a safe place to think on your next move."

Still looking down, she starts to pick at her fingernails. "My next move is simple. I leave San Diego." Even with her head bowed, I can tell she's only just holding back tears when she sniffs.

My eyes narrow, sensing something deeper is going on. "What's worrying you?"

"Where can I go where I'll be safe? Duke's found me once. There's nothing stopping him from finding me again."

I wonder whether on some visceral level the idea that she's my old lady has taken root in my brain when the acknowledgement flits through my head that I really don't want her to leave. Not the clubhouse, and not San Diego.

"Then the answer is to get Duke off your back," I suggest.

She shoots me a look as if doubting my ability to do that. "I thought he wouldn't be looking," she states, shaking her head. "Sure, I knew he'd be angry, but after all these months, why's he pulling out all the stops? I didn't think he'd try that hard to find me."

Grimacing, I tell her the brutal truth. "Men like that don't want to lose, Saffie. With him in the picture, you'll never be able to stop looking behind you."

"Where did I go wrong?" Her voice turns to a wail. "I thought I did it right, Niran. I did everything that the Freedom Trail people told me. Then I trusted you, and your guy betrayed me."

"You did nothing fuckin' wrong," I growl, angry at myself as she's right. If it hadn't been for me, Duke would still be in the dark. "As for us trying to get info, well, we do that on anyone who the club comes across. Token knows what the fuck he's doing. Duke must have a fuckin' good hacker on his payroll or access to one."

She huffs. "Duke has everything on speed dial, but in this

case it's closer to home." Her brow wrinkles in disgust. "Grit. He's the security man for the Crazy Wolves MC. He's ex-FBI if you can believe that. He got kicked out when he was consorting too closely with White supremacists and found something he liked with the Wolves. When he joined, the club gained all the skills they needed." Her voice breaks off, and she shakes her head. "Whether he's good enough to track down my new name, I wouldn't know, but he's all I can think of."

As an ex-fed, he well might, or have contacts who could help. I hone in on why Duke's club had attracted him. "Crazy Wolves a White club?"

Her eyes roam over my face. "Let's just say you'd never get a step in the door."

Her answer isn't unexpected. Hell, it was only just before I joined that the Satan's Devils removed the colour clause restricting membership. When I'd first joined, I'd expected some flack as the token Black member, but here no one is judged by the colour of their skin, it's the heart beating beneath it that matters.

Something occurs to me. Something important. "And you, Saffie? You buy into the White shit?" I hold my breath.

"Me?" Her eyes widen. "Hell no. Niran, I might not know a lot about you, but from what I've seen, you're hands down better than any man in that club." Shaking her head, she adds, "There's no sense in judging a man by his colour. It's just one more excuse for them to bind together and do the shit they do."

She's got that right. Problem is, there are far too many who hide under that umbrella, believing anyone looking different to them is a threat to be removed. For a moment, my hands clench as I force myself to put issues of race aside that have so often been the blight of my life. A White man can walk down any street unmolested, as if there's a flag saying 'I'm no threat' above his head. A man such as me? Most of the time, I'm a suspected criminal until proved innocent.

I take a moment, then get back to the point, and one which annoys me no less. "The Freedom Trail needs to tighten up its shit. The only thing that makes sense is that this Grit hacked into their database and discovered your new identity." I make a mental note to talk to Stormy and get him to check Grit out, find out exactly what kind of threat he is. At the least, if she moves on, next time Stormy and his crew need to do better.

"To be safe, I need to move away without leaving a trace. How the hell am I going to do that, Niran? What's to stop Duke from finding any new name I choose again?" Saffie covers her eyes with her hands and rubs them.

I repeat to her what Token had told me when he'd caught me finding the tools to put on her lock. "This time we'll make sure your new identity will never be discovered. It won't be shared with the Freedom Trail nor anyone else. Once you're relocated, we can destroy all records and traces of it. There's ways for you to disappear completely if it comes to it."

Sadly, she shakes her head, then turns watery eyes to face me. "Does that mean you wouldn't be able to find me either?" It means exactly that. Earlier Token had suggested her new identity might not be shared even with me. Something I find abhorrent. All I can do is hope it doesn't come to that and persuade her there's another route she can go down.

For now, though, I give her that comfort. "If we do this right, Saffie. Then no." She must know I'll never betray her. But she needs that confidence that she'll disappear without a trace. Even to those who have innocent reasons to find her.

Turning away, I know I can't bear the thought of her once again having to rebuild her life. A hard thing to do at any time, but with her still immersed in her grief? Hell, I wouldn't rehome a dog unless it was fully fit, and probably not even then.

She can't leave. I offer the alternative. "You've got another option," I tell her. As her brow creases, I continue, "We get Duke out of the picture." Her lips narrow, but I don't give her a chance to speak. "If you accept the protection of the Satan's Devils MC, then we can deal with him for you."

Her face, which hasn't got much colour to start with, pales before my eyes. She even takes a step back. "You forget, Niran, I know how an MC works." Her words sound forced, almost staccato. "Unless the MC is being paid, protection is only offered to property. I'm not a whore, I've never been, and will never be." Tears once again leak from her eyes.

"Fuck, Saffie. How could you think we'd ask you to repay us by working on your back?"

"Well what else do you want?" she snaps. "You've probably found out that I come from a wealthy family, but there's no chance of them paying you to protect me. For all I know, I'm dead to them now."

"Saffie." I try to keep my voice low, particularly when I hear feet walking past the door. I'd close it for this conversation, but now's not the time to give off the wrong signals and make her more scared than she already is. "We're not asking for money."

"You want me to believe you're doing this out of the goodness of your hearts?" She's growing angry. "You think I'm stupid? You think your club would go to war for me? If Duke finds out you're protecting me, he'll come for me, and he doesn't take prisoners. Or is it the Devils who have lost their minds? Are you so far away from a normal MC, that you've forgotten the blood that can be spilled? You, your brothers, would be putting your lives on the line for me if you go up against Duke." She gets to her feet, shakily, but there's determination in her eyes. "Your men…" She waves her hand. "You tell me you're different from the Wolves, if that's true, you've no idea what you're up against. Duke wouldn't come for a conversation, he'd come in with all guns blazing. And when push comes to shove, you think your brothers would give their lives for a woman who's basically walked in off the street?"

"We're not fuckin' stupid," I hiss, ignoring her accusing finger pointed my way. "Nor weak."

"If everything you do is legal, perhaps you've forgotten how to fight. Duke hasn't, I assure you."

She's pressing my buttons and I'm getting riled. It's my temper that pushes the fateful words out of me. "You're fuckin' right, Saffie. My brothers wouldn't go to war for just anybody. It's property that's protected. That's why I've claimed you as my old lady."

She gasps and retreats once again. A trembling hand rises to her face, and she shakes her head as if wondering if her ears are working. In a growl, she rasps, "Say that again."

I've gone and fucked up. I know it. I shouldn't have spat that out, should have kept it to myself. Another woman would have believed we'd help because we were sorry for her, but Saffie's got too much experience with MCs. The Devils might not be the Wolves, but we work to many of the same principles.

Tonight should have been a time for her to rest and settle in. Fuck, that's why I came to secure her door. Instead, what I've said could get her running for the hills, and I wouldn't blame her.

"Saffie, listen to me." I brush my hands over my head, linking my fingers together behind my neck. "Before I knew about your connection with the Crazy Wolves, I was gutted by the problems you were going through and wanted to help you. I wanted to be there for you, just as a friend. But throw in Duke and his MC, that's not enough. You need more than just me on your side, you need my club." Breaking off, I shrug. "Taking you as my old lady ensures your protection."

"I'm not a fucking dog you rescued from the pound," she throws back. "I'm a human being with wants, needs and desires all of my own. I'm not someone who can just be claimed. Hell, even Duke asked me first."

"You'd have said no if I asked you." Christ, I can't believe the words that come out of my mouth. I should be conciliatory, but each of my utterances seems designed to make matters worse.

Her eyes widen and fill with horror. "You've already done this? Claimed me? Voted me in?"

I grimace. "The prez and VP know." I don't add it was their suggestion. Knowing it hadn't been my proposal and I'd been virtually forced into it would hardly have helped.

She stomps her foot. "Well, apart from a vote which I presume you'd have, that makes it official doesn't it?" Now her face has colour in it. I wish that it didn't as her cheeks blaze red. "What happens next? You want my name tattooed on your body? Yours on mine? Well, if you do, you'll have to cover up Duke's name first. You want to fuck me to seal the deal? Well, I've got news for you, asshole, you'd have to force me into your bed."

Her cheeks are puffing out and receding as she draws breath after angry breath. As I go to speak, she holds up her hand. "I've had it up to here," she raises her hand to her chin, "of people making decisions for me. Of not having a choice. I thought you were a good man, Niran, but here you are, acting just like Duke. All I know is I never want to be an old lady again, not even a wife. I belong to myself, and no one else."

My teeth grind together. "It works both ways, Saffie. You agree to be mine, then I'm yours, and that includes everything I bring along with me, including my Devil brothers. Think before saying no. I can't see you're in any position to refuse."

"We barely know each other. And you've given no sign of being attracted to me. Are you that shallow?" Her eyes widen. "Perhaps things are different in the Crazy Wolves MC. There, men take having an old lady seriously. Do the Devils take them and swap them like a dirty pair of underwear? Doesn't that title mean anything to you?"

"It means the world to us," I protest, realising if that's true, I'm jumping in with both feet. I'm telling her I'm viewing this as a permanent arrangement.

She's not stupid. She challenges my declaration. "You really want me? Want me in your life? Want me riding behind you, and in your bed every night? You really want that, Niran?"

"I want you to be safe!" My shout rings in the air and my fingers curl into my fists. That's all I want. The other stuff? Nah, how can I say whether I want that or not? I don't really know her, what she likes or dislikes, whether we're compatible in bed or out of it. When the thought of taking an old lady crossed my mind, it would have been me heading into it with every pertinent i dotted and t crossed.

Dart and Lost had forced the situation upon me, and I'd agreed only so she had protection. I hadn't thought anything further than that. *But I hadn't put up much of a fight about it.*

"Saffie." I calm my tone. "Look at it as a pretend situation. I call you my ol' lady, and you'll have the Devils at your back."

Her head drops again, she takes a few breaths, then she looks up. "You're not thinking straight, Niran. Your brothers won't have your back for a fake relationship, nor offer their support to me. And you wouldn't ask it of them. And even if you ask me to play the part, I'm in no place where I can do that." Her hands wrap around her empty belly. "I don't even want to think about having another man in my life."

She doesn't want me. That hurts more than it should.

"Staying alive is important, Saffie." I don't want her dead but have to acknowledge the points she's made. How could I ask my brothers for support if this was all a lie? I'd be asking my brothers to risk their lives for someone with no connection to the MC. Unless this has at least a chance of becoming real, there's no point in starting the pretence.

I gaze at her standing there, weighed down by her fear and her grief, undernourished and a shadow of the woman I expect she could be. Would tying her down be unfair?

I can't pile more problems on a woman who's carrying a weight no one should be asked to bear. Not only trying to come to terms with the loss of her child, but her past. Whether the Devils are different or not, how would she ever be happy associated with another MC? Even if I were in the position to declare undying love for her, it would be too much to ask.

I start to pace, one side of the room to the other, then back. My hands brush over my head, then do it again.

Damn it. How can I do this to her? I should step back, let her leave, go somewhere that I could never find. Let the tech guys burn all trace of her, let her leave me behind.

But I feel such a pull toward her. The thought of her disappearing and me never seeing her again, never knowing if Duke's caught up with her, how could I live with that on my mind?

But how could I trap her in a relationship neither of us wants?

Damn being fair, that's the last thing on my mind. I want this broken but strong woman in my life. Being there, at my back and my side, and one day, when the time's right, it would be no hardship to take her into my bed. Stopping my pacing, I take a step toward her, not too close, but enough so she can read the sincerity in my face.

"Saffie. Say you'll be my ol' lady. Stay with me. Accept the protection of my club. Anything more than that, we'll take one step at a time." When she gives a sharp dismissive shake of her head, I continue before she can stop me. "I want you, Saffie. I want to protect you. I want you on the back of my bike and to be part of my life."

"You don't know me." Her eyes close briefly, then reopen again. "You've only seen me at my worst, maybe you won't like my best."

"Hell, Saffie. Don't you think seeing you cope with the shit in your life gives me some sense of your measure? Don't you see how fuckin' strong and capable you are, just to be still standing on both legs after all you've been through?"

"You love me?" she challenges.

My mouth snaps shut. How could I know? It's far too early. Like, respect, but love? How do I even know what that emotion feels like?

She snorts. "Even Duke could lie when it came to that."

"I'll never lie to you, Saffie. I like you, one hell of a lot. I think there's a basis for something to grow on."

Her hand rises as if it's going to touch my face, but never makes contact. "I don't love you, Niran. I like you as a friend. I've been burned so badly, I don't know if I'll ever want another man again, and certainly not to be his property. Even if I did," her hand drops to her flat stomach, "now's certainly not the right time." She grimaces. "I can't make you any promises or give you false hope, not when I feel dead inside."

I'm a bastard for pushing her. I should have kept everything quiet. I've fucked everything up. I'm selfish, only thinking that losing her would leave a hole in my life. Have I been considering her at all, or my own desires and wants?

"You're right," I finally concede, my face falling and something dying inside. "I won't claim you. You stay with us for a few days while we get your new identity sorted and the rest of your life worked out."

She glances around the room, her eyes landing on the meagre possessions she brought with her, then she straightens her back.

"Niran," she begins, softly. "I do appreciate you trying to help. I'm in no place to consider a relationship, even if you feel something on your part. To stay one step ahead of Duke, I'll have to leave San Diego, and all of the friends that I've made." She emphasises the word *friend* to let me know that includes me. "I'm grateful. I do need help to set up a new identity, but that doesn't mean I need to be here while that's done."

"Saffie—"

"Being here isn't good for me." She turns to face me. "I'm scared, Niran. Whatever you say, however nice Patsy is, I keep waiting for the Devils to act like the Wolves."

"What do you intend to do then?" Now she's implying she's not even going to stay for the time to get her ID sorted.

"I need to go back to my apartment, to pack everything that I can take with me. Then, I'll leave. Go to a motel, or something. One that takes cash."

"You got the money?"

She shrugs. "I've got enough. I'm not looking for luxury, just somewhere to crash."

"Saffie," I try again. "You shouldn't be alone right now." Apart from the fact there's a mad man after her, doesn't everyone need a friend? Especially after what she's been through.

"I've been alone for months, well, five years to be exact." She shrugs. "As long as Duke doesn't know where to find me, I'll be alright."

That feels like a kick to my gut. It's not because I was expecting her to jump at the chance of being my old lady, hell, I wasn't exactly thinking I was going to have to fight her off, but she doesn't even want my shoulder to lean on.

Why should I have regrets about a woman I barely know? Why should I find her announcement so devastating? Dart and Lost would probably think it's the best thing for the club. As for me? She's damaged, she's not whole, she might never be again. But I hate the thought I'm going to lose all contact with her.

But what can I say? I dove in with both of my overlarge feet, I should have expected her reaction. I've chased her off.

What do I do?

"Stay tonight," I tell her, unable to think of anything else. "I've put the lock on your door. If you're still of the same mind in the morning, we'll make sure you get home safe, and help you get relocated elsewhere."

Her yawn suggests she might be weakening. And indeed, it's not long before she agrees. "Until morning. But Niran, I'm under enough pressure as it is. Please, don't keep trying to wear me down. I've made my decision. I won't go back on it." She pauses, then adds the killing blow. "That goes for Patsy, Mary and anyone else who thinks they can help. I need to do this alone."

Because—my head adds in the missing words—that's how she'll be going forward and preparing to start all over again.

"Saffie." Words come out of my mouth before I'm conscious I've come to a decision. "If you go, I'm coming with you." So she's left in no doubt, I add, "I'll leave the club." To show her I can do it, I take off my cut. More than that, I let it drop from my hand onto the floor.

"Niran!" I've shocked her. "Niran?" she repeats, and her eyes narrow as though assessing me as a man without the cut.

Is it enough? Will that convince her? Will that stop her from walking out of my life?

"Think on it, Saffie. I'm yours however you want me."

She seems lost for words.

"Say it, Saffie. Just say you'll think about it. Wherever you go, you could have me with you. However you want me. I won't put pressure on you, but you won't be alone anymore."

Time ticks by. How many minutes, I'm not sure, but eventually she says, "Okay, I'll think about it."

As she turns her back on me, I realise I've said all I can for tonight. I've laid bare my soul; shown her the extent I'm prepared to go to. In the morning, if she says yes, I'll have to make good on my promise to leave the club.

Leave my brothers who've become so important to me.

But I've made the offer, I can't pull it back.

Hating that she's indicating the conversation is over, and there's nothing more I can do, I take a step toward the door, but before I get there, she calls me back. When I turn, she's staring at my cut as though it's a snake poised to strike her.

Going back, I pick it up, but fold it over my arm. Just one word from her, and tonight will be the last time I wear it.

A sound in the corridor has my head turning, but before I can investigate, Saffie speaks again.

"Niran… I do appreciate you."

Sure. That's what I want from her. Fucking appreciation. I raise my chin, and exit the room, hearing her close the door, engage the lock then shoot home the bolt.

I check the hallway, but except for footsteps on the stairs, there's no one.

For a second, I lean back against the door, my eyes closed, and my head shaking. *Why did I fuck it up?*

Could I really leave the club?

I straighten and shake out my shoulders. If that's what it takes, that's what I'll have to do. The alternative of not knowing where she is, and that she's safe, is unthinkable.

To never know if she's happy, or even alive? To think of her finding a new man eventually? Hell, I'd go mad.

I take a few breaths, my momentous, impulsive decision not settling easily. Then my sixth sense warns me, I'm not alone. Snapping my eyes open, I turn my head and see someone approaching.

"The fuck you doing here?"

"I was looking for you." Cyn bites her lip. "I didn't know where you'd gone." Her eyes widen, and her mouth forms an unattractive smirk. "Were you with her... Saffie?"

"What the fuck has that got to do with you?"

"I'm your sister. I don't like her. She's no good for you." She postures as though she's got rights in the matter.

Hell to the no on that. Putting my hand on her chest, I start pushing her back toward the stairs. "Just get out of here, Cyn. I'm your brother in name only. You've got no claim on me other than blood." To make it clear, I add, "You've got no say in what I do, or who's going to be my ol' lady."

"Old lady?" she gasps. Her pretence at being soft and nice

disappears. Her nails come up and she launches at me scratching. "You can't take an old lady. I won't let you do that."

I'm more of a match for her, catching her hand and holding it. "The world doesn't revolve around your wants and needs, Cyn, and it's time you learned that."

"But Niran…" She pouts. "You're my brother."

"And you're my sister, God help me. I've got nothing for you, Cyn. I've given you a place to stay, my time, I've been there for you. But now someone else needs me."

She casts a look up the corridor behind me. "Don't you dare try and talk to Saffie, you hear me? You try and come between us, then you're fuckin' dead to me."

Turning her around, I push her toward the stairs. With one backward glance toward me, she huffs out a breath, and at last seems to get the message and leaves.

I watch until she disappears, hanging around a few minutes more in case she tries to come back. Then when I'm sure the threat's abated, I swing on my heel and take myself off to bed.

CHAPTER TWENTY-NINE

Saffie

Niran had completely overwhelmed me, making my head spin until I didn't know which way was up.

I'm indignant, how dare he say in that off-handed way that he'd claimed me, when he knew I never wanted to be property again. Sure, Niran's not Duke, or not on the surface, but who knows what would happen if I allowed myself to be claimed? Bikers live by their own code, and from what I know, it certainly doesn't appeal to me.

Even if Niran's views of an old lady are different to the experience I've had, I've had enough of controlling men and being kept under the thumb. I didn't escape from Duke just to go back to another dominant man.

Maybe if he'd spoken to me, explained his reasons before claiming me in front of his prez… No, not even then. If getting help from the Devils involves me tying myself to a man, then I'd rather take chances and do it on my own. From what I gather, my new papers are already coming along and shouldn't be tied to any agreement or otherwise I have with Niran. My only option is to take them and run, and this time, try to disappear completely.

Even with the lock on the door, I know I won't settle here.

However much I try to tell myself the Satan's Devils are differ-ent, the sounds they make, the clothes they wear are too reminis-cent of what was my life for the past few years. One part of my brain tries to tell me I'm better off staying, while the other, and larger side is acting purely on instinct, and telling me I'm a fool to seek sanctuary in a lion's den. What didn't help was Niran acting like a Neanderthal, and proving by his words, that under-neath, he was just like the men I'd been running from. *How dare he claim me?*

I'm scared, on edge, and even staying here a couple of days will be too much for my already stretched nerves.

If I return to my apartment, there's a risk Duke will find me. But I've been careful about who knows my address, lying and giving my old one. I'd even lied on my hospital records. There should be no way he knows more than the name I'm using and that I'm somewhere in San Diego. Would he even set out with no more knowledge than that?

I know I'm banking my life on the answer being no.

Being equally scared of staying, and going back to my apart-ment on my own, the latter wins out, or at least, that's how I'm feeling currently. If I manage to sleep, I can rethink everything when I wake up. Things often look different come the morning.

If I stay, would I weaken?

I pace the room, trying to get the image of Niran out of my head. If I'd met him before Duke, yes, I would have fallen for him. Who wouldn't? He's handsome, kind, thoughtful and considerate, and while I'm certainly not in the place where I think he, or any man would ever arouse me, if I were to get there, I'm sure I wouldn't turn Niran down.

My problem is, I'd felt the same with Duke when I'd first met him, unable to see that it was all a ruse. I don't know how I can shake the thought at the back of my mind that the same thing is happening again. But what would Niran get out of it?

Niran offered to leave his club for me.

The disrespectful way he'd thrown down his cut and the immensity of his offer had astounded me, and I can't understand either gesture. Was it an indication of what I've come to mean to him? But why? Ever since he met me, I've been a hot mess. I've not led him on, nor for one moment let him think we could ever be more than friends. Yet he seemed set on providing his personal protection.

Or was it a ruse to get me to stay?

An offer to leave a club isn't made lightly, and that's if he even can. Knife would have had any man killed who'd expressed a desire to give up his cut. Are the Satan's Devils different? Maybe they are, but they can't be by much. Loyalty is earned, and once given, it's one hell of a snub for whatever reason to wish to leave a club.

Does Niran really think that much of me?

If he does, I'm not in a position to reciprocate.

When I was with Duke, I wasn't allowed to be me. Even with my first husband I was pretending to be the perfect wife. While I was pregnant, I had to think of more than just myself. I was going to be a mom with another person dependent on me.

That would have been fulfilling, and oh how I wish it had worked out. But sacrificing for a child is different to revolving your life around a man. Much as I miss my baby, and wish things hadn't turned out as they had, there's something inside me screaming this is my chance and I should take it. There's something attractive about standing my own ground and starting a new life with the chance of it being whatever I make it. For that, I'd be right in turning Niran down.

But in the cold light of day, will the dawn remind me that I'm not unencumbered? I've a man intent on finding and hurting me. Alone means vulnerable in these circumstances, so maybe I shouldn't be so hasty turning Niran away.

Maybe Niran and I could make a go of it. I'd be using him,

sure, but perhaps in time, I'd find myself as a woman again, and hell, I'd be hard pushed to find a better man.

But who would Niran be once he was a Devil no more? Who was the man without his club? Even he must know taking on Duke and the Wolves by himself would be suicide. We'd be looking over our shoulders for the rest of our lives. We'd always be on the run.

It wouldn't be fair to make him live that way. Duke's closing in. Finding me once makes it almost certain he'd find me again, even with a new identity. Much as I hope changing my name again would be sufficient protection, I doubt it.

Without the support of the Devils, I'd be back to square one, and Niran dragged down alongside me.

Do I need them too? Much as I don't want to admit it, only another MC would be able to take down the Wolves and get Duke finally off my back. But to get them onside, I'd have to agree to be his old lady.

No. No way. My body freezes when I even think it. My heart palpitates, and my lungs gasp for oxygen as if all the air has disappeared. Just the term has such strong connotations I don't think I could ever shake myself free of the nightmares in my head.

As for Niran, I don't believe he wants to be an old man, and certainly not mine. He's either offering for hitherto unknown ulterior motives, or out of a misplaced sense of honour which it would be wrong to accept.

It's been over an hour since Niran left, and I'm in no mood to go to bed. My brain's whirring, trying to work out what to do for the best. I sit on the bed, holding the key to the lock that Niran had installed for me, still wondering what to make of his sudden declaration and whether I'm right to dismiss it.

No one has ever offered to give up anything for me. My ex before Duke hadn't given up much, not even the women he'd kept on the side. Duke? Hell, he just slotted me into his life and carried on like he had before. Niran's the one man ever to offer to make a sacrifice.

Loud footsteps sound outside my door, and the lock rattles as whoever it is passes.

"Hey, Kink!" someone shouts out, his words slurred.

"What?" is called back, slightly more soberly.

"You really got a bitch tied up in your room?"

"Sure fuckin' have," is called back.

The footsteps recede, and so do the voices.

I though, am having a full-blown panic attack, trying to get air into my lungs. My heart's beating frantically, and blood drains from my head, making me feel faint. My shaking legs won't support me, so I drop to the floor.

They're Wolves in disguise.

Thoughts slam into me one after the other.

They brought me to the clubhouse when they had no real information that Duke was closing in, but the threat was enough to make me fall in with their plans. If Duke's still in Nevada, I could have stayed in my own apartment until I had a new identity.

Why was it so important to stay here?

Suddenly, Niran's offer to leave the club, the one thing that had made me start to trust him, has become more sinister. Was that just one last desperate ploy to stop me running away? Maybe their only reason to get me to stay was because they knew Duke was coming for me, but their motive wasn't to keep me safe.

I'd trusted Duke.

I'd trusted my ex before him.

I'm a terrible judge of men.

My life depends on me not making a mistake again.

My revelations make me run for the bathroom, vomiting up the meagre dinner I'd forced down. *It's happening again.*

No, Niran wouldn't do that.

But I heard it myself. One of the brothers here has a woman tied up in his room. That sounds to me like a sex slave. Just like the Wolves.

Stop! I instruct myself. Chest heaving, heart racing, I pull myself up. *Deep breaths.* I concentrate on calming myself. *It's just the compound getting to me.* Stay, I should stay, voice my fears to Niran tomorrow. Be an adult about this.

My eyes flick to the door, then my brow creases. There's a note that's been slipped under it. Wondering what it is, I go pick it up, unfolding it and holding it under the light.

Ask Niran about his old lady.

What? I read it again, but the words don't change.

Old lady? Had he had one before? He'd never told me. And if he had, what happened to her, and why had he kept it a secret? Bile rises in my throat as another thought occurs to me. *What if she's still around?* That would mean I was right, and he'd been lying to me.

Why?

Fuck knows, I don't, but I doubt there's any good reason. I'd been on the cusp before, and this is the final straw. There's only one thought in my head, *I've got to leave.* With shaking hands, I pick up my bag, throw the few things I'd taken out back into it, then I start my escape.

Tiptoeing along the corridor, I walk to the side of the stairs, stepping as quietly as possible. When I reach the clubroom, I freeze. There's a prospect tiredly wiping down the bar.

He glances up, eyes my bag, and I slump, knowing I'm going to be escorted back upstairs. But all he does is give a shake of his head, and nods toward the door.

"You leaving?"

Incapable of speaking, I nod my head.

"I'll open the gate from here."

CHAPTER THIRTY

Niran

I might go through my nightly routine and slide under the covers, but that doesn't mean I sleep. My conversation with Saffie plays on repeat.

Did I mean what I said? The pros and cons go around and around my head as I toss and turn all night. *Leave the Devils?* It would be like starting all over again, and what the fuck would I do with my life? I'd already failed once as a civilian, and nothing has changed.

So I'll tell her I didn't mean it. Stay here and live the ride. I stare at my cut hanging over the chair, thinking how much I disrespected it last night.

What the fuck kind of man am I? I'd be leaving her to start all over again by herself, just because that was exactly what I was too afraid to do.

Would I resent her if I left my brothers behind? I would hope not but suspect that I might.

Maybe we can reach a compromise?

Fuck. What do I want? *My cake and to eat it.* I snort. Yeah, well, I'm not getting that. And I'm not going back on my words to Saffie. Fuck knows why, but for her, I'll upturn my life just to be able to stay in hers whichever way she wants it. The restless night has only strengthened my resolve.

Having only dozed lightly, I wake early and dress and shower fast, wanting to be around when she wakes up. I pass by her door, tapping lightly. When there's no answer, I'm not surprised, we'd spoken until late. Poor girl must have been exhausted.

I'll have something to eat first, I decide. Let her get the sleep she needs and deserves. Then once she's rested, I'll find out which option she desires. Somehow, I don't think it will be agreeing to become my old lady.

I broaden my shoulders. So, I'll be leaving the club, making a fresh start. I'm a fuckin' Marine, for fuck's sake. I got this. I can fuckin' deal with civilian life.

"Saffie have a good night?" Kink slaps my shoulder with his one free hand, in the other, he's carrying two brimming cups of coffee, and heading for the stairs.

"I presume so. There's no sound from her room so I take it she's still sleeping."

He nods, grins, then tells me, "Best get off, I've got a pet waiting," and disappears to the second floor.

"Er, Niran."

"Yeah, Curtis. What do you want?" I go to walk past him, the aroma from the cups Kink was carrying making me thirsty.

"Saffie's gone. She went in the middle of the night."

I stop dead in my tracks. *Gone?* "Why the fuck didn't you stop her?" I round on the prospect. *She's gone?* I feel like I've been slapped in the face. *I'd offered to give up everything for her.*

Curtis's eyes narrow. "Because I didn't think she was held fuckin' prisoner. I'll do all the shit you want, Niran, but I won't take the blame for a woman leaving the compound. I was given no instructions to the contrary."

"You've got a brain in your head." I swear he won't be

getting my vote now. "You should have guessed we wanted her to stay."

"How the fuck was I to know?" Curtis retorts louder than he should.

"What the fuck's going on?" Salem roars, thumping down the stairs. "Prospect! Show some damn respect. Niran, explain now."

Glaring at Curtis, I turn my back on him. "Saffie's gone," I explain. "She left before dawn."

Salem shrugs. "Girl didn't seem comfortable here, which is understandable. We can't do anymore. At least it means we don't need to go head-to-head with the Crazy Wolves. Must admit I wasn't sure how to square that in my head."

"Where's Saffie?" Patsy demands as she comes down the stairs. "I stopped to check in on her. Her door was unlocked, and everything's gone from her room."

Luckily, Lost is following her. "Prez?" I shout out. "Can I have a word?"

"Niran?" Patsy insists. "Where is she?"

"Her apartment I expect," I snap at Patsy, causing Lost to emit a warning growl.

"My office, now, Niran!"

"Give me a minute, Prez?"

"One minute," he offers, piercing me with his eyes.

I stomp out of the clubroom and into the morning air. I breathe deep. I'm angry, but it's not all at her. It's also at me and how I couldn't keep my fucking mouth shut. She must have heard the word property and ignored that I'd offered to leave the club for her.

Another breath and I'm feeling slightly calmer. I take out my phone dial her number.

It rings, once, twice then again. Just before it rings out, *thank fuck,* it's answered.

No greeting, no hello.

"Saffie, are you alright?"

"Niran. Please, leave me alone."

"Where are you? Are you safe?" I thump my fist into the wall.

"I'm at my apartment. I'm sorting stuff out."

"I don't like you being there. Not alone. Can I come over?"

There's a pause, an indrawn breath, then, "No." Her voice sounds shrill. *She's upset.* Then she spits the words out one after the other. "Niran. You and I would be a great mistake. You're not what I want. I can't be with someone like you, either at the compound or anywhere." There's another pause, as though she's sitting herself down. "I don't want to see you."

There's something about her tone. "Saffie—"

"No, Niran. I've done a lot of thinking. I'm not right for you, and you're not right for me. We wouldn't work. It's best you just let me go." The words tumble out one after the other.

Is that a sob I hear? "Why the fuck not, Saffie? I thought we were friends."

"We're not friends!" she cries. "Please, Niran, leave me alone." She ends the call.

I scratch my head. *What the fuck just happened? What's gone on between me leaving her with promises last night and now? Why did she leave without talking to me?* I thought she'd told me she'd stay. While last night I put the discussion on abeyance, I thought this morning I could pick it back up. In the light of day, her thoughts might have become clearer. Apparently they have, but not in the direction I wanted.

And now I've got to go see Lost and tell him how I'd fucked up. *Fuck my life.*

"What the fuck happened, Niran?" Lost asks as I enter. "Patsy's upset and I don't like that one fuckin' bit." He waves me to the seat in front of his desk.

What do I care about the distress caused to his old lady, or that he might not get any until this is cleared up? *My* old lady is alone and missing. And it's all my own fucking fault.

Sitting forward, clasping my hands, I give it to him straight. "Last night I spoke to Saffie. She's too savvy about club ways, Prez. Knew we couldn't just give her protection without there being some strings attached. She was scared she would be expected to be a sweet butt, so I came clean. I told her I claimed her."

Lost rolls his eyes. "Which went down like a lead balloon, I take it?"

I shrug. "What could I do? She was right. Giving her a place to stay while her shit gets sorted is one thing, going head-to-head against another club is something else."

Lost wipes his hands down his face. "I'm going to have a hard job holding Patsy back from going after her. But I'm not putting my ol' lady in danger."

"I appreciate that, Prez. I'm having enough difficulty stopping myself." I would, but I know from our recent conversation, Saffie wouldn't take kindly to me turning up.

Lost leans forward and picks up his phone. He taps out a message. Almost before he's finished, the door opens.

"Ah, Toke. I was hoping you'd already be up."

"Up? I ain't gone to bed yet, Prez." Token grins, hooks his foot around a chair pulling it out, then sits. "Whatcha want?"

Lost sighs and simultaneously rubs at his temples. "Niran, the stupid fucker, opened his big mouth and shoved his foot right in it. Saffie took a dislike to becoming property again. She's taken off. We need to know where the Crazy Wolves are on tracking her, and ultimately, how much time we've got? In that, do we leave her in whatever hole she's bolted to, or drag her kicking and screaming back?" He shoots a glare full of accusation my way. "I take it despite her objection to becoming yours, you're still willing to help?"

In answer, I give a sharp nod. Yeah. It's stung my pride, but that's not going to stop me wanting her safe.

Token grins and sits forward. "You're in luck. I spent the night seeing where we were with her. As Niran," he winks at me, "is claiming her, I decided to see if I could track back and see exactly how much info the Crazy Wolves have got."

Ignoring his reference to the woman who's unlikely ever to be mine, I sit straighter. "What did you find?"

"I'm assuming they've hacked into the Freedom Trail database, but that only holds info about her alias and her previous San Diego location. When she moved, she was careful not to leave a forwarding address, and continued using the old one. All official records show her previous location." He raises his chin as though impressed as he adds, "Saffie was good at covering her tracks." Leaning back, Token folds his arms. "And, as we've been over before, it's likely he knows she was pregnant. If I were him, the hospitals would be the first place I'd start."

"Have you checked what address she gave the hospital?" I ask.

"Sure. As you know, it's child's play to access their database. But no worries there, Saffie gave them her prior address and not the recent one."

"How the fuck was she getting her mail? Was she going back to collect it in person?"

Token rolls his eyes. "No need to, Niran. How much snail mail do you receive? Nowadays most shit is sent electronically."

"Rent records?" Lost presses. "That might be somewhere she's slipped up."

Token barks a laugh. "That apartment block? The fuckin' landlord doesn't want records any more than she does."

"Taxes?" Lost rubs at his forehead again.

"Last address. As well as her medical insurance. That's part of what I was doing last night. Checking absolutely everything I could think of."

"So all he knows is that she's in San Diego," I point out, thinking maybe she is safe for now.

"It's a big fuckin' city." Lost seems to be on my wavelength.

Token's eyes soften. "You certain you and she aren't going to make a go of it, Niran?" I give a sharp shake of my head. "Pity." He purses his lips for a moment. "Anyway, after our conversation yesterday, I put out all the feelers I could." He sits forward again, this time lifting his laptop and balancing it on his knees. "I tried to put myself in Duke's head. We already know he's willing to offer money for information. If I were looking for someone, I'd post their picture all over the web, reward attached. I found nothing."

"Good news?" I could do with some.

He shrugs. "How else would he find her? Yeah, for now, even at her apartment, I think she's safe. At least in the short term. I can't think he's given up, but my reading is, he's not close." He glances at Lost. "I'm getting on okay with Stormy, surprisingly. I know Utah wanted her with us as a precaution, but we can't keep her prisoner. They must understand that. I'll update him and impress how we need to get her a new cast-iron identity straight away."

"And this time not fuck it up," I blurt out. "Do you really trust Utah to be able to do that?"

Token looks at me sharply. "Hey, Utah's tight. This isn't their problem. It was the Freedom Trail's system that proved to be the weak link, and they for certain won't be getting any more info on Saffie."

"Presumably they know their system's vulnerable?" Lost demands, his eyebrow raised. "Wouldn't want this happen to any other women they protect."

"Or men, or kids," Token corrects. "And yeah, of fuckin' course. Stormy's dealing with that end of things. Though, I have to admit, it wasn't a novice that was able to hack in."

"Saffie said Duke's man Grit is ex-fed," I inform him.

"Yeah?" Token's eyes rest on me, and his head dips and rises. "That makes sense."

Lost sighs, this time with relief. "I don't like letting down another club when they made a direct request of us, but it seems we're covered. Of course, we wouldn't be in this shit if Niran hadn't fucked up and made us look like fuckin' amateurs."

He doesn't know the half of it. I'm still reeling. I'd fucking offered to leave the club for her, and she didn't give that suggestion the time of day.

Maybe it's a mistake, but I decide to come clean. "It wasn't just me implying that she'd be my property, Prez, that sent her running away. Before I left her last night, I'd already taken that back. I gave her another option. Our last words were about…" I pause, summoning up the strength to admit, "me leaving the club and disappearing with her."

For a moment there's silence.

Then, "You like the bitch that fuckin' much?" comes from Token, while Lost looks incensed.

"You lost your fuckin' mind, Brother? What do you think the Satan's Devils are? Boy-fuckin'-scouts, where you can dip your toe into the water and walk out if find you don't like it? No one fuckin' leaves the club, except in a box. You know that. It's what you signed up for."

I wince at the anger in his voice. "I was hoping you'd make an exception."

Lost, normally a genteel and calm man, smashes his hand onto the desk. "You fuckin' know what happened to this club, Niran. We lost nine fuckin' men. Did you stop to think your leaving might be taken as a betrayal? That your brothers weren't fuckin' good enough?"

"It's not about you or them," I defend myself, rasping out, "It's about Saffie."

"Club before bitches," Token spits out with disgust.

I glare at him, then turn back to Lost. "What if it were Patsy?"

Lost stills, a flicker of something akin to sympathy flashes across his face, then it's gone. "You go ahead with this plan of yours, and a fuckin' beatdown is the least you can expect. And don't expect the brothers to go easy on you."

My suggestion to Saffie had been made on impulse, and it's true I hadn't for one moment considered the effect it would have on this particular chapter given its so recent past. Nine men had for one reason or another thought this club wasn't good enough, or not in its then incarnation. I hadn't taken into account the effect me turning my back might have on my brothers.

"Prez," I cry out earnestly. "If it comes to it, I'll take any punishment you see fit to dole out. You think I want to do this? You think I'd turn my back on the club and my brothers who mean fuckin' *everything* to me if I had any fuckin' choice? She's important to me, damn it." By the time I finish, my chest is heaving. I thump one of my fists into the palm of my other hand. "At the end of the day, it doesn't fuckin' matter. That she fuckin' left without speaking to me says volumes about her views."

As my final words ring in the ensuing silence, Token regards me, his expression not that of a computer nerd, but a man full of feelings and sympathy. Suddenly he puts his ever-present laptop to one side and sits forward. "You care for her, Niran, if you were prepared to give up so much. It must sting like fuck that she didn't want that. But hey, I'll work with Stormy. We'll keep our ears to the ground. I promise wherever she goes, she'll be safe."

He's right. I do care for her, care what happens to her. Fuck knows why, I couldn't explain if I wanted to. There's just something about her vulnerability and situation that tugs at my heartstrings. But not only has she pushed me away, she left without saying a word. Seems as clear as night and day that she doesn't want me anywhere near her.

There's only one thing I can ask. "Keep me in the loop, Brother."

"You got it." Token raises his chin toward me.

Lost's still staring at me, seemingly unable to give up on the previous conversation. "You serious about turning in your patch?"

Could I tell him it was just words said in the heat of the night? I grimace and give him the truth. "Fuck it, Lost, I am. If that means I don't lose her, then if it came to it, I would do that. As it turns out, I've no choice in the matter."

As he continues to stare, I wonder whether I've burned my bridges. Stay or leave, I've already shown my loyalty could be divided when it comes to the club. Once again, I should have kept my mouth shut. I'd give anything to be able to wind back the last twenty-four hours.

After a torturous silence, Lost breaks it. "Utah asked us to keep eyes on her, you've fucked that up. I'll ring Snatcher, come clean. See if we can get Vegas and other friendly clubs to keep an eye out for a herd of Wolves heading our way. And if they do," he raises a finger and points it at me, "someone will have to make sure she gets out before they arrive." He breaks off and looks at Token. "You keep on at Stormy, but I'll step in as well. I'll prepare Snatcher and impress on them the necessity to speed up her new paperwork." Reaching into his pocket, Lost pulls out his phone, then hesitates, his eyes landing on me, then Token. "Haven't you fuckers got some work to do?"

"He might." Token points to me with a grin. He stifles a yawn, then adds, "Me? I've got sleep to catch up on." With his laptop under his arm, he walks out.

Lost puts his head down and pulls some paperwork toward him. Feeling dismissed, I stand.

"We okay?" I ask, hesitantly.

It takes a couple of seconds, and then Prez's face turns up. Grimacing, he states, "You tell me."

With a clenched jaw, I step to the door and open it. After closing it behind me, I breathe out. *Fuck it.*

This isn't a job you resign from, it's a way of life, a lifelong commitment once you accept the patch. This club saved me when I thought I had nothing, gave me a purpose and only asked my loyalty in return. Hell, they've accepted my pain-in-the-ass sister, and all our current problems are down to me. They were prepared to go to war with the Crazy Wolves over Saffie, a woman they'd never have met were it not for me.

And what have I done? Shown I'd throw all that back in an instant, all for my own selfish needs.

Saffie doesn't want me, her running off without a word made that clear. Now my inner thoughts were out in the open, what if the Devils decide they too no longer want me? It's not like I'm a long-time member, I've only been patched in two years. The disrespect I've shown could see me losing my patch and being declared out bad.

Damn it.

I'm a grown man, yet my eyes water. I've fucked up. With my club and with Saffie.

Is there a way to come back from this? I can't see it. Especially as I know, were Saffie to indicate that she needs me, I'd go with her in an instant. Full of regrets and wishes of what might have been, but it's her I put first.

What do I do?

What can I, but go through the motions? I ride to the shop on autopilot, trying to put the question of my future with the club out of my head. What will be, will be.

Instead, I focus on the reason that's brought me to this place. Saffie. Should I take her gesture as the final answer, or should I override her objections and try to see her? But to what end? What good would more talking do? Her actions have told me plainly she wants nothing to do with me, whether or not I'm a biker.

What danger is she in?

If Token's to be believed, and I've no reason to doubt him, Duke hasn't enough information to locate her. Maybe some time to calm down is all she needs to sensibly think about the offer I made. Perhaps her initial reaction doesn't mean she's said no to me forever. There's still time before her paperwork is completed, and she'll be ready to leave.

Backing my bike into a parking spot, I've still no answer, and no way forward decided.

"You're late." Grumbler spies me immediately.

Straightening my back, I approach him. In a few short sentences I tell him only that Saffie had walked out on me, effectively thumbing her nose at both mine and the club's protection.

Once I've assured him Token's pretty certain she's safe, he guffaws, finding amusement in me having the shortest spell of having an old lady in history. I do a good job of pretending I don't give a damn, wanting to end the conversation quickly. Then I volunteer myself for a tricky job which will hopefully focus my attention.

But however complicated the fault is to find, Saffie stubbornly stays on my mind. It doesn't help that I can picture the apartment she's living in. *Will she still go to work? Is her car still running?* Fuck, she didn't even let me help with that. Another thing to show she's had enough of overbearing bikers controlling her life.

The day passes slowly. When I return to the clubhouse, she's still on my mind. Rumours are rife about the woman who appeared yesterday evening, only to bolt in the middle of the night. Saffie, and her vulnerability, had touched many hearts. It doesn't help that Eva, Patsy and Mary all seem to give me the cold shoulder. I want to defend myself, but keep my mouth shut. It was she who walked out. She who turned her back on the safety I could offer her.

Grumbler, it appears, isn't much better off. Mary seems to be blaming him by association.

"I don't understand why the club can't help," Mary comments theatrically loudly in passing while I'm speaking to her old man. "Saffie should not be alone in that apartment."

"Club business," Grumbler retorts. The way his old lady tosses her head as she walks off, I gather tonight he will not be getting lucky. His glare my way confirms that thought.

After dinner, I head out on my bike, just riding to nowhere to get Saffie out of my head. It proves impossible.

What I should do is forget her, but I can't. Despite there being no rational reason for her I offered to upturn my life, then have to face she had no such reciprocal feeling. We were just passing ships in the night. I barely know her, and have no responsibility for her, not now she's turned my offer down flat.

"You look like shit," Kink remarks on my return.

Yeah, I probably do. Riding, for once, hadn't helped. Maybe I should get drunk instead, but I forego the spirits and stick to beer, wanting to keep a clear head in case she needs me and calls. *Fuck, I'm a fool.* Sliding onto the bar stool adjacent to his, I place my bottle in front of me.

"It's Saffie," I tell him, leaning in close so I can speak confidentially. "She's got me twisted in fuckin' knots."

He snorts. "Don't talk to me about knots, Brother. I can talk about them for days." Despite myself, my mouth quirks. "You ever been this worried about a woman before?"

"Never come across one in such dire straits," I answer. "It's so fuckin' hard to accept her doing everything alone."

"Kind of got that when Token said you'd offered to turn in your patch."

"Token's got a big fucking mouth," I growl, wondering now whether everyone knows.

"Is it true though? She means that much?"

"I'm sorry, Kink." He's one I'd be letting down if I did. "Seems she does."

He studies me earnestly. "Then I don't fuckin' blame you, even if I don't think you'd be right. You were born for this life, Brother. And she'll still be a tough nut to crack, whether or not you wear a cut. Her fear of bikers will always be against you."

"The boat has sailed," I tell him. "She doesn't want me to go near her. She'll be moving out of town, hell, out of state. What I should be focusing on is whether I've still got a place here."

"Should be, but you're not." His lips thin. "Thing is, Niran, on the home front, I don't think you've got much to worry about." I shrug. He hadn't seen the disappointment in Lost's face. Still, at least Kink doesn't seem to be holding it against me. "You know your mistake," he continues. "You're giving her what she wants, not what she needs."

"Fuck off," I retort but without any malice. I pick up my beer. "You screw up my head with that dominant shit."

He snorts as I walk off and take my ass off to bed.

Despite that I pride myself on being able to drop off anytime, anywhere, I spend a restless night with thoughts of a certain woman circulating around my mind.

The next day, I get up and do it all over again.

Today, it's even harder to stop jumping on my bike and going to check if she's alright. Only one thing stops me. She asked me to stay away, and I'll abide by her request. Of course Kink's words lodge in my head, but who am I to say what she needs? I start to hope Token will soon report he and Stormy have got her new identity sorted out, and that she's relocated somewhere far away. Maybe that will get her annoying presence out of my head.

I take another long ride this evening. I force myself to stop and admire the sun setting over the ocean, trying to focus on the reds and greens instead of Saffie's dark hair as it falls around her shoulders. It only works to a small extent.

On returning to the clubhouse, I get myself a beer, then

survey the room, wondering whether a game of cards would hold my attention, and how much I could afford to lose if it doesn't.

I watch Salem dealing out hands to Pennywise, Wrangler and Deuce, hoping one of them will fold soon, enabling me to take their place. Unlike my usual hypervigilant self, I don't see her before I feel the hand on my arm.

Startling, I twist around.

"Susie," I state, the word tasting like poison in my mouth.

"That woman hasn't come back, then?"

"What the fuck do you know about *that woman?*" The words had sounded distasteful coming out of her mouth. "And why are you fuckin' here? Salem told you to get lost and never come back."

"Pfft. He didn't mean it. Hey, your sister is a hoot. We've been getting friendly."

"You fuckin' stay away from my sister." I don't want someone like Susie anywhere near Cyn. Cyn's a bad influence as it is. The two of them together, well, I don't even want to think about that combination.

Susie shrugs. "I heard a rumour that woman let you down. You don't need to miss her, lover, not when you've got me around."

What the fuck?

"You been listening where you shouldn't have?" I snarl. Or just what the hell has Cyn been telling her?

She glances around, as if looking for someone. "It's not my fault if I overhear shit. The brothers do talk loudly." Susie flicks her hair over her shoulders and pouts.

Do they? Or is it that she sneaks around listening? It reminds me how I thought I heard something outside the room Saffie had been in that night, while we'd been having our conversation. *Had it been Cyn? She had appeared soon after.* I don't think it was Susie, I didn't think she'd been in the clubhouse.

"Whatever you fuckin' think you heard, what I do and whoever I want is none of your fuckin' business."

She flutters her eyelids. It does nothing for me. "Well, she doesn't want you, but I'm here for you, baby." Pouting, she adds, "I could be a real good old lady." She inches closer and her overpowering perfume makes me want to choke.

Pulling away, I snarl, "Susie, whether or not I have or am thinking about taking any woman as my ol' lady, it's got fuck all to do with you. As one thing's for fuckin' certain, if you were the last woman on earth, it still wouldn't be you." I can't put it clearer than that.

"We could have been good together. That night was great," she protests, trying to rewrite history. I don't have the slightest memory of that night, good or otherwise, except for the bad taste in my mouth that it had left, along with the feeling that somehow she'd tricked me. If it hadn't been for the evidence of my raw cock, I'd say it was all in her imagination.

How far would she go? For the first time, I wonder whether my drink had been spiked. If so, Susie's more dangerous than I thought her to be.

"Susie," a voice says sharply. "What the fuck are you doing here? Niran's told you before, he ain't interested, and I, myself, told you to get and fuckin' stay lost."

Salem's eyes question me over her shoulder, a slight tilt of his head toward the door and a firming of his lips speaks volumes. When I give a determined nod, he moves to stand in front of her.

"I banned you from the clubhouse once already. I don't take kindly having to do the same thing twice. This time you're gone and you ain't never coming back. You get me, bitch? If I see your face again, I'll happily rearrange it. You hearing me now?"

"What? No." She looks at him, then to me in horror. "Niran..."

"Susie, just go." I want nothing more to do with her, so turn and walk off. As I reach the card table, Pennywise grins, then seeing something over my head, his eyes narrow, and he sighs deeply. "Seems you've got more woman troubles."

Turning, I spy Cyn. Ruefully shaking my head, I spin around. "Whatcha want?"

"Susie would have made you a better ol' lady than Saffie. Why is Salem being so nasty to her? I saw him dragging her out. She was my friend."

What? "What the fuck, Cyn? And this is your business, how?" I walk away for privacy. She follows, then stomps her foot.

"I thought things would be better now that bitch Saffie has gone. But you've still no time for me."

"First, she's no bitch, Cyn. And second, think of someone other than your damn self for a while. Ever thought I might have shit on my mind?" Sure, I've been distant over the past couple of days. In truth, I haven't forgiven her for the comments she'd made about Saffie that night.

"I've missed you," she protests. "I thought it would get better now she'd gone. But you've got no time for me at all. I might as well not be here."

Oh yes, please. "You going home?"

She huffs loudly and marches off. *Guess she's not. I wouldn't be so lucky.*

Hell, I suck at this big brother gig, but who could blame me when my sister is Cyn?

Damn it. I need something to take my mind off women. Seeing me staring his way, Pennywise jerks his head to the cards on the table in front of him, kicks out a chair then when I sit, deals me in.

Accepting soon becomes a mistake. On a losing streak, I throw my cards in with a sigh before I completely empty my wallet.

When I go to the bar, Kid pours me a drink without me asking.

"Drinking alone again?"

"Go away, Kink. I'm not in the mood."

"Nah?" He ignores me and takes the stool next to where I'm standing. "You're hurting, Brother."

Raising and lowering my shoulders, I shake my head, not even bothering to refute his observation. "What can I fuckin' do, Kink?"

"You can obey your fuckin' nature for a start. Go and see her."

"There's no point," I tell him. "I offered to leave the club for her, Kink, give everything up. If that wasn't enough, I don't know how else I can persuade her."

"You're falling into a trap." As my eyebrows raise, he continues, "First rule of being a Dom is giving the sub what she needs, and not what she wants."

What Saffie wants is for me to stay far away from her.

Now it's his turn to shrug. "You being willing to turn in your patch shows the depth of your feelings for her. She needs someone like you in her corner, whether she realises it or not. What's to lose, Brother?"

"She's leaving, Kink. Either I let her, or I go with her." And right now, it looks like she's made her choice about going it alone. My wants don't even come into it.

He purses his lips together. "Or you find some middle ground. She needs you, Brother. Go to her."

Staying away, hoping she'd come to her senses and contact me hadn't worked. I could sit on my ass and feel sorry for myself or do something about it. What would it hurt? Another refusal isn't going to make me feel any worse.

I lower my gaze to my glass, then lifting my eyes, raise my chin toward Kink. "You're right. I'll go visit her."

CHAPTER THIRTY-ONE

Saffie

In the cold light of day, I realised I should have confronted Niran, should have allowed him to explain what that note meant. Questions abound in my head. Who could have put it under my door? Were they trying to warn me? Or was it someone up to mischief trying to push me away? Whatever the reason, that's the effect they achieved.

I could have challenged him when he'd called, but I didn't. I was too afraid I wouldn't be able to separate truth from lies. Not given my past and all the mistakes I've made.

When I'd run, I hadn't been thinking at all, nor remembering that the reason I left the apartment was because Duke was getting close to finding me. It was only when I got back to my apartment that I realised this wasn't the safest place for me.

Then Token had called reassuring me, for now, I had nothing to worry about. Duke didn't know how to find me. Not yet, he was sure about that.

When he asked questions, I listened and responded.

My new name? Something totally different this time, I don't care what. Location? I don't care where. Sure, New York sounds big enough for me to disappear. I'd stick out in a small town.

What had mattered was when everything would be ready. *Just a few more days.*

Was I suspicious he was part of the plan to keep me locked down for Duke? Hell yes, of course I was. But I was also exhausted, worn out, and heartbroken. My baby's loss is a constant physical ache, now there's another gap in my life that hurts almost as much. God help me, but I miss Niran. Half of me wishes I'd given him a chance to have his say, the other half congratulates me for leaving his cheating ass.

I feel in limbo, having neither the strength to go forward nor back. I'm too tired to do more than let things play out as they will. If Token's to be believed, I'll have my future sorted out in a few days. If he's lying, Duke will be coming for me.

As it is, I'm tired of watching my back all the time. What will be, will be.

Now two days have passed since I ran from the compound. Two days of me returning to normal. A normal where I'm living by myself, thinking only about what I want and nobody else, which is simply a polite way of saying I'm lonely.

I miss Niran. Miss his large presence which made me feel safe. Miss him just being there. I try to tell myself I had a lucky escape and thank my lucky stars I found out what he was in time. It doesn't help.

I should be used to Niran's absence, I'd already had a month without him being around to prop me up, but then I'd always known he was just at the end of the line should things get too much. This time, I'd burned my bridges and told him to leave me alone. And in case I became weak, I'd deleted his number from my phone.

He's already got an old lady. Or was he planning to kick her to the kerb? I was hardly the best substitute. I didn't want him in my bed.

When my mind circles back to the note, things don't seem to add up. Niran hadn't acted like a man who'd already had a woman he'd patched. When I'd refused to be his old lady, he'd offered to leave his club. What biker does that?

My immediate conclusion that he was doing all he could to ensure I stayed until Duke arrived, was beginning to dissipate as the days pass and Duke still hasn't turned up.

Did I take the excuse as soon as one had been offered to me? I'd rejected becoming his property, but its more than that. I never want to be dependent on another man again, and Niran's insistence that he wanted to be with me, even to the extent that he'd move with me and start a life somewhere new, had terrified me. How could I, Saffie, with all her problems, hold any attraction for a man like him?

It's been forty-eight hours since I last saw the man, and he still haunts my thoughts.

A fresh start would do me good. My apartment's still crap. The arguments still go on around me as if I'd never been away. My neighbours still have noisy sex, feet continue to stomp past my door all hours of the day or night and loud music constantly blares. It's not too much different from the clubhouse, except no one wears leather, and dealers and druggies tend to be the ones skulking about.

If I leave, I'll never see Niran again. But I won't anyway. I've no way of contacting him, and he's not bothered to follow up with me. Of course not. He's got an old lady waiting in the wings. But the more I try to tell myself that, the more I think that note was a sham. But what does it matter now?

As I knew I'd be leaving in a matter of days, I quit my job the first day I was back, in reality not wanting the bother of going anymore. Without any reason to go out, time hangs heavy on my hands and I'm left with far too much time to think and far too many of my thoughts involve Niran.

If I sit on the couch, I remember him sitting next to me. When I go to the kitchen, I recall him making coffee or pulling some food together and encouraging me to eat. His presence is somehow constant, making me wonder whether I've made a mistake. But I know I haven't. A man like him wouldn't be good for me, he'd want more than I'm prepared to give. Even if the note writer lied and he hasn't already, he'll soon find someone more appropriate for him.

I go through the motions, doing laundry out of habit, washing up the few plates I've used, putting things away to keep the place tidy, basically just ticking along.

Having finished my tasks, I stand in the middle of the living room. I've got to start packing as I'll be leaving soon. But what to take and what to leave? Will I have transport to take furniture with me, or just take what I can fit in my car? Of course, if it's New York I'm going to, my car will never get me there. In that case, I'll more likely be limited what I can carry in a suitcase on the plane.

Telling myself I need to know before I can begin, I leave everything where it is. I've just sat on the couch, my head leaned back and my eyes closed when the doorbell rings and startles me.

Who would come calling?

Pulling myself to my feet, I go to the door and stare out of the peephole.

It's Niran.

I don't know whether to be pleased or dismayed. My initial instinct is to pretend I'm not in. I don't want to see him; don't want to hear what he's got to say. I don't want to give him the chance to persuade me to stay. All my reasons for not seeing him remain valid.

But he's persistent, ringing again, and this time also knocking loudly. When I hear my neighbour start to complain, I get angry he's got the nerve to come here, and for bringing attention to me. Before I can have second thoughts, I fling open the door ready to give him a piece of my mind, words on my lips ready to tell him to go away and stop bothering me, but he strides straight in without giving me a chance to say anything.

I stand, my hands on my hips, my mouth open.

"We need to talk, Saffie." He eyes my apartment with a twist to his mouth, then grinds down on his heel.

Another cockroach? I feel my cheeks burn with embarrassment as I hear the giveaway crack. Although I can keep my place clean, they flood in from other not so kempt apartments.

While I'm stifling the need to apologise for the unsanitary conditions, he turns his eyes to me. The depth of his penetrating stare makes me feel uneasy. I look away and address the wall instead of the man himself.

Even though my heart gives a leap at seeing him again, I know how wrong he and I would be whether or not he's already tied. I could never give him what he wants from me. I decide to give my case straight from the start. "The only thing you've got to say that I'll listen to is if you're here to tell me the plans for me leaving are sorted."

"I'm not. I'm here to talk to you about us."

"There's no us," I mutter.

"Saffie, look at me." Stubbornly, I stay turned to the wall.

I hear him sigh. "Saffie, why did you leave that night? Why didn't you stay and talk to me?"

Because it's been all I can think about, I blurt out, "Because you've already got an old lady. I know, Niran. I know you've been lying to me."

"I got a what?" I hear confusion in his voice, then he growls, "What did you just say?"

There's a tremor in my voice as I tell him, "I said I know you have an old lady. And if she can't meet your needs, I certainly wouldn't be able to fulfil them. You're better off with the club whores."

"Old lady? Club whores?" He sounds perplexed. "Saffie, I certainly haven't got, nor ever had, an old lady and I've no clue why you'd think I have. As for the club whores, all they could complain about is that I never use their services. Once or twice, maybe, when I first joined the club. But never on the regular, and not once since I met you. I've not got my dick wet elsewhere either." A touch of anger taints his tone.

"I got a note," I spit at him. "It told me to ask you about your old lady."

"A fuckin' note? When? That night?" When I nod, he rakes his hands over his head. "Christ, Saffie." His eyes pierce me. "So why didn't you talk to me? Fuck, I thought we had something between us, and you go and believe that?" His face goes blank. "You just believed it," he repeats with resignation. Then his expression starts to change as his already dark colouring deepens, and his eyes fill with rage. His hands clench, his body vibrates.

Though I should be scared, I sense I've got nothing to fear from him. In fact, I roll back my head, defiantly staring up at him, daring him to contradict what I've been told.

"The note was pushed under my door. It was a warning to me. Who'd go out of their way to do that if it wasn't true?"

As fast as it came, he shakes off his anger, his face radiating sadness instead. "Fuck. No wonder you didn't want to talk to me." He shakes his head. "I'm so far from having an old lady, it's a joke. As for who, one person occurs to me. And if it's her, she's fuckin' dead. Saffie, I fucked a woman once, months back, and that was a fuckin' mistake when I was drunk. Since then, she won't leave me alone. Even the club girls have taken to chasing her off. Salem escorted her out of the club a couple of nights back. She's nothing to me and never has been. If it was her, she was only trying to stir up trouble between us."

Unreasonably jealous she's had a part of him I have not, forgetting for a moment I don't want it, I say cattily, "So you fucked her, didn't find her to your taste, and dropped her just like that?" I should have known. It's the way bikers act.

His voice rises. "I barely remember fuckin' her. I was *drunk*. If anything, it was she who took advantage. Good or bad, I have no recollection." He huffs. "What would you say if a woman was drunk, and a man forced himself onto her? What would you call it then?" He pauses, then shakes his head. "I didn't even know whether I used a condom or not, so got tested as soon as I sobered up. And that, Saffie, was the last time I fucked anyone. If I had an ol' lady, my damn hand wouldn't be so overworked."

I'm half full of hope, half disgust at myself, knowing I'm lapping up his explanation. The words he's saying make me want to believe him, when maybe I shouldn't. Turning around I face him, my hands fluttering in the air. "Who can I believe, Niran?"

His dark eyes, full of anguish, settle on me. "Not an anonymous note writer for a start. If you don't trust me, Saffie, then you were right to leave. I thought I'd shown you enough that you'd never doubt me. You never came and asked me for the truth." He wipes his forehead and looks at me sadly. "You really thought I had an old lady in the wings I was cheating on? How could you believe that of me?"

He's been moving, either his fingers across his hair, or using his hands to gesticulate at me. Suddenly he stills. "Fuck. How could it have been Susie? Even if she dared return to the club, she wouldn't have known where you were staying that night. It has to be Cyn. My own fuckin' sister."

His sister? "Why would she lie, Niran?"

He visibly slumps. "Remember I hadn't shut the door that night? I didn't want you to feel trapped. I thought I heard someone outside, but dismissed it. After I left you, she appeared. She could have been eavesdropping. If she had, she'd have heard me offering to turn in my patch and leave the club."

"And that matters to her?" It kind of makes sense, but I'm not convinced. Okay, I hadn't taken to Cyn when I'd met her briefly, and knew she'd taken an instant dislike to me.

Niran rubs his nose as though trying to think of the answer. "She's as possessive as fuck about me. And I suspect, she gets a lot from me being in the club. If I left, she wouldn't be welcome there. And I sure as fuck wouldn't have her coming with us."

"But she must have known she'd hurt you."

"I honestly don't think she gives a fuck." He steps closer to me. "Saffie, I swear, whatever she said, it's for her own reasons."

We've been arguing, I've thrown accusations, and he's refuted each and every one. Never once have I felt at risk, as I might have done with another man. I also feel certain that were I to tell him that having heard everything, I still want him to leave, he would. Instead of judging him on what I've been told, I judge him on evidence instead. He's never hurt me, and I don't think he ever would.

There's something comforting about him being with me in my apartment. The noises don't seem so threatening with him around. I feel the most at ease than I have since I returned.

He could be with me forever if I just reached out.

I let the tension ease from me, my shoulders dipping as they relax, and my breath comes more evenly. "I think I believed the note as it was easy. I wanted an excuse to think you weren't the man I made you out to be. You scared me when you said you'd claimed me. And then when you said you'd leave the club… You've offered so much when I've nothing to give you. We've not even had sex."

He looks at me sharply. "Sex? Hell, darlin'. Sure, that's part of a relationship, but not the be-all and end-all of it. You, you're different, like nothing I've known before. From the moment we met, there was something inside you that called to me. If you ask me what, I couldn't explain." He smooths his hands over his face, drawing down the skin below his eyes. "I wanted to be there for you, not sexually, but as a friend. I respect you, that's the difference. I wanted to get to know the real you, to be there for you while you couldn't be strong for yourself, to see you become the confident, strong woman I know you are under all the burdens you carry. In the meantime, you needed something from me, something that was my gift to give, my protection. It wasn't a hardship thinking about making you my old lady, even if we hadn't taken the next step yet, nor knowing when or if that was ever going to be possible."

His words are hypnotising, poetic, and on the face of it, reasonable. I point out what's wrong. "But you didn't ask me. I don't know you, and you really don't know me. You know a…" I pause to choke back a sob, "a now-not-pregnant woman who's got a ton of shit to sort out. I don't even know myself, Niran. I know I've changed since I left Duke, and I know I'll need to change again if I'm to survive."

He chuckles softly. "I know all about needing to change, darlin'." Tapping his leg, he continues, "I know all about regrets. Maybe I haven't lost something as precious as you have, but I do understand how difficult it is to reverse everything you thought you had straight. Yeah, circumstances led to the idea of us skipping a few steps and heading straight for the old lady part, but I didn't walk into it blindly."

I can't lead him on. "Nothing's changed. I'm still leaving."

"I know." He drops his head into his hands. "Offer still stands, I'll come with you."

"No, Niran, you can't. You'd come to resent me. Your club's your family, and I could never replace that."

The look he gives me, followed by his defeated sigh, tells me I'm right and he knows it.

Suddenly I want to address the other side of the coin. "What, what would you do if I stayed?" Part of me wonders if I'm mad. Whether I should have jumped at the chance of being his old lady with both feet. I'd be protected, and safe. *But I'd be associated with a club of bikers and I couldn't get away from that.* I'd be property.

"If you stayed? Well, fuck, I'd call you my old lady, but we wouldn't rush into anything. First, we'd eliminate the threat, get Duke off your back. Then, I'd date you. Take time to get to know you, then, if things went right and when you were in the right headspace, I'd show you how good we could be together in bed."

My stomach twists at his words, but not unpleasantly, and though getting rid of Duke should take foremost place, it's the rest he offers that almost draws me in. He'd take things slowly, woo me. Somehow, I doubt he wouldn't have to try too hard.

But how far would he go? "And what if," I gulp, trying to address the topic without tears, "I was still carrying another man's baby? What if I'd kept it, what if he'd been healthy?"

His eyes crease. "You're you, Saffie. And I'm man enough to take on another man's kid. Blood isn't what makes a dad."

He's saying all the right words. "Do you want kids?"

He meets my eyes, and without hesitation, says, "If the woman I'm with wants them, I'll move heaven and earth to fulfil her dreams."

CHAPTER THIRTY-TWO

Saffie

Oh my God. What am I doing turning this perfect man down?

Curling my fingers into my palms, I convince myself to think of my options. I can't stay while he's a member of his club, and he can't leave, not without it changing the person he is.

What if I stay, give it time, see if a relationship could evolve between us? But with Duke closing in, without the club, it won't just be me that's unprotected, it would also be him.

Best I should keep to my plan and leave. Alone. *Damn Duke. It's him that's forcing my hand.* It's he who's making me give up maybe the best thing to ever happen to me in my life.

Maybe I could enjoy Niran's presence for the days or maybe just hours until Token gets me my new papers and it's time to go.

"Is there news of Duke?" I bite my lip.

"Nah. Not yet. Token's still trying to find out how much he knows. But so far there's nothing to say the Wolves are on the move."

"How would you know?"

"Token's got his fingers on the pulse, checking all the electronic methods which Duke could use to find you. And we're utilising old-fashioned methods as well. It isn't foolproof, but we've got our Vegas Chapter and friendly clubs ready to alert us if there are signs they're heading this way. It's a five-hour ride or so, someone should pick them up en route and in enough time to give us some warning."

Five hours. Not much notice to run for my life.

His mouth twists. "I'm not going to lie to you. If you were at the club as my old lady, the brothers would be standing guard and ready to defend you and the compound. As you're not, and if you don't want me with you, you've got to accept that you're on your own. Should we get word Duke's in the wind, then you'll need to move on. Utah will send us instructions, we'll set you on your way, then you'll be met, just like with the Freedom Trail."

I shudder and look around me. I want to retract all previous statements. I want Niran to come with me. Though even as the thought enters my head, I know it would be wrong to use him that way. Steeling myself, I take a breath, and reply, simply, "Okay."

He grimaces. "I'll fuckin' hate saying goodbye."

So will I.

As we reach an uneasy impasse, Niran gets to his feet and goes into the kitchen. "Christ, woman, what d'you eat? You've nothing here."

There didn't seem much point in stocking the cupboards, not when I'm going to be leaving, so I don't answer him.

"Can I borrow your phone?" he asks as he reappears.

"Sure. Yours dead again?"

He gives a twisted grin. "Fuckin' battery just dies when I don't expect it." He takes mine and dials a number. "Kid?... Yeah... Can you pick up a couple of pizzas, bring them to Saffie's... Yeah, that'll do. Thank you."

"There was no need for that." My eyes widen. "I could have gone out and gotten something, or we could have ordered in."

"Saffie," he says, tiredly, staring at his phone once again as if it's offended him by being dead. "You've packed shit. If you're leaving, you've got to decide what to take with you. As I said, you might not get much notice. As much as you can fit in the car is all you'll be able to take. Kid can help you get shit ready, carry it down the stairs. I need to go back to the clubhouse and get my charger and speak to Token to get an update. Kid will be here while I'm gone."

I stiffen. "I don't need babysitting."

"He's not a fuckin' babysitter. He's your resource for you to direct."

A prospect doing my bidding? Never heard of that before. "I'm fine doing it alone," I insist.

He sends me a look that speaks volumes, that I've done such a good job of it already. "I'm sure you are, but humour me, okay?"

In my heart, I know I don't want to move on. But he's right. I could get the signal any moment. One thing him turning up has done is focus my mind about Duke and jerk me out of my state of lethargy. It might not be Niran, but in time I could have a future with someone, even another baby perhaps. Duke's stolen so much from me. I don't want him to take my future too.

Noticing my sad expression, Niran closes the gap between us, resting his hand gently on my cheek. "The boys know where I am if something urgent comes up, but I'd like to get a feeling for what's going on."

"With the Crazy Wolves?"

He doesn't use words to confirm, but the compassionate look in his eyes makes me shiver. *I need to get gone, away from San Diego.*

As if he can read my mind, his hand moves, raising my chin slightly, so I'm forced to look into his eyes. "I wish there was some way I could persuade you to stay."

"Duke knows I'm in San Diego. He's already closing in."

"The offer still stands. You could still be my ol' lady."

Twisting out of his grip, I snap back, "And I've already told you, I don't want to be anyone's old lady, property, wife or possession again."

"It wouldn't be like that," he replies sternly. "I wouldn't ask anything you're not prepared to give. We're friends, aren't we? Who knows what could develop?"

"I'm going, Niran. Alone." The spark in my eyes challenges him, but my mind is made up.

His mouth opens, but at that moment, there's a knock on the door and Kid's voice shouts through it, "Food delivery."

With a shake of his head, Niran approaches the door and opens it. When Kid enters, he goes to close it again. He's got it almost latched when it's kicked in, so violently, Niran's knocked off balance, and falls to the floor as his prosthetic leg slips out from under him.

I watch as it happens in slow motion. Kid stands, mouth open, boxes dropping from his hands as Duke storms in, followed closely by Slit, Croak and Grit. As if they'd choreographed every movement, Slit drops to the floor beside Niran, holding a gun to his head and Croak rushes forward and puts his arm around the scrawny prospect's neck.

Duke gives a sharp nod. Croak raises his other hand and twists. There's an audible crack, and Kid's only got time to widen his eyes before he falls to the ground. Sightless eyes meet mine, and I know that he's dead.

The ensuing silence seems loud. I'm the first to react, turning and vomiting nothing but bile over the couch. *Not again. Not another prospect losing his life.*

"Whoops." Croak grins unapologetically as he eyes the body at his feet. "Don't know my own fuckin' strength, do I?"

Duke gives a hearty laugh as if it's the best joke he's ever heard.

"Bastard!" Niran roars.

Quick as a flash, Slit pistol whips Niran, making him fall back to the ground, then sinks his weight over him, pinning him down, his gun inches away from Niran's ear. "Don't fuckin' move. I doubt a shot would worry the residents in this fuckin' dump."

"No one else here," Grit states, emerging from my bedroom.

Duke gives an assessing look around, seeming satisfied he's in control of the situation. He holsters his weapon and approaches me. His hand rises, and his fingers take a painful grip of my chin forcing me to my feet.

As I stand, I stare at Niran horrified. When his eyes meet mine, I read apology in them. For a second, I want to rant at him, telling him the Satan's Devils' assurances had, in the end, been worth nothing. Then the thought comes to me that this is what he wanted all along, for Duke to catch up with me.

I don't know what to believe. But the way Slit's guarding Niran doesn't suggest he counts him as a friend. I try to find comfort that whatever part he played, Niran will be dead soon anyway.

Then simultaneously, I want to scream at them to let him go free, unable to believe he had any role in this.

Duke has yet to speak to me. When he rectifies that omission, he does so first with his fists, not his mouth. I stumble, fall, my cheek burning, my ear ringing, and my stomach throbbing in agony.

"You killed my fuckin' kid!" he yells. "My kid, Sapphire."

The accusation surprises me. I had no idea he'd known I was pregnant. But his claim gives me the backbone I hadn't expected to exist. "You did that," I retort with a scream. "What you and your brothers did to me meant he couldn't survive. I had no choice, Duke."

"What I did to you?" He backhands me again, sending me to my knees. "If you wanted my baby, why did you take the pill for years and hide it from me? Why, when I planted my seed in you,

you ran away and made sure it was killed? What did I do to you, Sapphire? You tell me."

I should heed the warning in his eyes, but the events of yesterday make me want to fight back, if only verbally. "I didn't beat myself, Duke. I didn't feed myself drugs."

"You took them fuckin' willingly," he snarls.

I brace for the next blow, but it doesn't help. This one makes me see stars. Falling prone, I can't move, just gasp for breath. For good measure, he kicks me viciously in the thigh.

Then he appears to lose interest. "Who the fuck are you?" he asks Niran. "Why are you with my ol' lady? You fuckin' her? Oh fuck it, I don't even care." He nods at Slit who cocks his gun. "Just kill the fuckin' nigger. I don't want him breathing the same air."

Red

When I was young I had no desire to become a member of a motorcycle club.

If I envisioned a future, it would be a replica of the family life I'd had, finding a wife, getting married, and spitting out a couple of kids. I'd do some kind of blue collar job just to put some money in my pocket and food on our table.

But fate had other plans, and drove me into the arms of the Satan's Devils MC.

From then, I never looked back.

Now I'm the prez of the Vegas Chapter and I've achieved more than I ever expected, respect and loyalty from my brothers. The only thing missing is the woman I'd always thought would end up by my side.

I live for my club. That's more than enough. Isn't it?

Cheryl

Oh, the decisions we make when we're young which with age we regret.

At the time fear had me turning my back and walking away. There were men in the sea aplenty, surely a special one would turn up?

But as time moved along and I grew older, I couldn't forget the man I'd been unable to get out of my mind. What would my life have been like is I'd been braver? What if I'd said yes?

Would I have ended up a weary almost forty-year-old croupier in a Vegas casino with no man by my side?

Do we get second chances? How I'd love the answer to be yes.

OTHER WORKS BY MANDA MELLETT

Blood Brothers – A series about sexy dominant sheikhs and their bodyguards

Stolen Lives (#1) Nijad and Cara

Close Protection (#2) Jon and Mia

Second Chances (#3) Kadar and Zoe

Identity Crisis (#4) Sean and Vanessa

Dark Horses (#5) Jasim and Janna

Hard Choices (#6) Aiza

Satan's Devils MC - Arizona Chapter

Turning Wheels (Blood Brothers #3.5, Satan's Devils #1) Wraith and Sophie

Drummer's Beat (#2) Drummer and Sam

Slick Running (#3) Slick and Ella

Targeting Dart (#4) Dart and Alex

Heart Broken (#5) Heart and Marc

Peg's Stand (#6) Peg and Darcy

Rock Bottom (#7) Rock and Becca

Joker's Fool (#8) Joker and Lady

Mouse Trapped (#9) Mouse and Mariana

Blade's Edge (#10) Blade and Tash

Heart Mended: A Satan's Devils MC Novella

Truck Stopped (#11) Truck & Allie

Satan's Devils MC Boxset 1 Books 1-5

Satan's Devils MC Boxset 2 Books 6-8

Satan's Devils MC Boxset 3 Books 9-11

Satan's Devils MC - Colorado Chapter

Paladin's Hell (#1) Paladin and Jayden

Demon's Angel (#2) Demon and Violet

Devil's Due (#3) Beef and Steph

Devil's Dilemma (#4) Pyro and Mel

Ink's Devil (#5) Ink and Beth

Devil's Spawn (#6)

Satan's Devils MC - Next Generation

Amy's Santa (#1) Wizard and Amy

Hawk's Cry (#2) Hawk and Olivia

Twisted Throttle (#3) Throttle and Gwen

Satan's Devils MC - San Diego Chapter

Being Lost (#1)

Grumbler's Ride (#2)

Satan's Devils MC - Utah Chapter

Road Tripped (#1)

Stormy's Thunder (#2)

ACKNOWLEDGMENTS & AUTHOR'S NOTE

I know readers (including myself) are not keen on cliffhangers, especially when they come as a surprise. So first an apology.

I didn't set out to write a book in two parts. I thought Niran's story would be quite straightforward and never dreamed it would overflow one book. But as he kept talking, the words just kept coming. It reached the point where I knew this had to be split into two parts.

I missed my publishing schedule so I could release the second part without having too long to wait, and titled the books so that the abrupt end would be expected.

I do hope you'll forgive me.

As always, a massive thank you to my beta readers, with particular mention to Sheri and Danena who both have a large input to my books. Honestly ladies, I couldn't do it without you. Mention, of course, to the other betas, Jo, Tami, Alex, Nicole, Terra and Zoe. It's so encouraging to know at an early stage that the plot works and that you enjoy the book.

Maggie Kern, you are an amazing friend as well as a brilliant editor, and I can't wait to meet you in person again. Once more you have my grateful thanks and appreciation. Thank you for not holding my book hostage until you had the second part.

Massive thanks to Darlene Tallman who stepped in at the last minute to proofread Avenging Devil Part 1. I can't thank you enough for doing it, for meeting my timescales and the work you put in to giving the book a final polish.

The cover image was provided by Golden Czermak of Furious Fotog. As always, he had the perfect model, Curtis Presley. The cover was again brought to life by Dar Dixon of Wicked Smart Designs. Thank you all.

Finally, last as always, but definitely not least, thanks to all of you, my wonderful readers who've taken a chance on this book. If it wasn't for your encouragement, I wouldn't keep writing. I have recently received messages and emails telling me how much you like my books, and I love reading every one. A positive message inspires me to write more.

This book, like all of my works, has been to beta readers, through editing twice, to a proofreader and then to ARC readers, but there could still be the odd typo that's crept through. Please message me if you've found anything so I have a chance to correct the book. I love to hear from readers, even if you're pointing out something I've got wrong.

If you've enjoyed this book, please consider writing a review. Reviews are essential to us authors, and I appreciate and read them all.

Avenging Devil is already available for pre-order.

Amazon.com https://amzn.to/34RyVqM

Amazon.co.uk https://amzn.to/34Pz7qn

Amazon.com.au
https://www.amazon.com.au/dp/B095PNLXS9

Amazon.ca https://www.amazon.ca/dp/B095PNLXS9

STAY IN TOUCH

Email: manda@mandamellett.com

Website: www.mandamellett.com

Sign up for my newsletter to hear about new releases in the Satan's Devils and Blood Brothers series.

Facebook reader group: https://www.facebook.com/groups/mandasbadboys/

facebook.com/mandamellett

twitter.com/manda_mellett

Photo by Carmel Jane Photography